Paris Adieu

COMING OF AGE IN THE CITY OF LIGHT

ROZSA GASTON

PARIS ADIEU. Copyright © 2012 by Rozsa Gaston. All rights reserved.

Library of Congress Cataloging-in-Publication Data: 2012910568

Gaston, Rozsa.
Paris Adieu: Coming of Age in the City of Light/ Rozsa Gaston.
p. cm.
ISBN-10: 0984790616
EAN-13: 9780-9847906-1-6
1. Paris (France)—Social life and customs—20th century.
2. Americans—France—Fiction
3. Dating (Social customs) —Fiction
4. Women—France
5. Self-perception—France
6. Paris (France) —Description and travel
7. Food habits—France—Paris
I. Title

Cover design by Rob Mohan

www.parisadieu.com

CONTENTS

PART III BEING WHERE I BELONG

For Ardeo
Je t'aime éternellement
(It's all fiction)

ACKNOWLEDGMENTS

My deepest thanks go to the following:

Sharon Belcastro, my agent, for passionately loving this book and bringing it to the light of day. Terri Valentine, my friend and mentor. Ella Marie Shupe, for her encouragement and support. Rob Mohan, for his inspiration and artistry. Laura Mews Brengelman, without whose careful edits, I would have been sunk. Ariana Csonka Kaleta, Baroness von Trautenegg, for critical feedback and scintillating friendship. Edie Glass, my memoir-writing teacher, who got me hooked on writing.

Leslie Gueguen, Victoria Kann, Caroline Leavitt, Susie Piturro, and Laurence Siegel. My daughter Ava, who inspired the name of my main character. Most of all, thank you Bill – please don't read the book.

PART I

BECOMING

CHAPTER ONE

Escape

The year I turned nineteen I came down with lack-of-plan-itis. It was a long-drawn out illness with no apparent end in sight, made worse by constant solicitous inquiries from family and friends of family.

"Ava! Nice to see you. Home from school?"

I'd shrug, hoping they'd get the message to lay off. Mostly they didn't.

"Not at school? What are you up to then?" neighbors out tending their lawns would ask in one form or another as I passed their houses on my way to the house where I grew up on a horseshoe-shaped drive in West Hartford, Connecticut.

I was working as a cashier at a twenty four hour self-service gas station – which I didn't really feel like talking about – so I cut back on visiting my grandparents to escape the nonstop questions that started even before I made it into their house. Once I was inside, things got even worse. My grandmother would punctuate her stone-cold silences with snappy references to the year's worth of college tuition they had just thrown away on me at music college where I'd been studying to become a music teacher until I dropped out.

It wasn't my fault their plans hadn't been mine. I'd been trying to hint at that all along, but the symphony of my grandmother's own perfectly laid goals for my life had drowned out the tiny tinkling of whatever ideas of my own had been slouching toward self-expression. They held the moneybags, and I didn't. That was the gist of most of my grandmother's lectures. It was hell not to have a plan at age nineteen.

I had screwed up since finishing high school in Maine. And that was after I had screwed up beginning high school at a private school.

I had loved ninth grade at the all-girls' private school. But at home, there'd been endless fights with my grandmother. "This is my house, and you'll do as I say as long as you live in it," didn't offer much room for maneuvering. We sparred over why I couldn't wear blue jeans, "Young ladies do not wear blue jeans." How I should wear my hair, "Nancy Shelton told me the other day you could be such a pretty girl if only you'd stop hiding your eyes with that shaggy hair." As well as why I couldn't do just about anything else a normal teenage girl might want to do in the late twentieth century.

Finally, I got shipped off to Maine to stay with my aunt and uncle for my remaining high school years. I'd made the best of it and graduated fourth in my class at a public high school Down East (that's the area along Maine's coast from Penobscot Bay to the Canadian border) then returned to Connecticut to attend music college, where I fancied myself some sort of budding concert pianist. It took only one week of classes to know I lacked both the talent and focus to consider a classical performing career at the keyboard. By spring semester, even my piano teacher, a vivacious Pole who bounced and grunted on the piano bench when she performed, suggested kindly to me that I might have more strengths as a writer than a pianist after reading yet another of my well-thought-out notes explaining why I had not been prepared for our lesson. The simple fact was I didn't have the concentration necessary to sit around and practice a Bach fugue or any other piece of classical music hour after hour, day after day. I enjoyed playing pop songs or improvising on chord progressions, but contemporary music was scorned at my traditional, classical-music curriculum college. Besides, I was too distracted by the whole, wide world out there, just waiting for me to discover it.

At the end of my first year, I dropped out. My grandparents wanted me to become a music teacher, but I wasn't the teacher type. Who wanted to put up with nasty public school children who might not want to be in a music class anyway? One of two things I took away from music college was that teaching surly junior high-schoolers would be a surefire way to lose one's love of music. The other was that I wasn't a specialist. I was a generalist. Liberal arts colleges were created for people like me.

After spending the summer cashiering at the gas station, I needed to come up with a plan for the next school year while I went through the winter-through-spring process of applying to liberal art colleges – the ones I should have applied to during my senior year of high school instead of letting my grandmother talk me into music college. If I got into a good school, maybe my grandparents would help pay for it. If not, there were student loans and scholarships I could apply for. But if I didn't get into a top college, I knew what was waiting back in West Hartford for me – secretarial school.

I'd rather kill myself.

My grandmother's idea of a career path for a woman consisted of teaching, secretarying or marrying up. I'd heard her talking to my grandfather behind closed doors one Sunday afternoon when I'd arrived early for a visit and let myself in unannounced.

"And that's the last penny we spend on her," she'd said as I crept to the other side of the dining room wall where she couldn't spot me through the entryway to the sun room.

"Well, Helen, we'll see if she's interested. Maybe she doesn't want to go to secretarial school." My grandfather's mild voice warmed my heart.

"We'll do no such thing, Walter. She needs to learn a trade so she can get out and support herself."

"First, she needs to figure out what it is she wants to do."

"Not with my hard-earned money she won't."

My grandmother hadn't worked a day in her life, unless you count a year or two spent as a part-time teenage fashion model before she'd married – up, of course.

I tiptoed back to the kitchen and let myself out the back door. It was best to make an announced appearance at a moment like this. I ran around to the front of the house and rang the doorbell. My grandfather let me in, and I silently blessed him as I kissed his cool, smooth cheek. He'd been my champion. But no one could oust my grandmother from her high horse.

Now that I knew what she was cooking up for me, I began to work on a plan to leave my current job behind in the dust without getting roped into becoming a secretary. Not that there was anything wrong with being a secretary, but these were times of feminist awakening – I wanted to become someone in my own right – not an adjunct to someone who was *someone.*

I began to think about what I could do to support myself that would allow me to get away from my grandmother's endless disappointment.

At night I prayed God would show me a way to escape my current stalemate. I was too young to have my soul deadened by my grandmother's bitterness with life. Her minor-key dirges didn't sing to me at all. I needed out as soon as possible.

❧

About two weeks later, on one of those aimless days that figured largely in my life at that time, I took the bus to downtown Hartford for pretty much no reason at all.

I was wandering around the Woolworth's Five and Dime store when I got a very bad idea to shoplift a pair of dangly pink and gold earrings. The second I got the idea, I knew I needed to get out of the store. But I didn't.

Fingering the delicate filigreed hoop earrings, I held them up to my ears and looked in a mirror, then made a great show of putting them down again. The trick was that I only put down one pair of gold and pink earrings, not the two pairs I'd picked up. Don't ask where I'd learned that technique – this is a story about my future, not my past.

I walked up and down the aisles of the main floor, passing the jewelry, cosmetics, sunglasses, and sewing goods sections, until there was pretty much nowhere else to go other than out the door or back to the jewelry section to return the pair of earrings. Attached to a small rectangle of plastic backing, they nestled in the palm of my right hand, dangling next to the big, roomy right pocket of my green army pants.

They were mighty close – those earrings and my loose, empty pocket. All I needed to do was relax my grip for those earrings to deposit themselves deep in the folds of my pants. I decided not to think about it, just see what happened.

"Hey," a deep, male voice said close behind me. A smell of hair grease assailed my nostrils.

I jumped sideways, almost smashing into the display case I was standing next to. Every muscle of my body tensed, including my right hand. Instantly I put both hands up to my chest to protect myself. I could feel the posts of the hoop earrings digging into my palm. Ouch.

"Hey sweet thing, how 'bout a kiss?" The man before me was in his forties or fifties, graying, disheveled, and glassy-eyed. Yuck. His right arm shot out and grabbed my own. I struggled to get away from him as he leaned toward me, leering.

"How 'bout it, honey?" The smell of his breath was even more nauseating than the smell from his greasy hair. He pushed his face toward mine until I could feel the air expelled from his mouth on my lips. Revolted, I twisted violently, then stamped my right foot on his as hard as I could.

"Bitch, watch it!" he yelled as I pulled my arm free. I bolted down the aisle, followed by a string of foul epithets.

"You got it coming, girlie. You was asking for it. I'm gonna get you and your sweet pussy."

I ran to where I thought the nearest exit might be, dropping the earrings on the floor of the store.

"Serves me right, serves me right," screamed in my head, drowning out the feeling of the man's fingers digging into my arm, his fetid breath inches from my mouth.

Outside, I fled down Main Street, looking wildly for a safe place; somewhere the man behind wouldn't follow. I passed the library then Hartford's largest department store, G. Fox & Company. He could follow me inside both places, so I kept running.

"Oh God, Oh God, Oh God. I'm sorry, I'm sorry about the earrings, I'm sorry." Then I switched to "God help me. Help me now."

Past the department store, a dark, stone building with large, marble columns in front loomed ahead. It looked vaguely familiar. I glanced at a small, elegantly lettered sign on the front wall, *Hartford Racquetball Club*. It was a place my grandfather had taken me once for some sort of reception with our next-door neighbors the Sheltons — a private club for Hartford's finest families.

Up the steps I ran with the speed of light, almost colliding with the uniformed man opening the door for me.

"Yes, Miss?"

"Excuse me, but may I use your restroom?"

"This is a private club, Miss. I'm sorry."

"Yes, I know." I pulled myself together, straightening my back and looking him right in the eye. "Listen," I lowered my voice, "I'm being followed. A man is chasing me, a homeless guy. Just let me use the ladies' room. Please." My eyes bored into his, willing him to understand and respond.

He hesitated, looking less certain. I could bet they didn't care for scenes in a place like this.

"Please. He won't follow me in here. I'll just be a minute." I tried to look like the kind of person who wouldn't make a scene, the daughter of the kind of person who might belong to a club like this.

His face blanched as he shifted uncomfortably. "Well, if it's just for a minute."

"I promise, thank you." I craned my neck around him to see where the ladies' room might be.

"To the left at the end of the hall," he said quietly, his eyes discreetly indicating which way.

I flew down the hall and around the corner. The *Ladies' Room* sign was on the left. I ran to open the door.

Locked.

Ugh. Turning, I looked around. On the other side of the hallway was another door with a sign over it, *Ladies' Locker Room*. As I watched, a trim, blonde woman with a ponytail walked out, duffle bag and large handbag in hand. She reached into her handbag for something. As she did, I grabbed the door handle to hold it open for her.

"Thank you," she said, not making eye contact, still rummaging in her bag.

"You're welcome," I said, a tight, WASPy smile on my face in case she looked up. She didn't. *And thank you.* I sped into the locker room and entered the nearest bathroom stall to recover myself.

After a few minutes, I calmed down. Conflicting emotions chased each other through my head and nervous system: guilt, disgust, relief. I was disgusted by the gross man who had accosted me in the store. But hadn't my own actions before his arrival been just as gross? Which was worse, being a lecherous homeless guy or a shoplifter?

Had God used that repugnant man to save me from breaking a commandment? "Thou shalt not steal" had no qualifiers attached such as "Thou shalt not steal items valued over five dollars." I'd been rescued from my scumball self by a gross, homeless person. They weren't kidding when they said that God moves in mysterious ways.

Exiting the bathroom stall, I moved to the sink to wash the guilt off my face. The mirror told me that I looked the same. It lied. I was older and scummier than I was an hour earlier. I shook my head in disgust at the image of my round, unmarked pink and gold face – the same colors as the earrings I'd almost stolen.

I passed into the anteroom between the washroom and the door. A vanity stood on one side, a couch and two chairs on the other. I glanced at the notice board.

Announcements of candidates for membership were posted: *Gerard Aldrich (Vice-Chairman - Travelers' Insurance Corporation) and Penny Aldrich (wife) have been recommended for membership by Gaddis Newton. They have three children and reside in Avon and Nantucket.*

Farther down the board, a summer home in a place called Provence was listed for rent. Below that, more mundane listings for housekeeping and childcare were posted. My eyes swept over them: *Mature nanny, F/T for two children under age four in Farmington, five years experience min., must drive. Housekeeper available; excellent references.* Au pair *wanted for Anglo-American family in Paris; native English speaker only.*

Au pair? I had heard the term before. That was a babysitter for a family in another country. Most of the au pairs I'd heard about were college students or in their early to mid-twenties. Just where I was headed. My hand tingled. The same one that had squeezed then released the pink and gold earrings less than an hour earlier.

Looking around, I spotted a notepad and pen next to the house phone on the vanity table. I grabbed them and jotted down the phone number for the au pair listing.

At the front door, I nodded to the doorman as I slipped out. He looked relieved to see me go.

On the steps I scanned the sidewalk; my drunken rescuer from commandment-breaking was nowhere in sight. I shivered, thanking God for saving worthless, pathetic wretches like myself from myself as well as homeless lechers. Then I went straight home where I took the longest hot shower of my life as soon as I got inside the door.

Right before leaving for work I called the number for the au pair. A voicemail message came on, a woman's voice with a clipped, airy British-inflected accent. I left my name and number, careful to speak clearly to exhibit that not only was I a native English speaker, but one with a best-in-breed American accent.

Two days later, one of my roommates handed me a message. Someone named Annabel something-or-other had called about a babysitting job. I guessed immediately the Anglo-half of the Anglo-American family was the mother. How many American women were named Annabel?

I called the number again. This time, a live person answered.

"This is Ava Fodor returning a call from Annabel about an au pair job," I said, wishing my roommate had gotten her last name. I didn't want to sound too informal to a prospective employer, especially a British one.

"I see. What did you say your name was?" Her commanding voice told me I was speaking with the female head of the household.

"Ava. Ava Fodor." I enunciated each syllable clearly, careful to make the right first impression.

"And who was it at the club that recommended you?"

No one. What was it about clubs and recommendations? Thinking fast, I said "Mr. Shelton." He was the one who'd invited us to a reception at the Hartford Racquetball Club years earlier, so I hoped he might still be a member.

"Mr. Shelton?" The woman at the other end wasn't giving anything away. I couldn't blame her.

"Mr. Fred Shelton?" I offered weakly. *Please God, let the Sheltons still be members. Please, God.*

"Oh, you mean Fred and Nancy Shelton?"

"Yes. They're our next-door neighbors," I said, emulating her English accent. Inside, I gasped with relief. *Thank you, God.*

"In West Hartford?"

"Yes. On West Hill Drive."

"I see. And what are your parents' names, dear?"

"Walter and Helen Rusk." They were my grandparents, but so what?

"And do you have any babysitting experience?"

"Oh yes. Quite a lot." Now I was using British syntax: "quite" instead of "a whole lot."

"Have you ever lived with a family as a babysitter?"

"Well, I lived with the Sheltons for a summer while I took care of their daughter."

"Do you mean Rebecca?"

"Oh, you know her?" *What a relief.* "Yes, I looked after her a few summers ago down in Renwick."

The woman on the other end of the phone gave a laugh like tinkling bells. Had I said something funny?

"Just a minute." I heard the murmur of a male voice in the background. After some sort of interchange I couldn't make out, she got back on the line.

"Hullo?"

"Yes, I'm here." I tried to sound erudite, cultured, worthy of keeping her children's English up to snuff.

"We're looking for someone to look after our three children. There are two boys and a girl: ages six, eight, and eleven."

"That would be fine." It was hard to sound enthusiastic as well as British. Something about the two didn't go together.

"Then I'll be in touch, dear." She clicked off before I could respond.

That was it? Why hadn't she asked more questions? Had she been laughing at my pathetic American accent? My face flamed as I put down the phone. It was so hard to interpret someone from another country.

I spent the rest of the day despondent; knowing I'd blown it with God, blown it with the British lady, blown it with everyone in general. Still, it occurred to me to call the Shelton's just in case I hadn't entirely blown it and a friend of theirs named Annabel asked about me. Then I remembered they were down at the beach that weekend. I couldn't afford to call long distance so I decided to wait until Sunday evening when I planned to visit my grandparents for dinner.

That Sunday the Sheltons weren't back yet when I got to my grandparents' house.

"Nana, do you know when the Sheltons are coming back from the beach?"

"Why do you want to know?" my grandmother snipped, looking at me suspiciously.

"No reason. I just thought I might take Ginger for a walk when they get back," I explained, referring to the Shelton's dog. "She'll probably be desperate to go out after a long car ride."

The practice of hiding almost all personal information from my grandmother had become ingrained in me. She had a way of using whatever I told her as evidence of my misguided ways. I wouldn't mention the au pair job unless something came of it.

"Well, Nancy mentioned some sort of benefit they were going to this afternoon in Renwick, so I doubt they'll be back until late.

"Okay."

I hung around after dinner, long after my grandmother retired to her bedroom with a thimbleful of Dubonnet to watch the Ed Sullivan Show. Finally, I heard the Shelton's station wagon pull into their driveway. Not wanting to force myself on them after a long drive, I watched from the window until I saw Uncle Fred come out the back door with Ginger on her leash, straining and raring to go.

Quietly, I slipped out the front door then walked in the other direction, knowing I'd run into him halfway around the horseshoe-shaped drive, out of sight of my grandmother's bedroom window.

Within five minutes, his courtly, medium-tall figure loomed in sight. He was scratching Ginger's ears as they rested by the stone fence that bordered West Hill Drive from Farmington Avenue. I ran to him.

"Ava, what a nice surprise to see you." His face broke into a smile as he spotted me.

"Hi, Uncle Fred. How are you?"

"I'm fine. Nancy and I were just talking about you with our friends today."

"You were?"

"We saw the Griffiths this afternoon down in Renwick, and they asked about you. Do you remember them?"

"I – uh – I'm not sure." The Griffiths? Weren't those the folks with the trampoline in their backyard?

"Nancy told Annabel Griffith what a terrific job you did babysitting Becca a few summers ago."

Annabel Griffith? The same woman I'd spoken with on the phone?

"Is that the lady with the English accent with the trampoline in her backyard?"

"That's the one." He nodded thoughtfully, looking approvingly at me. His eyes on mine offered an antidote to my grandmother's baleful glances.

"They mentioned you'd spoken to them about a job babysitting their children in Paris for the school year."

"That's just what I was going to ask you about, Uncle Fred. I – I gave them your name as a recommendation."

"Already done, dear. Nancy raved about you to Annabel."

"Uncle Fred, you're too amazing!" The thought of a year in Paris made my heart pound. My face tingled as I imagined a whole world full of foreign cultures and countries to learn about. Much more appealing to generalist, adventurous me than deconstructing a Bach fugue.

Our eyes met, his filled with kindness and love. Everything was perfect for one shining moment, until my grandmother's face popped into my head. How would she receive the idea of me going abroad for a year? Any proposal coming from me was out. It always was, on principle.

"Umm – if Mrs. Griffith wants me for the job, how should I handle telling my grandmother?" Very few people outside our immediate family knew what a prickly character she was. To outsiders, my grandmother presented herself as a paragon of Southern warmth and charm. Even I was impressed by the incredible snow job she did on my friends. "Your grandmother is sooo nice," they'd trill after meeting her and being offered a piece of homemade fudge or a brownie. But Uncle Fred was one of the *cognoscenti*.

Although my grandmother was Boston-born, she'd been raised all over the place: Charleston, West Virginia; Los Angeles and La Jolla, California. Her father had been a hotel manager. Her mother ran off before my grandmother was old enough to remember her. After an unsettled childhood, she had enjoyed five years in Athens, Georgia with her first husband, a professor of agricultural at University of Georgia. Then he died of leukemia at age thirty, closing the chapter on the happiest years of her life. When she came north as a young widow her identity as a Southern woman had firmly cemented itself in her soul. To this end she occasionally referred to African Americans as 'darkies' and had a feminist sensibility mired deep in the Antebellum South.

"Don't say anything to your grandmother. If the Griffiths offer you a job I'll have Nancy speak to her," Mr. Shelton advised.

"Oh, Uncle Fred, thank you so much! I love you," I said, truly meaning it.

We both knew if the idea came from me she'd veto it. Coming from the Griffiths via Nancy Shelton, her socially prominent neighbor, my grand-mother would probably swoon with pleasure at the proposal.

On the way back to my apartment, I recollected memories of the Griffiths. I'd met them down in Renwick – a private enclave next to Old Saybrook, Connecticut, the summer I babysat Rebecca Shelton. The Sheltons owned a beachfront cottage in Renwick, three houses down from the Griffiths. Everyone in Renwick was very rich or related to someone who was. It was all inherited wealth, something I knew because my grand-mother had harped on the topic countless times as in, "Fred Shelton can afford to be nice to Nancy because he's never had to work for a living." My grandmother never had to work for a living either, but in her case she'd never been nice to my grandfather, whom she barely tolerated.

Mrs. Griffith was young, pretty, blonde, and British. She walked around at the beach in a teeny tiny bikini showing off her unbelievably slim post-third child figure in an effortless sort of way. I'd admired her hugely, although I never dared speak to her. It went without saying that anything I said to her would sound stupid, and then I'd sound even more stupid when she replied in her British accent and I wouldn't be able to understand a thing.

I was fourteen, about to enter ninth grade, the year before I'd been shipped off to Maine. The Griffiths were the perfect sort of all-American-with-a-European twist family I longed to be part of. My own family was twisted all-American except for one exotic European kink in the form of my father, a Transylvanian poet my mother had married at the tender age of twenty-four.

Poets, by and large, do not bring home the bacon. My father suffered the added disadvantage of not speaking English. Three months after arriving in the United States, at age forty-seven, he met my mother at a party thrown by a friend and patient of my grandfather's. My father had found work as a janitor at the Hartford Theological Seminary, a job he'd got through a sym-pathetic priest with a Hungarian background who'd read about him in the newspaper. He'd been photographed stepping off a plane in February 1957, an exiled Hungarian refugee persecuted in his own country for journalis-tic views he'd expressed against the new Communist regime. My mother melted at his dashing ways; hand kissing, smoking with a cigarette-holder, and wearing his jacket flung over both shoulders. What more could a girl ask for?

Apparently, a lot. My grandmother was not amused. The way she'd spit out the "'p" in, "Your father, the poet" came out as if she'd said "Your father, the pauper" or "the pickpocket." There went Robert Frost, Emily Dickinson, and John Donne, all out the window of my grandmother's estimation. If you couldn't make a good living or marry someone who did, you were no one in her book.

Predictably, my parents' marriage fell apart soon after my mother tired of life with a man twice her age who didn't speak English and had no money. They divorced when I was four and my father now lived in Yorkville, the Hungarian-German neighborhood on Manhattan's Upper East Side.

My mother resided in Greenwich Village in New York City with my younger half sister and brother, having divorced her second husband, an Italian-American man from the Bronx who hadn't worked out well either. We were vaguely aware of each other, but since my grandparents took me at the age of fourteen months for a summer babysitting stint that lasted the duration of my childhood, my grandmother hadn't been understanding of her daughter's lifestyle choices. After two disastrous marriages, both to men my grandmother deemed unsuitable, my grandmother washed her hands of her only daughter. I'd received Christmas and birthday cards from my mother throughout my childhood, but no visits after age five, when my grandmother made it clear she was no longer welcome. My grandfather had gone along with her to keep peace in his home.

The Griffiths summered in Renwick and wintered in Paris. How cool was that? Paris, to my fourteen-year-old imagination, was someplace beautiful and elegant where people ate croissants for breakfast on balconies festooned with intricate, curlicue designs outside grand, high-ceilinged apartments. At age six, my grandmother had taken me to see the film *The Red Balloon*. My bookcase was filled with *Babar the Elephant* books I'd read as a child and couldn't bear to give away. I knew all about Paris.

While the Griffiths were in residence at their summer beach house, their trampoline was available for any of the Renwick kids to jump on during the day. Most of the time, the Griffiths weren't home. They were at the beach or the Club playing tennis or golf. My young charge, Rebecca and I would drop by almost every day to jump on the trampoline.

That summer, I fantasized I was the eldest child from a family such as theirs, jumping up and down on my own trampoline. Rebecca was my adorable, blonde, five-year old sister. We lived in Renwick in the summer and in Paris in the winter. I'd jump with a dreamy expression on my face, hoping I'd spring into another life altogether like Alice down the rabbit hole.

A week after my conversation with Uncle Fred, my grandmother called. It was unusual for her to call at all since I'd begun living on my own with a group of other girls all connected up with the music college I'd bombed out of. Four of us rented the first floor of a three-family house right down the street from the gas station where I worked. It was six blocks from my grandparents' street, right over West Hartford's town line in Hartford where the bad neighborhood began. It was close enough that I could still walk over to their place for the occasional non-fun family get-together, but far enough away to ensure I didn't bump into them or anyone they knew.

"Ava, I have something to ask you," she said, sounding strangely formal, as if she were playacting or something. Usually, she never asked family members anything, she just told us what was what. I immediately knew something was up.

"Yes, Nana?" I asked, praying this might be the follow-up to Nancy Shelton's talk with Annabel Griffith.

"Well you certainly don't deserve this, and I have no idea why they thought of you, but do you remember a family down in Renwick by the name of Griffith?"

"You mean the family with the trampoline and three kids?" I could hardly contain myself, but I needed to act surprised.

"Yes. Win Griffith's father is retired head of Aetna," she said, referring to Hartford's biggest insurance company. Who knew? Who cared?

Apparently, my grandmother did. "Well you must have made quite an impression on them although I don't know how," she continued. The faster my grandmother's put-downs flew, the better the news would be. Her compliments to family members were routinely served with a sizeable splash of vinegar. My heart thumped in my chest.

"Well, they've asked Nancy Shelton to ask you if you'd be interested to babysit their children this school year in Paris."

"Oh wow! In Paris? Yes! I'd love to." I tried to sound as if the idea hadn't already occurred to me, been engineered by me, in fact.

"They wouldn't pay you much, but it would be a way for you to stay out of trouble."

The thought of the amount of trouble I could get myself into on my own in Paris compelled me to sit down, phone receiver trembling in hand.

"I'll spend the year applying to colleges, Nana. You'll see. I'll get into a good school."

"You already got into a good school thanks to your grandfather's and my connections, and then you threw it all away."

"I'm going to do it this time without your connections, Nana. I want to do it on my own." Hadn't I just set up this babysitting job on my own? Her recurring mantra on my grandfather's medical degree flashed into my head. *Your grandfather only made it through Harvard Med School because of his photographic memory.* Whatever either of us achieved, we could never win with her.

"You'll do it this time without our financial support, Ava. We're done tossing good money after bad. First your mother, now you. When you come back from your year abroad you'll either go to secretarial school or get a real job." My grandmother's plans for me were always plans for herself. In her eyes, my gas station one didn't count and for once, I was in agreement with her.

In your dreams, lady, not mine. "Okay, fine. I accept!"

"Then get yourself over here for dinner tonight, and I'll have you run over to Nancy with the news. Make sure you thank her profusely. She must have told the Griffiths some whoppers about you for them to offer you a job."

"Nana, I did actually babysit Rebecca for an entire summer. Maybe that had something to do with it."

"Be here by six. And if I were you, I would pick up some flowers for Nancy. She went out of her way for you." *Even though you don't deserve it* lingered in the air, unspoken.

My grandmother was artwork. Even if I hadn't wanted to spend a year in Paris, I'd have gone anyway, just to get away from my substitute mom's bottomless well of negativity and not-really-well-meaning advice.

❧

The next few months flew by like white lightning. On a golden late September evening, I boarded my flight to Paris – excited, exuberant, and ready for adventure. Goodbye West Hartford, goodbye gas station, goodbye Nana, goodbye to all that.

And *bonjour*, City of Light.

CHAPTER TWO

Au Pair in Paris

Working for the Griffiths turned out to be a dream job. Mrs. Griffith was not only gorgeous, but nice, and fond of wearing Laura Ashley dresses. She taught pottery classes. Mr. Griffith was a Yale grad, now president of the American College in Paris. He was tall, athletic, and pleasantly attractive in that "hail fellow well met" sort of way I'd come to France to escape. He was the only adult male I ever saw, in our neighborhood of École Militaire, who carried a gym bag to and from work with a squash racket sticking out of it instead of a *porte-documents*, or briefcase.

Then there were the two stunning blond boys, Winston and Cole, ages eight and six who appeared to have stepped off the pages of a Ralph Lauren catalogue. Their less ethereal eleven-year old sister, Reid, was a gangly brunette whose imperfections I could better relate to.

Mr. and Mrs. Griffith were hip, relatively young, and very rich. Their guidelines for my job would have made any other au pair drool with envy. I was to show up twice a week in the evenings to look after the children while they went out; no weekends, no trips to their country home unless I wanted to come, no cleaning because they employed a full-time

Portuguese housekeeper, no cooking. Mrs. Griffith did all that and left dinner for us in her own handmade pottery containers in the fridge. No plastic Tupperware for this family. The salary was measly, but so were my duties.

I spent babysitting evenings on the couch with the two oldest children telling me stories in clipped British-inflected tones about the international school they attended, while the youngest cuddled in my lap as I stroked his curly, platinum-blond hair and rubbed his back. A glutton for affection, he was my favorite of the three.

Given the choice of taking the spare room in their seventh *arrondissement* flat (translation – very good neighborhood) or living on the top floor of the building in the maid's quarters, a room the size of a postage stamp with a Turkish toilet (that's a hole in the floor with a pull-chain – it was 1977) in the hall and a sink outside the wash closet with only one cold water tap, I took the maid's room.

Privacy, it's all about privacy when you're nineteen years old and have only been post-virginal for a matter of months. To hell with weekends in the countryside with the family. Paris was my oyster, my aphrodisiac.

I hoped the Griffiths' family would forgive me for my appalling lack of interest in hanging out with them. They were the most well-appointed, genetically enhanced family I had ever met, precisely the reason I had no desire to spend more time with them. A big, bad, dirty, dark world awaited – the world of my newfound womanhood. And where better to explore it than the sexy, smelly City of Light?

I'd been in Paris for four months. Men pursued me relentlessly on the street: Algerians, Moroccans, Tunisians. Then there were the sub-Saharan Africans from Senegal or Cote d'Ivoire. The names of the countries appealed to my sense of exoticism, but not the type. I was looking for a Frenchman. What was the point of spending a year in Paris if not to meet an actual Frenchman? I didn't want to get tied up with another foreigner who was in the city for reasons similar to my own.

I signed up for a course on French language and civilization at the Sorbonne. My weekly budget roughly averaged out to twenty francs a day, about four dollars. At the start of each month, I'd purchase a *carte orange*, the monthly bus and metro pass that afforded me my main source of pleasure, exploring different neighborhoods in Paris and, above all, people-watching.

My French language class was given three times a week on an ancient, crooked side street, Rue Cloître Notre Dame, off to one side of the famous Notre Dame cathedral. The lectures on civilization took place at the Sorbonne itself on Rue des Écoles in an enormous auditorium filled with wooden seats and pull-up desks with graffiti etched into them dating back to the nineteenth century.

Thanks to the desktops and bathroom stalls at the Sorbonne, I figured out some key expressions that didn't figure into my French language lesson books. *Bordel*, for example, didn't mean bordello, but more closely resembled mess or fuck-up. *Fous le camp* was another popular one, loosely meaning, go fuck yourself. I didn't yet know what my plan was for the rest of my life, but at least I was picking up an education. And who could argue with "studying at the Sorbonne" on a college application form instead of "cashiering at a self-service gas station"?

Blonde, slightly chubby au pairs such as myself were a dime a dozen. We were walking targets for the single North and West African males who roamed the streets. Their opening lines were all the same, *"Vous avez l'heure, Mademoiselle?* Do you have the time, Miss?"

Come to think of it, that was the line Jean-Michel used, too. But his blue eyes, pale skin, Jean-Paul Belmondo boxer's nose and wavy light brown hair relaxed my guard. The chances were good that he was a Frenchman. For once, I did have the time, and I gave it to him.

The first moment Mrs. Griffith laid eyes on Jean-Michel was when he picked me up at the servants' entrance to the kitchen of my employers' flat. The look she gave him could have frozen over hell. As I watched her jaw clench, I understood for the first time the expression "recoiled in horror." He was thirty-two at the time, four years younger than her. It was clear that she knew what he was there for far better than I did, and she emphatically did not approve.

These being pre-e-mail days, I wondered if a telegram might be sent to my grandparents warning them I was up to no good with a much older Frenchman.

Frankly, they had nothing to worry about. I was not under the illusion that just because I knew next to nothing about sex, birth control, or pregnancy, I couldn't get knocked up. I wasn't a doctor's granddaughter for nothing. I had taken the precaution of putting myself on the pill not only before arriving in Paris, but one month before my first sexual encounter the summer before.

I was also prepared to turn away from Mrs. Griffith as she tossed a couple of eye-glance daggers at Jean-Michel then shut the door smartly in a manner that told me exactly what she thought. It was one of those moments when I knew I was no longer a child trying to please the adult authority figure in my vicinity. I was on my own, moving into unknown territory, and ready to go. This was no easy feat for a former Girl Scout who had heretofore sought approval from important adults in her life. Teachers, my favorite uncle, my high school guidance counselor – I'd tried hard to impress them all as a child.

As Mrs. Griffith shut the door harshly in our faces, I turned to Jean-Michel and gave him a poker face to let him know I knew what she was thinking, but I was thinking differently. So *allons-y*. Let's go.

It was a cold late January day on Boulevard Saint Michel, or Boul' Mich as it is commonly known, when Jean-Michel and I first met. I was bundled up in a shapeless L.L. Bean winter parka over overalls, my feet shod in dead giveaway "I'm-not-a-Frenchwoman" clogs. My morning lecture at the Sorbonne on French culture was over and I was hurrying home. I'd absorbed absolutely nothing from the lecture, given entirely in French – a language I could only vaguely understand if spoken ten times slower than any French person spoke it. Instead, I was thinking about which pastry to choose when I got to my favorite patisserie around the corner from the Griffith's flat. Zeroing in on making contact with a creamy hazelnut *Breton*, named for Brittany, a region in France to the west of Paris on the Atlantic coast, instead, I bumped into a *Normandien*. That's a man from Normandy, an area between Brittany and Paris.

"*Excusez-moi, Madamoiselle, avez-vous l'heure?*" he said, using one of the few French phrases I understood perfectly, having been accosted so frequently over the past five months by men with the same hackneyed line. It was as if I wore an invisible sign reading, "I am a naïve foreigner, please try to pick me up."

Preparing as usual to blankly stare past the annoying *boulevardier* – a man who tries to pick up women on boulevards, also known as *drageurs* or draggers – I noticed out of the corner of my eye the dark blue eyes of the man addressing me. Different. Very different from all the rest.

"*C'est une heure et quart*," I said, letting him know it was a quarter past one.

"*Merci*," he responded, falling into step beside me.

After a brief pause, during which time I processed his pale skin and a bump in his nose telling me it might have been broken, the inevitable question followed.

"*Vous êtes Americaine?*"

To be honest, I also frequently got, "*Vous êtes Hollandaise?* Are you Dutch?" and "*Vous êtes Suedoise?* Are you Swedish?"

Both guesses probably were due to my clunky workman-style clothes left over from high school years in Maine, a state not known for its high-fashion sense.

"*Oui*," I replied, sticking my short, turned-up nose into the air and away from him while I picked up my pace. The male of the species could be deadeningly predictable at times.

Some other idiotic questions followed, such as "You are a student?" and "Do you like Paris?" Then, a practical one: "Would you like to go for a coffee?"

For once, I would. I was cold, I had been thinking about stopping for a coffee before arriving at my bus stop, and this guy appeared to be French. I was dying to meet an actual Frenchman. I hadn't met any French women either, but they were not my focus other than as style icons to emulate.

I turned and looked at him briefly before replying, "*Oui, pourquoi pas?* Sure, why not?" I answered, a response I would never have given in English. But the whole blasé thing was so very French and that was what I was here to learn about, wasn't it?

Of course, I didn't smile. Why should I? I hadn't spent the past five months studying the *froideur* or haughty demeanor of Parisian women for nothing.

Jean-Michel gave only the faintest of smiles, then silently led the way to a café near one of the many entrances to the Saint Michel metro station.

Inside the café I sat down, carefully concealing my excitement. I had done it! Across from me sat a genuine Frenchman, perhaps the one thousandth *boulevardier* who had accosted me in the street since I'd arrived the previous September.

Jean-Michel was not overly talkative. I liked that right away. He wasn't leaning over the table breathing into my face. He didn't attempt to touch me. He wore a gray wool jacket with a burgundy and navy striped scarf around his neck – something my grandfather would wear. Sitting slightly sideways from the table, he crossed one slender, muscular leg over the other. He had an athletic, skinny build, not too tall, very French.

We introduced ourselves. I told him I was from Connecticut, which he'd never heard of. He told me he was from Normandy, which I had. Finest butter in the world. Once I'd tasted it, I was ruined for American butter for the rest of my life. Great cows are bred in France, the greatest in Normandy.

Wide pauses punctuated our questions and answers. Jean-Michel didn't fill up airspace asking the kinds of irritating questions I was always getting back home, "What are your plans?" The whole tedious, "What are you going to do with your life?" line I was currently allergic to.

I didn't know it at the time, but questions about what a person does aren't usually asked in Europe, especially within minutes of meeting each other. Europeans generally don't have a huge choice as to what they end up doing with their lives.

Jean-Michel's classically European, non-interrogative approach to conversation worked like a charm on me. No wonder cafés were invented in Europe. They offered both time and space to talk, or to observe and not talk.

I've always loved space: space between musical notes, space between people on a crowded sidewalk, space and time to think about something that just happened.

Now something was happening and the man across from me was giving me time to digest it. Was this a pick-up technique he'd perfected? Or was he just naturally intuitive when it came to women?

I thought it could be either. Whichever it was, I was impressed. He wasn't breathing down my neck, trying to get my number and address, or tossing out ridiculous, embarrassing compliments. I wasn't particularly self-confident at that moment in my life so no amount of observations from a man on my pretty face, my blonde hair, or my cute upturned nose would have had much of an impact on me. I was perfectly aware that my broad-boned Hungarian face was too round, my hair prone to frizziness, and my ridiculous perky nose at least two millimeters too short to have any *gravitas* or seriousness, at all.

I hadn't yet learned to listen to what a man might tell me. I was too busy fending them off.

After a relaxed quarter of an hour, we'd finished our coffee. I'd had time to absorb Jean-Michel's smashed-in boxer's nose, navy blue eyes, and mild manner. While I studied his shoulders, broad but not too broad, he scribbled something on a piece of paper. I knew what it was before he handed it to me.

He paid the bill, gave me the slip of paper and told me to call him sometime. There was no pressure at all. He did exactly what I wanted him to do. He let me know he was interested in seeing me again, but he gave me space and time in which to respond. I could already see he knew his way around women.

I took the bus home, forgot to pick up my usual pastry, and went up to my room. There, I had a long think. It lasted almost a week.

∽

Night and day, I wrestled with whether to call Jean-Michel. Nightly, I'd decide to call, the following day, I'd panic. I was in the Lenten period leading up to my birthday. Every year at that time, I'd reflect on my shortcomings. The year before, I had reflected on the idiotic burden of my virginity and vowed to cast it off as soon as possible post-birthday.

I accomplished my mission five months later, methodically and purposefully one sultry July night with the Portuguese-American boy I was seeing. I liked making love – sort of – but the experience was so new. There was all this unexpected noise and sweat, not to mention hair in unexpected places. Had he noticed I didn't have breasts like Barbie? Who knew some guys had hair on their derrières? After he'd leave, I'd go out on the back porch of the house I shared with the girl grads from music college, none of whom had found jobs in their field, and crank up Bruce Springsteen's *Born to Run* album on the record player. After a month of frequent assignations, I was definitely ready to run or at least back off in order to absorb all the new information our trysts had provided.

The minute the Griffiths offered me a job, I told him we needed to break up so that I could get ready for my new job in Paris. Sounded good, huh?

That had been my nineteenth summer, but now I was about to turn twenty. It was time to take an active approach to my sex life again – grab the bull by the horns, so to speak. I wanted to shake off my passive book-worm identity, get out of my shell, and get out there. A phone number had been handed to me by a man who understood my need for maneuvering room, and he wasn't unattractive. The ball was in my court.

Two days after my birthday I called. He knew who I was immediately and didn't waste time. Would I like to meet him at the entrance to the Louvre Museum workshop at Trocadéro at five on Friday? I would.

He gave me directions, letting me know this was his workplace. This also let me know he probably wasn't married or currently carrying on with an active girlfriend. If he was, why would he suggest meeting at a place where his colleagues might see me?

Relieved, I spent the next four days planning how things might go. I decided to forego my usual overalls and wear my most flattering jeans; the ones that showed off my curvy backside – the one asset I had that trumped the rear ends of most Frenchwomen I'd seen. I washed my hair the day before, slipping into the Griffith's apartment during the daytime to take a shower with hot water.

On the appointed day, I decided to walk to our assignation. One of the great joys of living in Paris was how pleasurable it was to walk almost every-where. Buildings gleamed with pride, the most gorgeous of which were illu-minated at night. Attractive people sat at outdoor cafes twelve months of the year. There was something to study wherever I looked, and, for the most part, my eyes settled on beauty. Traversing the Champs de Mars, barely throwing a glance at the touristy Eiffel Tower, I crossed the Pont d'Iena, one of six bridges in Paris which traverse the Seine, and made my way up the slight hill to the twin towers of the Palais de Chaillot also known as Trocadéro after which the film *Madwoman of Chaillot* was named, starring Katherine Hepburn from my birthplace of Hartford, Connecticut.

Paris, like the rest of northern Europe, was gray and dreary in the winter-time, and it was now mid February. But the gloom of the late afternoon did nothing to diminish the beauty of the approach to the Palais de Chaillot – two long, stately buildings each terminating in a tower stood above a long, oval pool with multiple fountains. Skateboarders practiced on ramps on either side of the pool leading up to the grand plaza in front of the twin palaces. I climbed the stairs to take in the view of the Seine, which I had just crossed from Left Bank to Right.

Everything felt right. Going around to the back of the Palais, I searched for a few moments, then found a modest door cut into the solid granite building with a discreet sign saying *Atelier du Musée du Louvre* in small letters. Nothing flashy. Before I had time to get nervous, the door opened, and Jean-Michel came out. His blue eyes flared as he spotted me. Coming over, he leaned down and kissed both of my cheeks. A combination of not-unpleasant male sweat and faint cologne helped me make up my mind instantly if this was going to go somewhere or not. It was.

We walked to the balustrade of the plaza of the Palais, from whence I'd just come. I'd just leaned over its wide marble surface as a young, clueless foreign girl – drinking in the sight of the Seine and the Eiffel Tower beyond without being in any relationship to it. Now, I was standing next to a Frenchman whose male scent was playing in my nostrils, with whom every potentiality stretched before me just as the wide park of the Champ de Mars did on which the Eiffel Tower was situated. Everything had changed in the space of five minutes, or rather, had the potential to change, given what I chose to do about it. The gods had handed me a cup, and I was ready to drink.

Just as at our previous meeting, Jean-Michel played it cool, there beside me, reassuring me with his presence and an occasional glance from his dark, blue eyes, but not frightening me away with overwhelming intensity or male interest in my young, nubile self. He was a regular New Englander of a Frenchman, perfect for a Connecticut Yankee in the Court of the Sun King.

Slowly, we strolled to a café across the Trocadéro traffic circle. It was cold, with a hint of dampness in the air. Night was falling. We ordered a carafe of red wine. My stomach warmed from the first sip. Our conversation had nothing to do with content and everything to do with checking each other out. Acceptably youthful, virile, and not overwhelming male smell. Check. Moderately good looks. Check. Cool, unhurried style. Double check. Shoes clean and polished. Double check. (Mental note to American males:

pay more attention to your shoes on first date.) Hands, medium-sized with long, rather wide fingers, sort of truncated at ends. Check.

Once we'd gotten through preliminary inspection, Jean-Michel suggested dinner, to which I agreed. We hopped on a bus and traversed the Seine back to the Left Bank, from whence I'd come.

We went for couscous. Paris is similar to New York; all the low-budget restaurant choices are ethnic. If you want to eat out affordably you choose North African cuisine or Vietnamese. If you want to eat a French meal, you prepare it at home or else pay a small fortune.

The Moroccan restaurant he led me to was in the neighborhood of Montparnasse, less than half an hour's walk from the Griffith's apartment. It would be an easy escape homeward if necessary.

Dinner was a continued dance of assessment. At the end, after ordering a plate of sticky sweet North African pastries he insisted I try, he asked if I'd like to drop by his place for a cognac. It was right around the corner. I wanted to but I was scared. What if I wanted to leave, and he wouldn't let me?

Nothing about Jean-Michel up to now indicated he was that kind of guy. But I told him I wasn't sure. He shrugged. We began to walk down Boulevard Montparnasse in the direction of my home. Nothing needed to be decided for the moment.

He put my arm in his. The smell of his wool jacket pleased me. I was drowsy and warmed from dinner.

At the corner of Boulevard Montparnasse and Avenue Le Clercy he stopped. "Shall we drop by my place for a *digestif?*" he asked again, using the French word for an after dinner drink meant to aid digestion.

I choked, then cleared my throat. I wanted to, but I wasn't ready yet. Of the myriad things I wished to say to him to explain why I wasn't ready to visit his apartment, I could express none of them in French. This worked out fine, because the only thing I was capable of saying said it all.

"*Pas encore.* Not yet." I shook my head just the tiniest bit playfully, my mouth in a tight little New England line.

"Shall I call you?" he asked in French.

"I don't have a phone." This time my mouth twitched. I did so want him to call me.

"Do you want to meet again?" he continued. This time, his eyes flicked over me like a man who could take a punch.

"Yes." I nodded.

His radar was good, his pace unhurried.

He looked down to hide his smile, pulling a packet of Gauloises from his inside jacket pocket and offering me one. I declined. He lit a cigarette carefully. Then, he loitered. I did too.

After a few minutes, it seemed too cold for further loitering.

"I should get home," I said.

"Come on, I'll walk you to the bus stop."

"I think I'll just walk back." I had a lot to think about and as long as I was moving, it wasn't too cold.

"Come on then."

We fell into step beside each other, the cold February night stinging our cheeks and crystallizing our thoughts. We were both thinking about the same thing, of that I was sure.

In a short half hour, we were at the corner of Avenue de la Bourdonnais and Rue de Belgrade, the street on which I lived. The way Jean-Michel looked over my building told me it was a very good address indeed, as if I hadn't already known. The Griffith's across the hall neighbor's Porsche was parked curbside, it's sleek frame low to the ground, like a tiger ready to pounce.

"Here we are," I said. "Thank you for a nice evening." This time, I felt my eyelids half close, my body betraying my interest in this not being the end of the story.

"Shall I come up?"

I shook my head. Not ready yet. Need time to think. *Too much of a thinker and not enough of a doer* a voice inside taunted.

"Shall I cook you dinner Sunday evening?"

Before I'd probed the entirety of what I was agreeing to, my head nodded up and down. What was there to say no to? I like to eat dinner and the concept of a man cooking one for me was altogether novel. The fact that this was a French man I found attractive, offering to cook a French meal made it impossible to say no. Also, I'd rejected him enough for one evening. Wasn't it time to say yes to something? I tucked the thought that the meal would be at his place into a dark corner of my brain.

"How about if I pick you up around three? We'll take a walk in the park then I'll make a special dish from Normandy for you."

My head kept nodding, up and down. I had time between now and Sunday afternoon to think about how Sunday evening might go. It was just what I needed, time and space to digest the unspoken plan between us.

"*Bonne nuit*," I whispered.

"*Bon dodo*," he whispered back, the way parents said goodnight to their children in French.

This time, the two kisses he gave me on either side of my face were slower, the velvetiness of his lips lingering on my skin. The smell of him was strong, fresh, male. Then he was gone, his back turned to me. I could see the movement of his arm as he reached into his jacket pocket for a cigarette.

❦

The first half of the weekend passed quickly. My conscience smacked me around non-stop – or maybe it was my id. *Get with the plan, Ava. Stop living in your head, and start living your life.*

I went through my wardrobe and found a soft, stretchy black and gold top to wear over black jeans. I shaved my legs, propping up one at a time on the sink with the cold water tap. It wasn't easy.

Miraculously, I held off on my usual two pastries a day habit. Something bigger than the appeal of flaky croissants, melting *pains au chocolat*, or the numerous other works of edible art displayed in the windows of the *boulangeries* or bakeries had taken me over. The ancient call of the wild beckoned; a summons I'd only recently awoken to and didn't really know how to answer. Jean-Michel's dark blue gaze told me he would know how to fill in the considerable gaps in my sentimental education.

At three on Sunday afternoon, I was on the sidewalk outside my building. Jean-Michel was prompt. This time, he wore a leather jacket. He stooped to kiss me twice, and we set off toward the Champ de Mars, the park next to which I lived. Its entrance lay twenty yards from my building. He had a sort of tough guy walk, no nonsense with a slight swagger. It appealed to me in a shivery sort of way.

At the entrance to the park, as if on cue, he took my arm and slipped it under his. The rich leather of his jacket smelled good. Combined with the faint scent of Gaulois cigarettes and the less faint smell of male sweat, it all beckoned to me. *Come on, Ava, cross over to the other side of the tracks. Stop standing on the sidelines and get on the train.*

I folded my fingers around Jean-Michel's forearm. Underneath them, his muscles tightened. They whispered to me the tantalizing thought that similar muscles could be found all over his body, waiting to contract under my touch.

We walked slowly down the Champs de Mars past the children in the playground, the Guignols puppet theater, finally stopping at one of the four enormous legs of the Eiffel Tower.

"Have you been up to the first level yet?" he asked.

"No, never."

"Shall we go?"

"Yes." Suddenly, I had license to explore the Eiffel Tower. For months, I had avoided it like the plague, although I lived less than a quarter mile away. I'd regarded it as the most obvious symbol of tourist attractions, so I'd deliberately disdained it. I didn't want to be thought of as a tourist. I told myself I lived here – at least for the year.

Something inside now gave me permission to visit the monument. I was on a date with a real Frenchman, an actual resident of the most beautiful city in the world. The Eiffel Tower was Paris's ultimate symbol. There was no way I would visit it with another tourist. This was different. Saving myself for the right moment to visit with the right man, it had now arrived.

We climbed the stairs to the first level. As we came out onto the platform, I caught my breath. Even on the lowest level, the view was extraordinary. Beside me, he seemed to sense my emotion. Taking my arm, he led me to the right to view the city's northeastern quarters.

"You can see so much," I sputtered out, amazed at the beauty of the city laid out before us.

The dome of the Basilica of Sacré Coeur, Paris's second most famous church after Notre Dame, shone gold in the setting sun behind our backs.

"All the Queen's jewels are on display here," he said, surprising me with the poetry of his words.

"How is it we see everything, or it seems like it?" I began.

His other arm reached around my waist. This was a fast, new maneuver.

I was ready for it.

"You're right. We can see every monument in the city from here. Because buildings in Paris cannot be more than twenty meters tall."

"So nothing obscures the view of something beautiful behind it."

"Only La Défense. Disgraceful." His face puckered into a classic Gallic sneer, honed over centuries of French contemplation of what constitutes good taste.

"What's La Défense? Where?"

He steered me back in the direction of the staircase. Pointing north by northwest his finger led my eye to a cluster of skyscrapers far in the distance to the west of Trocadéro. To an American, they were nothing unusual at all, but they seemed out of place against the harmony of the rest of the low cityscape.

"How did such tall buildings get past the zoning laws?" I asked.

"They're outside the city limits. In Neuilly-sur-Seine. A mistake. It's a business district, doesn't belong here at all."

I silently approved, not yet having any sort of business district taking up real estate in my twenty-year old heart.

"I don't belong here at all either," I commented, the thought escaping my mouth before I could stuff it back into my private thoughts collection where it belonged.

He gave me a wry smile, something entirely outside the context of what was developing between us, then pushed a strand of my hair behind my right ear. As he smiled, the lines on either side of his mouth changed from ironic to something more wistful.

"That's for you to decide," he said, after a moment.

"Really?" I tilted my head to gaze at him. His eyes held mine playfully. Then, his arm once again snaked around to the small of my back. He pulled me closer, not too close for comfort, but in a way that offered support, as well as fueled my interest.

"It's for you to decide," he said again, his voice lower.

This time, we weren't talking about La Défense.

"I like that," I told him. And I did. I liked the way Jean-Michel kept tossing the ball in my court. It wasn't just him playing offense and me playing defense. It was a volley.

Jean-Michel was eliciting some sort of huntress in myself I hadn't known existed other than in my most basic urge to continue my new studies in the world of sex.

I leaned back into his arm. He quickly brought his other one around to support me better. I leaned farther back, testing him. He held me well, not trying to pull me toward him, just watching my face and waiting. *Maestro.*

After some moments, I turned around in his arms and surveyed the south of the city. Soon, he moved closer behind me. I leaned back against his chest.

Then, the most extraordinary thing happened. An entire hidden section of my body, some secret area behind and below my stomach, kindled then burst into flame. It didn't have anything to do with romance. I wasn't looking soulfully into his eyes at the moment. I'd been searching the skyline for the tower of Montparnasse while the lower half of my body began an entirely different search. This was raw lust, a physical connection bypassing the brain altogether. It was the fire numerous erotic novels I devoured had described. I wasn't forcing myself to experience something just to know what it felt like. I'd done that already and although it had been pleasant, I hadn't particularly related it to being on fire.

Now I was.

Nothing could have come between Jean-Michel's body and mine at that moment. The atomic bomb could have dropped nearby, and I would have scarcely noticed. All I could feel was an indescribable melting sensation, as if the core of my being was melting into the universe, becoming one with everything around it.

Jean-Michel didn't move. The late afternoon sun warmed us weakly. Nobody was about. It was the stillest, yet most electrifying moment of my life thus far. I was trapped in a painting, my own will holding me there. I knew enough about Jean-Michel already to know he would move away if I'd resisted in any way. So I didn't.

It crossed my mind that it was slightly strange to receive so much pleasure from a man standing behind me, not face-to-face. But there was no denying it. I found his presence behind me much more exciting than if he'd been staring into my face, eliciting my nervous lack of self-confidence. This was better. He was giving me the privacy to experience my own pleasure. At my own pace. Not to have to worry about his pleasure at all or how my hair looked or whether I had mascara smudges under my eyes. Privacy and intimacy whirled together in the face of the setting sun.

For the first time, I understand what women meant when they said, "I didn't love him, but I loved what he did to me." Up to then, I'd thought you automatically had to be in love with the man who did things to you that you loved. In a flash I saw it wasn't so. My relief was huge. I wanted so to experience sensations I might love from a man, but I wasn't ready to be in love. I just wanted to know what the fuss was all about without getting permanently ensnared.

When I finally turned back to Jean-Michel, we understood each other completely.

"Shall we go?" he asked.

I nodded, unwilling to break the spell. From the looks of his narrowed eyes and flushed face, he was under it too. I walked beside him to the staircase then down one hundred eighty-nine feet to the park below. An image played in my mind of us as an invisible, permanent statue left behind on the first level, his body behind mine as we looked out over the Seine. I decided that we would always be there, held in position by psychic forces so impressed by our ecstatic stillness that they decided to memorialize us forever.

Forty-five minutes later, we arrived at his building. It was old and in need of a facelift, nestled in a quiet side street off Boulevard Montparnasse.

Up five flights of stairs, trying to conceal my breathlessness, I understood one of the many reasons why Parisians were rarely fat. At least my own building had an elevator, albeit an ancient one.

Jean-Michel unlocked the door to his apartment; it was exactly as I'd pictured it, miniscule with a sloped ceiling. It was one room, tucked under the eaves of the building. I took in a narrow bed, a table with two chairs, a desk, and a single lowly electric burner on top of a bar-sized refrigerator.

On further inspection I noticed a bathroom with shower only. All in all, it was an upgrade on my own attic room with the Turkish toilet in the hallway outside and no running hot water.

Jean-Michel's student flat didn't surprise me at all. The problem was figuring out where to look without looking at his bed, the largest piece of furniture in the room. Jean-Michel took my coat and scarf, hung them on a hook on the back of the door, then motioned to the table. I sat at it.

Immediately, he busied himself with taking out various paper-wrapped parcels from the refrigerator, finding a pot then setting up the hot plate. In another minute, he had opened the bottle of red wine on the table and poured two glasses.

I drank, taking in my surroundings. They were humble but tasteful. Prints I'd guess were from the Louvre museum shop affixed the walls along with posters of past exhibitions. One of my favorite pastimes in Paris was to go in the shops with my Polish au pair friend from Birmingham, England, who lived around the corner and ask for the posters in the windows of exhibitions that had just ended. The shopkeepers more often than not gave us them, since they would just take them down and throw them away anyway. Elzbieta, who went by Elizabeth, was stunning; a petite Polish beauty with platinum blonde hair and eyes the color of cornflowers. Her magic worked better on male shopkeepers than female ones, so we targeted the men, almost always successfully. Posters in Parisian shop windows constituted art work. We knew how exotic and appealing they'd look to our friends and family back home. It was one of the few activities we could do on our days off that cost us absolutely nothing, perfect for our budgets.

Jean-Michel had clearly had the same idea. His poster collection was better than mine, but it reminded me of the decor in my own room, giving me a measure of comfort. When he went out into the hallway to take out the trash, I took the opportunity to use his bathroom. Running the tap noisily, I opened the cabinet over the sink. No medications. Good. A bottle of Denim aftershave. So that was the scent I enjoyed smelling on him, mixed with leather, wool, and manly sweat. I made a note to remember it. The wrong scent on a man would stop me dead in my tracks. It was far more about scent than it was about looks in my book. The nose knows.

Returning to the table I spotted something pinkish and serrated on the butcher's shop paper on the counter. Glancing at it, I recognized tripe. Lord.

For five months, I had firmly forced down my throat every exotic type of French food offered in my relentless quest to experience the real France. I was not in Paris for a year to eat hamburgers and pizza. I was here to try crêpes from sidewalk vendors, not a difficult assignment; escargot, delicious if one thought of them as snails rather than worms; and all manner of paté, also delicious in a smelly sort of way. Thank God, no one had offered me horsemeat. I'd heard it was a delicacy, but there was no way I'd eat the meat of an animal so beautiful.

Tripe was different. Cows weren't that good looking, and this was a particularly unattractive part of them, their stomachs. I'd heard tripe stew was a typical economy dish that the French prepared at home. I told myself tripe was nothing compared to say pig's knuckles or frog's legs. At least it wasn't brains, sweet meat, or the Scottish haggis or English blood sausages that Elizabeth delighted in describing to me, accompanied by grotesque facial expressions.

As if to soothe, delicious smells began to waft through Jean-Michel's apartment. I decided to go with the flow. If I wanted to continue eating couscous, I might as well have given the time that January day on the Boulevard St. Michel to a North African man instead of a French one. I'd gotten what I'd wished for, and now I was going to really experience a French home-cooked meal, bite by tripe-filled bite. I took a sip of wine to ease what lay ahead.

In another hour, dinner was over. The tripe had been bearable, disguised in a tasty stew. The *petits pois* had been delectable, and I'd washed it all down with several glasses of red wine. Jean-Michel looked pleased with my compliments on his cooking.

We were now on the smelly cheese course, the after-dinner offering in a traditional French meal, either in addition to or in place of dessert. Using a small, sharp knife with a curved wooden handle, he pared off pieces of cheese from three different wedges on the cheeseboard he'd brought out, to eat with either a piece of baguette or a section of a pear he'd cut-up. There was a sheep's cheese, soft and almost white, a hard and golden yellow one, then a creamy and soft yellow Chaumes cheese. I liked the Chaumes best, paired with the juicy pear. It was ripe, runny, and sharply smelly. Something told me it was the most French of the three.

In another minute, we were sitting on the bed. How this transfer occurred I have no memory. But what happened next, I'll never forget.

"Shall I brush your hair?" he asked, picking up a wide brush on the narrow counter that ran lengthwise between his bed and the wall.

I love having my hair brushed. How had he known?

"Yes, why not?" I said, tossing my longish mane over my shoulder. I answered as if men offered to brush my hair on a regular basis. Paris was beginning to rub off on me.

He proceeded to brush, which he did skillfully with gusto. It was as relaxing to my body as puzzling to my brain to ponder the idea of a man cooking dinner for me, then offering to brush my hair. Men like this one hadn't entered my life thus far. I had a hunch that I wouldn't find many of them back home.

The brush felt good not only on my hair, but also on the back of my neck. After several minutes, he gathered my locks into a ponytail, pulling it to one side. Then his mouth was on my neck. Another sensation crept over me, warm and tingling. Turning my head slightly, the soft, brown tendrils of Jean-Michel's wavy hair tickle my nose as he kissed and nuzzled a section of my body I'd never paid any attention to. Now, it commanded center stage. Vampire movies suddenly made sense.

After a long moment, I turned to meet his face. We kissed. His mouth tasted fresh. Somehow the combination of tripe, smelly cheeses and wine had worked together to create a rich and delectable taste about as understandable as why drinking wine and eating liver paté, heavy cream sauces, and buttery patisseries combine to make French people trim and fit. By some special alchemy, all the wrong ingredients turn out to be the right ones in France.

Lengthwise, we stretched out on his twin-sized bed as he switched on the radio next to his head. Classical music spilled out. I forget which composer. Jean-Michel didn't appear to be in any sort of rush. I was free to explore his well-muscled wiry arms, shoulders, and chest, something I wouldn't have been able to do had I needed to spend time defending my upper torso from being mauled. Jean-Michel took his time getting to know my hair, neck, shoulders, arms, shoulder blades, back, waist, and hips. By the time he turned his attention to my breasts, I was ready to reveal them to him.

It was a whole new way of going about things, different from what I'd experienced before in the mad rush to round as many bases as possible on the way to a homerun. Only one man before Jean-Michel had hit a homerun with me, and the only way he'd accomplished that was by being in the right place at precisely the moment I decided I wanted to cast off my virginity. He'd been in a rush, sweating and making a lot of noise. It hadn't been bad, but it hadn't exactly been an art movie either.

With Jean-Michel, we were like two statues coming to life, exploring each other's contours. At a point, he slipped the black and gold knit shirt over my head. Then, he traced the contours between my breasts up and down, then circling around each one. Finally, I put his hand on the modest mound of one of them.

Everything proceeded by mutual agreement that evening. It was a nice feeling to be in the co-pilot's seat for once. When he took off his button-down shirt, I saw his chest was slender but rippled with muscle. He had some hair on it, not much.

It would be disingenuous to say Jean-Michel didn't smell. He did, just like every other adult male in Paris. His room was small, there was no bath or shower in his tiny wash room, and he was a grown man. A strong male smell hung everywhere.

But I liked Jean-Michel's dried sweat mingled with Denim aftershave. It worked for me. Funny how that adult male smell most often drives a woman away but every once in a while draws her closer until she's surrounded by it in the right man's arms.

Soon, the rest of our clothes were off. He was uncircumcised, so he more or less unwrapped himself to introduce himself to me. Jean-Michel did not use profoundly imaginative words for the hidden parts of the body. He referred to both my parts and his as *le sexe*. At least I knew what he was talking about.

I thought *le sexe* belonging to Jean-Michel more or less matched the rest of him. Knobby and wiry, with a taut, scrappy build, a boxer's build.

The boxer's build appealed to me. Within seconds, I realized width had it all over length — a very pleasant discovery indeed. Making love this time wasn't rushed. It was deliberate and unhurried. After a time, Jean-Michel began to drive toward a goal. When he came, he was loud. My face buried in his neck after he collapsed on top of me, I had to smile. I was learning a great deal of noise, smell, and sweat surrounded some of life's most important events, such as child-making and childbirth. In a while, Jean-Michel began to recover from the cataclysmic event that apparently had just happened to him. I wondered if anything like that might ever happen to me. His kisses on my neck gave me shivers, and the sensation of his sex filling me entirely and knocking against the sides of mine left me pleasantly stimulated. But these agreeable sensations were in no way comparable to the earthquake that seemed to have just occurred for Jean-Michel. Something told me there was more to discover, but I was in no rush.

Thankfully, Jean-Michel didn't light a cigarette in our post-coital bliss (his) and pleasant feeling (mine). Instead, he leaned over me, propped up on one elbow, his hand cradling his sharp cheekbone.

"You have the apples," he commented.

"I do?" What apples?

"Women have either apple breasts or pear breasts." He traced the out-lines of my breasts with his other hand.

"Apples or pears," I murmured, thinking either sounded appealing. It pleased me he hadn't said large breasts or small breasts.

"Which ones do you prefer?" I asked.

Sometimes, women can be predictable, too.

"*Les pommes*," he answered with no hesitation. It was a good response, given the moment. He hadn't said he liked small breasts, like mine. That would have fueled my insecurities. I wouldn't have been able to hear the clear statement that he liked my breasts over the airfield-type roar in my brain telling me he thought my breasts were small. But he hadn't said they were small, so the whole topic was neatly moot. This man liked my apple-shaped breasts. There was nothing to feel insecure about. How rare.

"Good." I laid back and thought to myself how nice it was to receive a compliment. I could now think of my breasts as apple-shaped instead of small or inadequate, as I had up to that moment.

Walking past French pharmacy windows for the past five months had informed me the French standard for attractive breasts was far different from the American one. Every French pharmacy seemed to have at least one display of a topless Frenchwoman advertising some sort of breast cream product for *soins de seins*, care of the breasts – a marketing concept that received very little play in the U.S. outside of the La Leche League. I hadn't seen many ads featuring topless female models in France with breasts larger than mine.

Back in the land of Barbie and Playboy, I'd always thought I was practi-cally flat-chested. After five months in France, I'd gathered I was not, but now I'd had an actual Frenchman pronounce me apple-breasted.

My world shifted as Jean-Michel lazily relaxed next to me on his nar-row bed, tracing my outlines with his fingertips and letting me know with eyes and hands that my proportions were pleasing in every way.

CHAPTER THREE

Springtime in Paris

Back in my garret room, I reflected on the events of the past twenty-four hours. Everything that had just happened between Jean-Michel and me was significant, because I'd just turned twenty. I was on the verge of everything. No man could have entered my life at a more impressionable moment.

It was clear he enjoyed teaching me, but he wasn't didactic about it. With everything yet to learn, I was an empty vessel waiting to be filled with French learning and culture. He provided every bit of education I'd come to France for that lectures at the Sorbonne did not. There were ways to combine certain foods with certain drinks; oysters went with Pinot Noir, paté with a good Burgundy. Every cheese had its complementary wine pairing; white wine, my favorite, was the wine of choice for alcoholics as far as Jean-Michel was concerned. There were ways to tie a scarf or to shine one's shoes with spit if on the street, if far from a water source. The French were *exigeant*, strict or exacting, about just about everything. Something Americans mostly were not.

It was fun to discover the French way of doing things with Jean-Michel. While he showed me how to comport myself both privately and publicly, I was continuing down my checklist of what I wished to accomplish during my year abroad.

Have an affair with a Frenchman. Check.

Get into a good college. Working on it. I'd sent my applications in on time in early January to the four colleges I'd applied to. Sometime after April fifteenth, I'd hear back. Hopefully the glamour factor of living in Paris combined with a good academic record from high school would propel me into a four-year liberal arts college where young people with broad liberal arts focuses who were also interested in having sex were a dime a dozen. I would finally find my milieu.

About whether I was meant to be a musician or a writer, I was working on it.

My exploration into a new identity as a writer consisted of reading as many books by female authors as I could get my hands on. To this end, I spent afternoons at Centre George Pompidou, also known as Beaubourg, one of Paris's largest libraries. A sizeable English-language collection located on one of its upper-level floors was available for borrowing. I devoured novels by Françoise Sagan, Simone de Beauvoir, Madame de Staël, Doris Lessing, Margaret Atwood, and Jane Austen. Then, I turned my attention to novels written by men about interesting women: *Nana* by Emile Zola and Tolstoy's *Anna Karenina* in particular.

The story of Anna Karenina puzzled me only slightly less than it had the first time I'd read it at age fourteen. I hadn't understood Anna's passion for Count Vronsky then and I still didn't six years later. Why would any sane woman throw herself under a train because of a failed love affair? My New England sense of restraint recoiled at the thought of such excessive behavior. Didn't she have a child to live for, after all? Or at least a bridge club at which she was counted on to make up a foursome?

Something inside me had not yet woken up. My instincts told me Anna's passion was connected to Jean-Michel's facial contortions and loud moans right before finishing off lovemaking with me. Instead of understanding he was at the climax, I thought of him as being at the end of what we were doing together. I knew there was something huge I didn't yet understand, so I chalked up Anna's passion to something I was in no position to judge and made a note to re-read Tolstoy's novel in another half decade.

Jean-Michel and I usually met once a week. I would pick him up at the entrance to his workplace on Friday afternoons, and we would spend most of the weekend together. It was enough for me. Given that I had no telephone, it was perfect. I wasn't ready for the intensity of nightly phone conversations, especially in French, and frankly, with someone whose horizons I had sensed were more limited than my own.

Jean-Michel was a master of his own domain, a precise and well-defined life he'd carved out for himself in Paris after running away from home at age nineteen. I too had more or less run away at the same age, but I had plenty to run back to. Apparently, he didn't. He never spoke of his family, nor visited. He'd never traveled outside France and had no plans to do so.

My life-to-be was an open book. Soon, I'd hear from the colleges I'd applied to and vast new opportunities would open up for me over the next four years. There was no chance of something like that happening to Jean-Michel. He was thirty-two and had already arrived at his destination. He was not only a Frenchman, but now a Parisian. That was saying something. Once a Parisian, where else would you go? The struggle to carve out a life, not to mention a home, for oneself in Paris was comparable to what it took to be a true New Yorker. Once achieved, it wasn't lightly thrown away.

My time together with Jean-Michel had nowhere to go but Paris, and Paris was only going to be part of my life for a few more months. It was a perfectly contained relationship with a clear-cut escape plan. Nothing could have pleased me more.

As grim, gray February slid into somewhat less grim March, Jean-Michel escorted me about Paris, introducing me to neighborhoods and monuments as if they were his own. We visited Montmartre, where we climbed the more than one hundred steps to the Basilica of Sacré-Coeur. The enormous white Romano-Byzantine church stood above a park where dubious transactions occurred after dark, he told me. As he began to explain what some of these might be, a man ran out of the woods holding his arm, which appeared to be dripping with blood. *Sacre-bleu!*

Jean-Michel had made his point better than if we had been watching a movie. I held his arm more tightly as we strolled around the sacred grounds of Sacré-Coeur then descended to the less sacred terrain of Pigalle, the red light district directly below the famous Basilica.

Many sparkling sites of beauty in Paris stood in counterpoint to dubious neighborhoods around them of equal interest for far different reasons.

Sacré Coeur presided over the prostitute-strewn alleyways of Pigalle below. Bois de Boulogne looked delightful by day, mysterious at dusk, and ominous by night. One afternoon, we'd lingered there too long and were hurrying back to the metro stop as night fell. Suddenly large, garishly dressed, and made up women began to appear along the grand boulevard leading through one section of the park. There was no denying the excitement of viewing the trans-sexual prostitutes who'd begun to come out to exhibit their wares to the male drivers who slowly drove past every night. It was a sight to behold, something I'd never have had a chance to do without Jean-Michel by my side, safely guiding me through the dubious sections of both his city and my mind.

Time spent back at Jean-Michel's flat consisted largely of cooking and lovemaking. There were no books in his home. But his conversation was rich in content as well as opinion. He weighed in on just about everything we discussed. If I brought up a topic he knew nothing about, he would indicate to me within seconds this was not a subject worth bothering about. Case closed.

His tastes were one hundred percent provincial, but the province that guided them was the Île-de-France with Paris at its center. This was an area of interest not just to me, but the entire world. I was captivated by just about every bit of information he shared with me.

There was one exception to Jean-Michel's close-mindedness – his taste in women. He liked Americans. He also liked voluptuous ones, but not with enormous breasts. He was more focused on women's hips or *les hanches*. I knew because he kept mentioning mine when we made love. I'd always thought *of les hanches* as the sections of jodhpurs pants that stuck out unattractively, but Jean-Michel let me know again and again my *hanches* were A-OK by him. His feelings of warmth toward my hips were confirmed by his frequent presents of pastry he'd bring back to his place for me to try after dinner. One of his favorites was called *le petit cochon*, little pig, made of marzipan, which I didn't especially like. I'd take a bite to be polite then hide the rest under a napkin. Feeling reassured by his admiration of my body's generous proportions, I didn't mind when he began to tell me about some of his former girlfriends.

April was one of them. She was from Berkeley, California, and had spent time in Paris several years earlier. I wasn't jealous, either because I was not in love or because he'd shown me her picture and she was undeniably plump, a good twenty pounds heftier than me. Perhaps I was too young to be jealous.

When I commented rather crassly that April seemed a bit chubby, Jean-Michel corrected me.

"*Non. Pas du tout. Elle est une femme bien dans sa peau*. No, not at all. She is a woman who is comfortable in her skin."

I had heard the French expression several times already, never fully understanding it. Now was my chance. At the hands of my Pygmalion, I asked what he meant.

"A woman who is comfortable in her skin is never too fat or too thin. She is perfect," he explained. "It's because she is comfortable with herself that men find her attractive. She is like a magnet."

"Come on," I protested. "Even if she's fat? I mean, doesn't a man notice that? That she doesn't have a perfect body?" What Jean-Michel was telling me seemed too good to be true, especially for an American male audience.

"Men don't fall in love with a woman who is perfect. They fall in love with a woman who is specific. A woman who is comfortable with herself can be herself specifically. She is free to explore who she is, because she is not comparing herself to other women all the time, trying to be someone she's not."

Suspiciously, I eyed him. He had to be kidding. But the food for thought he'd given me stuck in my craw like half-swallowed chewing gum.

∾

One week later, strolling in the Tuileries gardens on a late March day, Jean-Michel alerted me to a woman who had just passed.

"*C'est une jolie laide*. It's a pretty-ugly one."

Huh?

I turned to catch the back of the woman's henna'd reddish purple hair and bony legs. He motioned to continue walking around the pond until we passed her again.

This time, I pretended to look at some children playing behind the smallish woman as we approached. Her sharp, vixenish face had a pleased-with-herself expression on it. Its most prominent feature was a long nose with a definite bump. Her bony legs were nothing to write home about. No textbook from any country would have categorized her as a beauty.

"She is beautiful, no?" Jean-Michel murmured to me, once out of earshot.

"Um, she's got something going on, for sure," I replied truthfully, a little envious. What woman, with any sense of how crooked and short her legs were would dress them up in designer tights and stiletto boots? Yet, she'd looked undeniably hot. Apparently Jean-Michel thought so too.

Instead of giving in to my preconceptions, I opened my mind to his. I had so much to learn from him, and besides, I was working on becoming comfortable in my own skin these days, wasn't I? I could at least fake it till I make it, I told myself.

"A *jolie laide* is a woman who is beautiful even though she is not. She has something that is considered ugly, but on her, it's not. It's part of her charm," he explained.

I was all ears. We circled the pond again, hoping the woman would do the same. She did. As she approached, I pretended to spot something on the ground while I studied the suede, stiletto-heeled black boots she wore over gray and black striped tights covering slim short, legs with knobby knees. The content wasn't amazing, but the presentation certainly was. *Brava*, I silently complimented her as we walked by.

What the heck could a pretty-ugly woman have that a just plain pretty woman didn't have over her? Apparently, plenty. I searched my mind to think of a *jolie laide* I might have known somewhere in my past. I'd never contemplated the concept before, but as soon as Jean-Michel explained it to me, I understood. Something niggled at me, reminding me there'd been a woman like that in my own short past.

In a minute, I had it. *Voilà.*

Joelle. She had been a waitress I'd worked with back in Hartford, Connecticut, the summer before music college at a French restaurant called La Crêpe. It was a chain of restaurants that served crêpes in the style of Brittany, the region next to the Atlantic Coast of France, west of Paris, where Celts had settled in the fifth and sixth centuries – probably because the food was better there than back in the British Isles. The waitresses wore cute blue dirndl skirts with suspenders, white lace blouses, and enormous white Breton head-dresses. They'd looked sexy in a sweet sort of way. I'd applied for the job, because I knew in an outfit like that I'd meet guys.

Joelle had been short, bony, and chic with a bump in her nose, just like the woman we'd passed in the park. The other waitresses were in awe of her. Her boyfriend picked her up every day after work. During her shift, she flirted with any male customer she found interesting, regardless of whether they were in female company or not. She had been in total command of herself. Not surprisingly, she was French.

I'd soaked up every move she made, marveling to myself that she was not even mildly attractive, but her perception of herself announced to the world she was a knockout. The men appeared to buy it. To me, it didn't matter if she was beautiful or not. She was powerful.

Joelle had been a *jolie laide*.

"I know what you mean," I whispered back. "Like maybe a bump in a certain woman's nose isn't just a bump on her? It's a beauty feature?"

"*Précisément*," Jean-Michel agreed. "It's precisely the feature about her that a man falls in love with."

Whoa. Another reference point clicked in my brain. The year before — avoiding piano practice — I'd picked up a novel by a Japanese author in the literature section of the music college library. It had been a contemporary story about a husband and wife who lived in Osaka in the post-World War II years. At the time of the story, the early sixties, images of the West had invaded Japan. Many Japanese women emulated Western styles, wearing short skirts and high heels. Yet the wife in this story chose to wear kimonos instead of Western dress.

The husband knew why. She was self-conscious about her thick, short calves, a section of the legs that tends to be shorter on Asians than other races. What the wife didn't know is her husband secretly found her most hated point charming. He loved her short, well-developed calves but most of all, he loved her more for her self-consciousness regarding that part of her body.

In the Japanese story, the husband is charmed by his wife's modesty over her perceived flaw. A French modification of this uxoriousness would be that the husband is charmed by his wife's utter chutzpah in playing up her weak points as assets. If the hair tended to frizz, why not display it in a mass of wild curls haloing the face? If the legs were short and crooked, why not dress them up in designer tights and high-heeled ankle boots? It was a way to say to the world, "Here I am, and if you don't like this particular part of me, *je m'en fou*. I could care less. Let me just flap it in your face."

It was almost the outlook of a teenage boy. I laughed inside, thinking how freeing it might be for an adult woman to exercise her inner teenage boy on a regular basis.

Frenchwomen were encouraged to be in command of themselves, comfortable in their skins, *bien dans ses peau*. I wanted to be like that too. But how could I, with my twenty pounds of puppy fat, frizzy hair, and less than knockout chest-size? The *jolie laide's* physical attributes were even less appealing than mine. Yet apparently, she didn't think so. And because she thought she was smoking hot so did everyone she came in contact with. I burned with jealousy.

Straightening my posture next to Jean-Michel, I stuck out my apple breasts and tossed a thick lock of frizzy blonde hair over my shoulder. Then, I bunched it up with both hands to make it stick out even more on either side of my head. I would no longer be taken for an inconsequential American girl with no sense of herself. Those days were over.

We exited the park and began to walk along the enormous traffic circle of the Place de la Concorde. At the next street crossing, a woman waiting next to me gave me a surreptitious once-over. Out of the corner of my eye, I searched for her expression.

It was scornful, dismissive.

Deflating like a balloon, I scolded myself for seeking approval from a complete stranger. If I'd been the *jolie laide*, I wouldn't have given a fig what the woman thought of me.

The light changed, but I didn't. I had a lot of work ahead of me.

☙

Spring began to break through the long, gray gloom of winter, just as so many new insights were breaking through the hard shell of my low self-image. Cracks were appearing everywhere. Jean-Michel's lectures, attention, and obvious predilections forced me to question my preconceived notions again and again. I was an Easter chick about to hatch.

It was glorious to have my ideas of what was beautiful, what was not, what combinations went together, which ones did not, all blown away in the soft, fragrant air of a Paris spring. By the time I left France, I'd be transformed into a Picasso-like rearrangement of myself, only far more put together.

Jean-Michel and I had gone to view the Picasso collection at the Jeu de Paume (literally "game of palms," a seventeenth century court-game that was a precursor to tennis) museum in the Tuileries Gardens. I'd wondered at the artist's depictions of some of his girlfriends, especially Marie-Thérèse Walter and Dora Maar. Parts of their bodies were rearranged in surrealistic ways, with sometimes peaceful and sometimes disturbing results. Had this been what having an affair with the short, fiery painter had done to them? Marie-Thérèse Walter looked more or less serene in most of his paintings, but Dora Maar's images were anguished and angry. I took them in as I thought about what Jean-Michel's effect on me would ultimately be.

"What kind of man was Picasso? Was he nice to his wife?" I asked.

"Wife? Which wife? He had wives, girlfriends, lovers all at the same time. You should read his biography by Françoise Gilot," Jean-Michel advised as we strolled from room to room.

"Who's she?"

"The only woman who left him. For another man," he responded.

"Really?" I liked her immediately. "Where's her painting? Which one is she?"

"He didn't paint her; only a few sketches. He was too angry."

"Because she left him?"

"For a younger man." Jean-Michel looked at me wryly.

"Did she leave him first or had he been fooling around while they were together?"After several minutes of explaining what fooling around meant, Jean-Michel laughed.

"Of course, he was fooling around. He was Picasso. Women loved him. He loved them. It was natural, *Minouche*."

"But not for Françoise." I liked it when he called me *Minouche*, meaning pussy cat or darling, but I didn't like the fact that Picasso had fooled around on Françoise.

My French boyfriend gave the classic Gallic shrug. The concept of fooling around while in a relationship was not foreign to the French male sensibility. However, it tended to irritate French females, just like any others. I was eager to know what kind of revenge Françoise had extracted on Picasso for straying.

I put Gilot's biography of the short, ugly, bald painter at the top of my list for my next visit to the library at Beaubourg.

Jean-Michel didn't seem the type to stray. He was too fond of order, too fastidious in his appearance – I'd noted how carefully he brushed and polished his shoes before setting off the day after a night I'd stayed over.

Sneakers were not a part of his wardrobe. When I asked if he had any, he sniffed and explained *les baskets,* French for sneakers, are for *le sport* only. They are not meant to be worn in public on the street.

I was in awe, thinking of how completely my grandmother would have agreed with him.

Within weeks, my theory of Jean-Michel's faithfulness was put to test. April had written to say she was coming for a visit mid-way through her namesake month. I would have a chance to meet her.

Jean-Michel hadn't mentioned where she was staying so I asked. He reassured me that she would stay with the family she had worked for two years earlier when she lived in Paris. By then, I'd read Françoise Gilot's *Life with Picasso*, and I wondered if April's visit would spell the beginning of the end for Jean-Michel and me.

Picasso had been a master of bringing a new woman onto the scene as a way of letting the present woman know her days were numbered. This had driven most of his women crazy except for two. There was Françoise Gilot, who stayed calm then did the same thing to him. And then there was the remarkable Marie-Thérèse Walter, who had proven an exception to the rest of his relationships, remaining serene and unruffled through just about everything Picasso did or did not do to her, including never marrying her. She seemed one mellow female to me, beyond comprehension. I was a novice in the world of jealous passion, clueless as to what kind of rage a woman might feel to be sexually betrayed. All the books and women's magazines said it was something not to be tolerated, so I knew I'd walk if it turned out April was about to re-enter Jean-Michel's life.

My relative calm over April's arrival was based on a few factors, some to do with Jean-Michel, most to do with myself. Firstly, being pre-orgasmic, I had no idea what all the fuss was about sex. Relations were pleasantly sensual between us, but the oxytocin that might have bound me to him like crazy glue hadn't yet produced in my brain. I was still riding the clueless train, which wasn't taking me to any particular destination other than on a pleasant journey I knew would end soon.

By the time April left, I'd know which colleges I'd gotten into. I'd accept admission to one – my grandparents would be either delighted or not – and my summer plans would evolve quickly from that point on. I'd probably go back to the States around the same time the Griffiths did in mid-June. My escape plan from Jean-Michel was in place should the occasion warrant it.

Despite my overall *sangfroid* in the face of April's visit, my nerves began to fray the day before her flight was due. Would I know if Jean-Michel had slept with her after her arrival and before I was introduced? Would I meet her in his apartment or on the street? If in his apartment, would the place smell skanky with obvious clues of sexual activity all over the place: an unmade bed, bits of lingerie in the bathroom, and knowing smiles on their faces? Is this what Jean-Michel wanted to happen? If it was, I was prepared. I would take the Françoise Gilot approach, not the Marie-Thérèse Walter one.

Above all, I wanted to look good for the meeting with April. In her photo, I'd seen she was pretty, but undoubtedly plump. I was pretty too, but not so plump. I was also younger. At age twenty, this was a decided disadvantage in meeting a rival female. I looked through my wardrobe for something to wear that would provide psychological armor. Deciding on a periwinkle knit top and peg-legged black jeans, I kicked my clogs scornfully into a corner. It was time to wear something on my feet that Frenchwomen wore. That meant pointy, spiky heels, the kind I could barely walk in. I didn't have any.

I went shoe shopping the next day, all the while wondering if Jean-Michel had gone to the airport to greet April and if she'd end up staying with him that night.

It didn't occur to me to lay down ground rules for this visit from his ex. I preferred to stay on the sidelines, watch the play unfold, then take action if it unfolded in a way I couldn't accept. I knew the term *ménage a trois* hadn't originated in France for nothing; something about the idea made me feel very all-American, a rare occurrence. If something rekindled between Jean-Michel and April, I was out of there.

After visiting five shoe stores and being made embarrassingly aware that I took one of the largest shoe sizes available in France, I found some ankle boots similar to the ones the *jolie laide* had worn in Tuileries Gardens the month before. I could barely walk in them, as 1978 was the tail end of the first wave of feminism to hit the United States so stiletto heels were politically incorrect back home. But it felt nice to suddenly be two inches taller. Granted, clogs made me look taller too, but when Frenchwomen glanced at them with disdain, I immediately shrank back down to size.

I practiced walking home in my new boots. Their sleekness caused me to tap assuredly right past my regular pastry shop at the corner of the Griffiths' building. I decided to have a coffee instead with the five francs I had allotted for my usual dose of creamy Bretons or melt-in-your mouth *millefeuilles*, literally, 'a thousand leaves' of the most paper-thin pastry, topped with a white dusting of powdered sugar. In a minute, I was installed at a table on the terrace of the corner café, enjoying the soft breeze of the April afternoon.

Someone small and blonde hurried by.

"Elizabeth," I shouted out. What good luck to bump into my Polish-English au pair friend in my hour of need.

She turned at the sound of my voice, putting a hand up to her mouth as if she didn't want to be recognized. Why was she acting funny?

"Elizabeth. Over here." I waved, pulling out the seat next to me.

Something about her eyes was opaque. I could tell she was hiding something. When she took her hand away from her face, I knew what it was. Telltale signs of white powdered crumbs framed the sides of her mouth. I guessed she'd stopped at the same pastry shop I was addicted to and had her own fix for the day. We were peas in a pod, one of the reasons I liked her so much.

"Ava, hallo! I've got to get home," she called out. "Mrs. Brown is going out tonight, and I need to fix dinner." She'd slowed down, but was still walking past me.

I knew Elizabeth too well. She struggled with her weight, as I did mine, and I had caught her at the wrong moment in her cycle of feast or fast. She was an avid dieter, which I was not, and although she looked as petite as any Frenchwoman, I knew from our conversations on dieting she thought of herself as the size of a wild boar. I was far closer to wild boar size, and it wasn't the right size to be in Paris, where women were mostly svelte or at least small-framed. Come to think of it, it hadn't been the right size to be State-side either, where images of Barbie-clones ruled advertising and *zaftig* teenage girls with occasional breakouts weren't featured in print media at all, except as losers in coming-of-age movies.

"Come on, have a coffee. My treat." I caught up with her, putting my hand on her shoulder, hoping she'd receive my unspoken thoughts of understanding and sympathy for her secret struggles with the crazy cycle of dieting and feasting she was caught up in.

"Listen, I really need your help on something." I lowered my voice to a whisper, hoping to coax her out of her embarrassment from being caught eating something on her absolute no-no list and move on to her second favorite topic: men and relationships. "Jean-Michel's ex is coming today, and I'm going to meet her tomorrow. I don't know how to handle it. You've got to help me."

Her eyes rounded. I had her.

"What? You're letting him introduce you to his ex? Why are you doing that?"

"Because – because – I don't know why, that's why I need your advice. Come sit down. You look like you need a coffee." I grabbed her shopping bag and led her back to my table.

"When did he tell you his ex was coming to visit?" Elizabeth's eyes became bluer as they rounded in indignation. She was a study in primary colors – yellow hair, cornflower blue eyes, and doll-like red lips – her coloring similar to Marie Thérèse Walter, Picasso's most serene mistress. I visualized what Elizabeth might have done to the likes of Picasso the first time he stepped out on her. Unlike the cow-like Marie Thérèse, she'd have unleashed hell's furies on him then walked away after stomping over his testicles in shoes similar to my new stiletto boots. Elizabeth was no pushover. She was a five foot tall Polish spitfire, armed with rapier-sharp British wit.

"About three weeks ago. He showed me her picture," I said.

The waiter came over, and Elizabeth ordered *un café crème, grande tasse*, a large coffee with milk. I was relieved to see she would make time to advise me. My only female friend in Paris, I loved her dearly, not in spite of her imperfections, but because of them: her penchant for gossip, her obsession with her weight, her scathing, but hilarious put-downs of French mannerisms and characteristics. She was a quick-witted, sharp-edged comrade. She'd help me sort out what to do about April or at least how to dump

Jean-Michel in grand style if it turned out he was playing some sort of game with me. Then, she'd be there to help me pick up the pieces.

"And? What did she look like?" she asked.

"Pretty. And fat." I stated succinctly.

"Fat? She's fat? How could she be pretty if she's fat?"

I'd now given Elizabeth the perfect combination of interests to chew on, weight and romance. It was fun to see her light up. The man at the next table seemed to think so, too. I watched him out of the corner of my eye as he took in Elizabeth's hair, eyes and lips, all set against the palest, whitest Polish female skin imaginable. In a minute, he'd be at our table, offering to buy the next round.

"She's got a pretty face. And long, straight brown hair," I told her. It was the kind of hair I'd always wanted but would never have.

"But she's fat? How fat? Like a cow? Or a little pig?" Elizabeth had an exhaustive range of descriptions for fat people. One of her favorite activities was ripping apart people we saw on the streets who weren't perfect physical specimens. She had the innocent looks of a Polish angel but her wicked sense of humor was one hundred percent British. No one could sum up, then smack down total strangers as well as Elizabeth. Her specialty was noting people with moles, something we saw a lot of in Paris. Hair on inappropriate areas of the body or differently colored on different sections was another topic of derision. She loved pointing out bleached blondes with long black hair on their unshaven legs, a common sight on Parisian female bus drivers.

On days off, we rode the *Bus Périphérique,* the bus route that circles Paris for hours at a time, using our *Carte Orange,* Paris's monthly bus and metro pass, until we decided on a place to hop off, where we'd have coffee at an outdoor café. There we'd continue our snide observations of total strangers, some of whom were undoubtedly engaging in similar comments about us.

"Umm, she looked sort of like a pretty cow," I tried to explain.

"How can a cow be pretty? Why was he dating a fat girl, anyway?" She looked at me suspiciously as if to say my boyfriend had very bad taste.

"I don't think he sees her as fat. When I told him she looked sort of plump, he got really upset."

"Really? Why? She was, wasn't she?"

"He said, *"à chacun son goût."*

"What's that mean?"

"To each his own taste."

"Huh." Elizabeth looked thoughtful. Our coffees arrived and she took a sip.

"That's what I thought too," I seconded her.

We sat in silence watching big, puffy April clouds drift across the pale blue sky. Each one was fat as a cow. And beautiful.

À chacun son goût, was something now working its way under my skin. I hoped for Elizabeth's sake, it would work its way under hers, too. Perhaps we had both been sent to Paris by unknown forces to learn something about tolerance not only for others, but for ourselves.

"Whoa, where did you get those boots, girl?" Elizabeth asked after a minute.

"I just bought them," I told her. "In Saint Germain. Two hundred francs." Her next question would be how much they cost, so I thought I'd save time.

"They're sexy. You bought them to wear to meet the girl, didn't you?"

"Yes."

"Can you walk in them?"

"Barely." I shook my head. "That's why I'm practicing wearing them now."

"All these bloody French women wear heels like that. If they can do it, you can," Elizabeth encouraged me.

I loved the way she said 'bloody.' It came out like 'blue – dee,' perhaps because she was from Birmingham, a city she told me was far north of London, in the middle of England. I hoped I would be able to incorporate the adjective into my speaking vocabulary by the time I left Paris. It would be so wonderful to show up for my freshman year of college with the hint of a foreign accent.

"I'll try. I hope I don't trip, walking over to shake her hand."

"Why do you have to shake her hand?"

"She's not an ax murderer, you know. She's probably a nice girl who happens to be the ex-girlfriend of my boyfriend." I crumpled the napkin in my hand. Why was I getting worked up?

"What are you going to do if he sleeps with her while she's here?" Elizabeth asked, getting right to the point.

"Ah, there's the rub."

"Well?" Her eyes slit into raisins.

"I'll be upset. Probably have a fight with him then dump him," I said.

"Really?"

"What else should I do?" I shrugged. The Gallic shrug was something I wanted to nail before leaving France. It would be so effective back home, and no one would know if I wasn't doing it perfectly.

"You should let him know before she arrives that you're not putting up with any hanky-panky," Elizabeth advised. "When does she get here?"

I looked at my watch. "This afternoon."

"Blue-dee hell! What if she spends the night at his place?"

"He told me she was staying with the family she worked for when she was here."

"Sure, she is. When are you meeting her and where?"

"Tomorrow afternoon. At his place. I think we're supposed to go to dinner together."

"You'd better check out the smell."

I could feel my face crumple up just thinking about it.

"You know what I'm talking about," she said, staring at me. "That's what I mean, girl. You told me his place is smaller than mine. That means you'll all practically be sitting on his bed together." Elizabeth began spelling out details of the imagined scenario in her inimitable way, each image a dagger to my heart.

Except it wasn't my heart being affected, it was my pride.

"Maybe I'll suggest we take a walk," I said weakly.

"You'll need one to clear the air, that's for sure." She wrinkled her nose in disgust.

I made a face at her, imagining again how the air might smell in Jean-Michel's tiny, attic room. I wasn't yet sure of my moral stance toward the situation, but I could count on my nose to lead my decision-making. If it smelled dubious, I was out of there.

Jean-Michel might be fastidious about his shoes, but my nose was as exacting as noses get. It had led me away from the wrong type of man several times before in my life. If Jean-Michel turned out to be one of them, I didn't need anything more than my olfactory senses to turn me off. Being a New Englander and raised as an only child, I knew nothing about fighting and making up. If I fought with a friend, I didn't know how to get back on track – even more so with a boyfriend. I'd had no experience with reconciliations. It would be over if my Frenchman cheated on me. My nose would let me know.

༄

The next afternoon at quarter past four, I rang the buzzer to Jean-Michel's flat. The swish of white glass curtains in the ground floor apartment told me the concierge had noted my arrival. I wonder what she thought of Jean-Michel's female American visitors. How many had she seen over the years? Just thinking about it made my blood boil.

In a minute, the catch on the door released, and I was inside. Each step of the five flights up to his flat lead me closer to possible defeat and humiliation. What if my rival had lost weight? Was I about to meet a gorgeous California knockout? Swallowing the bile in my mouth, I told myself I would be very French about the situation. I would exude haughtiness and *froideur* and act superior, even if I was about to meet the woman who would recapture Jean-Michel's heart. Then again, who was I kidding? I hadn't been especially interested in capturing it myself when I'd had him all to myself.

Jean-Michel appeared at the door to his flat. He smiled. When I reached him, he kissed me warmly, once on each cheek. Then, he motioned me in.

April sat on his bed. As I entered, she stood. Taller than me. Pretty. Not at all slim, but not as plump as she'd been in the photo he'd shown me.

I immediately understood why Jean-Michel had been attracted to her. She looked fresh, wholesome, unspoiled, and nonjudgmental, entirely unlike most Parisian women. In all honesty, it was a compliment to me that Jean-Michel liked April's type, because I was like that too, aside from occasional snide conversations with Elizabeth.

"Hi, I'm April," she said, her voice soft as the spring weather outside.

"Hi, I'm Ava," I said, modulating my voice to match hers. I could out-April her if I tried. But did I need to? Jean-Michel watched closely as we eyeballed each other. I needed to be comfortable in my skin at this moment, and that was all. He'd taught me well. "How was your trip?" I followed up.

"Long." She smiled. "I'll be fine by tomorrow." She turned and sat down again on the bed.

"How many hours was it?" For some strange reason, I didn't feel threatened to see her on Jean-Michel's bed. Why she didn't choose a chair to sit in, I don't know. But it didn't bother me. I decided to take one of the two chairs myself. Jean-Michel took the other.

"Let's see. About four to New York. Then, I had a two-hour stopover. Then, seven to Paris." She gave me a gentle, rueful smile.

Nothing at all about this woman was threatening. Plus, she was plumper than me.

"Ugh. You must be tired," I sympathized.

"I am. A little."

"I heard you worked for a family here?"

"Yes. And you're doing the same, right?"

I nodded as Jean-Michel poured three glasses of wine, handing us each one.

"Yes. I'm going to school at the Sorbonne. The language and culture course," I said.

"That's the one I took," she laughed.

Her laughter was like bells tinkling. She was the most ethereal, non-threatening tall, plump person I'd ever met. No way was I going to be able to accurately describe her to Elizabeth. The way her words floated when she spoke, she seemed closer in size to Audrey Hepburn than Queen Latifah.

After a few more minutes of conversation – during which Jean-Michel looked bored – I discovered April was now studying for a degree in occupational therapy at U Cal Berkeley. That was my mother's alma mater. As usual, once the conversation moved off Parisian turf and out of Jean-Michel's league, he wanted nothing to do with it. It wasn't entirely about the fact we were speaking in English. It was about the fact that Jean-Michel was a thoroughly provincial person. April and I were not.

After another five minutes I was sitting on the bed next to her, leaving Jean-Michel out of the conversation altogether. He went out into the hall, probably to empty the trash.

When he got back, we decided to take a walk. Out on the sidewalk downstairs, I noticed the graceful way April moved. She looked comfortable in her skin. I knew where she had gotten that from. She'd taken the

Comfortable in One's Skin 101 class, taught by Professor Jean-Michel Reneau. I wanted to graduate from that class, too.

Jean-Michel walked ahead and smoked, while April and I discovered how very much we had in common. She too had waffled before college, taking a year off after high school to lose herself in Paris, far from home. I wondered what her parents were like but didn't know her well enough to ask. Had they been a motivating factor in propelling her to Paris, as my grandmother had been? Her pronouncements on a woman's place in society had lit a fire under me to get myself into the best college that would have me so I could pursue being anything other than a teacher or secretary. But April was from Berkeley California. Perhaps her parents wanted her to become a social activist or go into the family marijuana-growing business. Had she been escaping some direction they'd pointed her in when she'd chosen to go east instead of hang out in the far west?

I didn't want to ask her how she'd met Jean-Michel, because I could already guess. There was no point in sullying the memory of my own first meeting with my French boyfriend by discovering he'd used the exact same technique to pick up yet another American girl two years earlier.

"Shall we go for dinner now?" he asked. He'd circled back without either of us noticing.

April's face tightened. "I can't actually. I need to get back to the Greniers."

Her response surprised me.

"I thought you were joining us for dinner tonight." Jean-Michel looked perturbed. He didn't like things to go differently from planned. "I want to take you to the place we used to go, with the *profiteroles* for dessert you like. Come with us, *Minouche*," he cajoled her.

My stomach dropped. That was the term of endearment he used with me. Now, I realized it had been all over town.

"I can't. I promised the Greniers I'd be back for their son's birthday party tonight. I'm sorry. Can we get together another time before I leave?"

So April had not been planning to spend her one-week stay in Paris largely with Jean-Michel. From the way his face closed in upon hearing her words, this was obviously news to him.

"As you wish." He grunted, striding ahead again. In a minute, he had lit another cigarette.

April switched into English with me. Her voice was low, conspiratorial. "It's not really that I'm busy. It's just that I'm on a diet, and I'm still jet lagged. I don't feel like eating a big dinner, and he'll try to stuff me with *profiteroles* like he used to do. No matter how many times I told him I didn't want to eat sweets, he was always buying them for me." She shook her head, not without affection.

So, she was on a diet. She wasn't as comfortable in her skin as Jean-Michel had made her out to be. A light bulb went on in my head. Jean-Michel had enjoyed controlling her. But now she was driving her own bus. April knew how to act French, but she was all American on the inside. Dieting. Just like me.

I wanted to be just like her. There was no way Jean-Michel was going to sabotage my efforts to lose weight before going home just because he liked plump women. Suddenly, I saw what all the comfortable-in-your-own-skin lectures had been about. He hadn't wanted me to change.

But I wanted to change myself. From that moment on, I was allied with April in mutual resistance to Jean-Michel's efforts to keep us both passive and plump.

A moment later, we reached the Boulevard Montparnasse. Jean-Michel again entreated April to join us.

"It's your favorite restaurant, April. Come on, the *profiteroles* are waiting for you," he tried again. No line could have been lamer. Her eyes hardened as soon as he mentioned the cream-filled pastry puffs drizzled with warm chocolate. What a moron. Didn't he know it had taken her years to move on from giving in to the urge for *profiteroles* to firmly passing them up? She hadn't spent time working on herself just to turn back into the unformed girl she'd once been with her controlling French boyfriend.

"No thanks, I can't. The Greniers are expecting me." The firmness in her voice was unmistakable, albeit delivered in a breathy Jackie Onassis way.

It was clear some sort of power struggle was going on and the usual outcome hadn't occurred. The sulky face he presented in profile confirmed it. Inside, I laughed. Who would have thought meeting April would provide me with a window into Jean-Michel?

We watched the back of April's form disappear into the metro station, then went on to the restaurant ourselves. I decided to play a game. Should Jean-Michel suggest the *profiteroles* for dessert, I'd refuse. Not surprisingly, he did.

"Have the *profiteroles*. They're superb." He motioned the waiter over.

"No, I don't think I will. I'll have an espresso if you want to order some."

"*Minouche*, you should try them. You'll die from pleasure. This is a special treat I'm offering you. What's wrong with you?" His tone changed from commanding to scolding.

Neither tone worked for me after meeting April and seeing how she'd resisted Jean-Michel. I dug in my feet. Besides, I wasn't just any old *minouche*.

"No thanks. I'm full from dinner. I'll try them some other time."

"I won't take you here again if you don't order them," he said petulantly. "That's the reason I suggested this place. Come one, Ava, try them. You know you like chocolate."

Yes, I did like chocolate. I liked it too much. In fact, it was a big problem for me. But at that moment, what I liked even more was resisting Jean-Michel. Something inside, more real than the puffy, plump, pastry-eating person I was on the outside, was stumbling to its feet to take a stand.

"I don't feel like *profiteroles* right now," I told him. *And je m'en fous to never coming here again*, I silently fumed. Turning to the waiter, I ordered an espresso. Approval gleamed in the server's eyes, before he flicked them from mine.

Jean-Michel looked as exceedingly displeased as I felt secretly pleased. For the first time, I had divined the meaning of the popular French phrase *je m'en fous* and made it my own. It literally meant, I could care less. Some would give it a more salty meaning, as in, I could give a shit, but it was all the same. The French delighted in using this phrase endlessly. Now, I knew why. It was satisfying. In the right situation, it rolled off the tongue, originating straight from somewhere deep in the vitals.

There was also its variation, *je m'en fiche*, which had a slightly nicer ring, something like, I could give a rat's ass. However, I'd noticed the French preferred *je m'en fous*, the nastier version. I'd wager every French citizen from age seven up used the term at least three times a day, often accompanied by a dramatic upward thrust of the forearm and hand in a dismissive gesture. Before I departed France, I vowed to have that gesture down, too. I visualized myself, a non-demonstrative New England girl, breaking up with a future American boyfriend who'd displeased me. While recounting the scene to girlfriends later, over Cosmopolitans, I'd thrust my arm in the air with the *je m'en fous* gesture to show I could care less about whatever he had offered to make me stay. They'd be wildly impressed.

Coffee was served, and predictably, the mood was gloomy.

"How long is April staying?" I asked. Anything to break up the silence.

"Who knows?" Grumpy Gaul responded.

"I thought she said a week."

"So if you know, why'd you ask?" he snapped.

"I really liked her." I ignored his tone.

"So did I," he said, not looking like he liked anyone or anything at the moment. He glared at me, then raised his finger in my face. "But she's changed. She was a nice girl. Comfortable in her skin. Now she's different."

Even more comfortable in her skin perhaps? Less willing to be led around like a docile cow? I nodded. What was there to say? I applauded the new April, my approval in direct counterpoint to Jean-Michel's disgust. Her arrival had shown me that Jean-Michel and I would be moving in different directions soon. Perhaps starting that very evening.

"Ready?" He stood up, tossing some bills on the table.

I got up, more than ready to get out of there and away from him as soon as possible. I didn't want to be the person on whom he took out his dissatisfaction with April that night. Or stubborn girlfriends in general. Ones who wouldn't follow his party line. After that night, I had Jean-Michel's number. And I wasn't sure I'd be calling it too many more times.

CHAPTER FOUR

Fake It Till You Make It

Over the next two weeks, following my meeting with April, I received the four college admissions office letters I'd been waiting for. Bates and Bryn Mawr accepted me but offered no financial aid. Bowdoin turned me down.

When the letter from Yale arrived, I knew something was up. It was bulkier than the others. I went upstairs before opening it, ignoring Mrs. Griffith's curious stare, encouraging me to open it in front of her as she handed me my mail that early evening on my way back from a day of classes. No way.

Upstairs, I unlocked the door to my room and sat down on my bed. This was big. Very big. The envelope in my hands was big, too. I began to sweat. I knew I had a chance. A lively Japanese-American lady in the office of American College in Paris had interviewed me, and we'd clicked.

I'd told her about being lost and confused the summer before when I'd been so ashamed about dropping out of music college. I'd been in between gigs, I explained, out of high school, self-ejected from music college and ready to experience life, not books or Bach. When I'd mentioned wandering around Guatemala on my own until a priest enlisted me to accompany him on visits to mountain-dwelling parishioners, I'd seen her eyes widen. She'd been intrigued by my story, which had the added advantage of being true, thanks to my father slipping me an employee-pass plane ticket to escape my grandparents while I figured out what I was doing with my life. Our conversation lasted over an hour, and at the end, my gut told me she'd liked what she heard.

That evening, Mr. Griffith asked how the interview had gone. I said, 'well' to which he replied that my interviewer was a former member of the Yale Admissions Committee. Her word would be gold back at headquarters in New Haven.

I said a short prayer. Then, I opened the letter from Yale Office of Admissions.

Yeow! I was in. *Sacré bleu de putain*! I'd come across the oath, meaning sacred blue of a whore, in a Victor Hugo novel. I'd never heard it spoken aloud in France. Thank you, thank you, thank you, God.

The news was so monumental, I couldn't breathe. It wasn't just that I'd been accepted. After the acceptance page, another letter from the Office of Financial Aid informed me Yale College would put together a financial aid package that would allow me to attend no matter what my financial resources were. *Putain du diable*! This meant whore of the devil, another French oath I'd seen in a book written over three hundred years earlier and never heard anyone in Paris ever say.

The rest of the evening was poignant. Bursting with the best news of my entire life thus far, I had no way to share it with anyone. First, I wanted to frame the letter and send it to my grandparents. My grandfather wouldn't be surprised, but my grandmother would figuratively fall on the floor. Then, she'd rush out, and in the guise of taking a walk around the block, share the news with every neighbor she bumped into.

I'd let my parents know next time I sent either of them a postcard. Not having anything to prove to them, there was no rush.

It didn't seem right to share the news with Mrs. Griffith first. After all, she was a Brit. What did she know about how significant it was to get into an American Ivy League college? Jean-Michel was out of the question. He was at work, I didn't have a phone, and I hadn't spent the past two months with him not to know how utterly provincial his outlook on such news would be. He'd probably sniff and say something like, "So when are you leaving?" as if he didn't care and just needed to make plans for his next round of American girlfriend hunting on the Boulevard Saint Michel.

It was a strange sensation to receive great news and have no one to share it with. Too excited to sit in my room, I decided to share my joy with Paris at large. Putting on my stiletto boots, I applied red lipstick – something I didn't ordinarily wear – and went out for an early evening stroll.

Paris would be happy for me. Another American here today, gone tomorrow. At least I'd be leaving with a flourish and a plan. And what a plan it was. I couldn't begin to fathom what four years at Yale College would mean, but I had a clue. It would be life changing.

As I walked through the Champs de Mars, my exultant mood turned to panic. I had met enough hot-shot prep school types in my years growing up in Connecticut to know how cool, composed, and self-assured they'd all act on campus. How could I compete? I had spent ninth grade at a private, single-sex school, and it had been an eye-opener. The girls were cut from some other cloth than girls I'd known in public school. The private school girls possessed a sort of unassailable smugness, a *sangfroid*, a *je ne sais quoi*. If one of them said something patently false, say "the sky is red," she'd say it with so much self-assurance I would want to believe it. I spent the entire year studying them, far more assiduously than academics.

Down East, it had been all about smoking dope by the river during lunchtime and scoring acid tabs at concerts in Bangor or Augusta on weekends. I was out of my element, so I retreated into books, eating lunch in the library, since I couldn't think of anyone to sit with in the cafeteria.

Fair Isle sweaters, pool parties at upper-class-women's homes during the summer, and traveling to prep schools all over New England as a cheerleader for away football games were over for me. But I had gotten a glimpse into the rarefied world of private secondary school education. I knew the prep school sophisticates would have it all over us poor public school slobs once we arrived on the Yale campus that fall.

My one advantage was that I would be coming to New Haven from Paris. Perhaps I'd get stuck taking another summer job as a self service gas station cashier along the way, but who needed to know that? I vowed to apply myself to picking up style tips everywhere I could before leaving Paris. I could swing the story of my own history to my advantage if I really applied myself.

Mindful of my vow to drop fifteen pounds before showing up on campus the first week of September, I marched past the pastry shop on the corner, averting my eyes from the succulent window display. Never mind ninety percent of my nutritional needs were met by frequenting the shop. Buying a baguette and no other item, not even one hot, flaky *pain chocolat* or *pain aux raisins* would be the first test of the new me. On my way back from my celebratory walk, I'd stop in, buy a demi-baguette and nothing else. Never mind that I would desire desperately to pick up the usual two-pastry supplement to my daily half-loaf of bread. I would pretend I only wanted a demi-baguette.

The phrase "fake it till you make it" suddenly sky-wrote itself across my brain. I saw its meaning in a whole, new light. It wasn't about being honest or genuine or not. It was about knowing where you were going, then pretending you were already there while you were on your way. Or in my case, still in the starting gate.

"Fake it till you make it" was my passport to the future. It would be my secret credo maneuvering around those other Yale freshmen, all fresh out of boarding school or summer internships at the Rockefeller Foundation or the National Quantum-Physics Lab, if there was such a thing.

Would there be any other poor, public school grads like me? I had a hunch there would, but I vowed not to walk around looking like one of them. I would be Ava Fodor, straight off the plane from Paris, daughter of a Hungarian poet/writer. Never mind all the other New England, Episcopalian stuff from my mother's side. That would be too common a background to put forward first. There would be dozens of New England, Episcopalian undergrads on the Yale Campus, all more polished, moneyed, and self-assured than me.

A woman eyeballed me as I sauntered confidently down the Rue de Grenelle. It was a shopping street, so she carried her fishnet shopping bag on one arm, half full of produce, as well as a bottle of wine, wrapped in brown paper. I was reminded of the evening I'd brought a bottle of red wine over to Jean-Michel's to accompany our dinner. I'd picked it up at the grocery store on the corner of his street. As usual, they hadn't offered a bag, so I'd held it unwrapped under my arm. As I came in his door, Jean-Michel took one look at me and scoffed that only prostitutes carried unwrapped bottles of wine in the street.

I hadn't yet acclimated to the fact that in France, one shopped with one's own shopping bag. The first time I'd gone to the grocery store, I stood like a dummy waiting for someone to bag my groceries, wondering why people in line behind me were grumbling and glaring. Finally, someone poked me, letting me know in angry French I needed to gather up my groceries and get out of there so the line could proceed. The cashier looked at me for the first time, immediately comprehended I was a foreign moron and held out a plastic bag, which she would not release until I gave her ten centimes. From then on, I tried to remember to bring my own fishnet, expandable bag, but it wasn't second nature. I frequently forgot and needed to buy a bag at the counter, the very thought of which burned my New England penny-pinching sensibilities.

Walking to the Seine, I descended the stairs to the cobblestoned pathway directly along the muddy, brown water. In a minute, I realized this wasn't a good idea in my high-heeled boots; the ones I'd bought for my meeting with April.

I took them off. Picking my way over the cobblestones carefully, I walked toward the next staircase at the other end of an underpass under the Pont d'Alma, where I planned to re-ascend. It was about seven in the evening, the shadows deep, with just a hint of daylight remaining. Scents of spring surrounded me on all sides. Another scent did too as I entered the underpass.

The usual urine aroma combined with something more. I picked up my pace as I made out something move against one wall. Then it moaned, a female voice, low and panting. As I hurried past, I couldn't help but notice the back of a man pinning a woman to the side of the cool, stone wall. Her legs were around his waist. *Mon Dieu*, it was barely dark! But this was Paris, and it was spring. I sped up, trying not to trip, intent on getting out of there before they noticed me – not that they would. Before I tiptoed away, the woman's moans picked up speed. Something was happening to her I didn't understand, aside from the obvious.

I wanted to know more.

Exiting the underpath, I slipped around the corner of one of the bridge's massive stone girders and stopped, listening. The moans were now catching in her throat. A moment of silence followed, expectant and ripe. Then, she screamed in the most unearthly way I'd ever heard. It wasn't the scream of someone being hurt, but rather being sent somewhere. Glimpsing into another world, I waited, while another kind of silence descended. This silence possessed weight. It was as if the heavens parted, and I was witness to something sacred I couldn't comprehend. The faceless woman behind me had just ascended to the summit of somewhere I'd never been.

Quickly I moved off, my stocking feet silent on the cobbled stones. In a minute, I had climbed the next staircase from the river pathway. At the top, I put my boots back on and resumed walking along the quay.

What happened for that woman that never happened to me? I wanted to know, desperately. Was it because she was French, and the French make love better than everyone else? But my boyfriend was French, and I'd never felt the way she obviously had. The moans I could fathom. The unearthly scream, I could not. Yet I sensed it was a scream worth screaming. Another clue on my path to understanding why Anna Karenina had thrown herself under a train.

On my way home, I stopped at a café for a coffee. I needed to think. Inside, I was shook up. My college acceptance letter of earlier that day no longer held center stage. Something big, very big, had happened to that woman, and I needed to get to the bottom of it. Using a napkin, I wrote down how the sound of her scream made me feel, to transfer to my journal when I got back to my room. I was afraid I'd lose the memory of it, the way I lost the thread of most dreams the moment I woke up. The scream was so different and otherworldly it was as if a message from another realm had been sent directly to me.

Wake up, Ava. There's something you're missing. Something you don't yet know. You'll scream like that one day, too, if you don't forget this moment.

On my way back to my room, I called Jean-Michel from a pay phone.

"Bon soir?"

"Bon soir, it's Ava. I'm calling because I got big news today. How are you?"

"I'm fine. What's your news?" His voice was even, neutral.

"I got into Yale. It's the college I told you I'd applied to, along with a few others. My first choice. I'll start in September."

There was a grunt. Then he spoke. "Are you coming to meet me at work on Friday?"

"Yes. Of course."

"Good. You can tell me about it then."

"Five o'clock?"

"That's it. See you then."

"See you Friday. Good night."

"*Bon dodo*," he concluded, his usual evening sign-off. He hung up.

Now, at least, he knew. He'd have a few days to digest the news, which he knew was on the horizon. Shortly after we met, I told him I was waiting to hear back from colleges I applied to. I vowed to be careful at our upcoming meeting not to make a big deal about news that for him meant one thing only – I'd be leaving soon.

I walked home in the dark, my thoughts moving again to the image of the man and woman in the underpass. It afforded me a window into an adult world I knew almost nothing about. Almost, but not entirely. I wondered why Jean-Michel wasn't moving me in that direction. Was it because I didn't love him? Or was it because he didn't know my body well enough? There were so many things to find out about before the world of academics swallowed me up again.

Over the next few days, I threw myself into babysitting duties at the Griffiths. Cole, the youngest, begged me to take him to the *guignol* show in nearby Champs de Mars. The weather was mild, and I felt nostalgic about my time with the children now its end was near. On Tuesday afternoon, when the two older children were at after-school activities, I grabbed Cole and headed for the park at the end of our street. We took in the show seated close to each other on a wooden bench, his head burrowed into my shoulder in his usual unabashedly affectionate way.

"I like to snuggle you. I love your squishy arms," he said, digging his chubby fingers into my equally chubby arm at intermission.

"Thank you, Snuggle Bunny," I replied, my heart catching at the six-year old's comment. Lord, I'd always hated my plump, non-Audrey Hepburn-like arms. But Cole meant to compliment me. Why couldn't I take his remark as such? Both grown men and little boys liked my squishy body. Why couldn't I? *Fake it till you make it*, a voice out of nowhere advised.

"Renoir liked squishy arms too," I whispered to Cole, giving him a squeeze. He looked like a little Cupid with his rosy round cheeks and golden curls.

"Who's Ren Wah?" the boy asked. "Is he your boyfriend?"

"No, Snuggle Pie. He was a painter. He painted pretty girls with squishy arms and blonde hair." I stroked Cole's cheek at its rosiest point.

"Like you!" he exclaimed, bouncing up and down on the bench.

"Exactly. Like me," I agreed as the curtain came up for the second act.

While we watched the final act, I pondered the pearls of wisdom the chubby, blond cherub at my side had handed me. Why was I still fighting with my body type? I was who I was. I should be *bien dans ma peau* instead of trying to transform myself into an Audrey Hepburn lookalike. It was never going to happen. *Surrender to who you are, Ava. Surrender.* I shifted uneasily trying to figure out how to accept myself the way my adorable charge did. "I love your squishy arms," he'd said. Why couldn't I love them, too?

On Friday, I arrived at the Palais de Chaillot a few minutes early. As I leaned over the parapet of the grand terrace overlooking the skateboarders on the sloping pathways of the gardens below, something felt different. I'd stopped fighting myself. Without huge sacrifice, I'd eaten only one pastry over the past three days, a *pain aux raisins* I rewarded myself with after spending two days on a *fromage maigre* regime. *Fromage maigre*, which means literally, weight loss cheese, was a high protein form of tofu-like white cheese with zero percent fat. It came in flavors, making it palatable. I'd eaten three of the strawberry-flavored ones each day for the past three days, surprised at how satisfying they'd been.

Would Jean-Michel notice a change? I decided not to share too much of my overriding thoughts about Yale during our time together. It was a world apart from the one he inhabited. And moving toward it meant moving away from him. I didn't delude myself that Jean-Michel was terribly in love with me, but we were attached. Loss loomed on the horizon.

When he came out of the doorway, I hugged him extra hard after exchanging kisses. He looked pleased, his dark blue eyes casting greenish-gray in the late afternoon light. We strolled down to the Cinémathèque entrance in the gardens of the Palais de Chaillot to watch the movie-goers line up for the early evening show. It was a well known foreign film theater in Paris. We'd never gone to a movie there ourselves, content enough just to watch the crowd line up for whatever foreign art film was currently playing.

In Paris, people-watching was an art form. Jean-Michel was a discreet observer of public conduct and style, unlike my friend Elizabeth, who was unabashedly snide in her commentary on the failings of other human beings, with her snarky British wit. I enjoyed time with Elizabeth until invariably I felt as if I were participating in some sort of vivisection of poor, hapless strangers who really weren't all that inferior to us. But with Jean-Michel, I learned a great deal from his restrained commentary on the people around us. He wasn't so much judgmental as he was instructional. Now, he motioned to a woman with henna'd hair standing next to a man in line.

"Look at the woman there," he said in a low voice. "You see her scarf?"

I glanced in her direction, pretending to survey the crowd as I caught sight of the long black, white, and gray scarf loosely slung around her neck.

"Yes. What about it?"

"That's how to wear a scarf," he sniffed.

"Do you mean long like that?" The scarf was generous, draped over one side of the back of her black jacket.

"I mean everything like that. The black and white is *chic* but would be too severe without the gray. The design is not too busy. And the way she wears it shows she knows how good she looks in it. The scarf has made her jacket come alive."

I'd never had a conversation like this with an American man.

"It is *chic*, isn't it?" I agreed.

"It's not the scarf that's *chic*," he explained impatiently. "It's the woman wearing it who is." He squeezed my arm in reprimand.

"Right. That's what I meant," I corrected myself, chasing away a tiny cloud of irritation. His fussiness annoyed me but he had a point. Who cared about a piece of clothing? It was the person who wore it who gave it whatever value it possessed. I wondered how I'd do in a black, white, and gray scarf. Immediately, I vowed to look for a similar one then practice draping it in the mirror.

Tugging at his arm, I led the way toward the placid pond in the gardens of the Palais de Chaillot. Fountains shot jets into the late afternoon air. The temperature was warm, the heat of the day still lingering as did the scents of trees, shrubs, and flowers bursting into bloom all around us. My eye wandered over Jean-Michel's rugged profile and leather jacket. Our relationship worked as long as he played teacher and I played student. Any other dynamic would upset his apple cart.

"Your thoughts?" he asked.

I smiled up at him. "You're just right for me," I said, leaving out 'for now'. Some things were better left unsaid. Especially things that couldn't be changed.

He smiled back, but something wry rather than joyful was in his expression. "You say that because you're leaving."

"Do I?"

He was right. I'd said it because I had a way out. Otherwise, staring into the face of a man perfect for me at age twenty would have scared the living daylights out of me. I was far from ready for perfection. Ahead of me lay a whole world to discover, mistakes to be made. I wanted a happy home life one day, somewhere far in the future after college, a taste of the work world, and more than a taste of whatever men loomed in my future, both perfect and not-so-perfect. At this point, the oyster shell of perfection didn't beckon to me as a permanent home. I just wanted to grab the pearl and make off with it.

We stared at each other for a moment, all the while the sound of the fountains soothing the harsh reality of where we stood. I thought he was perfect because I was leaving, and he knew it. I could only guess what his thoughts were. Perhaps he was assessing the harshness of my blithe, superficial heart, accepting but hardening his own heart against it. I had a plan and so did he. Mine was to enjoy a few more months in Paris in his company, his was to enjoy mine until I left, at which point he would resume patrolling the Latin Quarter for unschooled, chubby American girls.

I was having a relationship with a man whose company I enjoyed. This wasn't Anna and Vronsky or Romeo and Juliet. Who knew what Jean-Michel thought about us as a couple? His hard, blue eyes told me he was a realist about romance. It had a beginning, a middle, and an end. Suddenly, I wondered if he'd ever been head over heels in love.

I linked my fingers through his and waited to see what he'd do.

"You're a minx," he finally said, taking my chin in his fingers, giving it a little twist. It might have been an affectionate gesture, but the sharp way he did it spoke volumes.

"Ouch." I pulled away, wondering at his words. What was "minx" code for? Liar? A young, superficial, hard-hearted girl having an experience with an older man she would soon leave?

For the first time with Jean-Michel, I knew I was in the driver's seat. But I didn't want to be. I just barely had my driver's license. All I really wanted was to be a passenger while we passed some pretty scenery, then get out when the ride was over.

Unsure of myself, I avoided further references to Yale. What was the point of rubbing salt into a wound? Another idea came over me. I would explore what more Jean-Michel had to offer in the lovemaking department. Would a touch of urgency transform my moans into screams? I wondered if fear of abandonment might not light a fire under him I hadn't yet seen.

If I was to be a minx, although I'd never felt like one up to that moment, then I'd try to fit the part. I put my arm under his and squeezed. His bicep was evident, compact, jutting, and hard, like the rest of him.

"Let's go," I said.

"Where?"

"Back to your place," I whispered.

"Why not yours?" he asked, for the first time.

I'd never thought to invite him to my room. It was my inviolate, feminist sanctuary, the place where I read Simone de Beauvoir and Anaïs Nin while pondering self-actualization strategies. In the eight months since I'd arrived in Paris, no man had stepped over its threshold.

I made a face, hoping it was minx-like. "It's too small. Not comfortable."

"Your room is smaller than mine?" He looked startled.

"Not just the room," I teased.

"What else?"

"My bed."

"Your bed?" His bicep throbbed under my fingers.

"Your bed is nicer," I murmured.

"You like it?"

"When we're in it together, yes." I'd taken a page from his comments on the woman, not the scarf, being *chic*. It was all about human beings, not objects, wasn't it?

"What about dinner?" he asked.

"Let's go back to your place, then go to dinner."

"*Mais, c'est pas normal*," he reproved me, using the French phrase for, but it's not normal, or, it's not the way it's done.

"So what?" I challenged him.

I was fed up with hearing that phrase used over and over again by what appeared to be the entire French population. It was right up there with *je m'en fous*, or I could care less, a seemingly opposite sentiment. Apparently, the French cared a great deal when it came to doing anything differently from the way things were usually done. It grated on my freedom-loving American spirit.

He seemed shocked. "We dine, then go to bed." He looked at me as if I'd just suggested putting on our shoes before our socks. Another twinge of irritation ran through me. Didn't he realize I was trying to add some zing to our sex life?

"How about if we make love, then dine, *then* go to bed?" I suggested, thinking he might find the idea exciting. I did.

"*Minouche, c'est pas normale.* Now is time to eat, later is time for bed. What are you thinking?" He was practically scolding me.

What kind of man reproaches his nubile, thirteen-year younger girl-friend for suggesting they make love sooner rather than later? I was vexed. Was there a French word for fuddy-duddy? I'd ask someone in my French class the following week.

Jean-Michel was steering us in the direction of Montparnasse. All I could think of was how utterly boring and conventional life would be beside him. Here I was trying to juice up our Friday night routine, and instead of being pleased, he acted put out. Until that moment, he'd never heard me talk this way. In fact, we never talked about making love at all. We just did it.

I already knew he was prudish in some ways. It was consistent with his fastidious nature, the way he polished and buffed his shoes before going to work. Did I like it? Hmmm.

I, on the other hand, was only prudish because I was inexperienced. The encounter with the couple in the underpass a few nights earlier had unleashed a curiosity in me far outweighing any prudishness I falsely exhib-ited. I was eager to get back to Jean-Michel's place so that I could find out if there was something more our intimacy that night might awaken. The sands had shifted in the balance of power between us.

"Okay, let's get something to eat and then go back to your place," I agreed, squeezing his bicep again.

"Of course. That's what we always do," he agreed calmly.

And that's why this has nowhere to go, I added silently. For the first time, I identified something about the French that wasn't vastly superior to my own countrymen. It was their unquestioning sense of conventionality, the distaste for anything out of the established order, say, making love sponta-neously at an unexpected time of day, having something to eat on the street or outside of mealtimes, ordering the wrong wine with a dish, or just doing anything differently from the way everyone else did it.

Dull. Very dull. My inquisitive American blood simmered in indignation at the sheer, plodding conformism of it all. I wanted to try something new in bed with Jean-Michel. But he was a tough nut to crack. If nothing changed between us that night, then something would for me. Jean-Michel would not be the only one to test his partner in this *ménage*.

∽

Finally, dinner was over. Itching to begin my experiment, I waited for Jean-Michel to make the first move. When he pulled his chair closer to mine, I was ready.

He kissed my neck, making the short downy hair there stand up on end.

Turning my face toward his, I kissed him back below his left earlobe. Then, I used my teeth, digging into him.

"*Doucement, cherie*," he whispered. Go easy, sweetheart, was what he meant.

I didn't want to go easy. I wanted to go hard. Wasn't that what that couple had been doing in the underpass along the Seine?

"Bite me," I whispered back. "Go on."

He continued to nibble on my neck.

"Harder. Use your teeth," I insisted. It was a command, not a request.

"Shhh, *Minouche*. Don't be crazy," he said, as if trying to reassure me.

I wasn't looking for reassurance. I was looking for the stairway to heaven. It was nowhere in sight.

Later, I lay back on the bed, staring into the dark. Jean-Michel snored gently next to me. Our lovemaking had been nice. I'd moaned. But nothing moved me to scream. Probably Jean-Michel wouldn't like it if I had screamed. It might disturb his neighbors, which wouldn't do.

My thoughts whirled. If a woman had the capacity to scream like the woman in the underpass, didn't that mean if her partner knew she could go there, he'd want to be the one to send her? I mean, why stop halfway if you knew you weren't all the way to your destination?

If I knew anything about men, I knew they liked to know how things worked. What guy would put down a new piece of equipment until he'd figured out how to get maximum capacity out of it? I thought of the few males I'd dated back in Connecticut. They'd all been obsessed with their cars or motorcycles – Triumphs, Corvettes, Harley-Davidsons. You name it, they'd pulled them apart and put them back together again, then taken them out on the road to see how fast they could go. Didn't this innate tendency to tinker extend to their interest in women? In other words, wouldn't any red-blooded male want to see how high he could make his woman fly?

I pondered these thoughts and others as I thought about the nice time I was having with Jean-Michel and how to go about leaving him as pleasantly as possible. My mind's eye returned again and again to the image of the couple in the underpass. One day, a man would make me scream in ecstasy – it just wouldn't be the one sleeping beside me. He had no idea he'd failed my test. It was better if he never did. There was no reason to ruffle fond memories of the time we spent together.

CHAPTER FIVE

Le Petit Cochon (The Little Pig)

The month of May was gorgeous. I responded with a speedy yes to the Yale Admissions Office. My very uncertain future suddenly had turned into something concrete and bright. I shared news of my Yale acceptance with Elizabeth, but she'd been more impressed that I lost two pounds since the last time we met.

The weeks flew by flush with planning and anticipation. My diet was working, albeit slowly. I was becoming addicted to *fromage maigre*, much as I'd previously been addicted to the *pain chocolats, pain aux raisins*, creamy *Bretons*, and other delicacies in the pastry shop windows. The nutritional label on the side of the *fromage maigre* containers thrilled me. High protein content combined with almost no fat to make it an ideal diet food. I'd grown up with chops, steak, and roast beef as cornerstones of my diet. I'd also been slim until I hit age seventeen and somehow slid into a pastries and sugar addiction. My final semester of high school in Maine, I took a job at Dunkin' Donuts. My size six donut girl uniform no longer fit by April of my senior year. Around Easter time, the owner of the franchise diplomatically said nothing as he handed me a brand new uniform, size ten. I was straining it at the seams by the time I quit in June, graduating from high school and exiting the state of Maine to return to Connecticut, and civilization as I knew it, as fast as I could.

At the tiller of my own sailboat for several years, I'd steered it into irons. Now was the time to get out of them. I knew where I was headed, New Haven, Connecticut, first week of September, 1978. I just needed to be ready to arrive there.

On a Sunday evening in late May, Jean-Michel went downstairs for a few final dinner supplies and came back with a small white package stamped *Gaillard Patisserie* on the wrapping paper.

"*Un cadeau, Minouche,*" he said, handing it to me. I eyed it suspiciously. Was there ever going to be an end to his habit of presenting me with fattening presents? I had foregone further thoughts of flying to the moon with him when we made love, since it was clear circling around somewhere in space before coming back to Earth was as far as Jean-Michel thought I should be going.

My own behavior toward him was highly conciliatory, now that the end of my stay in France loomed in sight. Could I not receive a little consideration on his part when I told him I was dieting and pastries were not on the plan? How many times had I mentioned that I was trying to lose a few pounds?

Obviously, he didn't care. With a tender smile on his face, he instructed me to unwrap the surprise. I sullenly did.

It was a marzipan *petit cochon*. I didn't even like marzipan. And it was in the shape of a little pink pig. Is that what he thought of me? His plump little American pink pig girlfriend? The blood rushed to my head as I stood up.

"I don't want it," I said, handing it back to him.

"But *Minouche*, I got it for you," he cajoled, thrusting the pig back into my hand. "Isn't it cute? It's cute, like you," he continued, pleading with me.

"Thanks. I'll eat it later," I said, furious. I'd dump it in the trash on my way home the next day.

"No, *Minouche*. Eat it now. I want to see you enjoy it," he insisted.

It was enough to make me sick. Not only had he not remembered I didn't like marzipan, but he didn't care that I'd told him numerous times I was on a diet and off pastry and sweets. The moment of truth had arrived.

"I'm not eating sweets now. I'm on a diet. How many times do I have to remind you?"

"Dieting isn't good for you. You shouldn't be dieting. You should be *bien dans ta peau*, like April. Eat it, *cherie*. I got it just for you."

Comfortable in my skin like April, huh? I thought back to what April confided to me the afternoon I met her. She'd told me Jean-Michel was always trying to stuff her with sweets like the *profiteroles* he'd suggested at a restaurant that evening. She'd turned down his invitation. Whatever he thought she was, April was comfortable in her own skin AND on a diet.

As Jean-Michel moved back to the kitchen table to unwrap the rest of the groceries, my chance presented itself. Above us, the skylight of his sloping eaves roof was open to let in the soft spring air. With one quick swing, I tossed the *petit cochon* out the skylight.

"What are you doing?" he cried, grabbing my arm and shoving it down. "What did you do that for?" His eyes blazed and a vein in his neck throbbed out.

"I told you I'm dieting," I yelled. "You don't listen to me. I'm trying not to eat sweets, but you keep buying them for me. It's a problem. Understand?" I'd had it. This time, my tormentor wasn't my grandmother, and I was no longer ten years old.

Jean-Michel looked shocked, then incensed. I felt a brief flash of sympathy, thinking how nasty he must think I was to have tossed his present out the window. But there was a point to be made that hadn't gotten through in conversation alone.

"I can't believe you did that," he said, angrily flicking the dishtowel in his hands. "What's wrong with you?"

I stepped away from the dishtowel, not knowing what the rules of engagement were now. All I knew was that I'd broken whatever unspoken rules we'd previously had.

"Nothing's wrong with me, Jean-Michel. I told you I'm on a diet, and I'm sticking to it." A voice like steel sounded in my ears. It took me a few seconds to recognize it as my own.

"So you just throw away the present I gave you?" The muscles of his jaw line hardened. His face looked as if it was carved out of Mount Rushmore.

"You weren't getting it. I told you I'm not eating it, and you said eat it now. What else could I do?"

"I don't know. I just don't know." He threw up his hands and turned his back to me. "Do whatever you want. It's not my concern."

He sounded just like my grandmother at the end of an argument. But I was no longer a child in an adult's care. This was my opportunity to really do what I wanted.

I gathered up my jacket and bag, while Jean-Michel pretended to be busy stocking his mini-fridge. In two steps, I was at the door. Unlatch, open, and out. The click of the door shutting behind exhilarated me. Quickly, I sprang down the stairs, praying he wouldn't follow.

Out on the sidewalk, I took a deep breath. The early evening spring air breathed new life into me. I started for Boulevard Montparnasse. In five minutes, I was surrounded by lights, life, and action. Happy for the anonymity of the crowd, my body began to shake in reaction to what just took place. I was not normally a hugely assertive person, making scenes or dramatic gestures. But I'd just made one.

Who was I now? I slowed down my pace, searching for comfort in being one with the crowd. Relief, pride, and the tiniest twinge of fear churned my stomach. I'd stood up for myself.

Was Jean-Michel no longer my boyfriend? My heart turned over to think I would be the one to make that decision. I sniffed the fresh spring air of freedom and weighed my possible new status as an unattached woman.

Could I manage on my own? Yes. Would I be lonely over the next few weekends? Yes, but Elizabeth had a list of activities she'd suggested we do together before I departed for home. Would a break up throw me into a tizzy of pastry gorging and self-pity? Probably not. Wasn't it my own decision if I wanted to lose weight or not?

Bile rose in my throat as my mind closed against Jean-Michel like a steel trap. He wasn't just a *vieux garcon* – a fussy older man. He was a bully, too.

I began to relax. Looking at the couples around me, I wasn't as dazzled by their coupledom as I was before. Who knew how many single souls in a partnership were secretly trapped, longing to get out from under their partner's hold over them? For the first time since I'd arrived in Paris, I felt happy to be single.

A commotion sounded behind me. Someone was coming up on my left, running and breathing heavily.

"Qu'est-ce que tu as, Ava? What's the matter with you?" Jean-Michel gasped out, falling into step beside me. Was that all he could think of to say? Or was it all he knew me capable of understanding in my limited French?

Ugh. Just when I'd worked it all out and begun to savor my freedom. Now what? I felt embarrassed. What I wanted was not what the man beside me did. I wanted something more. Now that I'd recovered my usual New England composure, I was loathe to engage in any further scenes.

Walking on, I barely turned my head to acknowledge Jean-Michel. It distressed me to see him looking so flustered. I didn't want to comfort him, but I didn't want him to look vulnerable either. If only another former American girlfriend of his could have materialized at that moment to restore him to his usual *sangfroid.*

"I just want to go home, that's all," I muttered. *I just want to say goodbye* was what I really meant but didn't have the heart to say.

"Cherie, stop being silly. Let's go back to my place and have dinner. I bought *tournedos* for us," he reasoned, referring to the small, tasty steaks Mrs. Griffith sometimes prepared for her family. "Come on."

So now I was his *cherie,* his sweetheart. But I couldn't turn the enormous ship of my resolve back in his direction. Jean-Michel's birthday had passed a few weeks earlier. He was a Taurean, a fixed sign, but Aquarians were, too, just less obvious about it. My own rigidity was now fast revealing itself in the clarity of my resolve. I had savored my new independence for all of fifteen minutes, and I could live with it. What I couldn't live with was Jean-Michel telling me what to eat and with what drink, how to dress, how to behave, and how to be comfortable in my skin. For the past quarter hour, I'd felt extremely comfortable in my own skin. I wanted to further explore my new comfortably-skinned self, the one weaned from him.

"I just feel like going home. Don't try to stop me," I answered wearily, pushing on toward the Avenue de la Bourdonnais that led to the Griffith's building on Rue de Belgrade.

"Ava, stop it. Come back. I won't buy you pastries anymore," he begged.

I thought about it. Nothing inside me wanted to go back to his place with him. I wanted to be alone to digest the change in our relationship that had just taken place.

"I don't feel like it, Jean-Michel. I just want to go home," I said, repeating myself like an automaton. I was a homing pigeon returning to my nest.

He walked beside me in silence for a minute. Then the unimaginable happened. He began to cry. First, I heard sniffles. I glanced at him. His face was red and tear-strewn. I was aghast.

What was I supposed to do? I had no experience with men crying. I felt hugely embarrassed. But under my discomfort, a twinge of anger flamed. Wasn't he trying to further manipulate me?

The New England men I'd interacted with my entire life didn't resort to tears to get their way. God only knew what stratagems they used, but they weren't lacrimonious ones.

My heart hardened further as I quickened my step. I wanted to get out of there as soon as possible before some other unbelievable thing happened – like getting hit. I was walking next to a total stranger, someone whose reactions I couldn't gauge.

My adrenalin racing in fear of the unknown, I raised my hand in a backward salute. Then, I fled. This time, he didn't follow. In another fifteen minutes, I was in my own room, the door safely locked behind me. There, I flung myself on my bed, spent, and slept.

∾

The next day, I felt somewhat safer. Jean-Michel would be at work and unlikely to try to contact me until after five. Thankfully, I was to babysit that evening for the Griffiths, so I would avoid him if he tried to find me in my room. Still shaky from the night before, I dressed and set off for French class in the Latin Quarter. It was good to have a busy day ahead of me, a schedule to fill my first twenty-four hours of newfound singleness.

It was a soft, beautiful May day. Instead of hopping on the bus, I walked home from class. I needed time to think. Finally, I had a story with a real man. It was energizing to be in the midst of my own dilemma for once, not a girlfriend's or a character's in a novel or magazine. But it was puzzling too. Did I want to try to work things out with him? Not in my New England book.

The light May breeze mocked me for my thoughts as I crossed the street to the Seine. I slid my hand along the wide stone railing next to the sidewalk as I walked. "Fake it till you make it" was not my operative phrase on this day. Thrown me up against the hard wall of decision-making, I was resolved. Nothing in the world could make me go back to Jean-Michel. I wanted to enjoy my own company for my final days in Paris. It was enough.

∞

That evening, I went downstairs to babysit the three Griffith children. The youngest, Cole, draped himself across my lap as I stroked his longish, platinum-blond curls. Usually, I tired of his heavy head on my legs after a few minutes, but this time I let him linger, thinking how dear he'd become to me now I knew I was leaving. I studied his older brother, Winston's, perfect looks and manners as we talked about his plans for the summer. He'd be attending lacrosse camp back home. His bright prospects for life didn't seem so alien to me, now that I was on my way to Yale. When Reid, the eldest and only girl confided to me about yet another boy in school she liked, I felt hopeful for her for the first time. If I could get into Yale, then the object of Reid's crush could like her back. Miracles did happen. It was pleasurable to soak up the children's details, fodder for a revisionist version of my own childhood to new friends I hoped to make in college.

Couldn't I appear to have grown up as a Ralph Lauren catalogue-type child to my peers in New Haven? I had the WASP pedigree, replete with blonde hair and blue eyes. My mother was descended from John and Priscilla Alden who came over on the Mayflower. There was the small matter of my Transylvanian heritage on my father's side. Perhaps I could transform my father into a count rather than a penniless poet whose first job in America was sweeping out a barbershop. Couldn't he become a poet of aristocratic origins? The cogs began to turn, and I soaked in Reid's, Winston's, and Cole's details so that I could create from them a pastiche of my own.

Passing through Mr. and Mrs. Griffith's bedroom on my way to use the master bathroom, as usual I admired their low-to-the-floor, funky, hippy-style queen-sized bed. Then, I spotted a book on one of the two night tables. It was the *Talahari Book of Massage*. Picking it up, I leafed through it. It wasn't just any old massage book. A couple was massaging each other in the nude in various pen and ink illustrations. Wow.

I glanced back at the night table, where a bottle of massage oil stood next to where the book had lain. It was half full.

Fortunately, the children were watching a long movie, which had only just begun. I rifled through the pages of the book until I came to one where the couple was doing something I didn't really understand. The man was massaging a part of the woman's body above her *sexe*. His hand wasn't inside, it was on something. I read the text.

One of the surest ways to lead your partner to orgasm is to repetitively stroke the clitoris with the degree of pressure your partner indicates is most satisfactory to her. Do not assume you know what this degree is. Only your partner can tell you. The female orgasmic response typically takes longer than the male's. You should position yourself comfortably, use a generous amount of non-irritating, natural massage oil and settle in for the long haul. Be sure to ask your partner if she prefers clockwise or counter-clockwise strokes. Do not stop, once your partner begins to respond. Apply increased pressure and wait for her to tell you if it's the right amount. Ask her to let you know if and when she wants to pause. After a pause, do not stop. Resume stroking with slightly increased pressure, asking for her feedback on the level of pressure. Repeat the process of stroking and pausing until your partner has climaxed. You will find the path to her satisfaction after many tries. Once your partner orgasms, she should be able to climax more than once again very quickly. Enjoy the adventure of finding the path to your partner's orgasm. You can only gain true sexual satisfaction within a partnership when you have satisfied your partner as well as yourself.

Huh... I needed to get back to the living room before the kids began wondering what happened to me.

As Cole crawled into my lap and Reid related to me what I'd missed of the movie, I pondered the new points of information I'd just learned.

Women were able to orgasm more than once during lovemaking? I wasn't sure I'd ever orgasmed at all, but it was nice to know I'd be able to do it again and again once I finally figured out what it was.

For the first time, I had an inkling of why certain African cultures had a custom of cutting off young girls' clitorises. They wanted to protect them from becoming raving sex maniacs. Hmm. I had an intact clitoris, yet I was in no way a raving sex maniac. Was I missing something? What exactly was the big deal?

Apparently, the clitoris was some sort of very big deal. Yet Jean-Michel hadn't really focused on it – nor had my first lover. They had both gone in for the goal, so to speak. But whose goal were they after? *You can only gain true sexual satisfaction within a partnership when you have satisfied your partner as well as yourself* rang in my ears. How did you know when you'd attained true sexual satisfaction? Was it when you felt pleasantly sleepy after making love? Somehow I didn't think so. The memory of the woman in the underpass streaked through my brain once again. Her scream had seemed to make the Earth stand still.

The Griffiths returned around ten, and I greeted them with new respect. Clearly Mr. Griffith cared about Mrs. Griffith's satisfaction in bed. Or Mrs. Griffith cared enough about it herself to alert Mr. Griffith as to how to make it happen. I made a note to determine whose side of the bed I'd found the massage book on the next time I babysat.

On Tuesday, I went to the library at Beaubourg after morning classes. I looked for the *Talahari Book of Massage* in their English language card catalogue. It wasn't on file. Then, I looked up "female sexual response." Nothing in English. I tried "female orgasm." A book called *Female Orgasmic Response* was on file, but when I went to find it, it was gone. Too embarrassed to ask a librarian to help me locate it, I decided to read *The Story of O* by Pauline Réage instead, hoping the "O" in the title referred to the "O" I was after.

Leafing through the book took my mind off my grumbling stomach, which I hadn't fed since Sunday afternoon, other than with three containers of *fromage maigre* daily. I was determined to make my break up with Jean-Michel into a success story. I wouldn't be one of those women who consoles herself after breaking up with a boyfriend by eating boxes of cookies – or the contents of a pastry shop window.

Looking up, I checked to see if anyone was noticing the book I was reading. No one. A scattering of West African men with skin like polished mahogany sat buried in books around the reading room. I was sure they were there to hit upon the foreign girls in the room, most of whom looked plump and blond or blondish. I hoped I was looking on the less plump end of the spectrum at this point. Although I was starving, I was happy I'd squirmed my way into a size 40 pair of French jeans. When I arrived in Paris, I'd gone shopping immediately and was appalled to find the smallest size I could fit into was a 42 – on the higher end of French women's clothing sizes which ranged from 36 to 44 — roughly equivalent to an American size four to size twelve.

Now, I'd dropped a size. Just then, a West African caught my eye and smiled. I frowned.

Although I was no longer with Jean-Michel, the last thing I wanted was to be with anyone else. It was such blessed peace to regain my solitude. In January, I had been lonely. Now it was May, and I was no longer lonely, I was on my own. It was different. I returned to *The Story of O*.

After twenty minutes, I put down the book. There was plenty of sex, but not the kind I was looking for. The heroine O seemed mostly interested in submitting to bad treatment from various men her master lover introduced her to. I wasn't looking for a story about sex so much as I was looking for technical information on what exactly constituted a female orgasm. I wondered if any of the West Africans in the room knew anything about the subject. Were any of them from countries where they cut off women's clitorises? Since I was already at the library, I decided to find out which countries did. Returning to the card catalogue, I looked up "female circumcision." A few books were listed, one in English. In a minute, I found it.

Burkina Faso, Djibouti, Central African Republic, Ghana, Guinea, Senegal and Togo had all outlawed female circumcision. That was good, except it was also bad. Why would it be outlawed in those parts if it wasn't practiced there? I read on. Countries where it was common included all of the above, as well as Sierra Leone, Ethiopia, Eritrea, Somalia, and northern Sudan. At least the French-speaking countries, except for Sudan, had banned the practice. With the former French colonies of West Africa redeemed in my mind, I snuck another glance at the dark-skinned Africans in the reading room. Some of them were pretty good looking. All of them had long, lean, muscular builds. Why would they want their fellow countrywomen circumcised? I returned to my book.

Circumcision of the clitoris is meant to terminate or reduce feelings of sexual arousal in women so they will be less inclined to engage in pre-marital intercourse or adultery. The clitoris holds a massive number of nerve endings, and generates feelings of sexual arousal culminating in orgasm when sufficiently stimulated.

Aha. This confirmed what I'd read in the Griffiths' bedside massage book. Orgasm happened through clitoral stimulation. It was good to know. But puzzling to think so many African men didn't want their womenfolk to experience orgasm. Didn't they enjoy experiencing it themselves? Maybe that's why they were prowling in English-language libraries for young, foreign females with intact clitorises. I'd bet they wanted to experience sex with them in a way they were unable to with the women waiting for them at home.

Shutting the book, it was time to return to my room and think about where those men might be who did want their womenfolk to experience orgasm. There must be normal, reasonable men around who possessed enough logical faculties to reason the goose might want to experience the same sort of climax the gander did. But that would also imply there were men out there who were reasonable enough to realize loading and unloading a dishwasher, making beds, doing laundry, and cleaning bathrooms was something women were as equally not interested in as men. For the most part, I hadn't met any men who did.

As I exited the library, Jean-Michel came to mind. He was the only man I'd ever met who was actually good at activities I'd never seen men do back in Connecticut. He'd religiously washed the dishes after we'd eaten the Saturday or Sunday dinners he cooked. For a brief moment, I thought fondly of him, until my mind turned again to the weighty matter of female sexual pleasure. Why was Jean-Michel good at food-shopping, cooking, and cleaning, but hadn't yet figured out his way around the female clitoris? It didn't make sense.

On my way home, I had a moment of weakness while passing the pastry shop on the corner. I circled the block, slowing down when I arrived again in front of the luscious window display. It was too much for me. Two days of *fromage maigre* and nothing more wasn't enough. I needed some sugar and fat in my body. Ignoring warning bells going off right and left in my brain, I entered the shop.

"Bon soir, Mademoiselle," the clerk greeted me like an old familiar customer. A bad sign. *"Vous desirez?"*

What did I desire? So much that I couldn't even begin to say. To begin with, something fluffy, delicious, and satisfying to fill my empty stomach. Then, an orgasm or two or three, whatever they were. Finally, to fit into size 38 jeans before I left Paris in one month's time. Were all of these aspirations mutually exclusive? Would I be able to fulfill any of them?

Sighing, I pointed at the tray of Bretons, practically beaming at me in their neat, cream-topped pastry shells.

"One Breton, please," I said, wanting to say three. *Fake it till you make it* fought with *the pastry shop closes in fifteen minutes. This is your last chance to load up on whatever delicacies you're breaking your diet with today.* While warring thoughts battled, I pretended to the clerk I only wanted one Breton.

"Only one today?" she asked, clearly wondering why I wasn't ordering the multiples I usually did. She was on to me.

I steamed, aware she thought I was an out-of-control, fat American pig. I'd show her. Right then and there, I decided I was not.

Two months ago, I'd been the girl who bought a minimum of three pastries every time I'd entered the shop. Now, I was someone new, a mature, twenty-year old woman with a yen for something sweet. I was here to order one pastry only, to satisfy that reasonable desire. That was all.

"Yes. Only one," I responded firmly. *Fake it till you make it* beat out *the pastry shop is closing in fifteen minutes.* It was an enormous victory. One I'd won post-break up with a boyfriend who'd striven to keep me plump. A double triumph.

It took all the willpower I possessed to wait patiently while she wrapped up the lone Breton in white paper, tying it neatly with string, then handing it to me. Equally succulent confections were beckoning to me from all directions. *Take me home now. It's your last chance. Buy me now, you can eat me tomorrow. Don't you want to have something on hand in case you get hungry later, after eating that one measly Breton?*

It was enough to make a rock sweat. Turning smartly, I exited the shop. Behind me, the clerk sang out, *"Au revoir, Mademoiselle,"* in what sounded like tones of new respect.

Next, I picked up a few cartons of strawberry *fromage maigre* as well as a one and a half liter bottle of water. The urge to drink water all day long, as Frenchwomen purportedly did, had not yet taken me over, even after eight months in Paris. According to French fashion magazines, French women swore by drinking at least two liters of water daily to maintain their svelte forms. I would give it a try.

Back in my room, I sat down at my desk, unwrapping the creamy Breton as if it were a prize *objet d'art.* In my mind, it was.

Before lighting into it, I took three long swigs of mineral water. The idea was to fill my stomach so my appetite was quelled before I began to eat.

The long swigs of water had no effect on my hunger whatsoever. Unfortunately, my appetite was regulated not by how full my stomach was but how raging my desire for sweets was. This had to stop.

I sat there and contemplated the Breton: sniffing, salivating, and practically lactating at the sight of it. How could I convince myself this one lowly Breton was enough to satisfy my bottomless yen for sugar and fat?

"Fake it till you make it," I repeated three times, aware that no amount of stating my credo aloud could turn my desire for three Bretons in one sitting into a desire for only one.

Then I ate it. Delicious.

I swigged some more water.

I pretended I was satisfied.

I wasn't.

Sighing, I lay down on my bed.

Only one thing could get my mind off food.

I closed my eyes and began to think about the couple in the underpass. As I remembered them, my hands wandered over my body. I saw the woman's hand uncurl, then drop to her side as the man kissed her neck. Then, I imagined my own hand was his. He put it on her mound, circling and pausing, circling and pausing, just like the instructions in the *Talahari Book of Massage*. Each time he paused, the woman's breathing slowed down and grew louder. Which did she enjoy most, the strokes or the pauses?

Out of nowhere, my music college training came back to me, the words of my composition professor in my ears: *Ava, remember above all the space between notes is as important as the notes themselves. Too many notes together in a composition just clutter it up. The audience needs space and time to absorb the melody. Don't overclutter your pieces. Create a melody, then leave some space for the listener to absorb it. Notes all strung together without any pause between them don't have any meaning. They only make sense in short clusters, punctuated by pauses.*

Whoa. Had he been talking about making music or making love?

Intent on my circles, I wandered in the deep, pausing every few moments to find myself on a sort of plateau, moving higher and higher toward an unknown destination. I was as excited mentally as I was physically. At the third plateau, a noise in the hallway startled me.

I froze. Someone was out there – a rare occurrence.

The footsteps grew louder then stopped. Two smart raps sounded at the door.

Panicked, I sat still as a statue.

Two more knocks.

"Ava? Are you there?"

Jean-Michel's voice sounded strange, stating my name. He didn't often say it aloud, preferring to call me *minouche* or *cherie*.

He knocked again.

My heart pounded so hard I thought I would have a heart attack. Nothing inside signaled to me to do the normal thing – respond, then get up and unlock the door. I just didn't want to.

"Ava. You there?" He knocked louder, the door moving slightly with each contact. I was sure my heart was as loud as the noise his fist made on my door. But I'd already waited too long. It would be embarrassing now to open the door to him. I had nothing to tell him, other than I wanted him to go away. The knobby muscularity of him filled me with fear. He'd never shown himself to be violent, but he could be a bully. If it ever came to that, he seemed at least a thousand times stronger than me.

Silently, I willed him to go away.

My strategy seemed to have worked. After a long moment, I unfolded my leg from under me and pinched it. It had fallen asleep. About to put my feet down on the floor, a further knock paralyzed me with fear.

Bang. Bang. Now, he was pounding.

"Ava, I know you're in there."

A pause. Jean-Michel's breathing outside the door was audible. Or perhaps it was my own.

"Open the door. I know you're there."

The knob jiggled as I held my breath. The door held.

He could drop dead. How dare he pull that "I know you're in there" crap? How could he possibly know that? There was no way to see through the keyhole, because I'd already stuffed it in anticipation of a visit from him. I wasn't born yesterday.

Yet somehow, he knew I was home. Did it necessarily follow that I was obligated to respond and open the door?

Over my dead body, I would. This wasn't a board game we were playing. Perhaps I would engage with Jean-Michel at some later date, just to clear the air and formalize our break up. But not now. Not tonight. Our fight had been too recent. My only defense against him was to remain mute.

Finally, the pounding stopped. This time, I was taking no chances. The draft that had blown in under the door in winter months told me there was a gap there. If he lay down, he'd be able to see my floor and whatever was on it, nothing more.

I vowed not to touch my feet to the floor until at least twenty minutes of total silence passed. Within five, something crumpled and white slid under the door toward me. A note. I'd read it as soon as its author left.

After an interminable period, during which time I forgot I was still hungry, Jean-Michel appeared to have left. Just to be sure, I lay back on my bed and read two more chapters of my favorite Françoise Sagan novel, *Bonjour Tristesse*. She was the mistress of cool.

Finally, I lowered my stocking feet to the floor and crept to the door, where I squatted, retrieving the note. Moving back to my bed, I tossed it on the night table. Whatever its contents, I needed a break for a few more minutes from the shock of Jean-Michel's unwelcome visit. The whole breaking up thing had moved me into new territory. With my only previous lover, it had been so easy. I'd told him I needed time to prepare for my move from Paris, and he hadn't told me his ex-girlfriend was still calling. We'd understood each other perfectly.

What happened if the person you broke up with didn't agree to break up with you? It was so inconvenient being in a partnership. You weren't boss of your own actions anymore. Someone else was in the picture, interpreting them all wrong. Sighing, I picked up the note, praying its contents would confirm it was the end for both of us.

Ava, I dropped by to talk to you. I'm sorry I offered you the little pig. I won't do it again. Let's meet this Friday after work as usual. I kiss you. — Jean-Michel.

Ugh. He was trying to reconcile. Gloss things over as if nothing happened. Now, it was up to me to respond. At least we were engaging pen to pen, rather than face to face. It was much more my style. Face to face, I wouldn't be able to think. Instead, I'd react to the vein throbbing in his neck. It wasn't fair. I couldn't maintain my position in the face of histrionics. I'd back down just to keep the peace. Or run off. But what if this time, when he followed, he grabbed me? Then, I'd smell his Denim aftershave all over again, mixed with his sweat, and I'd melt into his arms. That wasn't my aim at all.

My plan was to enjoy my few final weeks in Paris, practice being comfortable in my own skin and faking it till I was making it. That didn't include faking interest in reconciling with my fussy French boyfriend. There were too many other more interesting points to fake. Like my sense of *sangfroid*, my *hauteur*, my *je ne sais quoi*, none of which I really possessed, all of which I wanted to. There was a whole world of mannerisms I needed to practice and adopt as my own before leaving Paris so that I could return home appearing clearly improved to my friends and family after nine months abroad.

Two days later, I walked over to Jean-Michel's place and pushed my own note under his door. It was short, to the point.

Jean-Michel — I need to find myself. You taught me so much, but now I need time alone to truly learn how to be comfortable in my own skin. I miss you but it is time to say goodbye. Thank you for all the moments we shared. You are the only Frenchman in my heart. — Ava.

PART II

BEING

CHAPTER SIX

Paris Four Years Later

Four years later, my Yale graduation took place. I'd done it. Not knowing whether I'd passed my Calculus of Two Differentials class until one week before graduation had been a nail-biter, but at least I'd taken it pass/fail so as not to screw up my grade point average.

No matter. I'd screwed up my GPA regardless. As my two suitemates shared their *summa cum laude* status with me, I was unable to offer back even the mention of a *cum laude* to crown my B.A. in history, subspecialty European intellectual history. This was largely tied to my receiving a B minus on my senior essay, the crowning achievement of a Yale undergraduate's four years. My topic had been Martin Luther. Never having nailed exactly what point I was trying to make about one of my favorite church reformers, I'd enjoyed researching the fact that he'd been an avid beer drinker and had married a former nun who'd become his housekeeper. They'd had six children together. I'd been delighted to report that Luther was one all-around man, but my senior essay advisor, a leading religious history scholar, had not deemed this an essential point of original scholarship.

My plans, post-graduation, were as up in the air as my mortarboard hat at the close of the graduation ceremony. Everything looked rosy. That summer, my mother was taking my sixteen-year old half sister and me on a tour of Europe. My revisionist version of my childhood was starting to look like it had worked. Mom was actually in the audience somewhere making nice with my father. My grandmother sat as far away from my parents as possible, looking for fellow respectable white Anglo-Saxon Protestants to exchange civilities with – having none to share with family members, with most of whom she was not on speaking terms. Instead, she trained her Southern-style warmth and charm on my girlfriend's younger Downs' Syndrome brother, whose family was sitting next to her. My grandmother was a saint to people less fortunate than she, so long as they weren't related to her.

It rained like hell. Campus security handed out black utility-sized trash bags for families of graduates to cover their fine spring outfits. The entire ceremony was outdoors. A tent covered our heads to shield us from the drenching downpour, but nothing protected us from the unbearable humidity of the late spring day. In photos taken that day female graduates were memorialized forever with hairdos turned to frizz. My long, blonde hair looked like puffy yellow cumulus clouds haloing my head. After four years of end-of-semester all-nighters and academic stress combined with social maneuvering on the order of membership in the late nineteenth century Hapsburg Court, I was no longer plump. Stress had burned off the puppy fat.

In just a few weeks, I'd be in Paris, where I'd meet my mother and half sister. From there we'd roam around Europe for three weeks.

My mother had just inherited a substantial sum from her uncle, who died childless. He was my grandfather's brother, the accommodating family member who hosted secret visits between my grandfather and his daughter, while she continued to be in the doghouse with her own mother.

One of my mother's finer points was her recklessness. For the first time in perhaps her entire adult life, she wasn't hovering above poverty level. She may not have been able to contribute a penny toward my Yale education, but she was now in a position to give me a traditional graduation present, a tour of Europe with herself and my half sister as companions.

It was a dream come true. We would have time to get to know each other in comfortable circumstances. No one would be worrying about money. Even my grandmother approved of the plan, probably because it was a traditional graduation gift she herself offered my mother when she'd graduated from U Cal Berkeley twenty-four years earlier.

I couldn't believe my good fortune. Many of my colleagues were entering law, medical, or business school in the fall, or working for their father's or father's friends Wall Street firms. But I was determined to live life for a few years before getting swallowed alive by academia again or the corporate world. My rebel streak was alive and kicking – perhaps an inheritance from my mother. It had lain dormant the past four years, buried under a steady stream of exams, papers, deadlines, and structure. Yale College was nothing if not structured. I had played the game well enough to earn my degree and now I wanted to kick up my heels.

Three weeks later, I was back in Paris, alone. I had to fly before the start of the summer travel season in order to use my father's employee pass. He had gotten a job at Pan Am airlines years earlier, and when we finally got back in touch when I turned eighteen, he let me know that I could fly free on Pan Am twice a year as his family member. My mother and half sister would arrive around the first of July. I'd contacted the Griffiths around graduation time to alert them to my plans and ask if my old room was by chance available in mid-June. It was. By the time I arrived, they would be in Renwick, but would leave the key to the top-floor maid's chambers with the concierge. I wouldn't be lonely, I'd be alone. In a city I more or less knew my way around and wholeheartedly adored, this wasn't a bad way to begin my post-college life.

It was strangely thrilling to be back in my old room with time and privacy to assess what had changed in the four years I'd been gone. Jean-Michel and I hadn't kept in touch, but I still had his number. I thought about calling him, but then I thought better of that plan. It was entirely possible he was no longer at that number or now was a family man with a child or two. Why not let sleeping dogs lie?

I went out to explore my old neighborhood. Entering the pastry shop, I was relieved that no one behind the counter recognized me. I perused the wares, bought a demi-baguette, and left. No longer a slave to sugar and fat, I could window shop, salivate madly then say no. If Yale taught me anything, I now knew "fake it till you make it" really worked. And if you're still faking it after you make it, does the world really need to know?

Mais non — of course not.

Next on my list was a visit to my old haunting ground, Shakespeare and Company in the Latin Quarter. The English-language bookstore was located behind the student quarter of Saint Michel, next to the Seine. It was run by a stylishly eccentric older man named George, who either liked you or didn't, just the way my grandmother did. He'd known James Joyce, T.S. Eliot, William Faulkner, Ernest Hemingway and others who'd spent time at Shakespeare and Company either throwing book launches or sleeping on one of the couches upstairs from the bookstore during down periods of their writing careers. I myself had passed a night in George's informal *pension* — when I'd spent one spring break from Yale on a ten-day Eurail Youthpass tour of Europe and neglected to find out if the Griffith's were home before my arrival in Paris with no place to stay. They were off on a ski trip to Austria, the substitute concierge informed me — someone I didn't recognize at all.

Instead of wasting my limited francs on a hotel room, I'd wandered over to Shakespeare and Company and chatted up George while petting his cat. He took note of the heavy backpack I'd parked just inside the shop entrance and ended our conversation with the suggestion I take it upstairs and stay the night if I had nowhere else to go. I did, gladly.

If George was still around, he'd let me know what, if any, literary-set parties might be taking place over the next few weeks within the Anglo-American community. They were usually hosted by older, expatriate English, American or Australian men, who had lots of younger male friends with literary aspirations as well as ones to meet footloose and fancy-free females traveling abroad.

That would be me.

As early evening fell, I wandered into the bookstore. An overgrown boy at the cash register informed me George was on vacation in Italy.

"When will he be back?" I asked.

"Around the beginning of next week," the boy replied, looking disdainful. The James Joyce style owl-shaped glasses he wore made him appear about twenty-two, trying to look forty.

'Out of your league, baby boy,' I telegraphed to him as I paid for a novella by Françoise Sagan I'd found in the cheap paperbacks box outside the front of the shop. I decided not to inquire about upcoming parties. No way was I going to any party the twit before me might recommend.

On the sidewalk again, my plans were vague. The night was warm and balmy. Students, intermingled with tourists, roamed the street paralleling the Seine. I decided to head down the maze of crooked streets behind Boulevard Saint Michel to see if my favorite poster store was still there. As I made my way, I assessed the smells coming from outdoor food vendors. The night whispered to me as I passed stalls of roasted lamb, crêpes, and Moroccan sweets made from pistachio, walnuts, and honey. The poster shop was still there, as was just about everything else I remembered in Paris. The city seemed impervious to change. Why tinker with perfection?

I went in and perused the walls. Old movie posters were mixed in with the usual Toulouse Lautrec Moulin Rouge reproductions. Sinister clowns on circus advertisements leered at me. The characters on the posters all seemed to be suggesting something hidden, provocative, *louche*. Instead of frightening me, I was attracted. I greeted them silently like old friends. They were there to offer a taste of Paris to the tourists patronizing the shop. What was Paris if not suggestive, provocative, self-assured, and just the slightest bit sleazy? If it wasn't, why would so many of us be madly in love with it?

After having my fill of browsing, I strolled back toward the Place Saint Michel and decided to check out the Seine from the vantage point of the bridge before heading toward the brightly lit café next to it. About midway across the Pont Saint Michel, I leaned over its wide stone balustrade. Down below on either side of the dark, placid water, couples strolled or sat. Some, I imagined were leaning against the wall, engaging in activities that still occupied a hidden room in my mind.

"*Woo-hoo. Regarde-moi, le guignol.* Look at me, I'm a clown," a voice sang out from the darkness. I peered toward the sound of the voice to make out two figures, one standing, one seated, on the stone staircase going down to the river walkway from the Île Saint-Louis. A tall man, with dark hair and white skin was pretending he was about to fall into the river. The other man held his ankle from his seated position behind, alternately yelling at him to stop, then to go ahead and jump if he felt like it.

I watched for a few minutes, amused.

"Should I jump?" the dark-haired one yelled up to me.

"Don't do it," I yelled back, in the off chance there was any seriousness to his question.

"Will you have a drink with us if I don't?" he shouted back.

I shook my head, the darkness hiding my smile.

"I'm going to fall. It's your fault, *Américaine*. Help...help!" He tried to twist away from his companion, who leapt up and restrained him by the shoulders.

"Don't jump. Stay calm," I called to him.

"I can't help it. There's no point in living if you don't have a drink with us."

Now that was a line that could only have been offered by a man with Gallic roots. Without thinking, I moved closer to get a better look at the jokers. The tall, dark one was good looking. But it was the other who caught my attention. Shorter and slimly well-built, he silently stood behind his theatrical friend, restraining his arms from behind him and peering up at me. His expression was relaxed, but inquisitive. I'd bet his friend pulled this stunt on a regular basis.

"I'm on my way to the café on the corner. If you want to come, then come on," I said, surprising myself. What was I thinking?

The shorter man looked at me steadily. His friend continued to clown around on the staircase balustrade, his body like a circus performer, twisting and turning into positions of imminent danger, poised to fall into the water below.

To make my point, I turned and walked toward the café, not looking back to see if they followed. In a minute, a strong, fresh smell of young masculinity overtook me on my left. They'd caught up.

"*Bon soir*, I'm Gerard," the clownish one said. He looked harmless — tall, handsome and goofy.

I shot him an acknowledging glance, then looked over at his friend.

"*Bon soir*. I'm Pascal." The shorter one had curly, light brown hair, and a tight, muscular body. Nothing to write home about. But his gaze was direct and unwavering. He didn't look caught up in his own cleverness, the way the taller one did.

"I'm Ava."

To that, Gerard took my hand and leaned over, kissing it with a flourish. Over his head, my gaze connected with Pascal's.

We made our way to the Café Saint Michel. Brilliantly lit and relatively crowded, it was a good choice should I need to make a fast getaway.

"Wine for all!" Gerard practically shouted to the waiter.

"No. I'll have a coffee," I corrected him. *"Un café crème, grande tasse,"* I told the waiter.

"Why not have some wine with us?" Gerard suggested, cajolingly. One thick, dark eyebrow rose higher than the other.

I sensed he was intelligent, as well as funny. But there was something in his demeanor that put me off.

"I don't drink wine with strangers," I told him.

"I'll have a *café crème* too. A large cup," Pascal spoke up.

I liked the way he matched me, overruling his showy friend.

"Okay, then. Coffee. *Un espresso,"* Gerard amended.

The waiter ambled off, bored with yet another American girl pickup scene.

Gerard took the spoon on the table and balanced it on his nose. Pascal and I watched. Then Gerard slipped the spoon above his earlobe. As we stared, it disappeared. We laughed. In a minute, it resurfaced in the inside pocket of his jacket.

"What do you do?" I asked Gerard, before it occurred to me how inanely American my question sounded.

He volunteered that he was a student of mime, had run away from the circus and made money from jumping in the Seine for the benefit of tourists during the summer season.

I looked at Pascal, who rolled his eyes. They were large, round, and hazel. I'd noticed the preponderance of hazel-colored eyes amongst the French. It was a mutable color, sometimes green, sometimes brown, sometimes gold, depending on the light. The changeable color seemed consistent with the French character, a people neither northern nor southern, but with Latin roots that gave them more of an affinity with their southern Mediterranean neighbors than with the Anglo-Saxons to the north or the Germanic folk to their east.

Pascal's eyes were now gleaming gold.

I tried not to stare.

"And what do you do?"

"Je travaille à un hôpital, comme un aide-infirmier."

I didn't understand. "Do you mean you're a nurse?" In Europe, male nurses were not uncommon.

"Pas exactement. Je suis un aide-infirmier."

"Huh." It sounded like he did something related to nursing. "What do you do at your job?" I followed up, realizing once again I'd stumbled into the American trap of grilling someone I'd just met about his career. Sooo gauche.

He shrugged. *"J'aide les patients, je fait leurs lits; je lave les morts et d'autres choses."* His eyes continued to glow at me, carrying on a separate conversation.

Not really following his long response, I filed it away to figure out later.

Satisfied Pascal was gainfully employed in a respectable profession and not caring that Gerard was not, I studied the quieter man across from me while his sidekick mugged for us. Gerard was entertaining, gregarious, and very good at engaging his audience. Soon, not only were we laughing but students at neighboring tables were, too. Yet something about him didn't attract me. I couldn't put my finger on it. He had charisma in spades over Pascal. But there was something Pascal had that Gerard did not. It might have been an attention span.

Coffee together was pleasant for the same reason that it had been pleasant the first time I'd met Jean-Michel four and a half years earlier. I wasn't required to talk, to spit out my life history or personal facts about myself that I didn't care to divulge to strangers. Neither Gerard nor Pascal pressured me to tell them anything whatsoever about myself. I felt comfortable and light-hearted, reassured that there were two of them instead of one. They played off each other, or rather Gerard play-acted, while Pascal hung back dreamily and looked at me.

We finished our coffee and left. I wasn't in any rush to get back to my room, so I agreed when Gerard suggested we walk for a bit. We strolled along the quay of the Seine in the direction of the Eiffel Tower as well as the Griffith's flat.

It was one of those warm summer nights when every adventure seemed safe. The idea that Pascal was some sort of nurse appealed to me. He was in the healing arts. How could he be dangerous? The more Gerard talked and jumped around, the more I was aware of Pascal's quiet presence next to me. It was as if we were on a first date, our bodies holding their own *entente cordiale* as we watched a stage performance.

"Where do you live?" I asked him.

"North of the city. In Saint Denis, just outside the Pèriphèrique," he said, referring to the circular ring road that defined Paris's borders.

"How far is it from here?"

"By the RER, about thirty minutes." The Réseau Express Régional was the rail line through Paris that served its suburbs.

Having no concept of any Parisian suburbs, other than Neuilly-sur-Seine, a wealthy enclave to the northwest of Paris which I'd visited one Sunday afternoon with Jean-Michel, I envisioned a well-ordered community of stately single family houses with filigreed balconies, majestic floor-to-ceiling French windows, and well-appointed gardens.

"Is it pretty?" I asked. I really just wanted to know whether Pascal thought I was pretty, which I already did.

"Bah — no, not really. It's like all the other suburbs around Paris." He retreated into silence, matching my pace and not feeling the need to clutter up the still, night air with conversation.

Gerard, meanwhile, was walking on top of the stone balustrade bordering the Seine, attracting attention. I watched as a muscular lone black male wearing a backpack stared at him. Gerard had a knack for getting noticed. It was fine by me as long as he didn't fall, splashing into the river below, or worse, splattering his brains on the stone pathway below. Pascal apparently had seen this stunt many times before, as he paid him no mind.

"*Gerard est un pédé,*" he said out of nowhere, reading my thoughts.

What? I'd heard the term before and knew it meant something less shocking in French than it did in English, but still shocking. Perhaps I'd heard wrong.

"What did you say?"

"*Il est un pédé. Un pédéraste, tu sais?*" " He's a pederaste. A homosexual, understand?"

Wow. He'd hit the nail on the head with his answer to exactly what I'd been wondering. Then why was Pascal hanging around with him?

"And you?"

"No. Never. " He shook his head violently. "I like women," he explained, making sure I got the point.

I did. But I didn't know too many straight guys back home who hung out with gay ones. Then again, I didn't know too many gay guys, period.

"How long have you been friends?" I asked.

"All my life. We went to school together. From the École Maternelle," he said, referring to the French state-run, free-to-all pre-school for children between three and six years old.

"That's nice," I replied, wondering if anything about Gerard's disposition had rubbed off on Pascal. It wasn't apparent, if it had.

"We're completely different. That's why we get along," Pascal continued. "He's funny, I'm not. He talks a lot, I don't. He likes men, I like women. *Comme ça.*" He stopped, raising his hands in Gallic gesture, as if to say "there you have it."

That was twice Pascal had told me he liked women. Message received.

I kept my thoughts to myself as we walked through the deepening night. One fact seemed indisputable. Pascal liked me, and I liked him. My rationalization skills took over. Wasn't this sort of triangle even better than a one-to-one liaison with a man from another country, another culture? At least with Gerard as gag man, I could laugh, let down my guard without worry that two men were interested in me, and appeal to him should Pascal prove to be something other than what he appeared.

I looked over at the shorter man. He seemed soft, gentle, dreamy, and intuitive. He was a professional caregiver. I'd bet anything, he knew how to cook. What Frenchman didn't?

"Are you in Paris for long?" he asked.

"Two weeks," I replied, wondering why I didn't feel the need to censor information with him, a complete stranger.

"Are you free tomorrow?" he asked.

I was. But wasn't it gauche to admit I had no plans? Guys were supposed to give you lead time of at least three to four days when they asked you out, where I came from. On the other hand, I was no longer in the country I came from, less than two weeks remained until my family joined me, and I had no agenda whatsoever.

"Why do you ask?" I hedged.

"Do you want to go for dinner?"

"With you?" I meant with him alone, but it hadn't come out right.

"If you prefer, I can bring Gerard."

Pascal had understood perfectly. Maybe I did prefer Gerard to join us. Pascal was the one I was interested in, but I didn't know him well enough to accept an immediate date. Yet there was no time for a slow and gradually unfolding getting-to-know-him period. Gerard could provide distraction as well as entertainment. Plus, he could be a foil, should Pascal not appeal to me twenty four hours hence, the way he was appealing to me at that moment.

I doubted that would happen.

"Yes. Bring Gerard."

"As you wish." He smiled.

A kinetic connection jumped between us. We both knew we didn't ultimately want Gerard around. But for now, we needed him to play chaperone.

Pascal moved closer to Gerard, engaging him in brief conversation, too fast for me to follow. In a minute, he returned to my side.

"Do you want to meet tomorrow around six?"

"Where?"

"I want to take you to a restaurant behind Saint Michel. On Boulevard Raspail. Do you like *crêpes?*"

"Yes. Definitely." My mouth watered.

"Shall we pick you up?"

I hesitated.

"If you wish, we can meet at the same café where we just had coffee."

"That's good."

"Around six then."

"Fine."

We continued to walk, the night quiet. Soon, we would be in my neighborhood. As much as my companions seemed trustworthy, I didn't want them to accompany me to my building.

"Listen, I should say goodnight here," I told Pascal a block away from Rue de Belgrade.

"Are you sure?" he asked.

"Yes. See you tomorrow at six."

"You promise, you'll come?"

"Promise."

"Could I have your phone number?"

"I don't have one."

Our eyes locked. *Don't worry, I'll be there*, mine said to his.

"Don't you want us to walk you home?" Gerard asked.

"No," I said simply, not taking my eyes off Pascal. "I'll see you tomorrow."

"But it's no problem," he pressed until Pascal cut him off, muttering something under his breath.

"As you like," Pascal finished for him.

Something inside zinged every time he answered 'as you like.' I could think of other things I liked that he might be interested in exploring with me.

"*Très bien. A demain soir, Ava*. Until tomorrow evening," Gerard concurred, changing course. He reached in to kiss me, once on each cheek. I accepted, a teensy bit put off by the wet, sucking feel of his full lips on my skin. Then, it was Pascal's turn.

"*A demain*," he said, stepping close to me. His mouth on my cheek was dry, firm, masculine. A faint hint of sandalwood hit my nose. Spicy, but subtle.

"*A demain*," I replied, suppressing an urge to inhale deeply. Quickly, I walked away, turning the corner to recover my privacy. There was a lot to reflect on. But all I could think of was Pascal's gleaming, gold eyes following me home; Gerard left behind, dancing on the banks of the Seine.

၁၆

At ten past six the next day I sat down at one of the outdoor tables on the terrace of the Café Saint Michel. The weather was warm and clear, so I tilted my head back to take advantage of the long rays of the late afternoon sun.

I wondered where my two new friends were. It wouldn't do to look for them. They could find me. Instead, I closed my eyes to feel the sun's warm rays dance on my lids.

In a minute, large, clammy hands stole over them. Ugh.

"*Bon soir,*" Gerard sang out.

I squirmed to release my face from his unwanted touch. I couldn't be too mad. It was just Gerard being Gerard. Like a puppy dog peeing on your shoe, he couldn't help himself.

"*Bon soir*," I greeted him, hoping I could escape the mandatory two kisses. I couldn't.

As he bussed me on each cheek, I looked for Pascal. Sure enough, there he was, standing to one side, wearing a clean, navy and white striped shirt and looking as if he'd slicked down his curly hair. He'd made an effort.

Our eyes met, his large, warm, and greenish-brown today. I didn't doubt the gold in them would return later. I'd make sure it did.

As he kissed me hello, a fresh pine scent filled my nostrils as well as the sandalwood I'd smelled the night before. He'd apparently used shower gel, a product Jean-Michel had disdained, along with deodorant.

I was dealing with a whole new animal here. On the surface, domesticated; underneath, I rather hoped not.

We sat down and ordered drinks. Pascal suggested a kir for me, ordering *pressions* – draft beers – for himself and Gerard. Feeling safe enough with the men to drink a small amount of alcohol that evening, I agreed. The kir was a refreshing combination of white wine and *crème de cassis*, black currant liqueur, a classic lady's drink. I was glad he hadn't suggested a beer for me too, because the aftertaste would have interfered with my fantasies of returning his kisses later – not the once-on-either-cheek kinds either.

We basked in the sun, Gerard keeping an eye out for a potential audience to entertain, and Pascal and I pretending not to be electrically aware of each other. There was something about Gerard's presence that heightened the excitement of the dance Pascal and I were now engaged in. It was as if having a chaperone was giving us permission to explore our attraction to each other that we wouldn't have had if I'd been a lone female protecting herself in the face of an advancing, unknown male.

After a lazy hour of watching the crowds, as well as each other's responses to Gerard's antics, we departed for the restaurant Pascal had mentioned. In no rush, we stopped to enjoy street performers along the way. Paris was at her best that evening. We applauded a magic show, impressed by a dog riding a unicycle. Then, we came upon some fire swallowers, just setting up for the evening. Gerard studied them intently, no doubt thinking of future revenue streams.

After another twenty minutes, we walked past the Cluny Museum at the corner of Boulevard Saint Michel and Boulevard Saint Germain. I pictured the tapestries of ladies with unicorns inside that had fascinated me ever since I'd first laid eyes on them in an art history book. Woven in the Middle Ages, there were six in all; depicting the joys of the five senses.

At the moment, all five of my senses were engaged. I imagined myself the lady in the tapestry, the star of a medieval tableau, courted by a minor knight of the court. We'd be chaperoned by the court jester who had been paid off by the knight to make himself scarce when the right moment arrived. It was an ancient rite we'd enact, one sanctioned by Paris, the City of Love as well as Light, the late spring night, and choruses of worldly angels singing suggestively to us from both heaven and Earth.

Unsure if Pascal was familiar with the Cluny tapestries, I kept my thoughts to myself. The European history I'd spent the past four years majoring in was present right here and now, not only in the ancient building that housed the Cluny Museum, but in the thoughts and desires of two people outside on its sidewalk, who might begin a history together that very night. My college education fell into place at that moment, my major perfectly chosen for the grown up adventure I was contemplating.

"Are you cold?" Pascal asked, noticing me shiver as we passed the ancient, thick walls of the Cluny fortress.

"No, I'm fine." I liked the way he tuned into my details.

If only he knew the swirl of excitement I felt at the combination of awe in the face of history and pleasure at being a part of it. No European could possibly understand the impact upon an American of walking past a fifteenth-century building and thinking of all the souls and all the stories that make up its past.

In another half hour, we arrived at the restaurant. Our long walk there had given me an appetite. Gerard opened the door for us, bowing as I passed. Again, I felt as if I was in a medieval tableau, a mystical rite playing out that evening in which each player knew his part and each savored the anticipation of its inevitable outcome.

The restaurant was provincial in style, dark and richly paneled in rough-hewn wood. It smelled of apple cider.

We were seated. At the Café Saint Michel, both the evening before and earlier that day, Gerard had sat next to me, with Pascal across the table. But this time, Pascal took the initiative, shouldering Gerard out of the way as he slid into the wood banquette seat next to me. *Bravo.*

"Would you like to try some Breton cider?" he asked.

"*Pourquoi pas?*" "Why not?" I agreed. I had no recollection of cider as an accompaniment to the crêpes I'd served as a waitress at the crêperie restaurant back in Hartford, Connecticut. But I was in France now, not New England. It was time to try something new.

Looking around, I took in the homey and rustic decor, like the maritime culture of Bretagne or Brittany, next to the north-Atlantic Ocean. It reminded me of Maine.

"What kind of fillings do you like in your crêpes?" Pascal asked.

I hesitated. There had been the crêpes back at the restaurant in Hartford, filled with ratatouille and shredded cheese. I hadn't liked most of them, truth be told. Then, there were the crêpes on the streets of Paris, which I'd practically survived on four years earlier, when I'd been an au pair. The cheapest ones had been sweet, with sugar and butter inside, or chocolate and coconut if I splurged. I loved those crêpes, but they hadn't loved me, especially not my hips.

"I'm not sure. I haven't really eaten a lot of crêpes," I lied. *Fake it till you make it*, my conscience reassured me. Or was it my id?

"Do you like cheese?" Pascal asked.

"Yes. Very much."

"Smelly cheese or mild?" Gerard chipped in.

"Smelly," I replied, thinking back to the cheeses I'd enjoyed eating with Jean-Michel. *Chaumes* had been my favorite. It had been orangeish, runny, and deliciously stinky.

Pascal poured me a glass from the large pitcher of cider the waiter set before us. I drank deeply.

"How's the cider?"

"Hard," I said, pleased with the taste. It was nothing like apple cider back in New England. This cider had a bite. It tasted robust, not too sweet, and most definitely alcoholic.

"Hard? What do you mean?" Now, it was Pascal's turn to be confused.

"I mean it has alcohol in it."

"Of course." This was France, after all.

"Not too much. But a little," he added, quaffing from his own glass.

I nodded as I took a longer swallow. It was delicious.

The waiter came over.

"*Vous-desirez, Mademoiselle?*"

I turned to Pascal. "Tell him I want a crêpe with the smelliest cheese in it he's got."

"*Très bien*," Pascal smiled approvingly. Then, he ordered two smelly cheese crêpes. One for me and one for him. Gerard chose a classic *jambon gruyère*, or ham and cheese, for himself.

Dinner arrived. It was delicious. Everything about our evening was zesty and zingy, like the Breton cider.

Pascal wasn't exactly a conversationalist, but he was attentive. Gerard chattered on, interspersed with occasional breaks while he perused the room. I felt warm, coddled by Pascal and reassured by the resonance of the decor with my childhood summers in Maine.

Dinner ended with espressos and shots of *calvados*, a fortifying apple liqueur from Basse-Normandie, near where the Allies landed in 1944.

After settling the bill, which Pascal paid, waving away my money, we spilled out onto the street. As we turned onto the Rue de Grenelle from the Boulevard Raspail, it was almost a straight shot home. This time, I didn't mind being accompanied. We linked arms, with me in the middle, swinging them as we walked. As we passed the grand open space of Napoleon's Tomb, known as Les Invalides, Gerard struck up a French song in a pleasant baritone, Pascal joining in on the choruses. On the far side of Les Invalides, we entered the quiet, well-appointed neighborhood of the Griffiths, the seventh arrondissement, a far cry from the Latin Quarter.

We lowered our voices. This was the neighborhood where well-to-do Parisians who preferred the more artsy Left Bank lived. That would include the Griffiths. I didn't want to bump into any of their friends in the company of my two new acquaintances, happy though I was with them. Mrs. Griffith already thought I had very bad taste in men.

"Where do you take the train to get back to Saint Denis?" I asked Pascal, wondering if their train station was anywhere nearby.

"We take it from Saint Michel," he replied, looked at his watch. He frowned, then mumbled something to Gerard.

"Is everything okay?" I asked.

"Everything's fine," he reassured me.

A quarter hour later, we stood at the entrance to my building. The concierge's light was off, to my relief. Time had flown. It was past midnight.

"Are you going to walk back to Saint Michel now?" I asked, wondering why I was worrying about them. They were two adult men, not children.

But there was something so childlike about Gerard – he elicited my maternal instincts, different from the ones Pascal stirred.

"It doesn't matter now," Pascal shrugged.

"What do you mean?"

"It's too late. The last train is just after midnight. We missed it," Gerard explained.

"What will you do?"

"Don't worry, *cherie*, we'll manage," Gerard said, giving an identical shrug to Pascal's of a moment before.

"Okay then." I shrugged back. They could take care of themselves. "Thank you for dinner. It was really fun."

Pascal's eyes bored into me.

"Shall we come up?" he asked.

I'd been expecting that. Only I hadn't expected what happened next.

"If you'd like. My place is small though."

Who said that? Not the me I used to be. I prayed I was making a good decision. It wasn't a wise one, but I'd become fond of them both, and they had nowhere to go until the first train of the following day began.

"It's okay. I don't mind," Pascal said, holding the heavy outer door for me as I led them through the service entrance to the elevator to the top floor where my room was located.

I'd never seen what my room looked like with three people in it at once. It was very small indeed. Pascal and Gerard took off their shoes at the door, and we all sat cross-legged on the floor, Pascal and I propped against my bed, Gerard facing us, against the tiny desk.

A cool, night breeze drifted in the one, small window on the far wall. I had a few bottles of mineral water on hand, so I poured some for everyone. Unfortunately, Gerard showed no signs of sleepiness, but Pascal was beginning to doze off. I pulled out blankets for both of them, then went to use the Turkish toilet in the hall.

When I returned, I was disappointed to see Pascal wrapped in a blanket on the floor next to the door. Gerard was stretched out in the middle of the floor, closer to the bed. That hadn't been my plan, but it was a safe one. There was no way I wanted to explore closer relations with Pascal with Gerard on hand.

I sat at my desk, next to Pascal on the floor, to take off my sandals and brush my hair. Finally, Gerard got up and left to use the hallway facilities.

The second the door closed behind him, Pascal sprang to life. Sitting up in his blankets, he rose on one knee.

"Ava," he whispered, putting his hands on my forearms.

"Yes?" His hands on my arms were dry, firm, the fingers pressing into my flesh. He was quick on the mark when action was warranted.

"Come to my place for dinner tomorrow."

"How do I get there?" I asked, rather inanely.

"Just come back with us tomorrow. You'll enjoy it."

I was sure I would. It would be fun to see a suburb outside of Paris, fun to have yet another Frenchman cook for me, and fun, most of all, to get rid of Gerard at some point the following evening.

I nodded as his hands pulled my face down to his. We kissed hurriedly, urgently. Then, the door handle jostled, and Gerard was back.

It was Pascal's turn to leave. Ignoring Gerard, I found my pajamas then climbed into bed.

By the time he returned, Gerard's eyes had closed. Pascal's gleaming, gold, tiger eyes met mine over his friend's inert body. As if he'd touched my mouth, I felt my lower face muscles form into a sly smile.

"Tomorrow," he whispered.

I nodded, indicating that he should turn off the light switch next to his head. In the dark, I wrestled with putting on my pajamas under my bed sheets, Girl Scout camp style. Fortunately, Gerard appeared to have drifted off. He was like a small boy, incessantly moving and talking until his head hit the pillow. Then he conked out.

The sound of Pascal's heavy breathing reassured me. *Tomorrow*, he seemed to exhale. *Tomorrow*, I silently exhaled back. In a minute, I drifted off to sleep.

CHAPTER SEVEN

Anna Karenina Understood

*T*he next day, I awoke to Pascal's sleepy eyes upon me. Gerard was still asleep. We looked at each other steadily, as I imagined waking up with him without Gerard between us.

"Tu as bien dormi? Have you slept well?" Pascal asked.

"Yes. Very well. And you?"

"Très bien." He should be, considering he was waking up in my room, if not in my arms. The golden ring was in sight.

In a minute, Gerard was up, and we all went out to greet the day. It was comical to see their drowsy, early morning faces. Gerard's eyes were puffy, with dark rings under them. Pascal's usually large, round eyes had taken on a slanted shape – exotic and sly. I didn't doubt his thoughts were both, his eyes on the prey.

Bypassing my usual boulangerie, as well as the patisserie shop, I led us to the working man's café on the corner of the Rue de Grenelle where I'd frequently stopped for a large cup of *café crème* on my way to French classes at the Sorbonne.

We had our coffees at the counter, and Pascal introduced me to a new custom. I'd often wondered why eggs were displayed on a vertical stand on café countertops, especially in the mornings. Now, I watched as he plucked three eggs from the stand, peeled, and salted one then handed it to me. The hard-boiled egg was fresh and delicious.

My English girlfriend, Charlotte, came to mind. I'd met her in Tokyo, where I taught English the summer between sophomore and junior years. She was ten years older, wildly sophisticated, with a penchant for black American Japanese major league baseball players; a male genre which enjoyed superstar status in Japan. Pretty, tall, and willowy, her complexion was as delicate as an English rain shower.

Her eating habits had been as carefully controlled as her love life had not. She was discipline personified. I'd soaked up everything she did, worshiping at the altar of her self-control. Every morning, she'd eat either one hard-boiled or soft-boiled egg with a piece of unbuttered whole wheat toast. She'd wash this down with a few cups of tea. I never saw her vary from this routine once. After we'd parted ways in Tokyo, she came to Yale one spring to visit me. At breakfast in the chaos of my residential college dining hall, surrounded by undergraduates wolfing down doughnuts, bowls of granola, plates of pancakes, eggs and bacon, she maintained her strict regimen by carefully unpeeling her hard-boiled egg and toasting her lone piece of bread. My girlfriends and I were in awe.

A good number of the girls in my class were anywhere from five to fifteen pounds overweight, except for the ones who were anorexic, bulimic, or naturally slim. My female colleagues and I sucked in our breaths as Charlotte rose from the table after breakfasting, her stomach flat, hip bones jutting out fashionably under her thin, flowered dress, with long slim legs ending in ankles you could wrap your fingers around. Everything about her showed us up. After dark, she was capable of drinking like a fish, another British character trait my Yale colleagues and I found impressive.

As I stood at the counter, enjoying my salted, hard-boiled egg, I connected up the dots. Pascal was showing me how to do something Charlotte had known how to do her entire adult life: carefully control her blood sugar in the morning so she didn't become enslaved to it for the rest of the day.

Finishing the egg, I washed it down with strong coffee with foaming milk in it. Suddenly the display case of flaky croissants farther down the counter had no power over me. If the counterman had slid it down to my end, taken off the top, and wafted the tray under my nose, I wouldn't have flinched. My one hard-boiled egg with coffee was enough. For the first time in my life, I felt like a Frenchwoman.

"You'll come back to Saint Denis with us, no?" Pascal asked.

"I have some things I need to do," I hedged. Like take a shower. Then I remembered I couldn't, because the Griffith's apartment was locked up for the summer. The thought of taking a cold-water sponge bath in the sink outside my room held little appeal.

"Why don't you bring everything you need, and you can do whatever you want at my place?" he asked.

Hmm. It was an idea. I could do lots of things in a fully-equipped apartment that I couldn't do in my room: take a hot shower, wash my hair, and shave my legs, rinse out, and re-insert my diaphragm... It sounded like a plan.

"I need about twenty minutes to get my stuff."

"We'll wait here for you," Pascal agreed.

Gerard was over near the pinball machines eyeballing another man having coffee at the other end of the bar. His fashionable haircut told me he might be on Gerard's wavelength. Secretly, I applauded Pascal for having limited fashion sense. Even Jean-Michel would have sniffed at Pascal's scuffed, dusty workman's shoes. But I liked them. They reassured me that they were holding up a standard-issue, heterosexual man.

I left the café and hurried back to my room. At the entrance to the building, the concierge was out on the sidewalk, sweeping.

"*Bonjour, Mademoiselle*," she said automatically, not even looking up as I passed. I sensed she'd seen nothing of my two companions of the night before.

"*Bonjour, Madame*," I rejoined, heading for the service entrance.

I wondered what Saint Denis would be like. Not having explored anything outside of Paris other than the posh suburb of Neuilly-sur-Seine, I was excited. Perhaps the suburbs were very different from the city. I wouldn't wear my high-heeled boots. Thus far, spending time with Pascal and Gerard had involved a lot of walking. Hanging out with them made me feel fit, fresh, and on fire – the last with exclusive respect to Pascal.

Within ten minutes, I had everything I needed loaded into my backpack, which was new, clean, and fashionable, a graduation gift from my cousins, the ones who weren't from Maine. It was black and gold, with 'Manhattan Express' written on the side. I tossed in my black and gold knit, long-sleeved jersey in case it got cool that evening, along with my bottle of Paloma Picasso perfume – also a graduation gift, and a book. I didn't know if I'd open it, but if Pascal cooked the way most French people did, preparing dinner might take a while. I was good for cutting up vegetables, but for the most part I had no idea what went on in French kitchens and was better off sitting at the table and complimenting the chef while sipping wine. If he tossed me out of his kitchen, I'd go read my book in the living room.

In another ten minutes, I was back at the café.

"*Ça y est?* Are you ready?" Pascal asked. The phrase literally translated: Is it done or are we there yet?

"*Ça y est,*" I responded. I've never understood why the response to *ça y est* was the same as the question, but it was similar to *ça va* or how's it going? In both cases, the same phrase served as both question and response.

We took off from the café and headed toward Saint Michel. I had never taken an RER train before. Roomy and comfortable, with royal blue upholstery and clean windows you could see out, it was unlike any American train I'd ever traveled on.

Our route was due north: first stop Gare du Nord, Paris's largest international train station, where we changed from the blue line to the green line. Gare du Nord was in the bustling, working-class twentieth arrondissement, where many North and West Africans lived and the best bargain shopping in Paris was to be found. Elizabeth and I had spent many Sunday afternoons there. Our next stop was outside the city limits.

"Is this it?" I asked Pascal, as ten minutes later the train pulled into a station.

"Yes. We're here." He took my backpack as we got up.

It was exciting to be somewhere outside of Paris. We exited the station, then crossed a wide boulevard toward what looked like a large supermarket. Graffiti covered its walls. This wasn't Neuilly-sur-Seine.

"We'll do the shopping later," Pascal said. "First, I'll show you the cathedral." We walked down the street, past graffiti-strewn walls, a school, and then a public pool. It was early in the season, but people were going in and out, carrying gym bags and large net bags of drinks. Most of them were young, in their late teens or twenties. Gerard scanned the crowd carefully as we walked by.

"If you want, we can go there later," Pascal said.

"Isn't it a bit cold to swim now?"

"No one goes there to swim," Pascal explained.

"What do they do then?"

He shrugged. "Hang out. Meet friends. Have drinks. I'll take you later, if you want."

It sounded like fun.

Directly across from us, a busy street scene was in progress, with outdoor vendors, each at their own stall.

"What's that over there?" I asked.

"Sunday is market day."

"Can we go see?"

"Sure. Come on." For the first time, Pascal took my hand as we made our way across the square. It felt natural, his hand warm and dry in mine.

I looked around for Gerard but didn't see him.

"Where's Gerard?" I asked.

"He had to go home. We'll meet him later." He'd melted away before I'd even noticed, perhaps by pre-arrangement.

"Do you live together?" I hoped he'd say no.

"Not really." Pascal shrugged again. "Sometimes he stays with me, sometimes with his mother."

Where would he be staying that night? I prayed his mother cooked Sunday lunch for the family so he'd be gone the rest of the day. It was time to see how much Pascal and I had in common without Gerard around.

We wandered among the vendors until Pascal came to a vegetable stand. He picked out a long skinny courgette, five tomatoes, and a good looking head of lettuce.

"What are they selling over there?" I asked, pointing to a stand run by North Africans. The aroma wafting from their direction was spicy and fruity at the same time.

"They sell sweets made with honey. Nuts, dried fruit. Do you want to see?"

"Sure."

The nut-filled pastries on display dripped in honey, an opulent sight for early in the day.

"Do you want to buy some for after dinner?" Pascal asked.

I shook my head. Instead, I bought two packets of incense; one sandal-wood, one musk. It would be my contribution to postprandial ambience that evening.

Finishing with the outdoor stalls, he led me to a row of shops on the street perpendicular to the cathedral square. First stop, the *crémerie* or dairy store. He picked up a small container of crème fraîche, along with six eggs, a carton of yogurt, and milk. Then we went into the *boucherie* or butcher shop, two stores down.

"Three hundred grams of *lardon*," he ordered, referring to the cubed bacon the French use to flavor many traditional dishes as well as salads.

The florid butcher behind the counter grunted as he gave me a level look.

"Are you making spaghetti carbonara for dinner?" I asked my curly-haired companion. It was a dish Jean-Michel had frequently made.

"Do you like it?"

"Yes. Very much," I exclaimed, with gusto. The day without Gerard was unfolding to tremendous possibilities.

Pascal's face lit up. It occurred to me that he was the type of person who got pleasure in giving pleasure to others. I would be the enabler of his happiness that day. It was the least I could do, considering he was going to prepare one of my favorite dishes that evening.

"I'll get the wine," I told him, caught up in the spirit of the occasion. "But you need to help me choose it."

"If you insist," he agreed companionably, dropping the packet of diced bacon into my backpack, which I'd unzipped and held out to him. We were like an old married couple shopping for dinner ingredients.

Outside the streets bustled with North and West Africans, mixed in with the local French population. The shoppers looked less fashionable than they did in Paris, more homey. Everyone jostled together, pinching fruits and critically examining wares. A young mother frowned at a bunch of flowers she deemed inadequate, until the stout vendor came around the side of his cart, bent down, and pinned a red posy on the little girl whose hand the mother was holding. The woman's frown melted into a smile as she reached into her purse to buy the bouquet after all.

"What's your favorite color?" Pascal asked, surprising me as we slowed down near the flower stand.

"Blue."

"Mine too," he said, deftly reaching into the midst of the flower display where he plucked out a fat bouquet of small blue flowers. He motioned to the vendor, who wrapped them in white paper.

"For you." He handed the bouquet to me.

"Because I like spaghetti carbonara?" I asked.

"Because I like you," he said simply.

We continued down the street until we reached a *super marché* on the corner.

"Let's get the wine in here," Pascal said.

"But I want to get something special," I demurred. How could supermarket wine be anything but rot gut?

"There's plenty of good wines to choose from. And the price is better here than at the wine shops," he said with authority.

We entered. Sure enough, an enormous selection of wines lined an entire wall. Prices ranged from very inexpensive to reasonable but somewhat high.

"What goes with spaghetti carbonara?" I asked, wondering if I'd elicit an inner pickiness in him I hadn't yet seen. Had Jean-Michel been representative of all French men or had he just been extraordinarily fussy?

"Whatever you like to drink, Ava," Pascal answered, sounding just like a standard-issue American male trying to please his woman.

"Shouldn't it be red wine?" I asked, wanting to seem sage as well as mindful of Jean-Michel's pronouncement that white wine was strictly for alcoholics.

"Not necessarily. If we buy white wine, we can put some in the recipe then drink the rest of it."

"Good. Let's get a bottle of white," I enthused. "You choose it." For once, I could indulge my preference for white wine in the land of wine connoisseurship.

Pascal nodded then began to study the labels in the section marked 'Loire Valley'. The French had remarkable similarity in the matter of what wines went with what dishes. It was a sacred topic with them all.

In a minute, he'd picked out a Sancerre and a Pouilly-Fumé. I felt the tautness of his chest as I took the two bottles from him, moving toward the checkout counter. Surprised at how reasonably priced they were, I paid then asked for a sack, remembering yet another of Jean-Michel's admonitions that only prostitutes carried unwrapped bottles of wine in the street. The clerk wrapped them in brown paper then put them in the sack, handing it to me approvingly.

Finally, our errands were done. Pascal's pace picked up as he led me to his home. After three turns, the streets became quieter, more residential. The sounds of the market disappeared, replaced by the laughs and cries of children playing in the park we passed. A final turn took us away from the park and onto a narrow side street lined with three-story buildings with wrought-iron balconies. I hoped his flat had one.

"Here we are," he announced, stopping abruptly in front of a modest structure.

He tapped a code into the keypad next to the door. When it clicked, he pushed in, and we strode through a drab inner courtyard.

"Up two flights," he said over his shoulder. "Sorry, the elevator isn't working right now."

I followed him lightly up the stairs, eager to see his home. At the top of the second set of stairs, he paused and unlocked the closest door. Down a dark hallway, we entered a large living room with light streaming in the window. It was just as I'd imagined, a large, double window from floor almost to ceiling, opening onto a small balcony. Before I could look at the view, Pascal motioned me to the kitchen, where we dropped our packages.

After Jean-Michel's tiny room, Pascal's flat seemed spacious. There was a living room, kitchen, bath, and another room down the hall, which I assumed was the bedroom. His home was tidy and pleasantly furnished. He appeared to be master of his domain, not mastered by it.

"Very nice," I said, sweeping my arm through the air to indicate our surroundings.

"Thank you." He looked proud.

"How long have you lived here?" He hadn't over-decorated. The flat was by no means cluttered.

"Four years, about. I moved in when I got a job at the hospital here."

We began to unpack our provisions. I was glad Gerard was no longer around to distract us from getting to know each other. Now that we were, I was finding commonalities everywhere. To begin with, he wasn't as picky about everything as Jean-Michel had been. I felt less childish in his presence and more in command of myself. Was it due to my being four years older now or because Pascal seemed younger than Jean-Michel?

"How old are you?" I asked, surprising myself. I wasn't usually so direct.

"Twenty-six," Pascal replied, not appearing to mind my question. "Something to drink?" He reached for a bottle of fizzy mineral water on the counter.

"Sure, but do you have something cold?" So, he was two years older than me, virtually the same age. Whatever happened between us, this wasn't going to be the May-November dynamic Jean-Michel and I had had. Although I didn't doubt Pascal was going to teach me a few things.

Pascal reached into his refrigerator then held up two bottles, one of mineral water, the other a bottle of crisp, chilled white wine, unopened. He looked at me, expectantly.

It was only two in the afternoon. On the other hand, we had no plan, other than to get to know each other better, and I wasn't in a rush to explore the non-swimming scene at the local public pool. There would be time for that another day, if this one turned out well.

My mouth broke into a smile, despite myself and I pointed to the bottle of wine. He smiled back then reached into a drawer for the *tire-bouchon*, literally pull-cork.

"Shall we make the spaghetti carbonara now?" he asked, pulling down two wine glasses from the cabinet then rinsing them at the sink.

I shook my head.

"A little snack, then?" He handed a glass to me.

"Yes." A little snack would be perfect.

"*A cet après-midi,* To the afternoon," he pronounced as we clinked glasses.

The wine was delicious, dry but not too dry with a fruity undertone of apples and blackberries. It would be perfect with some grapes and the right cheese.

Pascal opened the refrigerator again and began to take out small white packages. In a minute, a cheese tray was assembled. Everything we needed was there: red grapes, a soft cheese, a hard one, and a few slices of sausage. Silently, I applauded the domestic skills of French men. They knew how to gain entry to a woman's heart via the stomach.

He picked up the tray, along with a baguette, and led the way into the living room. Sunlight poured through the long, double-doored window, the beams dancing on the floor. I sat on the couch as he fiddled with the radio. In a minute, the strains of West African techno-dance music filled the room. I nodded in approval.

Pascal sat down next to me, the smell of dried sweat mingled with a faint whiff of eau de cologne. When had he put it on? I hadn't noticed it earlier. Then I remembered he'd disappeared for a minute when I'd first gone into the living room.

His eyes were warm and lively, the color his usual daytime brown, with hints of green. He put his left arm on the back of the couch, behind me. In his right hand, he held the stem of his wineglass. Then he put it down. The hand behind me began to play with my hair, wrapping a strand around his finger, then gently tugging. I rested my head on the couch back, giving in to his touch as I studied the specks of particles in the sunbeam path.

Soon, his fingers were on my neck.

"Umm." Without thinking, I closed my eyes. Pleasure was pleasure, and we were in no rush. No wonder Pascal had toasted to the afternoon.

"*Ouvre-ta bouche*," Pascal said, instructing me to open my mouth.

I did.

Gently, he deposited a delectable bite of soft, mellow cheese with a tangy grape.

"Umm," again came out from somewhere deep in my throat.

With one hand on the back of my neck, he pulled me closer. I opened my eyes just in time to see the gold-flecks in Pascal's as his face came up to mine. Then his eyes shut, and he kissed me.

The kiss went on for some time. His tongue probed but didn't over-power. I probed back. He tasted like smelly cheese, fruity wine, and some-thing more – the fresh, healthy taste of young, male virility.

Finally, we broke apart. I was pleased to see the shades of green in his eyes turn to gold. Instead of big and round, they had become slanted cat-eyes.

I took another sip of wine, then put it down. My hand went idly to his thigh. Immediately, he grabbed it and put it on his shoulder, near the neck. I squeezed, feeling the firmness underneath his cotton shirt. Tracing the line of the clavicle, I continued down over his chest. His heart thumped loudly as I pressed against it a minute. Then he pulled my hand away and laced his fingers in mine, kissing me again. This time, he took my lower lip in his teeth and pulled then released. It hurt.

Or did it? I did the same to his lip.

We broke apart. As I took another sip of wine, I felt my lip swell at the touch of the cool fluid. I imagined it puffing out, like a flower bud unfolding. Every part of my body now tingled, the blood circulating fast, then racing back to headquarters, my heart. Taking his hand, I put it there, giving him permission to explore. Soon, his mouth replaced his hand, burrowing inside the opening of my white cotton blouse. Teeth nipped my nipple, causing my back to arch in immediate response.

The hypnotic percussion of the West African dance tune locked us into its insistent beat. As we kissed again, his chest came up against mine, rocking me back and forth in subtle motion. Next, his hand found its way to the inside of my thigh and squeezed. Then it moved upward, the thumb making clockwise circles. Soon, the circles were on a part of my anatomy largely unexplored by my brief list of former lovers. The pressure felt good, repetitive and insistent. Suddenly, my body contracted, pushing away from him. But his hand came back, this time all four fingers together, circling patiently, hypnotically, in time to the music.

As the motion continued, he locked eyes with me, a dreamy expression on his face. His eyes flicked from my eyes to my mouth and back, watching and waiting for my response. He knew how to focus on another person. This was new for me. I was used to men focusing on their own pleasure. Although unsure of myself, I knew this was my moment to let him lead me to my own.

My mouth parted, and I felt my eyes slit into narrow orbs. Something about what he was doing reminded me of something from way in my past. I tried to reach for it in my mind, but his mouth again on mine distracted me. As we kissed, I felt him unsnap, then unzip my jeans. I lifted my body off the couch so he could pull them down. Then the fingers closed in again, under the thin material of my panties and then again under the hood of my clitoris. The second I felt them directly on my flesh, I jumped.

Pascal restrained me. With his other arm behind me, he pressed me back against his chest then continued the motion. Neither speeding up nor slowing down, he refused to stop, no matter what I did.

I moaned.

As his movements went on, sensation took over, and I could no longer think. A feeling of engorgement came over me, but the dam had never burst before. I was afraid to let it burst now.

"Stop – stop – you have to stop," I sputtered.

"For a minute, *cherie*. Only for a minute," he replied, relaxing his grip.

Relieved, I inched backward, seeking escape. Pascal put the wineglass up to my lips, tipping it gently to trickle into my mouth. The taste was refreshing.

Suddenly, I realized I was panting. I looked at Pascal in wonderment. Something was going on here that hadn't happened before. I had no idea where we were going, and I was scared.

"Don't be afraid, Ava. Just relax," Pascal murmured, his eyes as slitted as mine felt.

"You're going to make me scream," I told him, embarrassed.

"Good." He smiled slyly, his eyes golden. "I want you to."

I reached to take one more sip of wine, then fell back limply. His hand found my flesh again, resuming its clockwise rhythm, stroking and caressing the underside of the hood of this newfound most sensitive part of my body. Again, my mouth fell open, and I heard the pants escape me, then moans. It was as if I was another person, witnessing what was taking place.

Pascal's head moved down to rest on my belly. My hands were freed, so I sunk them in his curly-brown hair, my fingers digging into his scalp.

"Uhhh." It was his turn to moan.

My back arched rhythmically. As I thrust myself against his hand, my mind fought to get away from his relentless stimulation. I was at war with myself, mind fighting body for control. But control was slipping away and an inner voice whispered this was what was supposed to be.

Something new touched me. Pascal's tongue had found its way to the center of my pleasure zone. I screamed aloud, then covered my mouth with my hand.

His tongue flicked over me, again and again, until I felt something take shape like a small, hard kidney bean. My own clitoris was having an erection. Who knew such things happened? I marveled at the shock of having a virtual stranger introduce me to my own body.

As I stifled my cries, I felt Pascal reach up and pull my hand away from my mouth.

"Scream. Go on," he murmured then returned to the task at hand.

Sensing no embarrassment on his part, I gave way.

In a minute, I could bear it no longer. Squirming away from him, I fought to regain control.

Masterfully, Pascal allowed me my moment, then continued, his tongue now flicking slower, then teeth, gently pulling.

I cried out again.

Coming up for air, he raised his head.

"You're going to come soon," he said.

I was? Come where? What did he mean?

His fingers were on me again, tracing a clockwise pattern that was leading me inexorably to something, I knew not what. As I flinched, he grabbed my pelvis with his left arm, pinning me down. The fingers pressed harder, refusing to stop.

"Stop!" I screamed, feeling as if I was about to drive off a cliff.

"No, Ava. Come," he said calmly.

Where was I supposed to go? Wherever it was, I had never been there before, at least as far as I could remember.

One final time, I wrenched away from him.

"*Laisse*," I hissed at him. "*Laisse-moi*. Leave me alone."

"You're going to come now" was his only response as he patiently waited while I rested.

A potent pause took place. It was the richest, fullest pause I'd ever experienced. My eyes turned to the ceiling then closed.

Pascal touched me again.

Molten sensation engulfed me. I was helpless to control any of my bodily functions. My last conscious thought was whatever happened next, I couldn't be held responsible.

As if a giant funnel was wrapping every impulse and nerve ending in my body into the tiny bit of skin Pascal was stroking, I felt every ounce of my being compress into one swollen sensation that lifted and crested, rode the outer edges of sensation for several seconds – then shattered into a million shards of glass.

My God.

I had fissioned into one with the universe. My entire being split apart, into atoms and molecules that rocketed out in every direction, seemingly connecting with everything in their path.

"Ahhh," I screamed in a pitch higher than any moan, more like a dolphin's cry than something human.

"Good, Ava. Good," Pascal encouraged me.

Good wasn't the word for it. This was mind-blowing, Earth-shattering, a religious experience. For the first time in my life, I was centered entirely in the present moment. The past fell away, there was no future. I thought of God. This was how He wanted us to live, no?

My eyes widened as Pascal's face came back into focus.

"You came, Ava. Good," he commended.

I came? So that's what it was to come. To arrive. To be right here, right now, divinely dancing on the head of a pin. A multitude of analogies for what had just happened flooded into my mind. At the same time, my body felt magnificently relaxed. I was Aphrodite in full glory, Ares at her side.

Stretching, in the most glorious full-body stretch of my life, I lifted my eyes to the ceiling, asking heaven what just happened.

Then Pascal touched me again. This time, my body was primed and ready for blast-off. In less than sixty seconds, my soul again escaped my body and shattered into space. The most high-pitched, unearthly cry I'd ever uttered escaped from somewhere deep in my belly. Again, the glass pieces shattered into a million diamonds and I felt myself connect with every living being, my life-force poured out onto everything around it.

After the second moment of fission passed, I looked at Pascal with wonder. Were we still alive? And how was it this man I barely knew had unlocked the most elemental part of me?

I gazed at him. Were we in love now?

I was impressed with Pascal. Grateful to him. My heart was warm. He was the conduit to the new world I'd entered. At last, I was a woman.

It was crystal clear. I *was* in love. But with the universe all around me. The one I'd just connected with. Not with Pascal.

He touched me once more. I begged him to stop. He wouldn't. In a minute, I was speechless, in the trough before the storm. Then a scream rose again from my throat. Losing all control, I hurtled toward oblivion until sensation crested and I was flung over its top. Pieces of me rained down on all sides, landing on Pascal, on the street below, on flowers, grass and trees, fecundizing everything in its path.

So that was an orgasm.

Finally, I noticed Pascal's excitement at watching me shatter into a million pieces. He scooped me up in his arms and staggered into the bedroom. In less than a minute, he was inside, thrusting and withdrawing, deep, then detached, until I moaned and begged for his return. *Maestro.*

He came with a mighty moan that eclipsed my own. His sweat-covered, hairless chest crashed down on mine, fusing our bodies in an intimate oneness that differed from the universal connection with everything I'd felt a moment earlier.

We slept. When we awoke, we made love again. Wetness made the climb to heaven easier. I was still apprehensive, unused to the relinquishment of my own sovereignty to the hands and tongue of another, but I surrendered to Pascal's mastery. Together, we collaborated in my climb to pleasure, the plateau, again the ascent then one final ineluctable pause before hitting the summit in ecstatic explosion.

We fell back on Pascal's bed, spent. As we rested, I watched the long rays of late-afternoon sun play over us. My whole life had changed in the space of one afternoon. I understood so many things now, to begin with why Anna Karenina threw herself on the train tracks when her relationship with Count Vronsky soured. Clearly, he had sent her to heaven when they made love, when her husband hadn't.

I had finally discovered how to experience my own life in the present moment. I'd never really been there before – my mind always aware of the past in the midst of the present or racing off to the future the second something new took place. I'd finally experienced the joy of being one hundred percent in the present, fully connected with the universe, with no distinction between myself and what existed outside of myself. Was this how God managed His time? Nice.

Pascal opened his eyes and reached for me.

"Tu as faim?" "Are you hungry?" he asked, smoothing the ends of my wavy hair.

"Yes. Very." I must have looked like a madwoman or one who had just had seven orgasms in one afternoon. Would the average man on the street now be able to tell I was no longer a girl?

In the mirror over the bathroom sink, my lips pouted at me, swollen and bee-stung. My cheeks glowed, rosy and flushed. It seemed to me the cosmetics industry would go out of business if women used the time they took putting on make up to enjoy a few orgasms instead. Who would need make up with sheer bliss written all over their faces?

Showering, I tried Pascal's shower gel in a green plastic bottle. It smelled of pine and the outdoors. I lathered it over me, my mind bursting with newfound knowledge

I wrapped myself in a towel and went to the living room to retrieve my clothes. Charles Aznavour poured out of the radio, perfect for making dinner on a Sunday evening. I turned up the volume.

In the kitchen, Pascal was pulling salad ingredients from the refrigerator. I kissed him on the cheek then took the knife from his hand.

"Go take a shower. I'll make the salad," I said, newfound authority in my voice.

"It's no problem. I'll shower later," he protested.

"No. Go now. There's still hot water." I shoved him gently with my hip. He put his hand around my waist, then bent down and kissed the spot on my body where I'd just shoved him. I grabbed the curls at the nape of his neck and tugged. "Go on."

He left the kitchen obediently. How had I become so in command of myself in just four short world-shifting hours? As I washed the lettuce and chopped radishes and tomatoes, I looked forward to smelling cleaned-up, pine-scented Pascal again. We'd have dinner, then I could turn him into sweat-drenched, scent-of-sex Pascal. It was the cycle of life, and I was co-starring in it. Finally.

I swigged from the bottle of bubbly mineral water on the counter. Yuck. Having an orgasm hadn't changed my desire for ice-cold water, especially if it was carbonated. I put the mineral water in the refrigerator, and took out the bottle of Sancerre. Eyeballing the corkscrew on the counter, I realized I didn't know how to open it. Instead, I found our wineglasses in the living room, washed and rinsed them, and set them on the counter.

I wouldn't be a bona-fide graduate of the school of *savoir-faire* until I knew how to open a bottle of wine. When Pascal returned, I would ask him to teach me, now that I knew what a sensational teacher he was.

In ten minutes Pascal was back, wearing a navy blue bathrobe. Sexy. We wouldn't see more of Gerard that night, I knew.

I stuck one finger in the salad dressing I was making and held it up to his lips.

He tasted, sucking on my finger as he pulled me toward him.

"Wait," I protested. "I need you to show me something." I couldn't handle any more action until after we'd filled our stomachs. Burning off at least ten thousand calories over the past four hours, I'd turned into a race-horse: sleek and supple.

"What's that, *cherie?*" he asked, making as if to untie the belt to his bathrobe, a devilish smile on his face. His actions seemed more assertive and well-defined than before we made love.

I pulled his hand off his bathrobe tie. My actions were more assertive, too. Was that what having an orgasm did to you? I'd turned into a completely new, turbo-charged version of myself.

"Not that." I smiled, trying not to get too close. I knew if I looked, a tent would form. "Show me how to open this," I ordered, gesturing to the wine bottle on the counter.

"With pleasure." He took the bottle opener, unscrewing it slowly, until the two handles came up slightly like half-open angel wings. "This is how you begin."

"Okay."

"You place the tip of the corkscrew in the middle of the cork," he explained.

"Yes."

"Then you twist it in, in clockwise motion, slowly." Intent on his task, he didn't see me smile. Slow, clockwise motion would never be the same for me.

"The trick is to not twist too quickly. Just turn it slowly until you're at least halfway through the cork. You'll know you're done when the angel wings are fully open." He stopped then directed me to continue.

I grabbed the bottom of each angel wing.

"Now push the angel wings down slowly, until the cork comes out of the bottle."

He watched carefully as I pushed the wings down. The cork slid up the neck of the bottle until it ejected with a satisfying pop.

"So the secret is – " I began.

"To do it slowly," he finished.

Shivers ran up and down my spine as I watched Pascal carefully fill each glass only two thirds full. A fuller comprehension of what it was to do things slowly seeped through me from head to toe. I would never be in a rush again. At least not when I was climbing the stairway to heaven.

We clinked glasses, looking at each other through half-slitted eyes.

"Here's to doing things slowly," I toasted. His smile widened until his teeth showed. I felt them again on hidden parts of my body.

We dined in the living room at the table by the window. The remains of the day lingered in the sky, but it was dark inside, so we lit two candles.

The spaghetti carbonara was delicious. It had been simple to make, something even I could prepare with impressive results. When we were done, we moved to the couch.

Memories of time spent on the same piece of furniture a few hours earlier stirred us quickly to a re-enactment, this time more playfully. Pascal took his time as he moved me up progressive pleasure plateaus. I was still scared, but now I knew where we were going. The smile in Pascal's golden eyes trained on mine reassured me it was okay to arrive there kicking and screaming.

In the same way as before, he lifted me into his arms and carried me into the bedroom. Once my pleasure had exploded and his was ripe for fulfillment, I lay on his bed, welcoming his entry. As with leading me to pleasure, he took his time finding his own. Slowly, slowly he entered then withdrew, until I moaned for his return. Skillfully, he used his fingers this time, finding my secret spot under its hood, and stroking until I reached the final plateau then shot like a cannonball straight to heaven itself. His excitement skyrocketed, stimulated by mine.

Within seconds we came together in a bed-shaking frenzy of ecstasy. Pascal collapsed on top of me, and I stroked the lean, muscular length of his back. Each caress was like swimming in molasses. I was Marlene Dietrich, every move of my body sensuous and feline.

At night with Jean-Michel, I'd wondered if the pleasant state I'd usually felt after we made love and before we fell asleep was what was meant by bliss. I'd doubted it.

Now I knew what bliss was. There was no mistaking it. I melted back into the pillows and slept the sleep of the dead.

CHAPTER EIGHT

Life in the Present Moment

he next day, Pascal walked me to the train station on his way to work. On the platform, he kissed me on each cheek twice. We agreed to meet back on the platform of the 6:13 PM train arriving from Paris that evening.

On the train, I found myself surrounded by men in blue coveralls, their feet shod in work boots. Saint-Denis was evidently a working-class sub-urb, something I'd missed on Sunday when the working population was out of uniform enjoying their day off. At the train stop of Châtelet-les Halles, across the river from Saint-Michel, I got off. The day was beautiful. I decided to walk home.

For once, I took the route along the Right Bank of the Seine, not the Left where I lived. It seemed fitting to be on the opposite side of the river, now that I was on the far shore of womanhood. What had happened the day before had been far more momentous than the occasion of losing my virginity. Less than twenty-four hours earlier, my whole world had shifted from black and white to Technicolor.

Yet I didn't get the sense that there was any profound tie-in between my emotions for the person responsible for sending me to heaven and for the experience itself. Pascal had given me the most incredible, sensual experience of my life. But falling in love with him hadn't followed automatically.

Were sex and love only distant cousins? Or was I still too callow to have the capacity to fall in love? My adult education was only beginning. Perhaps getting down the mechanics of lovemaking preceded falling in love.

Putting aside theoretical speculation on whatever romantic love might be, I wandered back to considering what having an orgasm actually was: mind-blowing, earth-shattering, apocalyptic; the most profound spiritual experience of my life up to that moment.

I couldn't help mixing up the event with thoughts of God and eternity. How could the two not go hand in hand? Fusion and fission belonged together as much as love and death did. One was the ultimate creative act; the other, the ultimate annihilation. One necessitated the other. For the first time, I understood the connection.

All this had happened at the hands of an unassuming twenty-six year old nurse's aide who knew a thing or two about female anatomy. What had he said about his duties at the hospital? Now that I had experienced ecstasy, my thinking was clearer, sharper. The French phrases he'd used to describe his job the night we'd met came back to me, *"Je rangent les patients, font leurs lits; je lave les morts et d'autres choses."* What did that mean, anyways? I'd look up *ranger* when I got back to my room, but I could guess it meant to arrange or make comfortable. He made the patients comfortable, made up their beds, and washed the dead ones and other things.

What?

He washed the dead? Of course he did. He was an orderly, for God's sake. Who else did that sort of thing at a hospital?

Bordel de merde! The man whose hands had just introduced me to total sexual fulfillment used those same hands to wash dead bodies at his day job.

I thought about it long and hard. There was a lesson in there somewhere.

Meanwhile, the azure blue sky smiled down on me, and the river looked almost clean. I had just experienced my first orgasm. My lover and I had plans to meet again that evening. I would get through this moment.

I hadn't been raised in a doctor's household for nothing. Most of the time, I thought of my down-to-earth, New England upbringing as a mill-stone around my neck, but every once in a while, it came in handy.

My grandfather had taken me on occasional house calls when I'd been a young girl. I'd enjoyed them, holding the hands of blue-haired ladies in big homes filled with antiques and musty smells. On other occasions, we'd visit funeral homes, where my grandfather signed paperwork and chatted with the man in charge. Since my grandfather was relatively old, his patients were, too. It wasn't uncommon for one to die, whereupon my grandfather would be called in to confirm the death and sign the death certificate. While he was busy, I'd wander around the funeral home, invariably going over to the casket to check its contents. Usually, it would be another one of the blue-haired ladies in peaceful repose, eyebrows penciled in, wearing attractive pearls and immaculately applied red lipstick. Sometimes, it was a bald-haired old man, distinguished and proper, in an impeccable black suit, hands folded on stomach.

At the age of seven or so, I never found these tableaus morbid. They seemed natural, a sort of pleasant end to the prosperous lives most of my grandfather's patients led. My grandmother referred to my grandfather's practice as a society one, consisting of holding the hands of hypochondriac old ladies. She meant it disparagingly, but I saw nothing wrong with making a good living for our family by providing comfort to little old ladies.

I had met death head on at an early age, and it hadn't struck me as a big deal. It was part of the cycle of life, nothing more. My grandparents, as well as my great-uncle and aunt, had already made full end-of-life arrangements. They had their plots picked out, headstones chosen, and a file for final arrangements in their desk drawers, along with folders for taxes, wills, and stock certificates.

When they died, someone would come to wash their bodies if they were in a hospital, then someone else would take them to their pre-arranged funeral home of choice. Pascal was one of the workers involved in that process. What was the big deal?

As long as he washed his hands. Had I seen him washing his hands the day before? Yes, multiple times. Not only was he a good cook and a superb lover, but his flat had been tidy and clean. When I pushed him into the shower, he hadn't protested overmuch.

A part of me found the whole thing funny. It would be very funny indeed, if a girlfriend had related to me the news that her most phenomenal lover of all times had a job washing dead bodies, among other functions. What was so terrible about it? What if Pascal had a job washing newborns, was an average lover, and lacked the skill to bring me to climax? What then? Which version of Pascal would I choose?

I'd choose the Pascal who washed *les morts* in a heartbeat. Still, I made a tiny mental note to make sure I saw him wash his hands with soap that evening, before he went anywhere near any hidden part of me.

By half past ten, I was back in my room. I changed into fresh clothes, putting on a floaty, lilac summer top that was just the teensiest bit sheer. It would drive Pascal crazy. I was now a full-fledged woman, whose sex appeal had a destination in mind. For the first time in my entire life I realized the whole point of having sex appeal wasn't really about making men happy. It was about making myself happy. Who knew?

For the past six years, I'd thought sex was about men having a mind-blowing experience, and women enjoying a pleasant time with some messiness at the end. But the image of the woman in the underpass along the Seine had lingered in my brain. Her unearthly cry teased me, hinting at a secret I wasn't privy to, inviting me to share it with her when the time came.

Now, it had come. And so had I. *Brava*, Ava!

I stuffed a notebook, several pens, and a bottle of water into my backpack and went out again. Posterity commanded me to write down whatever I could articulate of the watershed event that had just taken place. I would show this notebook to no one. Or perhaps lock it in a safe deposit box with instructions to a future daughter to read it after my death, provided she was at least eighteen.

The day passed in a pleasant haze of writing, walking, sunning on park benches and shopping. I bought Pascal an Arab scarf, a red and white one known as a *keffiyeh*, in the small streets behind Saint-Michel. It was the least I could do for him after he'd introduced me to myself.

Soon I was on the 6:13 P.M. train, speeding back to Saint-Denis and my personal savior. Pascal had saved me from wasting any more years of my life wandering around in the Sahara Desert of sexual ignorance. How many women remained that way for a good part of their adult lives? I'd spent six years no longer a virgin but still an ignoramus. Was it possible that some women never got a chance to climb the stairway to heaven? I hoped not, for their sakes.

Pascal was on the platform, waiting for me. As I returned his four kisses – left, right, left right – I breathed in the aroma of fresh, pine-scented shower gel. He'd showered after getting home from work. Showering regularly was not altogether common among French men. Not only had Pascal washed his hands, he'd used them to wash his whole body, too. I thanked Saint-Denis, whoever he was, for the regular saint he'd sent me.

"How was your day?" I asked, hoping he wouldn't go into any detail. Who cared, when all that mattered was our time together?

"*Comme ça.*" he shrugged, meaning "like that" or "the usual, not worth mentioning."

It was the response I'd hoped for. We set off toward his flat, the day still in full swing, dusk nowhere near.

As we passed the café on the corner, a voice rang out.

"Eh! *Tête-bouclé!* Curly head!" Gerard called. He could have been addressing either one of us. I'd decided to let my wavy, frizz-prone locks go wild, now that I was a complete woman.

He sat at a table on the terrace, one leg swung over the other, his thick, dark hair slicked back in a leonine coiffure. We strolled over, kissed multiple times all around, then sat.

"*Ça va?*" Gerard inquired.

"*Ça va bien,*" I responded. Pascal echoed me.

"*Qu'est qui se passe?* What's happening?" Gerard continued, looking at Pascal.

"*Comme d'habitude.* The usual," Pascal responded, his voice flat.

The usual, my foot, I thought. My world turned upside down was more like it. I closed my eyes, lifting my face to the sun, as Gerard's inquisitive gaze moved slowly over me.

Gaze away, man. You'll never know the secrets I've got now. I was a woman of mystique – one way to Gerard, another to Pascal. Every man I passed on the street would sense an air of mystery about me. They would speculate, wondering what noises I made when I came: if I screamed, moaned, or cried. I had become a sort of female deity in the past twenty-four hours. To celebrate my newfound goddess status, I ordered a *kir royale* from the waiter. Pascal and Gerard got draft beers.

When our drinks arrived, I held mine by its delicate stem. Never again would I hold a glass by the body of its goblet. Fingers were made for delicate operations. Now, I knew what some of the more important ones were.

Over the rim of the champagne flute, I eyeballed Pascal who squinted back at me. We silently toasted the evening to come.

Gerard and Pascal exchanged small talk as I basked in the late afternoon sun, sunglasses hiding my mysterious eyes.

"Shall we meet Gerard at the pool this Saturday?" Pascal asked.

"Bah, pourquoi pas?" I said easily. Why not indeed? Pascal was making plans for us for the weekend already. What was wrong with that? Now that our nights would be filled with trips to the moon, who cared what daytime plans we made? He could have suggested we whitewash the outside of his apartment building that weekend, and I would have said fine.

No wonder Brigitte Bardot had looked so blissfully happy in that ratty little seaside town, in her pathetic, run-down apartment in the film that made her famous, *And God Created Woman.* She'd run around barefoot with her lips all puffed out from having them bitten by her husband. Domestic tasks hadn't annoyed her at all. Now, I knew why. She'd been having multiple orgasms every night. At the time I'd seen the film, I'd wondered what a knockout like her was doing married to a modest, little guy like her husband, played by the actor Jean-Louis Trintignant.

Now I could guess why. He'd probably possessed certain skills that had trumped his looks. Who cared what a guy looked like? What mattered was what he could do with his hands.

At the rate Pascal and I were going, I'd learn how to cook and enjoy it. Maybe I'd even go to the market the following day to shop for our dinner. I could squeeze a few fruits while screwing up my face at their lack of ripeness. The art of shopping skeptically was yet another French tradition I was determined to master.

After forty-five minutes, we said our goodbyes to Gerard in another flurry of kisses. Then we strolled home, stopping at the graffiti-covered *super marché* on the way. Pascal pulled a net bag out of his jacket pocket, and we filled it with small amounts of delicacies we'd have been better off to have picked up in specialty stores, which were now all closed.

We chose *paté de campagne,* a coarse country paté with enormous fresh peppercorns dotting its rough texture. Next was a bottle of *cornichons* or little pickles to accompany the paté. Some *saucisse de merguez,* a North African spicy sausage that went well with coarse mustard followed. Then there were the cheeses, not much of a choice. We picked a soft and a hard one. I promised Pascal I would go to the market the following day to pick up other cheeses at the *crémerie* where the selection was better.

Adding another bottle of wine and two bottles of water to our bag, we were done. We would picnic that evening in Pascal's living room. A bit of this and a taste of that would fortify us for the real feast to come once dinner ended.

I tried not to think about it as we stood in line, Pascal's hand surreptitiously on my left hip as he stood only centimeters behind me. His breath sucked in as he inhaled the scent of my hair.

Back at his place, we unwrapped our parcels. Returning from food shopping in France is like unwrapping presents on Christmas morning. Delightful smells and the promise of delicious tastes ravish one's nostrils at the unveiling of each item. We pulled small plates out of Pascal's cupboards and arranged the cooked *merguez* sausages on one, with a tiny bowl of coarse mustard to one side, then another plate with the paté accompanied by its own bowl of tiny *cornichon* pickles. Finally, the cheese tray was assembled, and we carried everything out to the small table in the living room.

I sensed that routine would be nice with Pascal. He didn't seem the type of man to tire of it. I would be more the problem in a cozy domestic scenario. But this particular domestic setting was tinged with exoticism. Not only were we enjoying our temporary ménage in France, a country as far apart in sensibility from my own as *cornichons* with *paté* were from dill pickles with pastrami, but when dinner was over, we would once again enter a new world to which I'd just been introduced. My senses sharpened, I tried to push away thoughts of later and enjoy the distinctness of the taste combinations spread before me on the table. Be here now, I told myself. God, how I would embrace that phrase in a few short hours.

"Close your eyes. I've got a surprise for you," I told Pascal the minute he pushed his cheese plate away. The silky command in my voice startled me. In two short weeks I'd graduated from clueless American college grad to woman of mystery.

"What's that?" he asked, sounding far more receptive than Jean-Michel would have been.

"Tais-toi." I ordered him to be quiet, using the French phrase that hovers between 'hush up' and 'shut up'.

He obeyed, shutting his eyes, and leaning back. A smile played on his lips.

"Be right back," I whispered, a trace of steel in my voice. The *keffiyeh*, the red and white Arab scarf I'd gotten him, was stuffed in my bag in the hallway. Quickly, I found it then returned. Pascal's eyes remained obediently shut.

I slid my hand across his face, thanking him silently for his freshly-shaven cheeks. Later they would rub my flesh without scratching it. Quickly, I tied the scarf around his eyes, securing it tightly at the back.

"What are you doing?" he asked laughingly.

"Come with me," I ordered, pulling him out of the chair and over to the couch. With my fingertips just below each collarbone, I pushed him down onto the soft pillows.

"What are you doing to me?" he asked again, his voice tinged with excitement.

"What I please," I stated firmly. He would be my slave for the next few minutes, until I inevitably became his.

It wouldn't do to let him call all the shots in one evening. Now that I was a full-blown woman, I was ready to call some shots too. I wasn't quite sure what they were, but one thing was certain: whatever part of him I touched at that moment, with whatever part of me, would turn him on.

I took his chin firmly in my hands and massaged upward along his jaw line.

"Hunh." The sigh that escaped his mouth as it fell open told me I was on the right track.

I circled his cheekbones with my thumbs. The right one stroked clockwise, the left counterclockwise. As I touched him, color flooded into his face below the blindfold.

"Umm," he groaned.

My newly minted goddess within lit up with pride in her seduction skills.

Gently pushing his torso forward, I slipped onto the couch behind him. Then I stroked his ears, moving down his neck to his strong, broad shoulders. Like heat-seeking missiles, my fingers searched for his flesh under the fabric of his shirt. I'd never been so turned on by a man before.

He leaned back against me, pressing into my breasts.

I moved my hands farther down his torso, circling his chest in a figure eight. Then, I slid them down to his stomach, finding the buttons on his shirt and unbuttoning them. When done, I slid my hand inside to feel the warmth and hairlessness of his taut physique.

Now, it was his turn. Taking my right hand, he moved it farther south along his firm belly, underneath his belt buckle into the area between his jeans and his jockey shorts. With his left hand, he unbuckled his belt then unzipped his pants. An enormous, rock-hard expansion had taken place while my hands had traveled from neck to male organ.

Using my fingers lightly, I explored. The male body was a marvelous piece of engineering. Was what had happened to my clitoris the night before similar to what was happening to him right now? Hopping off the couch, I pulled off his jeans to release the large animal inside, straining for air.

Pascal reached for my waist and lay me down in his lap, face up, to sketch the same designs on me I had just drawn on him. My hair covered his male glory. I wondered if it tickled. As usual, Pascal's focus was first on me, not his own swelling sensations. Still blindfolded, he closed my eyelids with his fingers, then traced the contours of my face.

I shuddered in response.

His hand moved farther down, covering my throat. With the middle and ring fingers of his right hand, he began to circle in clockwise strokes. Immediately, muscle memory kicked in. I responded in an area nowhere near his fingers. Forever after, I would respond to the right man's fingers stroking clockwise, no matter where on my body.

Soon, his fingers moved down to my breasts, encircling each with no hurry; a lazy, clockwise motion, as if to remind me where his fingers eventually would head. The thought of their ultimate destination was now making my insides turn over in pleasure and anticipation.

Were there women out there who could orgasm just at the thought of being stimulated in the right place? What a great skill to have. For the first time, I considered pursuing a post-graduate degree. Higher education had its perks, especially in certain arcane areas of study.

We continued to strum each other's bodies like a guitar duet. My hands grasped confidently, my strokes more sure of themselves. The remembrance of time slowing down after I'd experienced bliss the night before, made it slow down again until each caress I gave him was exquisitely languid. Now,

I knew where we were headed, and part of the satisfaction of getting there meant taking our time. We stood up and walked to the bedroom.

Pascal excused himself for a minute. While he was gone, I noticed something new. Over the bed, near the headboard he had written my name on the wall, then added some vertical lines below it. They looked like tally marks, eight in all. The first four had a fifth slashed through them, the other three in a separate group. It took me only a moment to figure out that he'd recorded the number of orgasms I'd had the night before. Not the number he had, which had been less. What a man.

He returned, and our explorations escalated. Soon, I'd be putty in his hands. It was hard to embrace the idea of surrender. My will fought against it. But the memory of surrender's blissful, explosive result kept my willful spirit at bay. Something told me there was a greater underlying lesson to learn, which my willfulness would drown out if I gave in to my usual instincts to control my surroundings.

Tonight, I would succumb to Pascal. He was a man worth surrendering to.

In a minute, I was on my back, pinned there by Pascal's arm across my torso and head buried between my legs. His tongue would not be deflected from its destination, no matter how hard I tried to push his head away. My will fought my body, as one sought control and the other surrender. Who was I?

The day before, a girl. Today, a woman.

One hour later, we lay intertwined, spent. My body, in a state of profound relaxation, pillowed Pascal's inert form, as he snored softly and regularly. But my mind hummed, turning over and examining the implications of what had just happened to me. It hadn't been just an orgasm or two or three. It had been a complete union of mind, body, and soul. I sought to relate the experience to what I'd spent the past four years studying.

It came to me that the highest truths presented themselves as paradoxes. I had focused on history, philosophy and religious studies during my time at Yale. When we'd studied truths at the highest levels, they always turned out to have some sort of built-in contradictions. In Christianity, one God manifested Himself three ways. Christ's surrender to death resulted in eternal life. Confusing, huh?

The first stage of Hegel's dialectic of existence was Being, followed by Nothingness. He then showed that the first stage actually was also the second stage, even though they seemed diametrically opposed. In other words, what was coming into being also was returning to nothingness. Finally, both concepts were united as Becoming. Wasn't that what orgasm was all about? First, a total movement of will, then a complete smashing into oblivion of the ego, that sense of fission at the moment of climax, finally followed by bliss, or the moment of becoming.

A concept I'd wrestled with in my history of philosophy class had been the actual definition of dialectic itself, something we'd studied before moving on to various examples of the concept offered by Socrates, Plato, Goethe, Hegel, and others. The term 'dialectic' was based on the concept that change moves in spirals, not circles.

I jumped at the image of spirals leading to change. Hadn't that been what had just happened to me? Wasn't the process of orgasm a spiraling upward of pleasure, punctuated by periods of rest, then ultimately leading to climactic explosion? The clockwise stroking circles that led me up the pleasure path weren't just two dimensional. They were three dimensional spirals or helixes that led to waves of pleasure after each interval of stroking and stopping, until finally the wave crested, and my being shattered into nothingness.

It was then that the Earth moved. That was the moment of change, of transformation. Something profoundly and permanently changed inside of me each time I had an orgasm. Nothing more exciting had ever happened to me before.

The concept of transformation had always stirred my Aquarian-with-Aries-rising nature. No wonder Jean-Michel hadn't wanted me to experience earth-shattering bliss. If I had, it would have connoted change, a shifting of who I was. He would have perceived such a shift as moving away from him, escaping the vision of me he had locked me into.

Pascal didn't seem to have a big problem with change. Perhaps he hadn't pondered the fundamentals of dialectic, so wasn't bothered when I changed before his eyes. Besides, how could he know I was changing if he hardly knew who I was in the first place?

As I lay beneath my lover's sleeping form, I marveled at the insights to which my eyes were now opened. It was as if the physical, earthly side of my being had manifested the theoretical concepts I'd learned but hadn't understood over the past four years. My education finally made sense. Metaphysical concepts weren't just posited for no reason. They were grounded in natural law. I fell asleep, at one with nature, fully arrived at the third stage of anyone's dialectic.

⌒〜

Three days later, I received a postcard from my mother letting me know their flight plans had been delayed by one week. My sister's passport had not yet arrived, but would be ready by the end of the following week. Their reservation at the Hotel Étoile was pushed back to July fifth through eighth.

The plan change gave me additional time to play house with Pascal – as well as rack up more tally marks on the wall at the head of his bed. We were both happy to hear the news.

I planned to introduce Pascal to my mom and sister. My mother had been an aficionado of the school of international affairs from way back. On her own grand tour of Europe shortly after graduating from U Cal Berkeley, she left the United States as an engaged woman and returned to break her engagement to the nice boy from Georgia of whom her mother had highly approved.

In one of my infrequent visits to my mother in Manhattan, she had regaled my sister and me with a hilarious rendition of what happened on that trip. She began with a frank confession that no thought of her fiancé had crossed her mind for the entire flight over from New York to Brussels – one of my mother's strong points is a complete absence of judgmental censure of anyone's behavior, including her own. She could tell a straight story about herself up to a certain point.

When she arrived in Brussels, she was greeted by the group's tour guide, a tall, strapping Austrian man in his mid-twenties. He wore a beret. My mother's sigh while describing him told me he'd been very handsome. I envisioned someone like Liesl's boyfriend-turned-Nazi, Rolf, from *The Sound of Music*. By the end of two weeks, touring the great monuments of Europe in the company of Rudi, my mother came to the realization that a whole world was out there for her to explore, with only her fiancé standing in the way. In her mind, the engagement was over.

Then, some sort of rupture occurred that incensed my grandmother, who had financed the trip. She'd sputtered and fumed about it whenever the subject came up during my childhood. I had never been able to piece together what actually happened, other than my mother had broken every rule in my grandmother's rulebook as soon as she'd gotten out from under her thumb on the other side of the Atlantic. I could hardly blame her.

My mother left the tour in Vienna and struck out on her own for a few days. It was the summer of 1955. Vienna had just regained its sovereignty, after a decade of allied occupation post-World War II. My grandmother raged over her daughter's astonishing naïveté and complete obliviousness to the dangers of being a virginal, twenty-two year old college co-ed wandering around Europe by herself.

I sensed there was more to the story. My mother was not a brash or foolhardy type, more a delicate English rose. She wouldn't have left the tour unless there had been a good reason.

Over a bottle of rosé wine, shared by my mother and me, while my sister drank a Coke, the truth more or less leaked out. Something of a romantic nature had occurred between her and Rudi, the tour guide. Then, something else, along the lines of a spat, had taken place, and my mother left the group. From that point on, it got hazy. A great deal of mysterious alluding and half-recollecting from my mother's mouth, punctuated by nervous giggles, led me to believe she wandered around completely defenseless and vulnerable for a day or two in Vienna, on her own, until, at some point, she sat on a park bench and some older guy tried to pick her up. The rest of the story blurred into laughter, along with the intake of a good deal more wine.

I didn't know my mother well, but I'd spent enough time with her to know when she giggled nervously like that, it wasn't because something was funny. It was her way of expressing hysteria. Something had taken place she couldn't share with us.

She never did. The upshot was, she never reconnected with the tour but returned home on her scheduled flight. Shortly thereafter, she broke off her engagement with her fiancé, a Southern Baptist man studying to be a career diplomat, whom she'd met at college.

Whatever happened to her, I hoped it was good. At a minimum, it rearranged her worldview so that she couldn't go back to being the same docile, affianced virgin she had left the United States as – precisely the point of an educational tour abroad, but not what my grandmother had in mind.

In a rare moment, I felt empathy for my mother. As the expression goes, "how you gonna keep 'em down on the farm once they've seen Paree?"

Indeed.

Her epiphany occurred in Vienna, mine in Paris. We were alike in ways I could never have guessed until meeting Pascal.

I knew the moment I introduced him to my mother, she'd see what was going on, add it all up, and smile to herself. She'd been there herself, half a lifetime ago.

There was no way she would condemn me for having a mad fling with a Frenchman. What was the point of being in one's early twenties, newly-graduated from college, if not to have a fling in a foreign country? It was basically an invisible bullet point on the European Grand Tour agenda, one American college grads had followed for over a century. Edith Wharton would have approved, with the proviso that such a connection have a firm beginning, middle, and end – especially an end.

Within seventy-two hours of my mother and sister's arrival, we'd be on a train out of the Gare du Nord, Paris's largest international train station, departing for Italy, where we planned to visit Florence, Rome, then Venice. It saddened me to think of leaving Pascal. He'd unlocked the door to my womanhood. He would always remain in my heart.

That weekend, we met Gerard at the neighborhood pool. The weather was warm, and the water swimmable. But as Pascal had predicted, almost no one swam. Clusters of young adults lounged everywhere, posing, checking each other out, smoking, and drinking coffee, mineral water, or *citron pressé* – lemonade, French style.

A few people were in the water, where they talked to each other, splashed a bit, leaned against the side of the pool while slowly kicking their legs – anything except actually swimming. I unloaded my beach bag, while Pascal and Gerard caught up with each other. I'd brought a *Paris Match* magazine, a notebook, and the latest slim Françoise Sagan novel which I hadn't yet read. All of her novels were slim and smart, as I imagined Françoise herself to be. Anyone who could come up with a title like *Bonjour Tristesse* at age eighteen was a genius, in my opinion. The book had been pretty good, too.

The next few days melted together in warm, hazy sensation, punctuated by nightly moments of acute, sublime passion at the hands of Pascal. I was at a crossroads of sensation meeting intellectual awakening. My mind was on fire, racing to articulate the birth of my womanhood into a philosophical framework for the new world of existing in the present moment I now inhabited. Heloise must have wrestled similarly with a desire to intellectually understand the physical sensations her tutor Abelard had set alight in her.

I could imagine them in a garret room on a narrow side street near the cathedral of Notre Dame, only a few dozen miles and eight hundred centuries distant from my own awakening with Pascal. The power of Heloise's intellect would have impelled her to articulate the sensations provoked by her tutor-turned-lover. I was mad to know what words she might have used to describe her physical awakening. On my next trip to the library at Beaubourg, I would research her. I hoped everything I really wanted to know wouldn't be written between the lines.

Fully alive and on fire, I lived each day in the present moment while Pascal was at work. It was a new way of being for me. Whether I chose an apple in the marketplace or decided on a cheese at the *fromagerie*, I was grounded one hundred per cent in the present moment, without thought for past or future. For the first time, I was living the mantra of the sixties spiritual teacher, Ram Dass – be here now.

Finally, I was.

Was this what having an orgasm did to a person? I wondered why every post-orgasmic female didn't dance barefoot in the streets with flowers in her hair like Brigitte Bardot had done in *And God Created Woman*. How could women walk around the next day concealing the wonder of what had happened to them the night before? As when I'd first been kissed at age twelve, I spent time looking in the mirror to see if anything in my face or expression had rearranged itself due to my newfound status. Nothing jumped out at me.

My mother and sister arrived on the appointed day, and I went to their hotel to meet them. My sister, technically half sister, was sixteen – a cute, Italian-American brunette, just beginning to turn male heads. Her obliviousness to such new attention was charming. I hoped she'd meet her own Frenchman or Italian one day who'd show her, as Pascal had shown me, how to step over the threshold of waiting to being.

"So what have you been up to?" Nina asked.

"Not much," I improvised. "Just hanging out with a French guy I met a few weeks ago. Going to his local pool, reading, that kind of thing." Was my poker face in place? My sister was still innocent. At her age, she didn't need to know exactly what I'd been up to.

My mother smiled discreetly. Something told me she had an inkling of what had been going on. Despite our separation in my childhood years, DNA bound us together. I was a chip off the old block.

"What's he like? Is he all suave and French like those French guys in the movies?" Nina probed.

I thought about it. Pascal was very French, but not exactly suave. It had been his lack of pretension in comparison to Gerard that had drawn me to him in the first place. My younger sister might not understand that one of my primary points of attraction to a man was a certain homespun sincerity or purity of spirit. Pascal had it. Thank God, he had other qualities, too, far less pure in scope and intent.

"How about if I have him meet us at a café, so you can check him out for yourself?"

"Oh yay," Nina shouted, bouncing on the narrow hotel room bed she was lounging on, surrounded by French fashion magazines she had cajoled my mother into buying. After a few minutes of primping, grooming, and hair-gelling, my sister was ready to go out and see the sights.

We descended in a miniscule elevator that barely allowed the three of us to breathe and proceeded directly to my sister's restaurant of choice, the Hard Rock Café on the Champs-Élysées, where she ordered a hamburger and fries and my mother and I ordered thin-crust pizzas. We would explore Europe, but within strict American guidelines, dictated by Nina's penchant for dining at six and ordering nothing other than burgers, pizza or pasta.

That evening, I returned to Pascal's place. He folded me into his arms the minute the door opened.

"How did it go with your *maman* and *soeur-cadette?*" he asked, using the French term for younger sister.

"Great. They want to meet you." I breathed in the scent of balsam *bain-douche* on his neck. He had been thinking about me, getting ready for my return. A good man. Purity in a man warmed my heart, but an indication of impure forethought could set it on fire.

"Sure. Why not?" He slammed the door shut with his foot, then bit me on the neck. It was all I could do not to faint. Pascal had a certain *je ne sais quoi,* or "I don't know what," in spades. He wasn't suave in a studied way, but the natural suavity of his moves in the heat of desire won me over every time. He was other-oriented. I was me-oriented. It was a match made in heaven.

Could lust like this last forever? I doubted it, but I was leaving town in a week. There would be no slow diminuendo to our red-hot tango. As Pascal lifted me into his arms I kicked off my shoes. We headed into the bedroom, where he tossed me onto the low bed. As he pulled his shirt over his head, I noted three new notches on the wall. He had been thinking about me, marking notches on his wall while waiting for my return. The thought of it turned me on astoundingly. Was it what he did that I loved or the way he did it? Before I could sort out my thoughts, we moved together toward oblivion.

The next morning, I pretended I was still asleep as I watched Pascal add three more marks on the wall. Idly, I wondered if my mother would detect anything in my face in Pascal's presence that would give away what we'd been up to recently. I hadn't been able to see it myself, but mothers were able to see things others couldn't, weren't they? If so, I knew she wouldn't give away my secrets. She had secrets of her own to treasure and hide.

Three days later, my mother, Nina, and I rendezvoused with Pascal at Café de la Paix in Place de l'Opera, in the center of Paris's Right Bank. I was irked that my little sister seemed under-impressed. I guessed it might take another decade before Nina figured out a standard issue cute guy is not always the guy who finds his way to your heart. Or your clitoris. She would learn.

My mother, on the other hand, took to Pascal right away.

"Ava told me you work in a hospital," she said in careful high school French. I was sure Pascal found it charming. "How interesting. Do you enjoy your job?"

"Bahh. Someone has to do it, *Madame.*" The look of puzzlement on his face told me he either didn't understand why she might think his job was interesting or why she would ask if he enjoyed it. Pascal was a working man, not an artist. The thought that someone might care if he enjoyed his job or not had never crossed his mind. For him, a job was something one did in order to pay the bills.

"What exactly do you do?" My mother wasn't a social worker for nothing. Her sweet, unassuming tone disarmed her listeners and resulted in getting the full story of their lives out of them, in fine detail. I'd seen her do it before.

"Oh-h, bah! A bit of this, a bit of that." Pascal's shoulders went up in the classic Gallic shrug. No mention of washing the dead came up, to my great relief.

While my mother and he chatted, Nina gave him less than ten seconds of a thorough glancing-over, then turned her attention to the ice cream sundae she was devouring. She was oblivious as well as cute. I wondered if we'd ever become close enough to share notes on the men in our lives. I hoped for her sake she'd let in ones like Pascal, whether they scored high on her cute-guy chart or not.

My mother seemed engrossed in whatever Pascal was saying to her. She appeared to bask in his attention. I knew that feeling. Pascal was good at giving his full attention. His conversation wasn't scintillating, but he was fully present in it. It was something not unimportant.

Glancing his way from time to time, I tried to see him through my sister's eyes. He wasn't exactly standard issue attractive. His nose was bulbous at the end and tipped slightly to one side. His light brown hair frizzed and showed signs of receding at the forehead. But his eyes stood out. They were again a different color in the late afternoon sun on the outdoor terrace of the Café de la Paix – amber, like tiger's eye.

And what a tiger he was. Truly. No one would ever know looking at such a modest, compact man.

"What an attractive scarf you're wearing. Is it from some special region in France?" my mother was asking. How could she not recognize a *keffiyeh*? Didn't she read the New York Times? Arab terrorists in *keffiyehs* were featured in the A section of the paper almost daily.

"No, *Madame*. It's a *keffiyeh*, an Arab scarf."

"How charming. Do you have some Arab in your background?"

My mother's considerable investigative skills were warming up.

"No, *Madame*, I'm French," Pascal responded, a tad quickly. "My family is from Alsace-Lorraine, near Strasbourg. The scarf is a gift –" He paused, turning to me, his face slightly red, either from embarrassment or irritation at being mistaken for an Arab. Then, he looked shyly at my mother, "from your daughter."

"Oh. Isn't that nice?" Something in my mother's face told me she sensed the extent of our involvement. I wasn't one to give men gifts, unless I was sleeping with them. If we were only at the courting stage, I'd limit myself strictly to receiving presents. It was some sort of unspoken rule.

Not wanting my mother to mine further information from Pascal concerning our activities of the past few weeks, I cut in.

"Mom, have you and Nina been to see the Dali animal sculptures at Place Vendôme? It's not far from here."

"No. Not yet," she replied and then turned to Pascal, who leaned toward her, as if eager to hear whatever she might say.

I swear she batted her eyes at him.

"Are you a fan of Dali's?" she asked.

Pascal stared at her uncomprehendingly. Nothing had been lost in translation. My mother and I were simply from another world than my non-Arab Frenchman.

"Bah, I could care less," he finally replied, using one of the gentler forms of the myriad ways the French used to express disdain. His eyes remained fixed upon my mother, as if to say when it came to Dali he felt one way, when it came to her, another.

I gave him points for honesty. Had my mother deliberately chosen to make it clear to me Pascal's world in no way adjoined mine? I doubted it. One of her strong points was her non-judgmental nature, an offshoot of her general lack of judgment. She'd married two men with whom she shared no cultural commonality whatsoever – one Hungarian, the second Italian-American. Divorce ensued both times, at her initiative.

I wasn't trying to marry Pascal, I was just trying to have as many orgasms with him as possible before I left town and we never saw each other again.

My mother's eyes met mine over Pascal's head. She liked him, I could tell. No warning flickered in them, only a twinkle. For one of the first times, I thanked God for her lack of standards.

"I see," she responded. "Well maybe we'll walk over there on our way to dinner. Will you two join us?"

"Sorry, Mom. We've got plans for dinner tonight," I answered for both of us. We had none, but I was determined not to give in to my sister's insistence on eating at six. After finishing her ice cream, she'd begun making noises to Mom about going somewhere for pizza.

"I hope we'll meet again," my mother said to Pascal as we got up to leave.

"Yes, *Madame*. I do, too," Pascal replied, looking as if he meant it.

My mother had certain sphinx-like qualities, an air of stillness or mystery about her that had its effect on men. A twinge of jealousy shot through me until I remembered that I, too, was a woman of mystery. I'd had to study to become one. My mother simply was one.

"Goodbye, Mom, Nina. Pick you up at the hotel tomorrow."

"Around what time then, dear?"

"Say, half past nine?" I suggested.

"Fine." My mother nodded. No mention was made of where I was staying overnight. I gave my sister a firm stare to squelch any urge she might have to ask.

Nina's mouth was already open, forming the question. I leaned in toward her, kissing her on both cheeks to prevent her from speaking.

In bed with Pascal that night, it hit me that soon I'd be saying goodbye to my Frenchman. *Bonjour tristesse*, hello sadness, washed over me. What if I never met another man who could activate my hot spots? I wouldn't let it happen. Now that I knew the difference between being squarely in the center of my own scene or not, I would make sure any man in my future who stopped short of putting me there would not be part of my life for long.

Before I'd met Pascal I'd known I was aiming for something beyond what I'd already experienced. Now that I'd experienced it, I'd never settle for anything less. As my grandmother had frequently commented, "Ava — you're too selfish not to get what you want out of life." And what was wrong with that? Wouldn't I be a nicer, kinder person to those around me if I was getting what I wanted out of life? Why shouldn't I make every effort to grab the golden ring when it was within range? Tenderly, my eyes drank in the lightly snoring man who'd introduced me to life as it should be lived.

"Thank you, darling," I whispered to his sleeping form, then leaned over to kiss his forehead. He stirred gently in his sleep. Soon, he would be part of my past, but what a place of honor he'd occupy in my psychic Hall of Fame. I welcomed him to roam there forever, checking in on my choices from time to time, always challenging me to remain the fully alive woman I had become with him.

PART III

BEING WHERE I BELONG

CHAPTER NINE

Paris Five Years Later

"Hey, could you do me a favor and play happy birthday for my friend over there when they bring out the cake?"

Groan. My job as the house singer/pianist at The Blue Willow, an upscale restaurant with a downtown clientele in Greenwich Village, would soon be over. That was fine by me. The only thing I found more annoying than being asked to play happy birthday at least twice a week, was being requested to play *Piano Man* by customers who would then tip me an entire dollar. The waiters at the restaurant made ten times the tips I made every night, and my base salary wasn't much higher than theirs.

"Uh – after we do the happy birthday thing could you play *Piano Man*? It's one of his favorite songs."

Too fed up to speak, I nodded as the young guy with the outer-boroughs accent slipped two dollar bills into my tip jar. I wrapped up the super-cerebral, intricate improvisation I'd been doing on the chord progressions for *Song for My Father* which no one recognized or cared about, and launched into *Happy Birthday* as the waiter came out of the kitchen with the lit-up birthday cake.

Until I'd gotten this job, I'd had no idea how banal it could be to earn a steady income as a house musician. It was right up there with playing in a wedding band or doing a hotel lounge gig. Top requirements for the job had nothing to do with talent or creativity. It was all about 1) starting on time, 2) playing customers' requests, and 3) not singing or playing too loudly so people could hear themselves talk.

The pendulum of my ongoing internal debate over whether I was meant to be a musician or writer had swung wildly back into the musician corner after slogging through four years of paper and senior-essay writing at Yale. One thing was for sure, I was my parents' child after all. I had picked up the impractical career aspirations gene from both of them. I thought by working as a professional musician, I'd been thumbing my nose at my Yale friends down on Wall St. working one hundred-hour weeks as investment banking associates. Contemplating my tip jar with the two dollar bills in it, I wasn't so sure any more.

As I launched into *Piano Man*, I was heartened by the thought that it would all be over soon. Milton Fine, my boss and a well-known Manhattan slum lord, had gotten his comeuppance from city authorities in their latest clampdown and lost his liquor license. I had until the end of June to figure out what to do with the rest of my life.

Finding another steady gig as a house musician in the heart of Greenwich Village would be next to impossible. No musician I knew had a steady performing job in Manhattan outside of a hotel lounge. I knew what that was all about, too. I'd done a gig at Novotel near Times Square the year before – another soul-deadening experience that had paid the rent for six months. Tired of being ignored by tourists in transit in the hotel lounge, I'd auditioned for a gig at the cocktail lounge of the Gramercy Park Hotel, farther downtown. It was known as a celebrity hangout, where many well-known bands stayed when on tour in Manhattan. I'd been thrilled when they offered me a two-night a week spot.

The Gramercy Park Hotel was supposed to be the kind of place where emerging artists get discovered. After I'd been there for three months, a hotel employee pointed out hotel resident Paul Shaffer, who was dining alone in the restaurant. He was the band leader on the *Late Show with David*

Letterman. I introduced myself to him as the hotel lounge pianist, to which he grunted unintelligibly then went back to his meal.

My next brush with fame had been one evening about a month later, when a short guy in a hooded sweatshirt and messy, day-old stubble on his chin came up to the piano and requested *Send in the Clowns*, stuffing a dollar bill into my tip glass. I played it, no one clapped, and the guy continued talking with his lady-friend over in the corner, unmoved by my performance. Later in the restroom, the cocktail waitress asked me if I realized that had been Bob Dylan.

My final celebrity encounter at the hotel had been when the band Kansas came in late one Saturday evening and asked me to sit with them after my set was over. As a child, I'd loved their biggest hit song – one of the most soulful rock tunes of the 1970s. Anticipating being invited to record with them, or at least join their touring band, I was less than thrilled when one of the band members, after downing multiple bourbon shots, asked if I'd give him a blow job. My feelings for the music of Kansas scattered like so much dust in the wind.

So when Milton Fine came in a few months after that encounter and asked to speak with me after I finished my first set of the evening, I was receptive. He was old and enormously fat, with hair growing everywhere but on top of his head. This kind of schlubby-looking guy in Manhattan frequently indicates two things – money and power.

I sat down with him, noting he'd hardly touched his drink, a sign he was there on business. He didn't waste any time getting down to it.

"Do you work here every night?" he asked.

"No, three nights a week usually."

"You like it?"

"I guess so –," I answered slowly to let him know that I was open to suggestion.

"You know The Blue Willow at the corner of Broadway and Bleecker Street?" he continued.

"You mean that restaurant with the high ceilings?"

"Yeah, that's the one."

I knew the place. It was exclusive, trendy, housed in a majestic, pre-war building. Its stunning exterior with twelve-foot high plate-glass windows had always intimidated me when I'd walked past. A Zagat review was posted right in the outer doorway.

"Yeah. I know it."

"I'm the owner."

My eyebrows shot up, but I held my tongue. Big deal. Restaurant own-
ers were a dime a dozen in New York City. It was time to talk turkey.

"You want a job playing piano there?"

That was more like it.

"How many nights a week?" I asked, as a warm-up. What I really
wanted to know was how much he would pay.

"I don't know. How many would you like?'

"I'd have to think about it."

"You do that."

"I've got to get back to work."

"I'll stay till your next break if you want to talk more."

"Okay," I said, playing it as cool as a cucumber. I'd absolutely love to
have a job at a fashionable, super-trendy place like The Blue Willow. But
the price needed to be right. I got up and walked away, my back straight
as a ramrod. 'Always maintain straight posture at critical moments,' my
grandmother had advised. This would be one of them.

Back at the piano, I mulled over what kind of money we were talking
here. Experience had taught me that if he asked how much I made at my
present gig, I would 1) lie and 2) know he was serious. When people talk
money in New York, they're serious. Otherwise, it's just talk.

He was still there at the end of my second set, nursing the same first
glass of wine – both very good signs. This wasn't the drink talking, whatever it was. I walked over, sat down and, bam, first thing he asked was how
much I made at my present job.

I gave him a number, slightly rounded up – okay doubled, I'd spent the
past forty-five minutes formulating.

He offered me fifty per cent more to come work for him, five nights
a week, as his resident house pianist. Just like that. Frankly, playing two
nights a week at the semi-sleazy Gramercy Park Hotel wasn't paying all my
bills. A full-time, five-night a week job at The Blue Willow with the salary
he'd just promised, would.

I agreed on the spot.

But after almost a year at The Blue Willow, I was ready for an exit plan.
Manhattan was eating me up and spitting me out in small pieces. I'd gotten
a gig that paid the rent – a situation every New York City artist dreams of

but only few accomplish. Most either worked as office temps or waited tables. I'd done both of those jobs, too. Why wasn't I enjoying being able to make a living working as a performer? Or to rephrase – how many more times could I stomach being asked to play Billy Joel's *Piano Man* or *Happy Birthday?*

That winter, a girlfriend of mine had brought in some French friends to see me play. Marceline and Henri had been delightful. Marceline was pint-sized and seriously chic, a true living Parisian doll. She'd worn pencil-slim black jeans in a size so small, I was sure she hadn't bought them Stateside. Her high-heeled suede boots had tiny gold buckles on either side announcing the brand of some fabulous French designer. The black, white, and gold print silk shirt she wore featured more buckles and horsey-motifs, vaguely identifiable as straps, bridles and harnesses. Her hair was a mass of dark, golden-blonde curls, her make-up subtle – some mascara and the tiniest hint of taupe lipstick. I'd studied every inch of her, admiring her effortless style. I wanted to look like that some day.

Marceline's husband, Henri, raved over my rendition of Peggy Lee's *Fever*, mentioning a place in Paris where he could see me performing. He'd given me his card, and I'd tossed it in the tip jar, not expecting to follow up in any way.

On one of those dull gray end of March days I went through my Rolodex, looking for career opportunities that would get me out of New York to someplace I'd be appreciated. After a few minutes, I found Henri's business card. In French, it said something about optical supplies. He'd told me he was an entertainment manager. Maybe pushing optical supplies was his day job.

I made an international call.

Henri Zidane remembered me. He agreed the French would love my repertoire of jazz standards; Fats Waller, Cole Porter, and Gershwin with a smattering of bossa nova and a few contemporary pop songs thrown in.

"Send your headshots and a cassette tape of three of your best songs, and I'll circulate it. I have just the place in mind."

"How soon could you arrange something?"

"When can you get here? If I can take you around with me, we can get bookings faster."

"By late spring or early summer." Milton had mentioned June 30th as the last day The Blue Willow would be open. There was no way I wanted to stick around for yet another sweltering Manhattan summer – even worse, in an unemployed state. I'd ask my father for an employee-pass round-trip airline ticket to Paris. It was the one really big thing he could do for me and he delighted in being able to fuel my love of travel and adventure gene. Undoubtedly, I'd gotten it from him. My grandparents had died, both passing peacefully in their sleep, well into their nineties. Nothing compelled me to remain Stateside.

Memories of Paris five summers earlier, when I'd met Pascal beckoned. God knew what he was doing now, but I'd bet he was married with at least two children, still living in working-class St. Denis, north of Paris. I treasured everything I'd experienced with him, but there was no point in tracking him down. Even during our intense few weeks together, I'd known we had nothing in common other than sizzling sexual attraction.

"As soon as I get your promo package, I'll get on it," Henri continued. "Do you have some good headshots?"

"Yes. I've got a few different poses. What kind do you want?" I had just had new headshots done for free in a barter exchange with a photographer-friend at whose fortieth birthday party I'd sung and played. Highly retouched, they looked pretty much nothing like me, just like the headshots of all my other friends in the performing arts.

"Send one of every pose. Soon. Go to the post this afternoon."

"You'll have them within a week." I couldn't believe my good luck. The stars were with me.

"You'll hear back from me within two."

Twelve days later, Henri called back.

"I've got you booked at the hottest club in Bastille," he said, referring to a neighborhood in Paris I remembered as roughly similar to Manhattan's East Village. "Six Friday nights from mid-July through the end of August. That'll give us time to find other club dates and get you settled in."

"What's the name of the place?" I asked, delighted.

"It's called Le Cactus Bleu, The Blue Cactus."

I was moving across the ocean from The Blue Willow to The Blue Cactus? My favorite color was blue. Apparently the stars had lined up.

"How much do they pay?" I asked. Despite the free plane ticket and no immediate prospects in New York, I needed to support myself. Paris was less expensive than New York, but not by much.

"Enough for you to get by," Henri said without specifying how much. "You'll make enough to live on while we line up bookings at other places.

And you can stay with us until mid-August. By then, we'll have you set up with gigs and a place to stay."

"Great." I got off the phone, shaking, unprepared for the future hurtling so quickly toward me. Now that I'd set the wheels in motion, I feared the consequences. With rashness one of my strong suits, I'd soon get over it. Plus, I'd forgotten to ask what the mid-August deadline was all about, but it seemed far away. We'd work out my housing situation once I got there.

Henri Zidane and his wife picked me up at Charles de Gaulle airport the second of July. He hadn't changed, his bony, medium-tall French frame honed through frequent cigarette usage, but Marceline was almost unrecognizable.

Félicitations, Marceline," I congratulated her as I took in her enormous tummy and bloated face. "When is the baby due?"

She scowled then grunted. She was no longer the sexy, chic Marceline I remembered from the winter before. Begrudgingly, she offered one cheek, then the other. Only two kisses this time, not four.

"The baby's due August fifteenth," Henri broke in enthusiastically. Bulbous light brown eyes looked me over then flicked back to his wife. She stared at him coolly, as if to warn him to keep his eyes off me.

In the car, I thanked them for picking me up. *"Je vous remercie, Henri, de me retirer de l'aeroport. C'est bien innoportun, je sais.* It was really inconvenient, I know," I tried to say in French.

"Pas du tout, Ava, pas du tout. Not at all," Henri replied.

Marceline nodded in agreement with me, giving Henri a baleful stare. I decided not to ask if pregnancy was agreeing with her. Apparently not.

"Je suis très excitée d être ici," I continued, meaning 'I'm very excited to be here.'

Marceline's head swiveled around abruptly. Her glare was unmistakable. Had I made a blooper? I looked in the rearview mirror for guidance from Henri's face. It was flushed, his eyes straight ahead on the road.

A strained silence ensued. I wracked my brain to think of something next to say. Then, it occurred to me. Exciter is one of those false friends from English to French. 'I'm excited' could mean a variety of things in English, but it meant only one in French – to be aroused. I'd just told Henri I was very sexually aroused to be there. No wonder Marceline was giving me the hairy eyeball.

"I mean it's very nice to be here," I amended, looking out the window to hide the enormous blush now covering my entire body.

Henri and Marceline's flat was near Bastille, a lively neighborhood with good nightlife where The Blue Cactus was located. I would stay with them at least a week until my first performance took place, the following Friday. The six gigs Henri had contracted for me over consecutive Friday evenings, guaranteed me an income at least until the end of August. After that, we would see. I set up my synthesizer in the spare room next to Henri's study where I practiced with headphones, ostensibly not to disturb them, but frankly so as not to be disturbed by Henri who was in the habit of interrupting me while working from his home office, which was most of the time.

"Did you bring that dress you wore in your professional photo with you?" he asked a few mornings after I arrived, as he stood in the doorway between the study and his office.

"Which dress?" I asked, although I knew immediately. It had to be the Norma Kamali dress I'd picked up at a sample sale. A skinny woman in the group dressing room had thrown it at me after pulling it off, saying "You should try this on. It would look great on you." She'd been right.

"Umm – the one with the – uh – cut outs. You know."

"The one I'm wearing in the photo with the big hair?"

"Yes. You brought it, right?"

"I've got it here. Why?" I nodded toward the closet door in the corner where I'd hung the slinky, long black dress to smooth out the wrinkles. The cut-outs on the shoulders and below the neckline gave the garment a bizarre appearance on its hanger. When I wore it, the effect was anything but bizarre. Stunning and devastatingly sexy was more like it.

"Maybe you could wear it your opening night."

Did Henri care about fashion? He was French, so perhaps he did. Still, the way his eyes shifted between the dress hanging on the door and my person, somewhere below the neck, told me it wasn't the dress, but me in it, he was thinking about.

"I had another outfit in mind. Something a little more chic," *and less provocative*, I told him. I'd worn that dress in my professional photos on the advice of my stylist, Mitchell, my gay friend back in the East Village. He'd told me it would help me score more gigs.

"You can try on a few outfits, then we'll decide," Henri answered, his eyes still on my torso. I wasn't exactly chesty, but this was France, world headquarters for connossieurs of small breasts.

"There's plenty of time to decide before the gig," I told him, hoping he understood it was going to be my decision and mine alone. The thought of trying on outfits and parading myself in front of Henri made me want to throw up. But that's what managers were for, wasn't it? They provided critical feedback on everything – not just the product, but the package the product was presented in. I was the product, he was my manager. Still, I vowed I'd find a way not to put on a fashion show for Henri Zidane. Something about the idea made my skin crawl.

By my third day in Paris, I was getting antsy. I needed to practice aloud, but the walls of most Parisian buildings were thin. Flushing a toilet or taking a shower in an old building in Paris was an event heard by all of its occupants; singing, or playing a keyboard instrument were in the same category. Henri suggested that I prepare my sets more or less *sotto voce* or under my breath, which didn't really help me to work on my voice, never mind practice with sound equipment – microphone and reverb units. I prayed the sound engineer at The Blue Cactus would know what he was doing and that we'd be able to go in for a sound check the day before my performance.

Marceline was at her job during the weekdays, but when she returned home, I had the distinct sense it had not been her idea to have me stay with them. Never having been pregnant, I had no idea what late-stage pregnancy in the middle of summer could do to a woman, but it was clear she was not in a good mood most of the time. At the sound of the key turning in the lock on weekday late afternoons, I'd run into my room before Marceline entered the flat. All sorts of sounds would ensue, indicating exasperation. The slam of her keys and bags hitting the counter would be followed by muttered complaints as she put away the groceries. After awhile, the banging of pots and pans, along with cupboards being forcefully shut told me she'd begun dinner. I tried to help the first day, but I put everything away in the wrong place then refrigerated the cheeses which were supposed to be left out for the evening meal. The scowl on her face after I put a glass in the dishwasher that was supposed to be hand washed told me it was time to exit the kitchen. After that, I made an excuse to get out of the flat every evening just to get away.

Mid-morning on the fourth day of my stay, I went into Henri's study to fetch a pen while he was out. I was making notes on the newest pop song I was working on, a smoky blues tune I wanted to rehearse full voice before Henri returned or a neighbor pounded on the door.

I reached over a pile of papers on Henri's desk next to his computer to grab a black pen. Something with a tip like a fine magic marker would make my orchestral notes on the musical score stand out. I couldn't find anything suitable on his desk, so I looked around. Glancing at the pile of papers, I saw the corner of one which had been marked up with a pen exactly like the kind I was looking for. It looked like a drawing. Curiously, I pulled it out.

It was a caricature of a nude woman with long, wavy hair, high perky breasts and a button nose. I'd know her anywhere. She was in the mirror whenever I looked.

Shoving the sketch back into the pile, I grabbed a black pen and retreated to my temporary studio, careful to leave everything in Henri's office exactly the way I'd found it.

Yuck. No wonder Marceline's default expression these days was one of stormy stares and unspoken recriminations.

After another half hour of practice, I went through my wardrobe, carefully stashing lingerie in the zippered compartments of my suitcase, out of sight of Henri's roving eye. What were the chances of Henri drifting into the room I was using as a bedroom when I was out? Probably as high as the likelihood of me visiting his office while he was out, as I'd just done. I would find somewhere else to stay as soon as possible. I needed a place where I could rehearse as well as not worry about what was going through the mind of my host.

As I hid the Norma Kamali dress with the cut-outs in the far corner of the closet, I came across my black leather postman's satchel, into which I'd emptied out my handbag the first night I'd arrived, retiring all New York-related items such as subway cards and gym passes, U.S. currency, and business cards of people I'd met at my performing job. Among the collection was the business card of an older American man I'd run into at the Blue Willow. He'd mentioned he threw parties at his Paris apartment for the literary ex-pat set. "Lawrence Pemberwick" it said in small, elegant script. No title, no company. Just an accompanying eight-digit Paris phone number and the address.

Less is more, I thought approvingly, along with Diana Vreeland.

I called. Going to a party would get me out of Henri and Marceline's flat. Besides, I could invite interesting people I might meet there to The Blue Cactus to see me perform.

Someone with an Australian accent answered to say Larry wasn't around but could he help?

"Well, Larry mentioned in New York that he throws parties from time to time so I thought I'd come to the next one if it's alright. Could I leave my name for him to call?"

"No need, dear. His salon happens every Sunday evening. Starts around sevenish. Potluck sort of thing. The more the merrier, especially if you're female," the voice chortled at the other end.

"What should I bring?"

"Beauty and brains, love."

It was my turn to laugh. A dose of Anglo-American wit would go a long way toward lifting my spirits, chilled by the frozen atmosphere of Henri and Marceline's flat.

"And a bottle of wine?" I offered.

"No need. We've got enough booze on hand to sink a ship. Bring a dish of something."

"Um, er, I'm staying with friends, I can't really cook anything to bring over. How about some dessert?"

"Marvelous. Something big and messy, like most of Larry's guests." His laugh boomed over the airways, welcoming and warm – definitely not French.

The Australian gave me directions to Larry's flat, including the metro stop. It was located in the east of Paris, near Parc de Vincennes, a section I was unfamiliar with.

The next few days flew by. I had something to look forward to. Wishing I had a girlfriend to accompany me to the party, I remembered an axiom my singer/actress friend Jessica had often mentioned back in Manhattan. She'd said the best way to meet a man was to go out alone. And the fastest way to scare one off was to go out with a pack of girlfriends. If I could maintain my self-confidence, there might be an advantage in going to the party alone. Just the challenge of going to a party where I knew absolutely no one increased my excitement. I was already in a city and a country where I knew practically no one. What did I have to lose?

I ran errands Saturday afternoon, picking up a *tarte de Breton* at the local patisserie to bring with me to the party. It wasn't messy, but it was large.

Nothing in Paris was messy other than foreigners who didn't belong there and would leave sooner or later. The city's very signature was precise, orderly, well-thought out and most of all – in excellent taste. The French word that summed up all these ideas was *exigeant* or exacting, demanding due to high standards. The Parisian personality was *exigeant* above all else.

Fortunately, foreigners had a pass not to be exacting. Even if they were, it wouldn't matter. Parisians would still look down their noses at them, whether they were travelling tourists or ex-pats who'd lived there for decades. It was wonderfully freeing not to have to even pretend I was exacting. Little did I know that years after leaving Paris I would realize how much the city had left its mark on me – thanks to my time there, I would forever after drive my family and friends batty in questions of taste. In Paris, I couldn't exercise my newly-acquired Parisian standards, since the Parisians would have none of it from an outsider. It was only back home Stateside that I got to exercise my true inner Parisian.

At half past seven on Sunday, I exited the metro at Porte de Vincennes and was immediately struck by how good the air smelled. The neighborhood was residential, close to Parc de Vincennes, where the city's zoo was located. Around me, leaves rustled on trees, lit gold by the remains of the day. They hinted at something, bobbing and waving as I walked past. Some sort of secret was being passed, one which involved me, but which I wasn't in on yet.

Feeling more light-hearted than I had since my arrival, I followed the Australian's directions to Larry's apartment. The lushness of the foliage, the density of the trees lining the sidewalk all increased my anticipation of the evening to come. In a minute, I'd found 59, Rue d'Horloge and buzzed the name of L. Pemberwick on the name directory next to the outer gate.

"Yah, come on up," a garrulous non-French, non-exacting voice responded. The gate clicked open, and I was in.

Up two flights of stairs flanked by a curlicue, wrought-iron staircase, the door to Fred's flat was already open. Inside, the crowd was dense, almost all male. Immediately my adrenalin kicked in. Or perhaps it was my testosterone.

I steeled myself and entered, willing my face into a proud, mysterious mask. Surrounded by men, I'd play my best defense – the enigmatic female card.

"And who do we have here?" a voice rang out. A stout, balding man with a good-natured, florid face greeted me near the door.

"I'm Ava Fodor. I met Larry in New York a few months ago and ..."

"Ava from New York, eh?" he announced loudly to the surrounding male masses. "I'm Sam. Come on in and get yourself something to drink." He took my patisserie box and motioned me in. "Make way for the lady, mates. We've got a live one here from New York. Shape up boys," he boomed out as he led me to the kitchen, elbowing bodies out of the way.

My nose pointing to the ceiling, it was all I could do to keep my composure or *sangfroid*. But that was the whole point of being back in Paris again, or one of the main ones. Maintaining *sangfroid* counted for a lot. It was another thing I was determined to learn how to do well and then take home with me.

"Some white wine, please," I told a middle-aged man in the tiny kitchen. He wore a cravat tucked into a pristine, white-collared shirt. His well-manicured eyebrows suggested he might be gay.

He handed me a delicately-stemmed glass, and I quaffed. It was good to be at a rollicking, roaring, Anglo-Saxon party; even better to have a few gay men in attendance just to keep the heterosexual males in check. I steeled myself to enter the main room, drawing on my performer's skills to maintain composure. A ship in full sail, I sallied into the salon, drink in hand.

After a minute, a few females became apparent, all with male escorts. They looked mousy, timid – unlike me. I would be queen bee of this crowd. Perusing the floor-to-ceiling bookshelves, I ignored the myriad male eyes upon me.

"Hi, I'm Scott from Omaha. Have you come to one of Larry's parties before?" a blond, corn-fed Midwestern guy asked.

"No." Not my type.

"Are you here with someone then?" he followed up.

"Yes," *as far as you're concerned*.

Over the din of the crowd, a sharp voice stood out. "The wisdom of life, my friend?" The accent was cultured, more Continental than French, although it was that, too. It belonged to someone well-traveled. "The wisdom of life consists in the elimination of nonessentials. For example – speaking with you now." A raucous laugh ensued.

Now that was rude. I swiveled my head to scan over Scott's shoulder in search of the voice's owner. What kind of brazen boor would say such a thing? He had to be drunk, completely ill-mannered, or talking to his younger brother.

After a moment I located him – tall and brash, a man with a high fore-head and golden skin tossed back longish, auburn hair. Dashing but raffish, I imagined he would take no prisoners in a battle of wits.

I willed him to look my way.

The face turned, and a mobile, full mouth rearranged itself the second he saw me.

I pretended to look beyond him. Fortunately, the man who'd greeted me at the door stood behind him, chatting with a group of bookish types.

"Sa-a-a-m," I called out, in my best Audrey Hepburn impression. I might not look like her, but I'd watched *Breakfast at Tiffany's* so many times I was confident I could channel her when the occasion arose. Pointing my small, slightly upturned nose toward the ceiling, I moved in Sam's direction, brushing past the reddish-haired barbarian as I passed. I made sure not to give him the tiniest glance.

He took the bait.

A low growl followed as I swished past. It was as if the air rumbled between us, making the hair stand up on my arms.

The man called Sam looked pleased but slightly baffled as I approached.

"What a delightful party," I sang out as I broke into his circle of friends, all with manicured hands and eyebrows to match carefully man-nered expressions. Gay, the lot of them, I'd surmise. Unlike the uncaged lion a few paces behind me.

"Thank you. Let me introduce you to Trevor, Henry, and Jean-Paul," he offered graciously, clearly unsure of my name.

"How darling to meet you. I'm Ava from New York," I said, loud enough for anyone in the general area to hear.

"And what brings Ava from New York to Paris?" a voice that was all angles rang out behind me. Sharp as a knife, it crackled with testosterone.

I turned slowly. No need to hurry. Something told me that whatever I was about to face would be part of my very near future.

"And what brings you to Paris?" I asked back. He was way too uncivi-lized to be a Parisian.

"I live here." he answered, in a voice that sounded like a challenge.

I shivered, then braced myself.

"But you're not from here, are you?" It was a presumptuous guess – as presumptuous as his greenish-blue eyes, now roving over me, insolent and unapologetic.

The floor cleared on both sides, as if a duel were about to take place.

At Parisian parties, strangers didn't introduce themselves by immediately asking personal questions such as 'where are you from?' or even worse, 'what do you do?' These were private matters to be uncovered slowly, perhaps through discreet inquiry of a third party. At most Parisian parties I'd attended, small clusters of French people stood in separate corners, eyeballing the crowd, whispering amongst their own group and disdaining to interact with anyone outside their own circle. When I'd made attempts to infiltrate a cluster of unknown Parisians by introducing myself and saying where I was from, the response would usually be polite, but not forthcoming. "Hello" might be followed up with "Hello, I'm Anne-Marie," but it was never followed up with "Hi, I'm Anne-Marie from blah blah blah. So, how do you know so-and-so?," whose party it was, or "what brings you to Paris?" Less drinking, less noise, and less interaction all added up to a lot less fun from what I'd observed.

"Entirely correct. I'm from somewhere else," he answered maddeningly.

"And where would that be?" I insisted. This was a party thrown by Larry for the Anglo-Saxon ex-pat crowd. Different rules applied.

"Where would you like me to be from? Take your pick. I'm yours to serve." He bowed, but not before raking me again with twinkling blue-green eyes that reminded me of my father's. Nothing else about him did.

"You mean *you're* at *my* service," I corrected him. He must have misspoke.

"No. You're at mine." His eyes gleamed.

What cheek.

"Well thanks, but no thanks." Feeling my face flame, I turned back to speak with the gay contingent but they had already faded into another group. I searched for Sam or anyone else who looked safe. Where was Scott from Omaha when I needed him?

"Thanks, but thanks, you mean," he shot back.

"I didn't say that." This time, I bared my teeth as I looked at him.

"No, but that's what you meant." His laughing eyes continued their sweep over my form.

"I think I know what I meant," I hissed.

"I think I know what you meant, too," he hissed back. His English was accented but perfect.

This time, I couldn't control the color that shot into my face and neck.

"You look nice in red," he whispered.

"I'm wearing blue," I looked down just to make sure. Whatever self-possession I'd faked from the moment I'd walked into the party was now in a puddle on the floor in front of me.

"I meant your blush," he replied maddeningly.

"I think I know what you meant," I countered, wondering how long I could keep this up. Conversations with him would be exhausting. We'd need to find something else to do. My racing blood told me that wouldn't be a problem.

"Blue suits you, too," he continued, not missing a beat.

"Do you think so?"

"I do."

"Well – I'd better get back to my friend," I ad-libbed. "Nice sparring with you." I turned to go back to the kitchen. After that encounter, I needed another glass of white wine.

"When's the rematch?" he asked, blocking my way.

"The what?"

"Part two."

"Was this part one?" There was no doubt it was.

"Wasn't it?"

He had me there.

"Do you want it to be?" We'd turned into characters from *Waiting for Godot*.

"Do I?" I threw the ball back into his court.

"Do you?"

"You tell me."

"You do." His tone was clear, manly.

"Do I?"

"Yes, you do."

"Well then – make me an offer." With this man, I'd never be in the driver's seat. But I couldn't help wanting to take the ride.

"Dinner next week?'

"Call me." I needed to be sure this wasn't just party talk.

"Give me your number, and I will." His voice softened, taking on intimacy.

"Get me a glass of white wine, and I might." I lowered my own to match his.

"Your wish is my command," he replied, taking the glass gently from my hands, his fingers brushing mine.

"It's about time," I replied, not too sharply.

His lean, muscular back flexed as he searched carefully among the already opened bottles, then looked in the refrigerator. After a minute, he took out a green wine bottle labeled in medieval German script.

"Here's something worthy of a Rhine maiden," he said as he handed me my filled glass.

"Do I remind you of one?"

He nodded, saying nothing, his compliment more effective by not following it up with yet another *bon mot*.

The wine was dry but sweet. It tasted crisp, like the barbarian's conversation. I didn't even know his name.

"I like it. It's crisp and snappy," I commented.

"Like me?" The man didn't lack confidence.

"Do I like you? Or do I think you're crisp and snappy?"

"Both."

I took another sip, looking at him over the rim of my glass.

"Perhaps one out of two."

"So we need to get to Part Two to establish the other." He took out a pen and pocket datebook. "Number?"

"I don't give my number out to strangers."

"Am I a stranger?"

"Do I know your name?"

"Ahh. Allow me to introduce myself. Arnaud de Saint Cyr." He took my free hand in his, bent down, and kissed it. "At your service."

His touch was warm and dry.

I smiled at the way he'd said his name. It had come out like 'Ar-know the Sincere', Ar-know the Insolent was more like it. Nevertheless, I was hooked.

He clinked his glass with mine. Then, I gave him my number, and we talked long into the night.

Two days later, he called. Henri and Marceline were out. The voice speaking into their answering machine crackled with energy.

"Arnaud de Saint Cyr here calling for Ava about the rematch. When, where, yours to decide. You can reach me at...."

"It's me. I'm here." I cut in, finally locating the phone receiver on the kitchen counter.

"Ahhh. Felt safe to pick up, finally?" Wit, intelligence, and audacity all flew through the air to my heart and brain, jabbing me with electric jolts.

"I – just heard your voice and realized it's you."

"So, what about our rematch?"

"When, where, yours to decide," I parroted back, eager to hear what he might propose.

"Where do you live?"

"I'm staying with friends near Place de la Bastille." Why was I giving him information about myself? He didn't need to know anything more about me than how to see me again.

"Do you know Café de la Bastille right above the exit to the metro there?

"Sure." It was un-missable, the largest café on Bastille's enormous traffic circle.

"Let's meet there tomorrow evening at seven. We can go to dinner from there."

"Um — tomorrow's not good, I've got a rehearsal." With myself of course, but no need to seem ridiculously available. The russet-haired barbarian needed to work hard to see me. I couldn't just fall into his lap. Although I wanted to.

"Hmmm. Thursday's out, I've got a meeting. What about Friday?"

"Sounds fine." Friday had always been my favorite day of the week – the threshold of the weekend.

"Any type of food out for you?"

"None. Well, perhaps head cheese or horsemeat."

"Favorite drink?"

"Excuse me?" That was a broad subject. Where might I begin, especially in France?

"Favorite summertime drink?"

"Umm, let's see – " A good question, showing attention to details. The barbarian had a civilized side. "I like sangria."

The following three days passed in a flurry. Now that I knew the full scope of Henri's interests, I was sure I didn't want him to act as my manager. But anticipation had replaced the fear I'd felt in the pit of my stomach the day I stumbled on the drawing in his office. Henri's interest in my career had gotten me to Paris. Marceline's interest in reeling in her husband would get me out of their apartment. And whatever interest Arnaud de Saint Cyr and I had in each other would set the stage for the next chapter of my new life in Europe. In the meantime, I had to figure out what I would wear to my meeting with him less than forty-eight hours away.

On Thursday, Henri and I went over to The Blue Cactus. Henri introduced me to the owner, a Monsieur Thibault who sported a handlebar moustache and whose first name I didn't catch. He spent less than five minutes with us, then had the bartender set us up with drinks while we caught the evening's performance.

It was less than stellar. A male guitarist played unmemorable background music while diners ate, chatted, and paid him no attention whatsoever. No sound equipment was in sight. Concerned, I asked Henri if there was indeed a house P.A. system with microphone, reverb, and sound mixing board available for the night of my performance.

"It will all be taken care of, Ava. *N'inquiète pas*, don't worry," he reassured me.

Back in New York, it hadn't taken me long to figure out the waiters and waitresses at the trendy Village restaurant where I played piano and sang, made more money than me. It was due to tips. Customers felt obligated to give a fifteen to twenty per cent tip in New York for standard service, but the tip jar on the piano didn't beckon to them as an obligatory stop on the way out the door. Still, I had big ambitions for a career as a recording artist and songwriter, so what did I care if playing piano in a restaurant was a dead end? I wasn't planning on doing it for too much longer.

"Do you want another cocktail?" Henri asked pointing at the tiny glass I'd emptied in four sips. Mixed drinks in Europe were both miniscule and expensive. I'd stick with wine the next time I went out – perhaps sangria with Arnaud the following evening. My stomach warmed at the thought.

"No thanks. I'm done," I said politely. The last thing I wanted to do was spend the evening drinking with Henri. He'd probably confess something to me I wouldn't want to hear, and then it would be even more uncomfortable returning to the accusatory eyes of his wife back home. I'd be an accessory to crime by providing him with the object of his fantasies. Against my will, no less. That's how the world worked for attractive, unattached young women.

I wanted to leave as soon as possible to get away from Henri. "Shall we go?"

"If you like." he shrugged, clearly open to further suggestion.

I'd offer him some food for thought. "You and Marceline have the flat to yourselves tomorrow evening. I'm meeting a friend."

His eyebrows went up. "Another musician?"

"No. He's a- a- a..." I had no idea what Arnaud did for a living. Who cared? No one talked about that kind of thing at parties in Paris. But it had been a literary gathering, ostensibly. "He's a writer," I finally said.

"Oh." One eyebrow lowered, the other remaining up, in a speculative expression. "I see."

I ignored him, as I got off my barstool and headed to the door. He didn't see anything. Even I didn't see clearly what the following evening would offer. The thought of it made me feel like a newly-sharpened knife, except for some part deep inside that went all quivery and mushy at the thought of spending time alone with Arnaud de Saint Cyr.

For a split second, I felt the tiniest bit sorry for Henri, about to go home to his grumpy wife. She was right to be suspicious. Irritable, uncomfortable, swollen, and exhausted, she had every reason to be. But that didn't stop her husband's eye from roving. I made a mental note to take extra care to keep any future partner well away from single, attractive females if I one day found myself in a heavily pregnant state.

The next morning, Marceline left early for work. Then Henri finally went out on an appointment. At the sound of his Citroën accelerating down the boulevard outside my window, I pulled out a black and white dress I'd brought from New York. It needed ironing. In the kitchen, I found the ironing board and iron, being careful not to set the iron on any surface that would burn. Marceline had already dropped several comments about minor infractions I'd committed around the flat, which Henri had relayed to me apologetically. The dollop of skin moisturizer for babies I'd used from a jar in her bathroom hadn't gone unnoticed. She'd been saving it for the baby and I'd inadvertently opened it for the first time. I needed to get out of there as soon as possible, to save myself as well as their marriage.

The form-fitting cotton/linen dress ironed, I tried it on. Everything about it screamed Audrey Hepburn, except the figure of the person inside. That was probably for the best. In my experience, skinny men liked women who weren't skinny. Arnaud de Saint Cyr was slim as a weasel, but with broad shoulders. I didn't yet know how much I wanted him to like me, but if it turned out I did, this dress would do the trick. Taking it off, I hung it on a hanger, admiring the way it retained an hour-glass shape without me in it. There was something to be said for good tailoring.

That afternoon, I rehearsed well. My mind focused, I was able to master some country western/pop crossover tunes I knew would appeal to a French audience for their exoticism alone. No one would know if I forgot a word or phrase here or there.

At half past six, the key turned in the door. Marceline and Henri came in together, their arms full of shopping bags.

"Want some help?" I called from my room.

"No, we're fine," Marceline called back, sounding cheerier than she had in days.

I continued drawing the finest of dark brown eyeliner lines above my upper lashes. Done, I admired my handiwork in the mirror on the bureau.

"Getting ready for your date?" Marceline stood in the doorway, a sly smile on her face.

I turned. She looked like the old Marceline I'd met in New York the year before – foxy and full of spice. For the first time since I'd arrived, I relaxed in her presence.

"What do you think?" I asked, genuinely seeking her opinion, woman to woman.

Henri must have told her I had a date that evening, although I'd simply said I was meeting a friend.

"I think he's going to like it."

"Thank you." I winked to cover my blush. What if it turned out I didn't want Arnaud de Saint Cyr to like me? What if he was a highly intelligent, raving lunatic? I was nuts to put this much preparation into a first date.

Marceline turned, humming a tune as she went to the kitchen. She was a regular wellspring of good cheer that evening.

Catching her mood, I continued preparations, putting on a subtle rose-colored lipstick that wouldn't look too obvious if it got rubbed off. There was a chance it would, *non?*

I sprayed Paloma Picasso on my neck, one wrist, and between my breasts. The black and white dress was so form-fitting that it created the tiniest hint of cleavage, even though it wasn't especially low cut. Mentally, I thanked its designer, vowing to make him famous when I became a smash-hit pop star, picking up my first Grammy Award wearing his design.

Henri had gone downstairs to park the car by the time I headed out the door. I waved goodbye to Marceline. No doubt, she would light a candle that evening to the patron saint of good dates in hopes this one would hasten my departure.

On the sidewalk, I turned down the first side street to escape Henri's notice. If he saw me in my black and white dress, I could only guess there'd be a new sketch of me forthcoming in his private collection. Despite being a performing artist, I wasn't entirely comfortable with putting my charms on display for the general public. The New England side of me bristled at such a thing. But making an impression on a private audience I found interesting was another thing. I looked forward to seeing Arnaud de Saint Cyr's jaw drop when we met. Or would he play it cool? Who was I kidding? There was no way that man was capable of playing anything cool. He'd probably say something outrageous, throwing me off guard. I vowed I'd get back on track quickly, if he did.

Never had I dated anyone with a wit like the blade of a sword. As much as the thought of sparring again with the man unsettled me, it excited me even more. My stomach tightened as I hastened my step.

In fifteen minutes, I was at Place de la Bastille, one of Paris's many large, round traffic circles. Four years earlier, I had read a book on the unusually high number of fatal traffic accidents that happened at Place de la Bastille. The author hypothesized that due to the location of the Bastille, Paris's most terrifying prison during the French Revolution, the souls of thousands of enemies of the revolution who had died violently within its thick walls were trapped in limbo in the area, leaving a collective psychic agitation, which led to a higher than usual number of traffic accidents. It made sense to me.

I slowed my gait, running a hand through my hair to smooth it behind my ears. Crossing the street carefully, I reached our meeting place.

It was show time. Arnaud would be inside the café at a window seat, on the lookout for me. Sauntering past the length of the café front, chin held high, I'd let him find me.

At the end of the terrace of the café, I turned and made my way back, this time even more slowly. I was ten minutes late, in other words – right on time. Where was he?

CHAPTER TEN

Mad Summer Night

"Ava," a voice rang out behind me.

I turned. Arnaud looked taller than he had at the party, perhaps a shade under six feet. His wavy, auburn hair flowed down on his shoulders like some sort of medieval troubadour. He wore a dark purple shirt with a Nehru collar.

"Arnaud?" Just saying his name was like singing.

"Did you just get here?" He sounded out of breath.

"Yes. What about you?"

"Thought I wouldn't make it on time." His gaze roved over my dress. "I was in meetings all afternoon."

"Did you accomplish anything?"

"Next assignment." He stepped closer — his scent woodsy, a trace of spice. "Ready for a drink?"

"Sure. What about here?" I gestured to the terrace of the café we stood next to.

"Let's go somewhere quieter."

"Fine." I fell into step beside him. In another five minutes, he stopped in front of a tranquil side street café with three tables out front. It was more amenable to conversation than Café de la Bastille would have been, directly on a busy traffic roundabout. We sat at a table outside.

"What would you like to drink?" he asked.

"You already know."

His blue green eyes twinkled, a half smile playing across his lips. As if on cue, a waiter materialized, and Arnaud ordered two glasses of sangria, while I studied his mouth. It was wide, with a noticeably curved upper lip – one I could imagine belonging to Tiberius or another of the especially cruel Roman emperors. Warning bells should have been going off in my head, but something else was instead, further south.

"So where are we going for dinner?" I asked.

"Dinner is for later," he said mischievously. "Let's be here now."

I nodded. There was nowhere I'd rather be. Sitting back, I pretended to survey the passersby in the street. At the same time, I watched him out of the corner of my eye.

"When's your performance?" he asked after a minute. "At that place you mentioned – The Blue Cactus?"

"I thought you wanted to be here now," I teased. Had I told him about my upcoming gig? Then, I remembered. It had been in the kitchen while we'd sipped white Rhine wine at the party.

"I do, but I also want to be there when you're singing or whatever it is you do."

"Well, it's a week from tomorrow. I start at eight, finish around midnight." It seemed like a year from whenever. My mind hadn't been on music since the previous Tuesday afternoon when he'd called.

"I'll drop by." His voice was low, intimate. The arrogant, self-dramatizing man I'd met at the party was nowhere in sight.

"That'd be great. It's near here. We can walk by it later."

Our conversation progressed easily. Arnaud was articulate, inquisitive, and one hundred per cent on fire. When he emphasized a point, his broad forehead bulged out as if synapses firing inside his brain were trying to punch their way through to the outside. I couldn't decide which I was more attracted to – his brain or the way he looked when he was using it.

Our drinks finished, we strolled out onto Rue de la Roquette, Bastille's most fashionable thoroughfare, taking in the sights and smells of early evening. Young, stylish Parisians and less-well-dressed tourists filled its sidewalks, a heady excitement in the air at the onset of a summer weekend.

We turned down another side street. In a minute, we came upon a small restaurant, the name *Agadir* hand painted over its entryway. Exotic smells drifted from its interior along with a slim, olive-skinned man with a full head of dark, wiry hair. He ushered us inside and out a side door to a table in the garden. Amber light streamed from lanterns, bathing the diners in a golden glow.

Arnaud sat next to me, instead of across the table. It was a very European thing to do. We'd be able to breathe each other in as we took each other's measure.

He ordered a carafe of sangria. Then, we sat back and surveyed the passersby. Be here now, he'd suggested. It was exactly the reason I'd left New York for Paris. Being here now never seemed quite enough in New York. In Paris, it did.

The waiter came to take our order. We both chose lamb *tagine*, a thick Moroccan stew served with couscous. While we waited, we sipped sangria. I was tempted to take out the pieces of orange, lime, and lemon with my fingers and suck on them, but my New England side counseled against it. Best to behave in a ladylike fashion on a first date.

Our dishes arrived in ceramic casserole pots with conical tops, also known as *tagines*. Inside, thick chunks of lamb nestled in a fragrant sauce side by side with apricots, golden raisins and almonds.

I dug into the stew. Soon, I was scraping the bottom of my casserole dish.

"I like the way you eat," Arnaud commented.

"What do you mean?" I tried not to blush. I had always been a good eater, especially when stimulated by both good food and company. Nothing ever put me off food.

"I mean you're not afraid to eat," he explained.

"It was delicious. Why would I be afraid to eat?"

"Some women just pick at lettuce leaves when they eat," Arnaud replied. "Or have one bite of something and that's it."

"I try doing that when I'm dieting, but it never works," I confessed.

No matter how much I wanted to give him the impression I was a larger, blonder version of Audrey Hepburn, it was as if I'd taken truth serum that evening. Authentic statements about my less-than-perfect self kept tumbling out of my mouth. Now, he knew I was both unsure of myself as a performer and possessed an appetite like a horse.

"Don't diet. You don't need to," he said with conviction.

Music to my ears. This man would light a candle to the Venus de Milo, not a stick-figure Giacometti. With deep contentment, I took a long sip of sangria. Then, I fished an orange slice out of my glass and sucked on it.

Despite my newfound pride in my hearty appetite, when the waiter came to ask about dessert, I declined, as did Arnaud. A minute later, the bill arrived, and I reached for my bag.

"My invitation," Arnaud grabbed my arm, pulling it back to the table.

"Thank you." I said, remembering my grandmother's advice to let a man pay if I wanted him to pursue me. He wouldn't be able to chase me if I met him halfway, would he? And I didn't want him to think he'd been relegated to buddy status. Au contraire.

"Let me take you somewhere I haven't been for a long time."

"Why haven't you been there in a long time?" I asked as we rose. My mind raced at the challenge of asking him questions as clearly and precisely formed as the ones he asked me.

"I wasn't with the right person."

Now, he was.

I took in his panther-like walk as we exited the restaurant. Like a hunter, his steps were silent, almost stealthy. I imagined him sneaking up on a woman in a dark alley, embracing her from behind. Trying not to allow my mind to wander down that alley, I failed gloriously.

We proceeded back to the boulevard and, after a few blocks turned down another side street even narrower than the one where the couscous restaurant was located. Ancient stone buildings leaned over the cobbled street, askew, their foundations warped with time. I was tantalized to think of the scenes they'd stood before over centuries. Could a European appreciate the awe struck in an American's imagination confronted by a building over five centuries old? For once, I felt lucky to be from the New World, so acutely appreciative of what the Old World offered.

Finally, Arnaud stopped before a hole-in-the-wall place with English lettering over the canopy. *Tequila Bar* was all it said.

Tequila was my downfall. Despite being a strong drinker, genetically pre-disposed on both the Hungarian and Anglo-Saxon side, I had to draw the line at tequila. It was the Mexican version of absinthe, the drink that proved the downfall of many French artists and intellectuals in the late nineteenth century. Both were spirits with hallucinogenic properties.

"Come on," Arnaud encouraged me.

"I don't do well with tequila," I demurred.

"Let's have one shot, then we'll go." He sounded less like a Frenchman by the second. I'd never met any French person who did tequila shots.

"How about if I just get some mineral water or a coffee?"

"One shot. That's all." This time, his voice was a whisper, his eyes veiled like storm clouds.

God knew how much more intriguing Arnaud de Saint Cyr would become after a shot of tequila found its way to the pit of my stomach.

Entering through silky, floor-to-ceiling curtains, we sat on the only two unoccupied stools at a miniscule bar. Exotic, trance-like music played from the P.A. system. Instead of overhead lighting, small lamps with fringed shades gave off a dim, golden glow. Arnaud had become Apollo at ease against the near-black backdrop of the room.

The bartender approached, and Arnaud held up two fingers. In a minute, two shot glasses appeared in front of us. The bartender filled them slowly with a clear liquid. Arnaud picked up his.

"Here's to what?"

The ball was in my court.

"Here's to secrets," I said.

"And?" He gazed into my eyes, his own clear, direct, intelligent.

"And?" I parried. I wanted to know what his 'and' was, since I already knew mine.

"Here's to uncovering them," he finished.

We touched glasses, and the tequila went down, raw and fiery, speeding our way toward the great unknown.

An hour later, we were outside, walking toward the cathedral of Notre Dame. Arnaud had been as good as his word, not pressing me to take a second shot. Instead, we'd had an espresso, accompanied by lots of water – neither had done anything to put out the fire lit deep in my stomach.

We turned into a side street off Notre Dame that I remembered from French classes at the Sorbonne. The classes had been held in a building on a narrow lane dating from the Middle Ages; now seemed a good time to wander down it again.

I walked ahead, keenly aware of his presence a few paces behind. He would be absorbing the ancientness of the thick-walled buildings on either side, the cobbled stones under our feet millions of souls had walked over through at least fifteen centuries. But his eyes would be on the hourglass curve of my body in the black and white dress. Unlike Eurydice, I was sure my Orpheus followed.

I slowed my pace, as the taps of his footsteps rang louder. *Warning, warning. Red code alert. Surrender is nigh.*

His hands closed upon my upper arms – his mouth on the back of my neck. Never before had I been kissed by a man for the first time from behind. I was electrified. His mouth sucked at my neck until I moaned.

A mouse in the talons of a hawk, I sank back into him. His arm came around the front of my neck as the other slid around my waist. I struggled to face him, but he held me in a vise-like grip.

Again I moaned, locked in his embrace. We were one of countless couples over the past fifteen hundred years who had passed down this ancient street. Heloise and Abelard had clung to each other here in the dead of an inky black summer night some eight hundred years earlier. Arnaud and I had become the couple under the bridge I'd stumbled across ten years earlier.

He turned me to him, his mouth meeting mine. His tasted warm and dry, his fresh virility cutting through any trace of tequila aftertaste. Beneath my fingers, tight sinewy cords marbled the broad expanse between his shoulder blades.

His hands slid down my shoulders and found their way to my waist. There, they squeezed me hard, then traced the outward swell of my hips and circled around to my back. The sharp intake of his breath told me he was mine, at least for the moment.

My hands were as fascinated to explore his torso as his were mine. I had never gotten this close to a man with both intelligence and an athlete's body. My tastes in men ran to the exotic, in direct contradiction to my desire for a close meeting of minds. Arnaud offered both.

The silent street shrouded us, muffling all but the pounding of our hearts – a bass accompaniment to our moans and sighs.

Finally, we broke apart, resuming our walk down the winding, narrow street, as if nothing had changed. But everything had.

At the end of the street, just before we stepped onto the large square in front of Notre Dame, Arnaud pinned me to the wall. With a hand to either side of my neck, he kissed me hard and then pulled at my lower lip with his teeth. I could feel it swell almost instantly. Henri and Marceline would know how our date had gone the minute they laid eyes on me.

Grabbing his longish, thick hair at the base of his neck, I pulled slowly. As his head went back, I slid my tongue along his well-defined jaw to his ear. Then, I nuzzled his earlobe.

He moaned.

Gently, I bit.

He moaned louder.

Releasing him, I stepped out onto the square into a beam of light from the streetlamp.

Finally, I saw his face. A wondrous expression shone on it. The thought that I had put it there empowered me.

"Want to walk down to the river?" he asked.

I nodded. Anywhere would be fine. The river divine.

In less than ten minutes, we were there. After midnight, the Seine took on a romance largely missing from its brownish-hued daytime aspect. We slipped down the steps of a massive stone staircase to the side of the black, shining water bathed in moonlight.

A reverence quieted our seething thoughts. I was enmeshed in a mid-summer night's dream with no desire to break the spell. Instead of walking hand in hand, we swung our arms until we came upon an empty bench, where Arnaud sat, pulling me onto his lap. I faced the river, mesmerized by the coolness of the breeze in contrast to the warmth of Arnaud's chest against my back. The night spoke to me.

"*Don't get too close,*" whispered the breeze from the Seine.

"*Guard your heart,*" the leaves on the tree above the bench rustled.

"*Less is more,*" the inky sky counseled overhead.

My desire was taking a different path with Arnaud than it had with other men. With him, I would need to retain my independence if I wanted to maintain power in whatever transpired between us. I leaned back against him, my eyes on the river, then the sky, until they closed in an ecstasy of sensation as his hands wandered up my torso, circling my breasts, then closing on them, squeezing hard.

Careful, Ava. Slow down, I told myself. Enmeshing my fingers in each of his, I brought one hand to my throat, the other to my thigh. His fingers were surprisingly fine, long, and well-shaped. There was something wild and savage about him that provoked me. His squeezes weren't gentle, they were shocking, as were his bites on my neck and lower lip.

I shivered. Something subversive simmered just below the surface of this man. I was dying to discover more. But I would have to play lion-tamer if I didn't wish to be eaten alive by whatever I found.

"Are you cold?" he asked, wrapping his arms tighter around me.

"No." I shook my head.

"What do you need?" he asked.

"Nothing."

"What do you want?"

A more interesting question.

"Everything," I replied. Might as well set up his expectations now. He would be both demanding and generous. I had not yet learned how to ask for what I wanted from a man. With him, I vowed I would.

He laughed softly. Then, his lips found a place behind my ear and under my hair. After his lips, his teeth.

"Ahh," I exhaled.

"*Ça te plaît?* That pleases you?"

"Yes." The lock of his hair still in my hand, I pulled hard. "Do you like that?"

"Yesss." His response came out like a hiss. In the Garden of Eden, we frolicked with the serpent. Would he hold it against me if I played tough with him? Yes, most likely. But there was no other way to play with Arnaud de Saint Cyr. If I didn't play tough, I'd be played. Or dangled and discarded. I'd dated good-looking, arrogant men before. It was much more complicated than dating average ones. One had to be meaner to them than one wished to be. Otherwise, they'd be mean to you. This one had the added advantage of being a Parisian. The only way to handle the situation was to dazzle him with my American freshness and charm. Coming from Manhattan increased my advantage times ten. I would work it.

Eons later, we rose from the bench and made our way back to Place de la Bastille. In random alleyways and at dark street corners, we took turns pushing each other up against walls, kissing deeply, then backing off without a word. It was as if we both understood perfectly the game we played.

As we approached Place de la Bastille, streaks of pale pink shot through the eastern sky. Delivery trucks rumbled past, and men in orange or royal blue workmen's uniforms appeared on the sidewalks. We stopped into a working-class café to toast the dawn with big cups of coffee with steamed milk. As we stood at the counter, I took pleasure in the discretion of the workmen, who barely glanced our way. Paris was a big, sophisticated city – just like New York or Tokyo. Some people began their day at five A.M. Others ended their evening of the night before. Paris was large enough to accommodate both, with no censure attached.

"Are you around this weekend?"

I nodded.

"I'll call you."

I sipped my coffee to hide my smile.

Leaving the café, we continued our walk up the Boulevard de la Bastille. It was light enough to read a newspaper by now, shops and cafés beginning to open here and there.

"You don't need to see me home," I told him as the metro entrance loomed into view.

"Are you sure?"

"Yes. Go home and get some sleep."

"I'll call you this evening," he said.

My eyes slit into cat eyes as I nodded then turned homeward. I didn't doubt him for an instant.

At my door, I let myself in as quietly as a jewel thief, then fell into bed. It was shortly after noon when I awakened. Marceline and Henri had already gone out.

The day passed in a blur. Mid-afternoon, Marceline returned in an exceptional mood, unloading packages of baby equipment in the living room, ordering Henri to assemble various items. Around seven that evening, the phone rang. Marceline's eyes passed over my still bee-stung lips as she handed me the receiver.

"How're you feeling?" Arnaud's voice was low, intimate.

"I'm great. How was your day?"

"It just got started. Do you want to get together this evening?"

Heat flooded through me at his suggestion. I did, but I didn't. I didn't know him well enough to proceed so quickly.

"I can't. I've got plans." I had none, other than a master plan to keep Arnaud on the hook, and not reel it in too fast. It would end in disaster if I did. I'd known that sort of thing since fifth grade on, not that I'd always been good at it.

"Are you free tomorrow evening?"

"What do you have in mind?" Yes, yes, and yes, but it never hurt to make a guy work.

"Dining outdoors on as many oysters as you can eat."

"Washed down with?"

"Pinot Gris. Or a good Sauvignon Blanc."

"Umm. I'm tempted." Oysters, an aphrodisiac. Was I ready for this?

"And the answer is?"

"*Pourquoi pas, Monsieur?*"

"*Très bien, Mademoiselle.* I'll pick you up at seven. What's your address?"

"Why don't we meet at café de la Bastille again?"

"Not ready for me to meet your family yet?"

"Uhh – not ready to reveal you to my friends. You'd overwhelm them."

His laugh was hearty. "I do that, I know. Am I overwhelming you?"

"No. At least, not yet."

"Do you want to be overwhelmed?" Another good question.

"I want to be heard." Somehow I'd managed to retain a thimbleful of self-possession in the face of Arnaud's crackling male spirit.

"Of course you do. You're a performer. You want someone to hear what you have to say."

"Sometimes overwhelming personalities don't hear quieter melodies." I didn't mean to worry, but would a man with such an outsized personality drown out everything and everyone around him?

"I do when they're sung by Rhine maidens from New York."

"*Très bien, Monsieur.*" No answer could have pleased me more.

We got off the phone, and I went to bed, imagining myself a Lorelei combing her hair on a rock in the river on a moonlit night. Poseidon would come along and pull me into the water with him. We would frolic, swim, and do other things.

Lots of other things.

CHAPTER ELEVEN

Huitres à Volonté (All-You-Can-Eat Oysters)

Huitres à volonté, or as many oysters as you can eat, washed down with Sancerre, a dry white wine made from the Sauvignon Blanc grape from France's Loire Valley, was one of my favorite summertime meals in Paris. It was all protein and booze – two of my favorite food groups.

I'd changed over the past ten years. Smoked salmon, pâté, deviled eggs, and other savory delicacies had taken the place of pastries in my heart. My new food choices didn't lead me down the road of overindulgence. I was learning to eat like a French person – well, but in small quantities.

A breeze rustled our hair as Arnaud and I stood on the sidewalk outside Café de la Bastille. Sunday evening had arrived, seemingly a split second after we'd parted early Saturday morning.

"Do you like oysters?" Arnaud asked, kissing me carefully once on each cheek. He stared at my mouth as if reminding me not to forget where else we'd recently kissed.

"I like all seafood. My family's from Maine," I told him. Oysters didn't come from Maine, but eating all types of shellfish was practically a requirement for living there. You weren't a true Down Easter if you didn't.

"From Maine? Is that where your Mayflower ancestors ended up?"

I nodded. I'd told him a bit about my mother's side of the family over dinner two nights earlier. He seemed to know a lot about American culture. I'd bet he'd spent time there, but I wasn't going to ask. It interested me more to let Arnaud set the pace for revealing himself to me. "What do you eat them with?" I asked.

"Lemon juice. That's it."

"Sounds delicious." Nothing could resemble a classic WASP summer dish more – something simple that required minimal fuss, other than shucking the oysters out of their shells, which someone else would do.

"I want to watch you eat oysters," he said, setting off butterflies in my stomach.

"Then *Allons-y*. Let's go," I replied, making a note to eat oysters the way Catherine Deneuve would, not like a girl from New England.

We made our way to the seafood restaurant and sat outside. Arnaud ordered a bottle of Gerard Boulay Sancerre Chavignol, commanding the waiter's instant respect. His deference gave me pause. It occurred to me Arnaud was *bien-élevé*, well raised. With a last name that included a "de," was he well born or as the French put it, *de bonne famille?* While I ruminated I watched the small, dark man shucking oysters at a station tucked under the restaurant terrace's dark green and white canopy.

In a minute, our plates arrived. I sampled my first oyster, followed by a sip of light, crisp Sancerre. Heaven. Not for the first time, I applauded the French obsession with correct food and drink combinations.

"I'd like to ask you something," Arnaud said, his expression serious.

"What?" My spine tingled.

"I'm going to my country house next weekend. Would you join me?"

I felt my eyes widen, his gaze dissolving my will to say anything but yes. *Yes, yes, and yes.* I just couldn't bring myself to say it aloud. Finally, I spoke.

"I'll have to think about it," the Queen of Cool responded.

Not.

Sweat pooled under my arms as I considered the ramifications of an overnight stay with Arnaud.

"You do that."

I smiled. What a sexy guy. Then, a practical thought jumped into my brain. The first one I'd had in a week, since the Sunday evening before when we'd met.

"But I have my gig next weekend," I told him.

"Which day?"

"Friday night."

"No problem. I'll pick you up around ten Saturday morning. It's about a two and a half-hour drive," he explained. "We'll return Sunday evening."

I nodded, mute. It was a lot to think about.

After three plates of oysters, I'd had my fill. When the check came, Arnaud paid. I didn't try to chip in this time. We rose from our seats, and as we made our way to the sidewalk, he took my arm.

"Are you happy?" I asked, nestling into his side.

For a response, he backed me into the wall at the corner of Boul' Saint Michel and a small side street and kissed me hard.

I rested my forearms on each of his shoulders to steady myself. Thoughts of the coming weekend swirled in my head.

"What about you?" His voice was muffled by my neck, which he was tasting.

"Yes." The smell of his sweat intoxicated me. It was pungent – worthy of a Frenchman, undisguised by any grooming products.

"Would you like to come to my place for a *digestif?*" he asked.

"I would, but not tonight."

"And why not tonight, *chère* Mademoiselle?"

"Because it is too soon, and I know too little about you, *cher Monsieur*," I shot back, my head trumping my heart.

"Shall we walk then?" His eyes flickered with either disappointment or approval, I couldn't tell which.

"*Avec plaisir*. With pleasure."

We strolled slowly back to my neighborhood, the lights from Bastille's nightspots twinkling up ahead. As we approached, the streetlamp outlined a woman coming toward us, her walk unhurried, swaying. She looked to be in her forties – her face remote, mysterious. Arnaud's eyes followed her, then flickered back to me. Annoyed with myself for noticing, I pretended not to care. It was France, after all. I could hardly expect a heterosexual Frenchman not to notice another female. It was a national pastime.

In another minute, we were outside Henri and Marceline's apartment building.

"Goodnight," I said simply, turning to him.

"I'll see you Friday evening at your 'gig' as you call it." He pronounced it 'geeg', making me giggle.

"My geeg?" My what? Wasn't a gigue some sort of ancient French dance from pre-Revolutionary days?

"Your performance."

Mon Dieu. I'd forgotten all about my gig. The reason I'd come to Paris.

"Oh sure," I recovered myself. "Do you know where it is?"

"Yes. We passed the street on our way here, *non?*"

"Yes." Had he known The Blue Cactus was on the Rue de Lappe, a side street off Rue de la Roquette? He must have done some research over the past week since we first met.

"Your photo in the window there looks nothing like you," he said with a low chuckle.

"I know," I agreed ruefully. Show business had its ridiculous side.

"You are more beautiful in person, but I liked your beeg hair in the photo," he remarked, embracing me.

"Thank you," I whispered back, at a loss to respond. We were in the same boat, betwixt and between the real me and the show-biz me. The man holding me apparently liked both.

"Until Friday then." His eyes seared me. This time, he was first to turn, walking quickly away.

I ran upstairs, anticipation wrapped around me like fairy wings.

Around four on Thursday afternoon, Henri and I went over to The Blue Cactus for a final run-through before my opening performance the following evening. The owner had assured Henri the night manager would be there to turn on the P.A. system and perform a sound check. Instead, no one was about, other than the cleaning staff and a bartender setting up for the evening – who didn't know anything about the sound system. Henri got the night manager's telephone number from him and called.

Something had come up. The night manager couldn't get there until after the restaurant opened for business, too late to do a sound check. He assured Henri he would be on site the following evening to help me set up. Henri got off and reassured me heartily that there was no problem.

The sloppy preparation didn't please me. I knew all too well what happened when musicians relying on electronic equipment performed in a new venue.

Two years earlier I'd had a New Years' Eve gig at a Chinese restaurant in Glen Cove, Long Island, a wealthy town on Long Island's north shore, not far from Queens. I'd gotten there at eight, set up my DX-7 synthesizer, drum machine, and reverb unit, ran through everything, and satisfied myself the sound was good. The food and beverage manager let me know that they didn't care what I played as long as I broke into *Auld Lang Syne* at the stroke of midnight. It was standard procedure for a New Years' Eve performance, the highest paying gig of the year for most musicians.

The first three sets passed uneventfully. Then, just before the stroke of midnight, after an uproarious countdown with the crowd going wild, someone on the restaurant staff hit the circuit breaker to turn out all the lights for dramatic effect, then on again the second the new year was rung in.

The effect on my synthesizer was devastating. Cutting the power mid-program meant it needed to be reset again. The process took several minutes, similar to a computer booting up. As I fiddled with the instrument panel, several hundred impatient guests all stared at me expectantly.

"Play *Auld Lang Syne*," an impatient voice shouted out.

"Hit the music," another seconded. The energy of the crowd turning against me was as palpable as a wave.

The food and beverage manager came over and hissed at me to launch into *Auld Lang Syne* immediately as discussed. His frown told me he wasn't happy.

Desperately, I fiddled with my equipment until it had warmed up and was functioning again. By the time I launched into the opening bars of *Auld Lang Syne*, it was too late. The momentum was gone, and the crowd angry. In show business, timing is everything, and mine had failed. Never mind the reason. When a performer screws up, it's always his or her fault.

I crept out of the restaurant the minute my gig ended at one A.M. No one asked for an encore. Unsmiling, the manager handed me an envelope containing the exact amount contracted for the evening. No bonus was included, even though a large tip was customary for a New Year's Eve gig. I was never asked to play there again.

Something similar could happen at The Blue Cactus Friday evening. But I didn't really care. If my performance was a smash success, Henri would negotiate to increase the number of weekly performances and extend my engagement beyond the end of August. Then, I'd be stuck with him managing my career over the next few months. What I really wanted to do was get away from him and Marceline, leaving them to have their baby in peace without a stranger in their household. A stranger Henri was drawing sketches of without clothes on. Ugh.

"Let's decide what you're going to wear when we get back," Henri said on the way back to the apartment.

"I've already decided."

"The dress with the cut-outs?"

"No, another one, I said curtly. "Trust me – it'll be perfect." There was no way I was giving Henri a sneak preview.

"Why don't I take a look at it?" he pressed.

"Non. C'est déjà decidé et c'est ça, It's decided already and that's that," I parroted a line I'd heard Marceline use, in exactly her tone of voice.

He turned on the car radio. I'd won my point.

I no longer wished to cultivate a following, encouraging adoring fans to fall in love with the woman they saw on stage. Instead, I wanted to discover the real Arnaud de Saint Cyr and have him discover me. Privately.

The next day, I dressed for my performance. More accurately, I dressed for Arnaud, who'd said he'd be there. The black and white dress I'd worn for our first evening together would do the trick.

To go the extra kilowatt show business distance, I added a black and white turban I had picked up in Manhattan's East Village that made me look like a cross between Carmen Miranda and Josephine Baker. The effect was edgy, downtown. Using black eyeliner, I drew upward curves at the corners of my eyelids to emphasize the slight slant of my Hungarian eyes, passed down from Attila the Hun and his crew when they'd arrived in Europe from the Central Asian steppes some twelve hundred years earlier.

Henri's eyes widened, when I came into the kitchen, but he said nothing. We went downstairs, where he loaded my synthesizer into his Citroën, then drove the five minutes to the restaurant.

The night manager hadn't yet arrived. With no one to help me sync my synthesizer to the sound system, I asked Henri, sitting near one speaker, if the reverb was on.

"What do you mean, 'reverb'?" he asked back.

"You know – the delay, the echo," I explained.

"The delay?" he repeated, shrugging his shoulders.

I didn't have my French dictionary with me.

"Never mind," I snapped, fed up not only with him, the missing night manager, but the entire live entertainment business in general. There was no way I could check what my voice sounded like from the P.A. system at the same time as sing into the microphone. That was the whole point of having a house sound engineer available. "Just tell the night manager when he finally shows up to check my reverb levels. Got it?"

"Sure, sure." Henri nodded.

He had no idea what I was talking about, which pissed me off *in extremis.*

I began on the dot at eight P.M. Years of experience with hotel and restaurant gigs had taught me management cared about one point above all else – starting on time. Talent, choice of repertoire, musicianship – all were entirely secondary to whether the band began on time. If they did, they were professionals. If they didn't, they were soon unemployed.

The first set I played mostly swing, with some bossa nova tunes thrown in. I loved singing in Portuguese, the sexiest language in the world. Singing bossa nova was like singing in the kitchen while mopping the floor wearing a black and white French maid's outfit. Astrud Gilberto had gotten started that way, minus the maid's uniform. She'd been humming one of her husband Gil's tunes in the kitchen when he'd walked in and realized he'd found the singer who'd make him famous.

Speculating on Astrud's royalty percentage from her first album, I executed a long instrumental riff on *Wave.* No one applauded at the end.

It was just like being back in New York. I could put out a tip jar, but what would be the point? The custom of tipping was almost nonexistent in France.

Satisfied with my version of *Wave*, I launched into the theme from the Brazilian movie *Black Orpheus*. It was a wistful, sensual tune. Playful yet poignant, a combination the French adored, if their movies or pop songs were anything to go by.

I sang as if I was Kit Moresby trapped in a harem in the middle of the desert in Paul Bowles's *The Sheltering Sky*, one of my favorite novels. My delivery was breathy, intimate. No one paid the slightest attention. The crowd dining, drinking, and chatting before me had not yet recognized my genius.

Finally, a sole pair of hands began to clap, followed by several others. I peered out, but was blinded by the bright stage lights trained on the elevated platform I was on.

Next, I chose a French tune, *La Vie En Rose*. Edith Piaf had made it famous. I couldn't sing like her, all four feet ten inches of nasal cockiness, so I sang it my own way. I hoped the audience would find my American accent exotic, much the same way I enjoyed hearing French or Brazilian singers cover an English pop tune back in New York. Satisfied with my arrangement, more of a dance tune than Piaf's version, I ended dramatically, cutting the drum machine off with my foot pedal at the final moment. In New York, this usually elicited a round of applause. Not here.

For a moment, there was only the background hum of diners talking. Then again, a sole set of hands began to applaud. A few more joined in, all from the same direction. It was break time.

Henri was nowhere to be found, as I moved off the platform. Had Marceline called to say her water had broken or her contractions had started? So much for getting feedback on the sound mix of keyboards, drum machine, and microphone. It was the usual not-yet-discovered musician's story: no one around to help, no one paying any attention, drinks flowing, a steady source of income not flowing.

"Ava, you were great,"

Arnaud 's voice floated alongside me. I hadn't seen him come in. My eyes adjusted to the darker lighting of the room, as I turned in his direction.

He smiled, his eyes boring into mine.

"You're the only one listening, but thanks," I laughed, relieved to see him. In the dim light, his eyes looked gray, mystical. They seemed less crystalline, more limpid tonight. I wanted to swim in them.

He motioned me over.

I followed him to his table and sat, breathing in his faint male scent.

"I liked your version of *Black Orpheus*," Arnaud commented.

"You're the only one," I observed dryly, but pleased nevertheless. At least, he'd recognized the tune.

"Am I?" he asked, lowering his voice.

"What do you mean?" There I was playing catch-up again in response to Arnaud's lightning fast conversational turns.

"Am I the only one?" he whispered.

I tried to think of a response as light and teasing as a kitten's cuff. Finally, I had it.

"It's a secret," I purred.

"I like secrets," he murmured back.

The next two sets flew by in a dream. At some point, Henri turned up at the bar, giving me a thumbs-up while sipping yet another miniscule cocktail. He hadn't bothered to approach me even once to let me know how the sound mix was.

I was tired of him, tired of gigs in dive restaurants or even nice ones, and tired of inattentive audiences and absent sound engineers. Maybe if I'd been a knockout performer, belting out hit after hit, I wouldn't feel this way. But I wasn't.

I was an Astrud Gilberto-type of performer, humming a whispery bossa nova tune in her kitchen, cooking for her man. Okay, that was going a bit far, but I could definitely see myself singing quietly while arranging flowers in a high-ceilinged apartment with ornate moldings shared with Arnaud in a fashionable Parisian neighborhood. I'd be warming up my voice while waiting for my driver to whisk me away to the recording studio, where I'd lay down a few vocal tracks for my latest album. Later that day, I'd dine with my manager and Arnaud at some completely 'in' restaurant where we'd go over choices for my debut album cover design and discuss marketing strategies for making me world-famous. Then, Arnaud and I would go home and make wild love in our canopied Louis XIV-style bed.

While I fantasized, I played instrumental improvisations on some of my favorite tunes. I riffed on *My Favorite Things* from *The Sound of Music*. Then, I went for a long keyboard journey and back with Paul Desmond's *Take Five*. I switched back to singing after it became apparent no one was noticing my fancy finger work, other than Arnaud, who faithfully clapped after each piece. For my final number, I covered *Black Velvet* by Alannah Myles, growling my way through the smoky blues number, a red-hot hit back home that past spring. No reaction from the audience at all. Apparently, it hadn't made the French pop charts.

Finally, it was over. Making my way off stage, Arnaud grabbed my arm as I passed by his table.

"Can you come with me now?" he whispered.

"Don't you need to get some sleep before you pick me up tomorrow?" I asked.

"No. Do you?"

"I need to unwind a bit, then sleep." There was no way a performer ever went home and straight to bed after a gig. It took at least a few hours to wind down after any live performance.

"I'll walk you home then."

I nodded. "Just give me a few minutes. I need to talk to my manager." I gestured toward Henri at the bar then walked over to him.

"Ava, great performance! You were a star," he congratulated me.

Underneath the big smile, I could see his rueful look. At least, he could help me pack up and take my equipment back to his place so I could be alone with Arnaud as soon as possible. The post-mortem on my less-than-stellar opening night could wait until the following day. All I could think about was getting out of there.

In less than ten minutes, we'd disassembled my synthesizer, drum machine and microphone. Henri lifted the heavy synthesizer case, and I followed with the smaller items, through the kitchen, out the service entrance of the restaurant to the sidewalk. The neighborhood of Bastille was in full swing, streets full, the July night balmy and mild.

"I'll get the car. Stay here," Henri said.

I nodded, too fed up to respond. To my knowledge, neither the night manager nor the owner had even shown up to take in my performance. I'd spent the past three months preparing for my Parisian performing debut, and it had gone over like a lead balloon. Fortunately, Henri had arranged six guaranteed bookings for Friday evenings through the end of August. After that, my future would no longer be so clearly laid out in front of me.

"Hey, I didn't feel like waiting for you in there. Can I help you with your equipment?" Arnaud came up beside me, the finger of his hand tracing a path down the outside of mine. I shivered. That was it. The future wasn't ahead. It had snuck up on me from behind.

"My manager's bringing his car around. Just help me get my gear in it, and we can take off." My eyes met his, my mood leaping as I threw off the dark shroud of post-performance letdown. *Je m'en fous*, I could care less, I told myself.

The sound of Henri's car announced his arrival.

He eyeballed Arnaud, as he stepped out and hurried to open the trunk.

"Henri, this is Arnaud de Saint Cyr," I introduced them. *No longer my future, meet my future.* "Arnaud, this is Henri Zidane."

"*Bon soir.*" Henri's eyes widened, as he shook hands with Arnaud. I wondered why.

"*Bon soir,*" Arnaud greeted him, just a tad formally. God only knew what socio-economic judgments were now being passed. Two Parisians from dissimilar backgrounds meeting for the first time almost guaranteed negative speculation. After a curt glance, Arnaud lifted the heavy synthesizer and swung it in the trunk.

Henri took the rest of the equipment from my arms.

"Henri, I'm going out with Arnaud now. Do you mind bringing the synthesizer upstairs when you bring it back? The rest of the stuff can wait," I said commandingly.

"*Bien sûr,* of course," Henri replied, looking a bit surprised at my sudden self-assurance. Usually, it was him calling the shots. But now, an unknown Frenchman with an aristocratic name was at my side. He and Marceline had been fielding calls from Arnaud for the past ten days and I'd stayed out all night for two of them. Marceline would be thrilled to see her husband return without me. For my part, I couldn't wait to get out of Henri and Marceline's life as soon as possible. My disappearance would be the best baby gift I could give Marceline.

As he got in the car and drove off, I turned to Arnaud.

"Hey." At last, we were alone.

"Hey," he mimicked my American accent. One hand came up on my back, touching my shoulder blade just above the low back of my dress.

"How are you?" he asked gently.

"Happy it's over."

"Your geeg?"

"Yes." Thank God, my gig was behind me. It hadn't gone the way I'd wanted. But instead of being let down, I was on fire at the thought of the weekend ahead. Arm in arm, we walked away from The Blue Cactus toward the sights and sounds of Bastille, still going strong at one in the morning. Life beckoned, and I rushed toward it.

෬

The next morning, Arnaud's car pulled up to the curb outside Henri and Marceline's flat at twenty past ten. I was already down on the sidewalk waiting. I hadn't yet told him I was staying with my manager and his wife. He would find out if he needed to, but, for the moment, it was a good exercise for me to match him in studied vagueness. I admired people who knew how to hold back. It was something I wanted to learn to do better. Princess Caroline of Monaco had once said "Never complain, never explain," in a *Hello* magazine interview. I'd later discovered the quote was attributable to Benjamin Disraeli, the nineteenth century British prime minister. I wasn't good at either side of that equation. But her advice was right up there with "fake it till you make it."

Sliding into the seat as Arnaud held open the passenger door of his Peugeot, I vowed to keep both maxims in mind that weekend.

CHAPTER TWELVE

La France Profonde

"*Ça va, ma belle?* How are you, my beauty?" Arnaud asked, as he gunned the car away from the sidewalk, at the same time popping some music into the stereo system. "*Tu as bien dormi?* Have you slept well?"

"*Oui, j'ai bien dormi,* yes I slept well," I replied, looking out the window to hide my blush. If only he knew what thoughts had lulled me to sleep – perhaps the same ones he'd had.

"*T'as la pêche?*" he continued.

"*Uh ... c'est quoi, ca?* What's that?" He'd either asked me if I had the peach or if I was a peach. I hoped the whole weekend wouldn't go like this. He had home court advantage so I needed to come up with some other sort of advantage fast. Being female and not yet bedded by him seemed a strong one. After the bedding part, I intended to hold an even stronger position, although I wasn't sure how. I counted on my inner goddess to advise me.

"It means, "are you feeling peachy today? In good spirits?"" he explained.

"Ahh. Yes. In fact, I am." He'd gotten that right. "And you?"

"*Mais oui. Certainement.*" He accelerated as if to prove his point. His pale pink polo shirt accentuated the gold of his skin and set off the auburn highlights in his hair. I longed to reach over and touch him. Instead, I touched the base of my throat as I rested my elbow on the armrest.

He glanced at me, saying nothing. This was a good sort of game to play to equalize the playing field. I'd touch whatever part of my body I wanted him to touch, he'd notice, and when the right moment came, *voilà,* his hand would replace mine. Our two-and-a-half hour drive would be the appetizer to the feast that awaited when we arrived. And who cared if we ate anything, although this being France, I knew we would both eat something and care about what we ate.

Once we got on the *autoroute,* I relaxed. We traveled south, on the A6 *Autoroute du Soleil* or Highway of the Sun. Even the name sounded promising.

"Where are we headed?" I asked.

"To the Loire Valley."

"Where the chateaus are?" The enormous chateaus of the Loire Valley built for various kings, queens and kings' mistresses were France's most magnificent.

"Not my family's village, but yes, some well-known chateaus are nearby. Have you been there?"

"No."

When it came to my knowledge of France, I was a big-city girl. Outside of Paris, except for Nice and Pascal's largely forgettable suburb of Saint Denis, I was a total neophyte to French regions, *un zero* as the French say, like a born and bred Manhattanite, completely out of one's element the moment one crossed the bridge or tunnel to New Jersey, the Bronx, or Long Island.

"Are we going to where you grew up?" I asked.

"For part of my childhood, yes." He shrugged.

"And for the other part?"

"In another place." He waved one hand as if to say it wasn't important. Cryptic.

"Arnaud, what is it you do for a living?" I bit the bullet and went all American on him.

"A little of this, a little of that." Another Gallic shrug.

"Yes, but what do you do for a job? To *gagner la vie,* I think you say."

"Ahh. That."

"Yes. That." I was contemplating sleeping with this man in a matter of hours. It was time to find out how he made his money.

"I'm a journalist."

"A journalist? How interesting." My father had been a journalist when he wasn't writing poems – a penniless one. "What kind of journalist are you? Do you write a column or are you a reporter?"

"I'm a traveling journalist."

"Do you mean you write travel articles?"

"I mean, I travel for my job."

"Do you mean you're a foreign correspondent?"

He nodded, eyes straight ahead on the road.

A faint alarm went off inside. How frequently did he travel? And to where? My head began to spin with questions. How available was he for a relationship? *Pull back, woman. Foot on the brake.*

"Ava, let's be here now," he said, as if reading my thoughts. He reached over and took my left hand in my lap. Stroking each finger, the tips of his own tickled mine like a feather.

I pulled my hand away, smoothing back my hair. When I put it down, he took it again.

Maybe he was right, just be here now. I was a twenty-nine year old American woman driving to chateau country in France with an attractive, intelligent, single Frenchman. What was the problem?

The green countryside hurtled by, the evanescent music of the Cocteau Twins moving our thoughts to delicate, fairy-like terrain. Arnaud was the only man I'd ever spent time with who had the Cocteau Twins in his music collection. They were one of my favorite groups, a Scottish trio who made more or less transcendental pop music.

We were now in *la France profonde* or deep France, the appellation given to the French countryside by French city-dwellers – above all, Parisians. At Cosne-Cours-Sur-Loire, we turned off the auto route and onto a country road. Arnaud visibly relaxed as we wound our way through pastureland where fat cows and skinny goats grazed. We passed through tiny, ancient villages, where buildings stood so close to the narrow street you could almost reach out the car window and touch the walls. Finally, a sign announced we'd arrived in Chavignol, which Arnaud explained produced a famous goat cheese, as well as some of the finest Sancerre wines of the region.

Shortly beyond the village, which we passed through in less than thirty seconds, we turned off the road and drove slowly down a long driveway lined on both sides by tall, lushly-topped trees. They looked like a welcoming committee of household staff lined up to greet us. Scenes from *Barry Lyndon* or *Brideshead Revisited* danced through my head. After about half a mile, we pulled up to a long, low stone farmhouse with faded blue-shuttered windows, instantly snuffing out my reverie. It was charming but rustic, with the accent on rustic. Quickly adjusting expectations, I sprang out of the car and looked for signs of staff or at least livestock that might come greet us. None were about.

Arnaud took my arm and led me up crumbling stone steps to the front door, where he fumbled around in the eave over the doorframe. After locating an enormous iron key, he opened the door.

Inside, it was cool. The smell of dried herbs with a faint musty undertone informed me no one had been there for some time.

"Let me show you around," Arnaud said, taking my arm again.

The large living room featured an enormous stone fireplace. We continued on into a big kitchen with a long wooden table in the middle and then toured two smallish bedrooms, each containing a twin-sized wrought-iron framed bed. Next, he pointed out the bathroom and water closet, separate in European fashion. Finally, there was only one room left to explore – the master bedroom.

It was large, with three sets of vertical French windows on two adjoining walls. Sunlight and warmth flooded into the room. I crossed to the closest window to take in the view of the countryside – breathtaking. Across the road below, a small path wound its way over a meadow down to a village. Goats dotted the landscape.

"That's Chavignol," he said. "We'll go there in a few minutes to do some shopping."

A queen-sized bed stood against the wall opposite the windows, four wrought-iron posts at each corner. The bed linens were white, the pillows nicely plumped. Quickly, I looked away.

While Arnaud attended to details of opening the house, I returned to the living room. Very few personal items adorned its walls or tables. Among the few, a small black and white photo of an older woman hung on the wall near the stone fireplace. In her late forties perhaps, I guessed it might be Arnaud's mother in younger years, although I didn't see a family resemblance. The woman's face was smooth but with sharp features; the eyes looked mischievous, the mouth petulant. She was beautiful, in a difficult sort of way.

"Let's go to the village," Arnaud called from the doorway. "The *boulangerie* closes early on Saturdays, so let's get there before it shuts." He held a large wicker basket, the kind Frenchwomen typically take to market with them.

"Is that your mother in the photo?" I asked as I brushed past him out the door.

"What photo?'

"The one on the wall in the living room. Near the fireplace."

Arnaud looked puzzled for a moment.

"*Ahh, non.* Not my mother. Here's a basket for you, too, *Minou.*" He handed me a second wicker basket that he unhooked from under the eaves next to the back door.

"Then who is it?"

"Who's what?"

"Who's the woman in the picture?" I insisted, incapable of sticking to my resolve not to play the nosy American.

"She was my mentor."

"Your what?"

"My guide."

"What does that mean?"

"*Cheri,*" He turned to me, putting a finger on my lips. "It means what I said."

What *had* he meant? No way would I ask if she was a former lover. I filed his words for future reference.

On the way down to the village, we stopped as a large herd of goats crossed the road.

"The goat cheese here, *Crottin de Chavignol,* is known all over France. It's been made here since the sixteenth century from goats like those," Arnaud said, as we watched the slender, white animals amble across the road.

"Will I like it?" I asked playfully.

"It's sort of nutty."

"Like you?" I didn't actually think he was nutty, so much as wickedly articulate and just a bit outrageous.

"Like me," he agreed. Then, he leaned over and kissed me on the mouth.

As I tasted his salty pungency, I was overcome by the thought that delicacies like goat cheese made since the sixteenth century had gone into creating the man kissing me. I loved the whole idea of it. *Careful, girl.*

He kissed me again, this time harder.

Dizzy, I pulled back, turning to look out the window. It would be unwise to get involved with a man who worked as a foreign correspondent, almost as foolish as falling for a foreign intelligence agent. Who knew, maybe he was both?

I would enjoy the countryside and the introduction to exotic, smelly cheeses, but I would keep my emotions in check, I told myself.

After the next kiss, I felt faint. Perhaps it was the heat. Probably not.

When the last goat passed, we continued on to the ancient village of Chavignol.

In a minute, we were there and had parked. As we walked toward the shops, the cobblestoned street affirmed my choice of flat sandals. My kitten-heeled Parisian ones would remain in my weekend bag.

In the bakery, Arnaud asked for a baguette, two croissants and two *pains chocolats* then suggested I pick out some small cakes for dessert that evening. As I examined the rows of artisanally decorated madeleines, macaroons, creamy Bretons, polonaises, montblancs, baba au rhums, and other individually-sized cakes, my mind flashed back to au pair days, when I'd been addicted to the pastries that had lain in wait for me all over Paris.

This time, they weren't calling to me at all, lined up like overdressed courtiers at Louis XIV's palace. I looked at them indifferently and realized I'd changed. Some sort of quiet revolution had taken place inside me over the past ten years, since I'd first come to France. Finally, I was beginning to think like a Frenchwoman.

"Let's skip the cakes and have that Chavignol cheese for dessert. Maybe with some fruit," I heard myself say. Change had come. I was surprising even myself on the threshold of my thirtieth year.

"*Avec des figues.* With figs then," he agreed, paying for our purchases then heading out the door.

Figs and goat cheese had replaced chocolate cream and *mille feuilles-*layered, buttery pastries in my heart. I'd entered then exited a French bakery without losing self-control. My elation knew no bounds. Change, even transformation, was indeed possible. I had arrived.

Next, we visited the *fromagerie*, where rows of small rounds of *Crottin de Chavignol* were laid out. They were sold by age, the older cheeses dotted with blue mold – the kind an American would return to the store for a full refund but a Frenchman would pay extra for. I laughed, explaining what an American reaction might be to the mold-covered cheeses.

"*À chacun son goût*, to each his own taste," Arnaud replied diplomatically, echoing Jean-Michel's words almost a decade earlier. He might have said, "What do Americans know?" but didn't. Bravo.

He picked out two rounds, one aged and covered in blue bumps, the other young. "*Une femme jeune, une femme mûre*," he whispered to me as the clerk wrapped them up.

"What did you say?" I asked once we were out on the sidewalk.

"I said 'a young woman and a ripe one'."

"What's a ripe one?" I asked.

"*Une femme d'un certain âge*, a woman of a certain age, maybe forty-five, fifty, who is still beautiful and likes to make love," he explained.

"And which is better?" I was slightly jolted to hear how smoothly he'd explained himself. I could just see him on assignment, holed up in a hotel bar with a beautiful local woman. Whatever her age, his suave lines would cover all bases.

"*À chacun son goût*, to each his own taste," he repeated.

"And what is yours?" I pressed.

"*Ça depend, Minou*." The French endearment was a variation of *minouche*, Jean-Michel's nickname for me. It meant little cat. Like a caress, it landed on my ears pleasingly. "It depends on the moment. Whichever one is in front of me I suppose."

It wasn't the answer I wanted to hear, but it was one worthy of a Frenchman, not to mention a foreign correspondent. I would have to take the good with the bad. There was no way I was going to meet a man here with the style of a Frenchman combined with the character of John-Boy Walton from my favorite TV show of the 1970s. John-Boy, played by Richard Thomas, had been my kind of all-American male – sensitive and seemingly forever faithful. Frenchmen and forever faithful didn't seem to go together. I didn't want to typecast, but a complaint I heard often from women I met in Paris was that French men cheated. It was well known. They had different tastes for different occasions in all sorts of categories

– cheeses, wines, before-dinner drinks, after-dinner drinks, desserts – why not women as well?

We picked up some paper thin slices of veal at the butcher, two bottles of red wine at the supermarket, as well as water, yogurt, capers, and a few household items. On our way back to the car, we stopped at a café where we sipped espressos and watched stylish, relaxed people watch us – a French national pastime. Despite only two hundred inhabitants, Chavignol enjoyed a considerable tourist presence in mid-July, so there were plenty of passersby to observe. Finally, we stopped at a fruit stand, where we bought a box of fresh figs and a melon, then headed to the car.

We took the long way back. Arnaud drove to Sancerre at the top of the hill at which Chavignol lay at the base. Famous for its wines, we stopped in at a winery and enjoyed a glass of crisp, light Sancerre le Chene Lucien Crochet, as we watched the sun begin its descent behind the Chateau de Sancerre, which Arnaud explained was a medieval castle rebuilt in 1874 in the style of Louis XII.

A re-enactment of medieval castle life took place daily just before sunset. We watched as three couples in period costume joined in a courtly dance. A mock jousting match for the men followed. Then it was the ladies' turn. Dancing a scarf dance, the women laughed and flirted with the audience with coquettish skill, apparently honed by the lack of much else to do for the well-born denizens of medieval court life.

Arnaud watched intently as the oldest of the three ladies pulled a green scarf slowly across the lower half of her face, hiding her mouth. Her eyes danced as they slithered across Arnaud's face. Quietly, I noted his reaction. As if hypnotized, he stood like a stone, returning her stare.

Trouble. Apparently, I wasn't the only female capable of hypnotizing the man next to me. I shifted uncomfortably, quelling my American desire to be the only woman in Arnaud's viewfinder.

In another minute, the performance ended, the actors disappeared, and all eyes turned to the sun setting behind the castle ramparts.

At the moment the sun slid below the horizon, we kissed – the woman with the green scarf forgotten. The evening at Arnaud's country house awaited us. We zipped home, past goat herders returning with their flocks, bells attached to the goats' necks. The tinkling sound they made urged us on to the day's denouement.

In thirty minutes, we were back. Here's where once again a French date departs ways from an American one. An American man takes a woman out to dinner on a date. A French man prepares dinner for her. *Vive la différence.*

As Arnaud cooked, I wandered around the gardens of the low, stone farmhouse, snipping flowers for the table. In a while, heavenly smells informed me that he was sautéeing the delicate veal slices we'd bought.

"*Ça y est*, here we are," he announced stepping outside, bottle of wine in hand, as I finished arranging our peony centerpiece. His hands gripped the *tire-bouchon or corkscrew*, the sound of the cork coming out of the bottle as satisfying as the moment of watching the sun dip below the horizon or hearing him say *ça y est*. It was a short, succinct French expression phrase that expressed satisfaction at the completion of something – in our case the first chapter of our acquaintance. The second, more formidable one was about to begin.

"*Ça y est*," I echoed, accepting the wine glass he offered. We toasted silently and drank, eyeing each other over the rim of our glasses. The image of the woman in the photo on the living room wall came into my head, but I flicked it away, like a summer insect. It was enough to be here, now. Nothing more mattered.

"Shall we eat outside?" he asked.

"Perfect."

Dinner was succulent. A simple salad followed paper-thin veal slices sauteed in lemon, white wine, and capers. When it was over, we fed each other figs, interspersed with bites of Chavignol's nutty goat cheese. Soon, kisses took the place of every other bite. Done, we stood up, clinging to each other. Together, we cleared the table. As I washed the dishes at the kitchen sink, Arnaud embraced me from behind, his arms encircling my waist.

When I finished, I dried my hands slowly, then turned to face him.

Taking my arm, he led me to the bedroom, extinguishing lights as we went.

At the side of the large, four-poster bed, he lit the two candles that he'd brought from the kitchen, placing them on the night stand. Then, he put his hand on my throat, precisely where I'd touched myself in the car on the way down. Delicately, but firmly, he pushed.

I fell backward onto the bed. As I lifted my legs to kick off my shoes, I caught sight of my shadow on the wall over the head post. Shapely calves and feet danced in the flickering candlelight.

"Look at the wall," I told him.

"I see," he said admiringly. Then, his eyes returned to mine, green like a tiger sighting its prey.

"Don't look at me. Only the wall," I ordered. The ceiling was at least nine feet high, giving us a sizeable stage on which to shadow dance. Ornate moldings adorned its perimeters, continuing down each corner. Slowly, I moved my arms and hands above our heads, enjoying the black images dancing on the wall.

Arnaud studied the effect, then began to move his own arms in tandem with mine. We were like children at play.

"Close your eyes," he finally said.

I shut my eyes, feeling the soft night breeze from the windows play over my hair and skin.

Shuffling sounds ensued, something on the bedside table was moved, and then the fey, otherworldly sounds of the Cocteau Twins wafted over us.

Arnaud bent toward me, kissing my left temple. Next, my forehead. Slowly, his lips moved down the side of my nose, to my mouth.

I returned his kiss. Now, he was on both knees beside me. I sat up, putting my arms around his neck.

We fell back on the bed, his steely taut thigh resting over mine. Instantly, I understood the reason parents didn't want teenage couples in reclining positions with each other. Nothing could have prepared me for the total surrender of my will in response to Arnaud's thigh on mine. I tried to take command of my actions, but another more feminine part of my brain suggested I give in. I complied.

Arnaud moved downward, over my throat, finding the tops of my breasts with his tongue. My sundress was silky, loose. With two fingers, he moved the vee of its neckline to expose my pink lace bra. Then, his tongue traced its border, in a minute, finding my nipple.

I sighed, my back flexing upward. Then, I reached up to unbutton his thin, white cotton shirt. One – two – three buttons undone. My fingers slipped inside to find a mass of luxuriant silky brown hair covering his chest.

Sucking in my breath, I pulled his shirt out of his jeans, undoing the rest of the buttons. The hair-trapped scent of him was musky and fragrant, undoing whatever reason I had left.

In a minute, Arnaud flipped me over. Now, he was underneath, pulling my sundress off over my head, quickly unfastening my bra. He pulled me down onto him. I shuddered with pleasure at the feel of my breasts against the forested floor of his chest. His hands came round the back of my waist and quickly moved down over my haunches.

He breathed in sharply.

In less than a minute, we were skin to skin, the hardness of him pressing against the top of my thigh. Instinctively, I thrust my hips up against him. There would be time for subtle exploration later. At that moment, there was nothing I wanted more than to feel the driving force of him inside me. I thrust again, twisting my hips and taking him off guard. The second he released me, I moved away. It was entirely tactical. The point was for him to come after me.

He did, ferociously. His hand dove between my thighs, parting them. Then, he lifted himself above me, a black hawk above his prey. I lay still, transfixed.

There was nothing subtle about his entry. He drove into me, fierce and unrelenting. I cried out in surprise, scrambling to get away.

His hands dug into my hips, holding me in a vise, as he drove into me again. The length of him surprised me, the tip of his penis hitting a back wall deep inside each time he thrust. The sensation was exquisite, engorging, and enflaming me, until we were like two succubi devouring each other.

His moans drowned out mine. The moment was his, and I was his ardent audience, the provoker and provider of his unbearable pleasure. Like a gargoyle high in the rafters of Notre Dame, his face contorted and contracted in the dance of the candlelight. It looked chiseled and hard, a visage like a falcon, his nose long and ever-so-slightly curved, his jaw line sharp and his blue-green eyes hard as diamonds. The utter, fierce masculinity of him took my breath away.

After a long moment, when time seemed to stand still, he gave an enormous groan, as if he were giving up the ghost. Then, he released his life forces into me in one, final push that lit a fire at the back of my womb.

I would be the star of Act Two of this performance but Act One belonged entirely to the *maestro* above me. I silently applauded his *tour de force* as he collapsed onto me, seemingly one step removed from death.

Beneath his spent form, I relaxed into the complete stillness of the night and marveled at the power of the performance I had just elicited from him. I wouldn't try to understand what it was about him that excited me so. Better to let the mystery be. As soon as he came to, Act Two would begin and he would find out about my own mystery. Whoever Arnaud de Saint Cyr had begun this day as, he would wake up a changed man on the morrow. Thanks to me.

In another minute, I was ready to fly heavenward. I gently rolled him off and to one side of me. It was not yet midnight, and our explorations had only just begun.

"Hello," I whispered with a low laugh, looking into his face.

His eyes were softer now, less hard and glittering than usual. If Delilah was going to cut off his hair, this was the moment.

"Hello," he murmured. "How are you?"

It was the moment of decision. I was ready to come. He needed to know that.

"*Je suis excitée.* I'm excited." This time, I meant it in the French sense of the word.

His eyes lit up.

"What do you want me to do?" His question was apt. The most appropriate question a man could ask at that moment. One a boy might not think of asking.

Taking his hand, I guided it to my clitoris. He moved it farther down. I moved it back into position, my body convulsing when he found the right spot. Immediately, he focused on the task at hand. Raising himself on one elbow, he slid his body down mine, putting one hand on my belly to prevent me from moving away. With his other hand, he covered my pleasure spot, his index finger flicking over it, back and forth.

I slowed down his motion, then pushed his hand away.

"Wait," I ordered.

He looked at me, puzzled. Then, I put his hand back where it had been. With an upward thrust of my chin I motioned him to recommence. He did.

Soon, he had taken charge of command central. He understood my directions, clear and monosyllabic.

In another moment my breathing turned jagged and harsh.

"Don't stop," I commanded, my body doing its utmost to jerk away from him.

His left hand like a vise on my hipbone, he threw his right thigh over mine, pinning me to the mattress. I couldn't move.

He got it. Instinctively, he knew to synthesize my conflicting behavior.

"Stop," I cried out even louder.

He smiled, pausing for a moment, then resumed. This time, he pressed more firmly, stroking faster.

I couldn't stand it any longer.

"Stop," I pleaded. But I was no longer in charge. My tormentor was.

He applied his tongue.

I arched backward, practically knocking his teeth out.

"Ahhh," I screamed out, splitting the silence of the night into crystal shards. At the end of the longest tightrope I'd ever walked, I fell into an abyss. It took me several minutes before I could open my eyes again, my lips parted in sheer bliss. Arnaud's eyes on mine looked intrigued. Perhaps shocked.

It was the moment to show sheer bravado. My mouth curled into a savage smile, teeth showing. I could feel the sheen of sweat on my face. It would not do to worry about embarrassment now. He might think I was an absolute maniac, but he would be impressed. Women could be falcons, too. If he hadn't known before, he did now.

"Are you okay?" he finally asked.

I nodded.

"You looked like the girl in *The Exorcist* when you were coming."

"The one whose head turns all the way around?"

"Right."

"Thanks." A matched response would come in handy. "You looked like a monster getting blown away by the Terminator," I countered.

"*Sans aucune doute.* Without a doubt," he agreed unashamedly.

"The best things in life aren't always pretty," I pointed out.

"The best things in life are the smelliest," he countered.

"Spoken like a true Frenchman," I teased.

"Do you agree?"

Good question. Back in the States I would have said, "Yuck, no." But this was France. I wasn't two-faced or a hypocrite. I knew what I liked, and I knew I didn't like strong smells on a man or from a cheese in the States, but I did like them here. I was discovering what suited me in one place wasn't necessarily the same as what suited me in another.

"There are strong smells that I don't like. Then there are others that excite me," I whispered, putting my fingers in his chest hair and twisting.

"Ow," he protested. He reached for my head, grasping it then pulled my hair back hard.

"Ouch," I echoed.

"You like that," he observed.

"So do you," I replied.

Over the next twenty minutes, he showed me how much he did.

There was something subversive about Arnaud de Saint Cyr that appealed to my own carefully concealed subversiveness. He elicited a high octane sex drive within me I hadn't known I possessed. Together we formed a turbo-charged team. It was almost too good to be true.

The drive back to Paris, the following day, was peaceful. I chose Erik Satie's *Gymnopedie* to play as Arnaud drove – an elegant, minimalist accompaniment that perfectly contrasted with the explosiveness of the night before as well as that morning. Arnaud was relatively quiet, showing a calm, thoughtful side that may have been the result of spending time in the countryside, but more likely caused by the four orgasms he'd experienced over the past twelve hours. Either way, it was pleasant. Wrapped up in blissful thoughts, I was happy to take a break from our usual verbal badinage.

At half past eight in the evening, we pulled up in front of Henri and Marceline's flat. Arnaud turned to me, his face remote, pensive.

"Why so serious, *mon cher?*" I asked, the endearment slipping out naturally. Did I have a right to use it? Yes, my heart sang.

He sighed. "I have to go to work tomorrow."

"But, that's normal isn't it?" What was the problem? Most people had to go to work Monday morning. Not everyone was a musician like me. Thank God, not my boyfriend, if that was what I could call the man now clasping my hand in his.

"I'm going to Thailand on assignment."

"You're what?" What had he just said?

"I'm leaving for Thailand tomorrow to cover a story there."

"Did you mention this before?" Stunned, I could feel my blood pressure rising. We hadn't spoken about mundane things such as work or careers. We hadn't gone near those all-too-American type topics. Now, I wished we had.

"No, *ma belle*. I didn't want to speak of it. I wanted to be with you, that's all."

"But we, but we just –"

"Yes. We did." He put one finger on my mouth to stop me from saying more. "And we will again. As soon as I'm back."

I removed his finger.

"It's just a bit of a surprise." A shock is what I meant.

"Ava, I'm a foreign correspondent. It's what I do for a living."

"So – you write news stories about places around the world?"

"Yes."

"And you go to those places to write them?"

"*Précisement.*"

My heart sank. I knew enough about his profession to know that it encouraged the same kind of loose living lifestyle being a performer or airline pilot did – a woman in every port, worst case scenario. On assignment for three months somewhere, back home for two weeks, next assignment six weeks somewhere else, and home for Christmas if no earth-shaking event occurred anywhere else. It was a peripatetic existence. Not music to the ears of an equally peripatetic musician who entertained occasional thoughts of settling down. Or did I want to settle down? I wasn't exactly sure of what that entailed, but I knew I was fed up with playing piano in restaurants for less money than the waiters were making.

"When will you be back from Thailand?" I didn't want to ask, but the words popped out regardless.

"In ten days. Two weeks at the most. It's a short project." He looked at me, his eyebrows arched into question marks.

Hell. That implied a long project might last a month or more. Did this work for me?

Non.

Would I finish things here and now between us?

Non. Impossible.

"*Bahhh...*" I used the famous French expression to hedge my response, unable to think beyond 'information rejected – rewind tape'.

"I'll call you, Ava. The minute I get back."

Great. He wouldn't even call while he was gone. It was unfair. How could we have been so close and now this? He would disappear, making me wait for ten long days, wondering if he would reappear in my life again. Shades of horrid Manhattan dating encounters danced through my head. Hadn't I left all that behind? Or was this some sort of modern-day phenomenon – the unavailable male available just long enough to get laid then pushing off into the sunset? Bastard.

"Do you have a girlfriend in Thailand?" I couldn't help myself.

"No. I have no girlfriend anywhere. My work doesn't permit me."

"Well now you do." There. I'd really gone out on a limb.

"Ava," he pulled me into his arms, practically impaling me over the stick shift.

I squirmed, trying to get away.

"Will you be the girlfriend of a guy like me?"

"What exactly is a guy like you, Arnaud? The guy you were this weekend? Or the guy you'll be tomorrow when you get on the plane?" I hoped there wasn't a difference, but I'd worked as a musician long enough to know there probably was one. From what I'd seen, when adult men and women went on the road alone, they didn't stay alone for long.

"Like the guy I am in both places."

"I can only know the guy you are here with me."

"Is that good enough for you?"

"Is it good enough for you to be with me now and not with anyone anywhere else?" I was getting ahead of myself. This was a conversation for down the road, not at the onset of a relationship. But he was leaving the next day. For a country filled with slim, dark gorgeous women with more manageable hair than mine.

"You're too good for me," he replied, not exactly answering my question.

"Great. I've heard that before." Why did that old, tired line always come up when a relationship was about to go bust? We'd just begun something glorious. I wasn't about to let whatever we had go up in smoke by engaging in a premature discussion.

"Will you wait for me?" he asked. Unfairly, I thought.

"*Ça dépend*, Arnaud." Nor would I promise him anything at that moment. 'It depends' was all he was getting from me. It wasn't a response from the heart, but my heart had gone into hiding from the moment he'd mentioned leaving for Thailand.

"*Ça dépend de quoi?*" he demanded.

"It depends on you."

He looked confused, exactly how I wanted to leave things with him – unsure and wanting more. Without a word more, I got out of the car then slammed the door shut.

Arnaud jumped out the driver's side, slamming his door with equal force.

"*Qu'est-ce que tu as, cherie? What's the matter with you?*" he asked. I knew that question from time spent with Jean-Michel.

"You know what's wrong, Arnaud. Could you open the trunk please?" I didn't mean to be upset, but him leaving for Asia for the next two weeks had not been on my radar screen of foreseeable events. At least, he hadn't said two months.

He complied, pulling my two bags out and placing them on the sidewalk. Then, he put an arm on either side of me and backed me up against the side of his Peugeot. All I needed now was for Henri or Marceline to show up. They were probably at the living room window that very moment, taking in the whole scene.

"I'll be back in ten days, two weeks at the most. *Tu me manqueras*. You will miss me."

What was that – a command? Had he just said I would miss him?

"No, Arnaud. You will miss me," I shot back, incensed by his incredible cheek.

"That's what I said, *cherie. Tu me manquera énormément*."

Had he just said 'You will miss me enormously'? Yes I would, but that wasn't for him to say, was it? Some sort of miscommunication was going on here. I needed to get away before everything we had just begun went up in smoke and flames.

"Goodbye, Arnaud."

"*À la prochaine*, Ava. See you next time."

Not trusting myself to refrain from escalating combat further, I picked up my bags, turned and smartly walked into the building. There would be plenty of time to sort out our parting conversation later. Ten full days, in fact – perhaps fourteen.

I fumed as I made my way upstairs. Thousands of miles from New York City, and here I was again dealing with flighty man problems.

❧

The next morning, I bumped into Marceline in the kitchen, all eight months along of her. She waddled toward the counter where I sat, coffee cup in hand.

"And how was the weekend?" she asked, looking curious.

"It was good," I said, avoiding her eyes.

"Then why so sad?" she followed up. She was right. I was in the dumps.

It wouldn't do to punch a pregnant woman. In any case, it was Arnaud I wanted to hit. I was still confused about our conversation curbside the evening before.

"Marceline?"

"Yes?" She looked surprised to hear me address her by name.

"What does *tu me manqueras* mean?"

She smiled.

"I will miss you," she explained.

"But doesn't it mean 'you will miss me'?" I asked, confused. That's what it had sounded like.

"It's a common mistake. In English you put yourself first. But in French you put the other person first. It's like *ça me plaît*."

"What do you mean?"

"I mean you say, 'I like that' in English, but we say *ça me plaît*, that pleases me."

"So do you mean to say if I say *tu me manqueras* it means I'll miss you even though it sounds like you will miss me?"

"*Exactement.*" The grin widened on her face.

"And what does *tu me manqueras énormément* mean?" I asked, although it was pretty clear. I just needed a native French speaker to confirm it.

"Is that what he said to you?"

I blushed. "I'm just asking what it means."

"Right. It means "I'll miss you a lot – enormously.""

"Oh." I stared into my coffee cup.

"Did he go somewhere?"

I nodded.

"For how long?"

"Ten days to two weeks."

"Oh." She took a deep sip of her coffee with milk. "That's not so long."

"It seems long to me."

"Try waiting nine months."

I looked at her and laughed. She had a point. "You're almost there, Marceline. It will all be worth it in a few weeks' time."

"If I can wait this long, then you can wait two weeks."

"But what if he doesn't call?"

"That depends on you."

"What do you mean?"

"How did you leave it with him?"

"I – uh – I was sort of mad." I shook my head, thinking of our dust-up on the sidewalk.

"Were you mean to him?" Marceline asked enthusiastically.

"Uh – *malheureusement, oui* – unfortunately, yes."

"*Très bien,*" she approved. "He'll call."

What was that supposed to mean? What if I'd been all nice and accommodating? *No problem, Arnaud. Call me when you get back, whenever that might be.* That would be a man's fantasy, right? I steamed, just thinking about it.

"But I wasn't very nice to him" I explained. "I was angry because he hadn't said anything about going away until we got back from the weekend."

"What were you expecting him to do? Say something before you went away and risk not having you come?"

"I guess not."

"You have to understand his point of view. He wanted something, and he needed to make sure he was going to get it."

"Just like a man," I agreed, disapprovingly.

"*Oui.* Just like a man, *naturellement.*" Marceline didn't look disapproving, just instructive. "And now it is your chance to behave just like a woman."

"Meaning?"

"You scratch. You kick. You meow. Finally, you leave. Shut the door in his face. *Bouf.*" She gestured violently as if slapping someone in the face.

"Wow." I studied Marceline with new respect. She might look like an overripe watermelon, but she had some serious moves. "What's all that accomplish?"

"You let him know he's just another *mec.*" She used the slang for "guy" in French. It had a slightly more pejorative spin.

"I do?"

"They're a dime a dozen." She shrugged. "He's gone for a few weeks? Who cares? Someone else will come along to take his place. Let him know there are plenty of other fish in the sea, all ready to swim your way."

"I like your thinking."

"It's only natural," she continued. "You need to take the advantage, so he understands it's his loss if he chooses to leave you for a few weeks. Why is he going away, anyways?"

"He's a foreign correspondent."

"A what?"

"An international journalist."

She made a face, as if I'd said he was a drug-runner or something. Then, she composed herself.

"Well, good luck with that."

"Yeah, thanks."

We parted ways – her to work, me to my keyboard. I tried to focus with renewed zeal, but too many loose ends flapped in the wind. Would I get booked for more gigs at The Blue Cactus after my six-week run was over? Where else might I find work? And would the man I'd just slept with for the first time call when he got back? While I rehearsed my repertoire, I vowed not to think about him.

Then I broke my vows repeatedly.

Had I expected Arnaud to be an accountant? Not likely, with his fast-moving mind and cheeky delivery. Foreign correspondent would have been one of the top ten on my list, if I'd had to guess what he did for a living. I just hoped beyond hope he didn't share the same sleazy habits many men picked up in that line of work.

My mind wandered back to the house pianist at the Watertree Crab House in lower Manhattan where I'd been a singing waitress until I'd found work as a singer/pianist hotel lounge act. I'd had a ridiculous crush on Jules. For months, I'd pined after him, until finally at the end of our shift one evening, he'd offered to walk me home. We hadn't ended up at home but instead at one East Village bar after another, until we found ourselves back at his apartment. Never mind about all the rest.

The next morning, he mentioned over coffee that he had pretty much bedded the entire waitressing staff of the restaurant where we worked. It was then that I knew male musicians in New York City had it way too easy when it came to women.

The ratio of heterosexual men to women in the performing arts in New York City was something like one to four. It hit me like a ton of bricks that I'd just given myself to a complete sleazebag. I took the walk of shame back to my own East Village apartment, wearing my clothes and tired makeup from the night before, while I tried to squelch any aspirations I might have had for our relationship to pan out. At work in the weeks following, Jules treated me exactly the same way he had before our all-night encounter, aside from an occasional smirk or lascivious stare.

The scales fell from my eyes after that encounter. Welcome to the New York dating scene, Ava – World Headquarters for Meaningless Encounters. On occasional Friday or Saturday nights at the end of my shift, Jules would offer to hook up with me again, which absolutely drove me up the wall. I wasn't looking for a hook up. I'd wanted a relationship, a love story. We weren't speaking the same language. Our tryst set the wheels in motion for my exit from New York City. No way did I ever want to be a musician there again.

CHAPTER THIRTEEN

L'Amour à la Folie (Crazy Love)

The next few weeks were among the most creative of my life. I was in love. I was in agony. Marceline returned home Monday evening with the news that her grandfather had suffered a stroke and she had to leave immediately to attend to him. Because of her advanced condition, Henri accompanied her, and they both took off for the grandfather's home outside of Paris. After a day, Henri called to say they would be staying on through the weekend as the house there was cooler than our stiflingly hot, un-air-conditioned flat. Blessedly, a week of solitude stretched out ahead of me. I would be alone with my music and my thoughts.

I made the most of it. At the top of my priority list was finding a performing job on my own so I could get out from under Henri's thumb as well as his flat. There was no way I wanted him managing my career. He hadn't known what a reverb unit was, he was about to become a first-time father, and sooner or later Marceline would come across an erotic sketch of me in Henri's office and all hell would break loose. For all of those reasons, Henri and I needed to part ways.

Days, I rehearsed in the mornings then broke for lunch. Every afternoon, I visited different neighborhoods known for nightlife. *Pariscope* was my guide, Paris's weekly entertainment listings magazine sold at every newsstand. I used the same technique I used back in New York to get a job – wandering into a place, getting the name of the manager or owner, then pretending to be my own agent as I presented head shots and a short recording of the sensational talent I represented: Ava Fodor from New York City.

My headshots were so dramatically retouched that no one associated them with the person who stood before them. I wore my glasses just in case anyone might have made the connection between me and the knock-out blonde with big hair and sharp cheekbones in the photos. No one did.

By late afternoon I'd return home, just as my creative juices began to flow. Other than preparing for my Friday evening gig at The Blue Cactus, I was free to focus on songwriting. Hands down, it was my favorite part of being a musician. The flat was more atmospheric without Henri and Marceline around. I threw open the windows, welcoming in Paris's street sounds for inspiration.

New songs came to me almost fully-formed, like Athena springing out of Zeus's head. The first night of my solitude I wrote *Au Bord de la Seine* sweet, wistful and as light as a bagatelle – a short, light-hearted piece of classical piano music.

The next night, I composed *Find Me* – a ballad. Thursday night, I mixed both songs. Then it was Friday, my gig. After observing male restaurant-goers salivate over my headshots in the front window of The Blue Cactus while I slipped by them unnoticed, a hard-edged tune popped into my head, *Through Men's Eyes*. I put it together after midnight, upon returning home from my unremarkable performance. On Saturday evening, I wrote my opus, *Scheherazade*. I thought it was at least as good as Madonna's *Holiday*.

Anyone other than a creative artist would find it hard to believe I could write music so quickly. But artists know too cruelly well that inspiration usually comes all at once or not at all. In my case, I was writing three-and a-half minute pop songs, not three-movement symphonies; verse, chorus - verse, chorus - bridge - verse, chorus - chorus. *Et voilà.* Done. It was a piece of cake, as Marie Antoinette more or less said.

By Sunday afternoon, I was lonely but exhilarated. I'd written music almost nonstop since Arnaud had left town. In a rare state of mind, I felt totally connected to my real self. Writing songs wasn't like performing them. I was writing them for myself. Unlike performing songs for an audience, when I wrote songs I wasn't trying to curry favor with anyone. I was just trying to express what I really felt – and I knew when I got it right – like hitting a nail on the head.

But when I performed, it was about how the audience received me. My job was to get strangers to like me – something that didn't sit well with me. Why should I try to get strangers to like me? Not only did it seem unnatural, it didn't seem very French at all. Not that I'd become French all of a sudden, but it seemed to me the French exhibited natural behavior in their distrust of strangers or outsiders. Why did Americans smile at total strangers anyways?

Sitting around the apartment in the final hours of privacy left to me before my hosts returned, it occurred to me that Larry would be having another soirée that evening. Someone there might know of a nightspot where I could find a gig. Why not go? As I dressed, I thought about social events Arnaud might have attended over the past week in bloody Bangkok or wherever he was. Foreign correspondents partied like fish swam – everyone knew that. I put on a more or less conservative sundress as a concession to him *in absentia* and made my way over to Larry's flat near Parc de Vincennes.

The party seemed more muted this time. Perhaps it was the lack of Arnaud's outsized presence. The usual suspects were there – the older, well-dressed gay guys and Scott from Omaha. I sought out Sam, hoping he might have some leads on where I might find my next gig.

"Ava! How have you been? Has Paris been treating you well?" he asked, propelling me into the kitchen, where he handed me a glass.

"Hi Sam. Yes, it's been delightful, thank you so much." I sipped, thinking how much I liked the older, courtly man. He made me feel welcome.

"Paris is always delightful. That is – until one day it isn't. But you're nowhere near that time, love."

"What do you mean?" I was curious. Was this drunken party talk or was he making a point?

"Don't worry, Ava. You have many more mornings to wake up to a Paris that's delightful."

"Will I know when the tide turns?"

He looked thoughtful. "You'll know. But the bigger question is – will you act on it?"

"What do you mean?" I didn't want to play the dumb American, but I hadn't a clue as to what he was talking about.

"Ava – just about everyone in this room is an ex-pat. You've heard the term?"

"Yes, of course." Everyone knew what an ex-pat was. It was someone who chose to live abroad. Glamorously, preferably.

"Some of us have been here for years. Decades. Do you think Paris is still delightful for us?"

"Ummm – I hope so."

"Dear girl. You are so very sweet and so very young."

"Not really, Sam, but thanks anyways."

"Every foreigner who comes here and stays for awhile wakes up one morning and realizes Paris is no longer in love with him or her. And never was. Then, it's decision time."

"You mean you need to decide whether to go home or stay?"

"Precisely."

"But don't you think you've made the right choice?"

Sam sighed. It was the deepest sigh I'd ever heard.

"Ava, have you ever been in love with someone who didn't love you back?"

I recoiled. How did he know my secrets? No one knew that. No one ever would. "Fake it till you make it" was my motto. "Fake it till you move on" was another variation I'd relied on at times.

"Umm – let's just say I know what you're talking about."

"So which is better then? To continue loving someone who doesn't love you? Or to move on, cherishing your memories but giving yourself a chance to be loved by someone a little less glorious?"

"I guess it depends on what type of person you are," was all I could offer. It would take years for me to figure out the answer to his question.

"*Brava*. I think you're right. And what type of person do you think you might be?"

It was my turn to sigh.

"I don't know, Sam. Many types. I thought of a *mille-feuilles* pastry, the "thousand-leafed" pastry that had contributed toward adding extra inches to my hips the year I'd been an au pair.

"But which type above all?" he pressed.

I thought hard. Artistic? I'd like to think so, but probably not. Intellectual? I'd met enough intellectuals at Yale to know I wasn't really one of them. Ethereal? Only in my dreams. Practical?

Yes.

"Well – I'm sort of a practical person at heart."

Sam nodded approvingly.

"Good. Very good."

"Why's that good?" I asked, curious. Talking to Sam was better than paying to see a shrink.

"You'll go home, you'll find someone to love who'll love you back. And for the rest of your life you'll cherish your memories of the time you spent here."

"But what if I want to stay?" I asked, rejecting his mapping out of the whole rest of my life. Who did he think he was?

"Many do. The dreamy ones, the aesthetes. Those who have no home to return to," he gestured behind his back to the corner where his gay friends clustered.

"But I *am* dreamy – I mean, I'm a songwriter. And I love beauty, too. I'm crazy about Paris!" I protested.

"Don't be too crazy, dear. Don't love *à la folie* as the French say. It won't get you where you need to go."

"But what if I want to stay right here? Why shouldn't I be crazy about this place?" Paris was the most gorgeous, elegant, well-appointed city in the world. Anyone with taste would be mad about it.

"That's the point, my dear. You're crazy about this city, but this city will never be crazy about you."

"How do you know that?" I was miffed. I would be the next Josephine Baker, except I'd be a singer-songwriter instead of a cabaret dancer.

"It's nothing personal, Ava. Don't take it amiss. You see – Paris is the Queen of Diamonds. She's so far above and beyond us all, she can't possibly partner with any of us."

That sounded like a lot of single women I knew back in Manhattan. "But isn't that sad and lonely for her?" I asked. Somehow Paris didn't fit the bill of a sad, lonely queen. Not by a long shot.

"Ava, you've just revealed why it is you'll ultimately leave."

"I have? No, I haven't! I haven't made that decision at all," I objected. What was Sam talking about? Maybe I'd stay in Paris forever. Sooner or later, I'd be discovered by a French record producer while playing somewhere like The Blue Cactus, just as the Gypsy Kings had been. We'd make a debut album together with at least one mega-hit. And depending on how things went with Arnaud, we might marry and live happily ever after in a high-ceilinged Parisian apartment with occasional visits to his country house. Our children would be French, and I'd learn how to cook *coq au vin*. Who was Sam, who didn't even know me, to predict otherwise?

"Ava, you're a smart woman. You won't waste your time beating your head against a stone wall. Paris has a heart of stone. She's the Queen of Diamonds, girl. Mark my words." He moved off, leaving me baffled.

I refilled my wineglass, mulling over Sam's parting words.

Putting aside his advice, I spent the next two hours chatting, drinking and information-gathering. The name of one nightspot in particular kept coming up – Teddy's. It was in the twentieth arrondissement – a largely African neighborhood in the north of the city, known for rollicking nightlife and good bargains by day. It was where young, hip Parisians had begun to hang out – mostly because it was affordable. I took down the address and decided to check it out the next day. If I got lucky, Teddy's might be a place like The Blue Willow back in New York, where I could line up a steady weekly gig as a house pianist.

On Tuesday afternoon I visited Teddy's. While waiting for the owner to show up, I sat down at the beat up, old upright piano and improvised on one of my favorite instrumental jazz standards. Then Teddy himself walked in.

"Is that *Song for My Father* you're riffing on?" he asked, his accent Liverpuddlian. I'd briefly dated a musician from there back in New York. Things hadn't progressed, partly because I had only been able to understand about forty per cent of what he said.

"Yes."

"I like your sound. Looking for a job?"

My heart jumped. Yes! This was the way things were supposed to go, but rarely did. As long as I could negotiate a reasonable fee with Teddy and when I should start, we'd be all set. On the spot, he booked me for Wednesday and Thursday nights starting the following week. His usual pianist was just about to leave to go teach English in Thailand. What was it about Thailand that pulled so many people to it? One day, I'd find out myself, perhaps with Arnaud at my side.

On Thursday afternoon, the call I'd been waiting for finally came.

"*Ça va, Minou?*"

"*Oui, ça va bien. Et toi?* How was your trip?" There was no way I would let him know how much I'd missed him.

"It was fine. Can you meet me at Café de la Bastille at six?"

"Uhhh." I paused, pretending to consult my engagement calendar, New York-style. I wondered if Parisian women did the same thing when dating a man. "Yes, six should be fine." I had no plans for the evening whatsoever. And if I had, I would have changed them. But he didn't need to know that.

Three hours and several outfit changes later, we met at our usual spot. I wore a coral and pink striped silk top with tight chocolate brown jeans that took me entirely too long to decide on wearing.

"*Bon soir, Minou. Tu es ravissante.* You're ravishing," Arnaud greeted me enthusiastically. He kissed me four times, then picked me up and swung me around in his arms. It was like being in my own hair commercial.

With a tan, he looked even more chiseled than he had before.

"Hello Arnaud," I said calmly, pretending I didn't feel like a golden retriever greeting her master returning from work. *Play it cool, Ava.*

"Did you miss me, *cherie?*" he demanded.

"*Bah – un tout petit peu.* A tiny bit," I teased him, just a tad put off by his reflexive question. Was it all about me missing him? What about him missing me? I reminded myself this was a Frenchman I was dating – not John Boy Walton who would have told me how much he'd missed me and left it at that.

We entered the café where we ordered *omelettes aux champignons,* mushroom omelettes and then talked nonstop for the next hour and a half. Movies, books, music, politics – we discussed everything except what he'd been up to in Thailand. Finally, he suggested we go back to his place.

It was small, like most Parisian apartments I'd been inside. Built-in bookcases lined the walls, loaded with books and magazine journals. The titles I recognized were like old friends to me, *Vol de Nuit* or *Night Flight* by Antoine de Saint Exupéry, the author of *The Little Prince*, and *Bonjour Tristesse* by Françoise Sagan – both among my top ten favorite books. I wanted to know everything there was to know about Arnaud de Saint Cyr, especially what roamed around the halls of his brain.

The next seven days passed gloriously, drenched in sensation and passion. Our connection went far beyond the physical. Each day I woke with wonder at what he would do or suggest next.

Arnaud's interests were eclectic, along with his neighborhood. He lived in the poor and ethnically diverse twentieth arrondissement next to the nineteenth, where Teddy's was located. Directly next to his flat on Rue Pierre Bayle was Paris's most famous cemetery, Père Lachaise. We visited it several times the first week of his return. A galaxy of Somebodies lay in repose there: Jim Morrison, Oscar Wilde, Chopin, Colette, Sarah Bernhardt, and a host of other notables. Even Héloise was in residence with Peter Abelard at her side. Separated for most of their lives after their love affair was discovered, they had come together in a final reunion.

By the end of the week, I wanted to stay by Arnaud's side forever. We electrified each other. His acquisitive, searching personality elevated me to a level of aliveness I'd never experienced before with a man. At times, it was exhausting, but only because I wanted to match him at every level, clever phrase for clever phrase, sultry pose for sultry pose. I was no longer just performing at my job, but also in my private life. We wandered around Paris's ethnic neighborhoods, which were filled with Arabs and West Africans, seeking out exotic shops, and cafés serving spicy teas and honeyed pastries I'd never seen in the United States. We took long walks through the magnificent environs of Opera, Place de la Concorde, then on up the Champs-Élysées to the Arc de Triomphe. But those areas ultimately left us cold. The shop windows were filled with consumer goods designed to appeal to the most *haute bourgeois* tastes, which neither of us possessed. We were much more interested in exploring the exotic, hidden, dark sides of Paris as well as each other.

New York and Paris were both cities where everything fun and affordable to do was from somewhere else. The best nightclubs were West African, the best restaurants either North-African, Middle-Eastern, Vietnamese, or Thai. The best bars were English or American. The only truly French establishments we frequented on a daily basis were Paris's sidewalk cafés and its parks.

We returned to Chavignol a few times in the month of August. Wrapped up in each other, we took long walks in the countryside, read books, made picnics, and visited a few chateaus nearby. The woman in the photo by the fireplace in the living room continued to taunt me, until my curiosity got the best of me.

"*Cheri,* tell me about the woman in the photo," I asked one rainy August evening, as we lay on the living room couch listening to Billy Holiday.

"What photo?"

"The one on the wall there." I pointed to it.

"What do you want to know?" Had he stiffened or was I just imagining it? It was like pulling teeth to get a word out of him about the woman with the hard, beautiful face.

"Well – was she someone from your past?"

"No. She is not from my past." He looked strained, as if he'd rather talk about something else.

"Then who is she? You said she was your mentor, your guide. What did you mean by that?"

"*Minou,* did you ever have someone you learned everything from? I mean – everything important there is to know?"

"Hmm." I didn't want to answer. Arnaud was the one I felt that way about. Pascal had taught me how to unlock my own body, but Arnaud's canvas was broader, larger. He painted ideas on it – not just how to love, but how to live; how to think critically.

"Perhaps," I finally said. I wouldn't give him the satisfaction of knowing he was the one.

"So when did you know this woman?" I continued.

"Is it so important for you to know?" he asked, stroking my chin and throat.

"Well – I'd like to," I ventured, then fell silent.

Arnaud's sigh filled the room.

Was I moving down the wrong track? Was this akin to the moment when the snake asked Eve in the garden if she'd like to eat an apple from the Tree of Knowledge? Did I really need to bite into that apple? What would it gain me?

Finally, he spoke.

"Would it be okay with you if I tell you I'd like to keep it to myself?"

"Uh – sure." I wrestled with myself, not wanting to come across as a pushy, insecure girl insisting on hearing more. I was a woman of mystique in full possession of Arnaud's heart right here, right now.

At least, I thought so. Perhaps one small follow-up question was in order, just to find out her name. As I opened my mouth, he pulled me toward him.

"*Je t'adore, Minou.* I adore you, little cat," he whispered, then kissed my moment of uncertainty into oblivion. It was the first time I'd heard him say those words, so compelling in French. I kissed him back, swept away by his confession of adoration. The rain beating on the window-panes serenaded us until rhythmic sounds of our own drowned out all others.

The next morning, as Arnaud loaded up the car for our return to Paris, I took one final peek at the woman in the photo. She stared back disdain-fully, baiting me with her cool imperturbability. I wouldn't bring her up again to Arnaud. It was between me and her now. But I needed to know who she was.

Quickly taking the picture frame off the wall, I pulled out the photo inside and turned it over.

"Mélanie 1986" was scrawled on the back. It was now 1988. I pushed the photo back into the frame and returned it to its place on the wall. Then I walked outside and hopped in the car.

In September, Arnaud got another assignment – this one, in Vietnam. By then, I was teaching English to French aeronautical students in exchange for a room over Teddy's Bar. John, the former pianist there, who'd left to teach English in Thailand for three months, had worked out a deal with me. Not wishing to give up his lucrative contract as an English teacher at an aeronautical school, he'd subcontracted me to take over teaching his students in exchange for the use of his tiny studio apartment. Our arrangement was perfect. I'd moved out of Henri and Marceline's flat the week before baby Simone arrived. In my own place, I was able to retain a modicum of independence from the man I was fall-ing in love with.

My grandmother had always advised holding back with men. "Let them chase you. Don't make it easy for them, otherwise they won't think you're anything special."

It was hard advice to follow.

"Are you sure you don't want to stay here at my place while I'm gone? You could water my plants, look after the cat, collect the mail," he'd suggested one night as we snuggled together in his bed.

"You don't have a cat, darling," I'd giggled.

"Yes I do." His finger stroked my throat. "Right here, *Minou.*"

Inside, I purred then flexed my kitty claws.

"If you want me to come over to water your plants, I will, but I'm staying at my place," I said, thinking *this cat can look after herself while you're away.* Arnaud had two plants, exactly. I had no desire to spend time in his apartment with him not there. I would miss him then think unreasonable thoughts such as why he hadn't invited me to join him in Vietnam. Better to stay busy at my own place, practicing new material and writing songs.

He left the second week of September just as the *rentrée* began. The *rentrée*, or return, was an annual event in France when the work and school year swung into full gear. Paris was abuzz, its rested, tanned population back from their mandatory four or five-week vacations. Teddy's was busy, with song requests coming with greater frequency than in previous weeks. The ex-pat crowd loved hearing Eric Clapton's *Wonderful Tonight*, and Carol King's *Will You Still Love Me Tomorrow.* Another huge favorite was Elvis Presley's sentimental *I Can't Stop Falling in Love with You;* the evergreen standard most people wrongly refer to as *Fools Rush In.*

One evening, a customer requested *Stand by Me* and to my amazement, people began to clap to the beat and sing along as soon as I played the opening lines. By the end of the song, the entire room was singing the chorus along with me. With the crowd hooked, I launched into Peggy Lee's *Fever*, motioning to the audience to snap their fingers to the beat of the single-note bass-line introduction. My listeners responded enthusiastically, fingers snapping, feet stomping, and wildly applauding at the end. The next night, I played the same two songs back to back with equally spirited audience participation.

"Play *Stand by Me* will you?" a man at the bar shouted out the following week. I recognized him from the Thursday before. This time, he was back with a friend.

"Play the finger snapping tune – the one you played last week," his companion added.

I lifted the wine glass on the piano top, shaking it at them. On its side, I'd handwritten a sign that said, "Tips welcomed – not drinks." The month before, someone had told me about a Nina Simone-type performer at a small club off the Champs-Élysées . Arnaud and I had gone to catch her performance, and I'd been dismayed to see what years of performing success had done to the older, female American performer. She played well, her singing style soothing, mellow and sensual. Fans in the audience sent over a steady supply of drinks to accompany their requests for favorite songs. An excellent, professional performer, her glassy eyes, wasted physique and remote air told me she was also a full-fledged alcoholic. I'd seen what downing free drinks did to house musicians as the years went by, and I vowed to myself that night I would never again accept another free drink from an admiring fan.

The man from the week before came over and put some money in my tip glass. I smiled and launched into *Stand By Me*. Then I played *Love Potion No. 9*, directing the audience to join me in shouting out the title of the song when it came up in the refrain. They responded with gusto.

The following evening, I brought in a clipboard with a piece of paper on it that asked "What songs do you like to sing along to most?" With a magic marker on a string attached, I sent it circulating along the bar, with instructions to the bartender to keep it going around the room. Sure enough, before the evening ended, the clipboard had made the rounds, with ten song titles added. My professional skills were now expanding into market research.

Over the next few weeks, I worked on adding new repertoire to get my audience more engaged. *You've Lost That Loving Feeling* by the Righteous Brothers took over the room the first time I played it. Maudlin and sentimental, it was an instant hit with the largely British Isles crowd. The Beatles' *Hey Jude* worked well, and Jimmy Buffet's *Margaritaville* gave everyone in the bar a chance to roar "Wasting away again in Margaritaville" then order margaritas from the bartender. In mid-October, when Teddy offered a regular Tuesday night spot in addition to Wednesdays and Thursdays, I was pleased to accept.

No longer was I a lonely, misunderstood performer playing for a disinterested audience. At Teddy's, we were in this together – a roomful of lonely ex-pats with a scattering of French customers who like to hang around with ex-pats. (In Paris there were many, due to the fact that many Parisians find hanging around with each other too socially draining.) Teddy's patrons were becoming my patrons, too. We were bonding over hackneyed, overplayed songs that weren't likely to score me a recording contract, but were at least gaining me a following.

I was becoming a sing-along, pub performer, someone I didn't really recognize myself as. How had Laurie Anderson or Annie Lennox gotten started in the music business? I couldn't imagine either artist pandering to pub audiences, churning out sing-along tunes. But I was finally getting noticed, and it felt a lot better than being ignored, the way I had been at the Gramercy Park Hotel lounge or The Blue Cactus. A not insignificant number of my fans were gay males, invited from Larry's parties. But the ones I secretly studied were the smattering of French women who accompanied their husbands or boyfriends to Teddy's. They dressed simply but superbly for the most part – unlike me in my "notice-me" New York performer's wardrobe.

"Ava, your turban is DEE VINE!" One of my gay fans gushed as he took a photo one evening, while I crooned *Fever* into the mic, my audience finger-snapping along with me.

The following week, he stuffed a ten-franc note into my tip jar along with the photo. I glanced at it during my break. Who was that over-the-top character in the black and white turban?

Neither did it look like me, nor did I want it to. I'd picked up the black and white turban at a boutique in Alphabet-land in the easternmost fringe of the East Village back in Manhattan. It took a lot of guts to wear it well, as it twisted into what appeared to be a super-chic antennae on top of my head, supported by a wire framework covered with boldly striped fabric.

My grandmother had always said, "When in doubt, and navy blue is out, wear black and white." The more time I spent in France, the more it occurred to me my grandmother should have been French. Although she'd never mentioned the name of Coco Chanel in my presence, she had absorbed much of the iconic French designer's sensibility – namely that less is more, and that black and white is always chic. When I'd been small, I'd watch her get dressed for an evening or afternoon event. Her signature perfume had been Chanel No. 5 and her signature accessory a scarf.

After she put on her dress, she would open her scarf drawer, whereupon out would waft the most heavenly scent of Chanel No. 5. A panoply of silk scarves in all colors and sizes would fill my eyes and imagination.

She'd try on one scarf after another, until she finally decided on one that would set off her outfit, most frequently a simple A-line dress in navy,

black, or black and white. Not only her choice of scarf, but the way she
wore it, would make her entire ensemble come alive. Satisfied with the
tying on of the scarf, she'd spray one final spritz in the air around her neck.
"A woman should never overdo her perfume. When in doubt, spray the air
around you, not on yourself directly," was one of her dictums. Then she
would sail downstairs.

I'd follow, transfixed.

Her final ritual before leaving the house would occur in the front hall
before the large mirror that hung on the wall next to the front door.

"Ava, whenever you're about to go out, look in the mirror one last time,
then take off one thing," she'd advise.

"But why, Nana? You're wearing so many nice things."

"That's the point. I'm probably wearing one too many. So I'm going to
take a look then remove one of them."

"But you spent so much time choosing what to wear," I'd remonstrate.

"Yes. And now I'm going to spend a bit more time choosing something
to take off."

"But why?" I couldn't figure it out. We'd just spent forty-five minutes
in her bedroom going over her final look in painstaking detail. "Are you
changing your mind?"

"No, darling. Just making a final adjustment." My grandmother rarely
called me darling.

After cocking her head, pirouetting in the mirror then smoothing
her already smooth dress down over her iron-flat stomach (thanks to the
full-support girdle she wore every day of her life), she'd take off a single
bangle bracelet, brooch, belt, or rhinestone hair comb. Whatever item she
removed, she'd hand to me.

"Here, darling, take this upstairs for me, will you?"

I'd rush upstairs, holding the accessory as if it were a bag of gold bul-
lion. Depositing it carefully wherever it belonged ("a place for everything
and everything in its place," was another of her dictums), I'd inhale one
final whiff of Chanel No. 5, then rush downstairs again, where I'd receive
a Chanel-bathed kiss and hug. If I was accompanying her, I'd grab my coat
and follow her out the door, imitating the way she sailed when she walked
on occasions she knew she was being noticed. She would be in a rare good
mood and so would I, because she was getting out of the house and away
from whatever it was that drove her up the wall about her own life.

Secretly studying the French women who came into Teddy's, I could see my grandmother's mantras put into action. "Less is more" appeared to be Parisian women's guiding fashion principal. Knowing how to wear a scarf was another. In the personal style arena, my grandmother could easily have held a candle to just about any Frenchwoman on the streets of Paris. How many American women could say that? Not me – although I was working on it.

Meanwhile, my outré gay friends loved me in my turban, and I didn't love me in it at all. Who was I kidding? I wasn't interested in being outré. I was interested to one day become a quietly stylish woman like the ones I saw everywhere in Paris; someone who carried herself like my grandmother.

There was something about the performing lifestyle that was turning me into someone I didn't recognize. I wasn't sure if I needed to catch up with the performing artist I was becoming or if I needed to rethink the whole idea of being one. Although I was flattered when my new fans made a fuss over me, deep inside I cringed. It didn't seem particularly me – especially the private, songwriting side of me. It also didn't seem particularly French. That ruled out both who I was and who I was interested in becoming. The kind of woman I admired was quietly elegant, a sort of toned down version of Holly-go-Lightly – if she'd belonged to a club and hadn't earned a living accepting fifty dollar bills to go powder her nose. Shouldn't I try to become the sort of woman I looked up to?

Arnaud returned from Vietnam in mid-October and we resumed our *ménage* or household together. I'd stay overnight at his place three to four times a week but return to my flat the night before work days to prepare and rehearse.

One day in late October, after we breakfasted on large cups of coffee with steaming milk into which we dipped pieces of buttered baguette, we crossed the street from his apartment to walk in Père Lachaise. Huge, ancient trees in regal fall foliage overhung the avenues and side paths criss-crossing the cemetery, laid out like a small city.

"*Elle se ressemble une belle femme mûre,*" Arnaud remarked. "It resembles a beautiful, older woman," he'd said, meaning a woman in full glory, at the apex of her beauty, charm and artifice, the apple at its ripest moment before its fall from the tree.

I liked his quintessentially French attitude. Americans referred to older women as moms, teachers, businesswomen and old ladies. France turned its older women into style icons, *grandes dames* who ran literary salons, *femmes d'une certain âge* who set high standards of grace and well-appointedness for the younger women who emulated them and the men who admired them. That was the kind of older woman I wanted to become.

Our next-door neighbor, Fred Shelton, had once remarked to me about my grandmother as we'd watched her return from a daily walk on West Hill Drive, the street where we lived. "Ava, your grandmother is one fine figure of a woman. She's like a ship in full sail. You should be proud of her."

If my grandmother could exhibit style worthy of a Frenchwoman, down to her fingertips back in West Hartford, Connecticut, never having set foot in Europe, then I could learn how to carry myself like a Frenchwoman, too. The only problem was, I'd never be accepted as French by the French themselves.

Eureka.

It suddenly struck me, sitting at Teddy's beat-up old upright piano playing *Inchworm,* while my mind raced in all directions, that the best place for me to present myself as French was back home in the United States. Back where I belonged.

I wouldn't actually be French, but I would be Frenchified. In fact, I already was. A certain Parisian mystique had already rubbed off on me. I vowed to make it linger in the air around me for the rest of my life, like the scent over my grandmother's open scarf drawer.

If I stayed in France, I'd forever be an ex-pat, mangling the French language, languishing in the style and *savoire-faire* departments, and lagging behind French women of my own age and social standing in every possible category. Or I'd learn to keep up with them in an exhausting daily competition I would more frequently lose than win.

"Do you think one day I'll be *une belle femme mûre?*" I asked teasingly, as we strolled down one of the cemetery's endless *allées* or paths.

Arnaud stopped and turned me to him. The branches of two tall trees on either side of the *allée* intermingled overhead, creating a canopy. Paris's autumnal glory was more muted than fall in New York. The reds, yellows and oranges seemed to be team players, rather than each vying for stardom as they did back home.

"If you grow into who you are, you will," he said, stroking the point of my chin with his thumb and index finger.

His words hit me like an arrow to the heart. It was exactly what I'd been asking myself at the keyboard over the past few months. I eyeballed the man next to me, who'd told me on the way to the countryside two months earlier that he liked women of all ages, young or ripe, depending on the moment. That was who Arnaud was.

But I wasn't someone who wanted to be someone's all-in-all for only a brief moment in their life. I wanted to be someone's all-in-all forever. Was that the American in me? Or was it just who I was?

"Tu es sage. You are wise," I murmured, my head resting against his chest. Arnaud was a match for me, the beauty of which I'd never experienced before. But the softly colored leaves that fluttered to the ground hinted at beauty's short duration.

CHAPTER FOURTEEN

Je T'adore, Je T'aime

wo weeks later, Arnaud set off on his next assignment, back to Vietnam. While he was away, business picked up even more at Teddy's. Paris's fall season was in full swing. My performances had been expanded to a weekend night too, usually Fridays, now my Blue Cactus Friday evening gig was over. I'd begun to weave in a few original songs to my evening repertoire, not that anyone cared. The crowd still clamored for the old standbys, the more sentimental the better. My visions of being the next Laurie Anderson were in constant conflict with the only way I gained recognition at my job – giving in to requests for crowd-pleasing, tear-jerker old standards. My performing career featured endless nightly compromise, but I consoled myself that at least I was working in my field, rather than office temping or waiting on tables. Soon cloudless, warm October days gave way to iron-gray, rainy, cold November ones. The memory of Paris's long, drab winter the year I'd turned twenty returned to me. Paris was nowhere near as cold as New York, but its skies were unrelentingly gray during the winter season, unlike the azure-blue brilliance of certain New York days in early winter. November to March in Paris was like one long month of February in New York.

Almost every day, I walked in Père Lachaise, where Arnaud and I had frequently strolled the month before. I began to notice the regulars who frequented the area: dog-walkers, couples, and lone walkers. All of us seemed shrouded in private thoughts – the cemetery a perfect backdrop for our self-reflection.

Upon entering the main gates late one gloomy, gray Friday morning I spotted a notice affixed to the lamppost next to the entrance. A print of a painting of a sharp-faced, aristocratic looking man announced an artist's opening exhibit at a local gallery the following day, Saturday, November fifteenth. Startled, I realized almost a month had passed since Arnaud had left. Even more shocked, I realized I hadn't thought about him very much over the past few days.

I examined the poster more closely. The man's petulant expression was similar to the way Arnaud looked at times. Almost guiltily, I admitted to myself I didn't like that side of him at all. It reminded me of the sharp-featured, beautiful woman in the photo in his country home. I didn't like her either. Suddenly, it made sense to me why he'd spoken of her as his mentor. They were most likely two of a kind – all angles, questions, and sharp edges. For the first time, I gave myself permission to accept how very different Arnaud was from me. I loved learning from him. But I wasn't like him at all. Why was I trying so hard to fit into the image of a woman he might fall in love with?

I continued on my way into the cemetery, where I passed the next hour deep in self-examination. *À chacun son goût*, to each his own taste, Arnaud had said. On my own, without him around, I was free to explore what my own tastes were.

I picked my way among the monuments and gravestones, mulling over the possibility that my own choices might differ from the man I was involved with. My thoughts were subversive. My mind tingled and raced. I was falling in love with a new person.

Myself.

As I made my way down the main boulevard toward the exit, a tall, lean-faced man walked toward me. His gait was awkward, as if he was just renting space in his own body and wasn't quite familiar with it.

As he passed, his eyes briefly made contact with mine. They were warm, strangely reassuring. Instantly, I felt a connection. Whoever he was, he wasn't polished, smooth, one hundred per cent self-sufficient and perfectly packaged like most Parisians appeared to be, foremost among them – Arnaud. This stranger seemed a bit out of his element, interested to reach out. He hadn't yet arrived, I'd guess. Just like me.

I shivered, hurrying on to escape my illicit thoughts. I was crazy about Arnaud's blue-green eyes. Why had I even noticed for a moment the warm, brown eyes of a stranger? Shaking my head to clear it from conjecture's cobwebs, I berated myself. Yet the thought remained. Arnaud's glance didn't reassure me. It was exciting, electrifying – but rarely reassuring. Was that what I really wanted out of a relationship with a man?

At Teddy's that evening, I mulled over my tiny mental betrayal of my lover as I finished my first set. Arnaud had been gone too long, that was all. I was lonely and just a bit fed up with our constant separations. Everything would be fine once he got back.

"Was that a Sade song you were playing?" a voice asked.

I looked up. Startled, my stomach churned as if a ghost stood before me.

It was the man from Père Lachaise that afternoon. Speechless, I couldn't reply.

"Was that Sade you were just playing?" he repeated, referring to the low-voiced, low-profile English singer of African origin who'd burst onto the pop music scene in the late 1980s, then disappeared, after three award-winning albums. She was one of my favorites, both for her spare song-writing style and sultry, mystery-laden voice.

"No. That was my own."

His English was good, with a slight French accent.

"You mean you wrote it?"

"Yes." My heart fluttered.

"What's it called?"

"*Method and Madness*." I was used to being ogled; admired for idiotic, exterior things like my hats or my Hungarian cheekbones that didn't seem intrinsically a part of me. My songs were.

"*Method and Madness?*"

"Yes."

He stepped back, cocking his head.

242 ROZSA GASTON

Mentally, I did the same. His hair was wavy and full, darker than Arnaud's. His face was less perfect in its proportions, a slightly too-long, too-thin nose and sharply angled cheekbones that jutted out so far they made the lower half of his narrow face look gaunt.

"Can you explain it to me?"

I smiled. "An artist shouldn't explain her creation. It's enough to just create it."

"You're right. It's enough just the way it is." He paused, looking at me gravely, nothing like the outrageous, joking but flirtatious way Arnaud had pushed himself into my life. "But I want to know more."

"Why?" I was pleased. Someone was actually asking about my original music. Not about where I was from, my astrological sign, or my availability for a drink later that evening. Although that might come.

"Because I'm a mathematician."

"Oh?" Now that was interesting. I'd never met a real mathematician before. "What kind of math do you do? – or – uh – study?" I wasn't sure if mathematicians did things or just studied them. Maybe he taught.

"I'm working on a project to define M."

"To define M? What's M?" It sounded like a good name for the kinds of songs I wrote.

"Bahh – ." His long, angular body shifted, while his large hands gestured in the air, cryptic and vague, as if engaged in a sign language neither he nor I could understand. "I can't really explain it."

I laughed. "That's exactly how it is with my own songs. I can't really explain them. You either like listening to them or you don't."

"I do." Hemming and hawing, his hands still attempting to define M in the air around him, he stood there looking gawky and interesting.

So what are you going to do about it, buddy? The minute the thought crossed my mind I knew how very American I was to the core. I'd never be French.

A French person wouldn't feel the need to do anything after engaging in a flirtatious exchange. He or she would just let it happen. An American would feel a categorical imperative to follow up.

Frenchmen flirted with women everywhere all the time. Married men flirted with married women, gay men passed compliments to straight women, and women critically eyeballed other women (in Paris that's a big compliment). In France, it was all about the journey, not the destination.

In my experience, American men flirted in order to get somewhere. They spent a lot of time rounding bases on their way to home plate. It was all about scoring – or at least thinking about scoring. French men didn't seem to interact with the opposite sex in those terms. They knew how to be here now. Or at least they knew better than American men how to be here now.

But the tall, awkward mathematician wasn't doing anything about us being there then, to my vexation.

"Good," I said in response to his appreciation of my original music. I got up and smartly disappeared into the dressing room behind the bar. There was no way I was going to help him make a next move. He'd have to figure it out all on his own. Anyway, I wasn't available, I reminded myself. Then, I scolded myself that I'd needed reminding.

When I came out, he was gone. Telling myself I could care less, I began my next set with Rodgers and Hammerstein's "I'm Gonna Wash That Man Right Out of My Hair."

The next afternoon, Arnaud called, surprising me. He never called when he was away.

"*Minou*, how are you?"

"I'm fine, darling. How are you?"

"Missing you." Something must have really gone wrong out there in Indochina. This was a first. "Are you missing me, too?"

"Sure I miss you," I lied. I'd thought about how his blue-green eyes didn't really reassure me, which far from qualified as missing him. "Why are you calling?" I asked, straight to the point.

"*Minou*, could you do me a favor?"

"Of course. What is it?" Why had I said "Of course?" What was I , his wife? *Non*. His hired assistant? *Mais, non.* A naïve American chick? *Certainement non.*

"My friend Pierre is in Paris. He's staying at my place. I told him about you, and he wants to hear your music. Just be nice to him if he turns up."

"Who's your friend, Pierre?" I asked, pleased to know Arnaud had mentioned me to his friends. I'd never met any of them thus far.

"He's an old school friend."

"You mean from the military academy – Saint Cyr?"

"*C'est ça*. That's it. He's a little weird, but you'll like him."

"How is he weird?"

"He's what you Americans refer to as a geek."

"How so?" I felt ready to defend the geek, whoever he was. There were times when I found Arnaud just a tad too polished, too smooth. Like when he was sliding in and out of my life on yet another assignment to somewhere I wasn't invited.

"You'll see when you meet him."

"How's that going to happen?"

"I told him what nights you play at Teddy's. He said he'll drop by."

"How is it out there?" I asked, careful to conceal how happy I was someone had expressed interest in hearing my own music.

"It's hot. *Affreusement mouillé.* Horribly humid."

"And how's the assignment going?"

"Slow, darling. Very slow and unexciting." A pause. "Like Pierre, I'm afraid."

"Then why are you sending him my way?" I asked, irritated.

"I told him you write songs. He asked what kind, and I said I couldn't really explain, he should just go and hear you perform."

"Okay, I'll look out for him," I replied, irked that Arnaud hadn't been able to come up with a single adjective to describe to his friend what kinds of songs I wrote. My articulate, intelligent boyfriend had been completely incapable of a single description of my creative work. A small balloon popped amongst the cluster I held in my heart to celebrate our love.

"I'll see you when I get back, *ma chère.*"

It was as if he'd said, "take care of yourself." Just something to say, with no meaning or commitment attached to it at all. I tried not to be disappointed, as another balloon burst.

"See you then," I responded, just a bit coldly.

"*Je t'adore.*" That was better. My heart sang. His words sounded so romantic, so French. What American man would tell his girlfriend he adores her on a regular basis?

"*Moi aussi.* Me too. *Au revoir,*" I answered and hung up.

That evening at Teddy's I didn't look up when a piece of paper fluttered into my tip jar. Why bother, if it wasn't accompanied by currency? A working musician's cynicism took over when I was on the job. It was just another gig after all, meaning I wanted to get paid for it, tips welcomed. When I finished the piece I was playing, I unfolded it.

"*Method and Madness, s'il vous plaît,* please."

I glanced around the room, my eyes focusing in the dim, smoky light. In the corner, the man from the evening before nodded.

He was back!

A tiny, naughty thought crossed my mind. Then, it decided to stay awhile.

Launching into *Method and Madness*, I lost myself in my latest composition. In the middle section, or the bridge, I extended the instrumental riff for extra drama. Caught up in the genius of my solo, I was startled when my boss's face suddenly loomed before me.

"Ava, could you play something everyone knows?" he whispered. It was the first time he'd ever commented on my song selections. Blood rushed to my head as I tried to prevent my cheeks from flaming. How dare he direct me back to yet another base, inferior top-40 cover tune? I was playing my own music for God's sake, something that would one day be famous!

"I'm playing a request right now," I hissed.

"That's great, but no one's ever heard of it. Could you play *Careless Whisper* again?"

I wanted to gag. It was my employer's favorite English pop song, one of the only ones he knew. I'd heard it one too many times to be able to enjoy playing it anymore. It was as if my boss had just asked me to toss out the vintage Mouton Lafitte Rothschild in his glass and refill it with Boone's Farm strawberry wine.

"Sure. As soon as I'm finished with this one," I snarled back. I needed to stand up for myself. But I also needed to eat and to earn a living in order to retain some independence from Arnaud.

Why did I need to do that when the man adored me? Because I just did, that was all. An artist didn't need to explain herself.

My eyes wandered back to the man sitting in the corner. He wasn't particularly good looking. But I liked the way he listened intently as I played my song. He seemed earnest, more like an American than a Frenchman. French men were all about smooth moves or suavity. They had it in spades. They practically majored in it back at *lycée* or high school.

The guy in the corner was now scribbling something on a cocktail napkin. For several seconds, I studied him as I launched into the dramatic opening riff of Teddy's request. It was nice not to be the star of whatever thoughts the stranger in the corner was caught up in at that moment.

Yet I wanted to know what they were. All of them.

By the end of *Careless Whisper*, the mathematician hadn't looked up once. Meanwhile, I received the first tiny, barely audible round of applause of the evening.

It seemed like a good time to take a break. Ignoring all my rules for *la chasse*, the hunt, I went over to the stranger's table in the corner and sat.

He continued to scribble on the cocktail napkin.

The more he concentrated, the more intrigued I became.

Finally, he looked up.

"*Bon soir,* Ava," he said.

"How did you know my name?" I asked, surprised.

His eyes danced. "*Ça va, ce soir?* How are you this evening?" He eluded my question, the first smooth move I'd seen him make yet.

"*Ça va très bien, merci.* I'm fine, thank you. And who would like to know, may I ask?"

"*Ahh, excusez-moi.* I am Pierre Castel. A friend of Arnaud de Saint Cyr. *Enchanté.*" He put out his hand to shake mine, American style.

"You're Pierre?" Incredulous, I pushed back from the table. This was Pierre? Arnaud had described him as slow and unexciting.

Not in my book.

"*Oui.* I am Pierre. And you are Ava. From New York, *non?*"

"Yes. Are you – I mean you are – you're Arnaud's friend from childhood?"

"We went to school together."

"To the military academy?" One of the few things Arnaud had told me about his past was that he'd spent time at a military academy that shared his name. When I'd asked if there was a family connection, he'd changed the subject.

"Yes."

"How fascinating. Does that mean Arnaud is some sort of – army officer in France?"

"*Bah, non, pas exactement.*" He cleared his throat. "Arnaud did not complete his studies at Saint Cyr. He moved in another direction."

That didn't surprise me. He'd probably dropped out. Or been thrown out. His outsized personality would definitely have gotten him tossed out of a boarding school back home. Nothing about Arnaud suggested "team player."

"So does that mean *you're* an army officer?"

"*Justement.* Exactly."

Now, I was in big trouble. I'd spent my entire life categorically rejecting every tenet of my grandmother's value system. Yet here I was, ready to
melt upon hearing the man sitting across from me was a military officer. I
could have kicked myself, except I was too busy soaking up Pierre Castel.
What would he look like in his military uniform? Would it have epaulets?
Badges? Or was that for Boy Scouts? Medals, perhaps? Would there be a
large hat with a horsehair plume on top?

I shivered involuntarily. My grandmother's voice sang in my ear. *Play
your cards right, Ava. And for God's sake get that hair out of your face.*

"Huh. Did you actually fight a war somewhere?"

"*Non.* France is not fond of making wars at this time in history." He
smiled, delicately refraining from mentioning other countries by name that
were.

"I see. So what exactly is the French military fond of doing at this
time?" Horseback riding? Fencing? Interbreeding with the locals? I was
all ears.

He smiled. "Do you really want to know?'

"*Mais, oui, bien sûr.* But yes, of course," I said, exactly as I'd heard the
French say when they found something strongly interesting.

"Then, why don't you join me tomorrow at my military canteen for
lunch?"

"Lunch at a military canteen?" I was dumbfounded. No one had ever
asked me on a date to a military canteen before. It sounded unappealing,
but in the interest of getting to know Pierre Castel better, I could put up
with a single, army-issue meal.

"Yes. There's one here in Paris, not far from Arnaud's place. I invite
you."

"Bah..." I thought I'd try out the French 'bah' expression to at least
pretend I was playing hard to get. Then I remembered. I was Arnaud's
girlfriend. This couldn't possibly be a date. It was just some sort of friendly
lunch, since we both knew Arnaud and were at loose ends while he was out
of town. "Well ... all right."

"*Très bien.* I'll pick you up at half past twelve, tomorrow. Where do I
find you?"

Pierre was getting smoother by the minute. Slow and unexciting? How
well did Arnaud know his childhood friend? And how well did he think
he knew me? On both counts, a tad too smug in his judgments, I thought.

"I'm here. I live in the apartment above Teddy's," I burst out, before remembering I was a woman of mystique.

"Good," he responded, smiling.

"Why didn't you tell me who you were last night?" I demanded.

"*Je m'excuse*, Ava," His smile widened, his expression sincere. "I just got caught up in – in your music."

Hmm. Just as I was getting caught up in his earnestness or whatever it was that hummed to me.

The manager caught my eye and tapped his watch.

"I've got to go, Pierre. My last set."

"I've got to go, too. See you here tomorrow, half past twelve?"

"Not here. Go to the door around the corner to the left of the front entrance. You'll see it. There's a little lantern outside. I'm at the top of the stairs on the first floor if I'm not downstairs already. Just knock."

"I'll find you."

"*Bon. A demain*. Till tomorrow."

"*A demain*, Ava." He stood as I rose from the table, giving me a taste of military manners. All the geeky awkwardness of him from the night before had melted away. He stood erect, practically saluting, as I passed on my way to the piano.

That night, I wrestled with my grandmother's angel before falling asleep. Memories of our neighbor Chip Hopkins, leaving for Naval Reserve weekends from his house across the street from us in West Hartford, filled my head. Once every three months or so, Mr. Hopkins would emerge from his house on a Friday afternoon wearing a crisp white jacket and trousers. Gold buttons, medals and gold and black trim decorated the front of his U.S. Navy Reserve jacket as he marched down the front steps. His blonde, slim, athletic wife Poppy would follow behind, practically bursting with admiration. She'd fuss over him, hand him his regulation duffle bag, affix his white cap on his head, then hug and kiss him a few times, making a huge public display of affection. My grandmother soaked this up in vicarious delight, as she spied on them from the couch next to the large, bay window in our living room.

"There's Chip going off on his reserve weekend. Poppy is one lucky woman to have a husband like that," my grandmother would sigh. *Unlike me*, every pore in her body would silently exhale. "Look at him in his uniform, Ava. Have you ever seen such a fine figure of a man? Too bad you couldn't have had a father like that." My grandmother knew how to drive home a point.

She'd swoon and moon over Chip, as he got into his Ford Falcon and drove off. Lithe, blonde, and suntanned Poppy in lime-green culottes would wave and blow kisses goodbye then turn to check on her flower beds. Poppy was one of those perpetually tanned athletic West Hartford ladies. She and Chip played tennis at their club. Twice weekly, they'd drive off on Chip's Vespa in their white tennis outfits, rackets stashed behind. They appeared to spend all of their time playing tennis or gardening when not tending to their three children, all of whom enjoyed effortless super-WASPy looks. The entire family had good hair.

I'd secretly disliked the Hopkins, whom I'd renamed the Snotkins. They weren't actually snotty, it's just that they pretty much represented every snotty value my grandmother possessed in her large repertoire of discriminatory and unfair social class distinctions. They were the 'It' family in her book, and we were the 'Not Its'.

However, I couldn't help but admire the white jacket Chip Hopkins wore on Navy Reserve days. It was an uncontrollable attraction in direct contradiction to my knee-jerk opposition to anything my grandmother stood for.

Sleep eluded me as speculations on Pierre intermingled with thoughts of Arnaud. As I drifted off, our phone conversation came to mind.

"See you when I get back" hadn't exactly thrilled my heart, but "*je t'adore*" had. Back to back, his two final lines had bewildered me. If a guy I was dating back in New York had finished a long-distance phone conversation with 'see you when I get back', I'd have taken it as a sign I was free to do what I liked in the interim. Yet, he'd finished off with "*je t'adore*." That meant he loved me, right? A little angry with him to have left me in such a confused state, I fell asleep.

The next day, Pierre picked me up on time, French-style. That is to say, ten minutes late. We set off for the military canteen. I'd opted for simple elegance in the form of a navy blue dress with scooped neckline. I'd added a red and white scarf, to match the colors of the French flag, along with the American one. Women in Paris dressed up to go to the market or take their small dogs out on the sidewalk for morning ablutions, so I wasn't taking any chances just because we were going to a military canteen. No Parisian woman would be caught dead in combat wear, unless it was the height of fashion chic that season.

We took the metro to Gare St. Lazare, a large train station centrally located on Paris's right bank, then walked three blocks, until we arrived at a large, distinguished looking building on boulevard Haussmann. Over the entrance *Le Cercle National des Armées* was etched in marble.

As we walked up the broad front steps, I felt my grandmother's cane prod the small of my back, as she'd done so many times on our walks around West Hill Drive. *Stand up straight, Ava. Posture tells the world who you are.*

Inside, paintings and photographs of famous French military figures lined the walls of the large foyer. I wanted to linger, but quickly we were ushered into a large and ornate dining room with twelve foot ceilings. The maitre d' handed us each leather-bound lunch menus announcing the set menu of the day. No ordering was required other than drinks. In a minute, sparkling water arrived, followed by soup, a main course of *cuisses de canard*, duck thighs, in orange sauce accompanied by *haricots verts* or tiny string beans, then salad, cheese, and dessert. It was a meal fit for royalty. We talked nonstop about music, math, Paris, and New York, where Pierre had once delivered a presentation at the City University of New York's graduate studies math department. Over the next hour and a half, Arnaud's name never once came up.

When it was time to go, Pierre signed the check, while I looked around the dining room. The couple next to us had recently sat down. They held hands across the table. The man leaned forward, his eyes gazing adoringly into the woman's. She was petite, dark, with short, straight precision-cut dark brown hair and expertly penciled-in eyebrows. My senses sharpened to their obvious regard for each other, my ears picking up their conversation.

"Je t'adore, cherie," I overheard, warmed to hear the same words Arnaud had spoken to me the other day on the phone. The man played with the bangle bracelet on the woman's wrist – a charming scene.

I looked at Pierre. His mouth had formed into a disapproving sort of *moue* or pout.

"What's wrong?" I whispered. "Don't you think they're cute?" I motioned ever so slightly to the couple next to us, oblivious to everything around them.

"Cute? If that's what you want to call it, yes, I suppose." He shrugged then rose from the table, motioning me toward the garden. In a minute, we were outside, strolling down an *allée* of plane trees flanking us on both sides like a military wedding guard.

"What was wrong with you back there?" I continued. "It looked like he was about to propose marriage. Wasn't it sweet?"

"He wasn't about to propose marriage, I can tell you that."

"How do you know?" I asked indignantly. What a killjoy. Was Pierre Castel was too much of a geek mathematician to understand romance?

"He wasn't serious about her."

"How do you know that?" I repeated. What was he, a body-language expert or something?

"Because of the way he spoke to her."

"What do you mean? He told her he adored her. Didn't you see the way he was smiling at her?"

"*Précisement*. That means he's not serious."

I stared at Pierre.

"How so?"

"If he was serious, he would have said *je t'aime,* I love you. And he wouldn't have smiled. But he said *je t'adore*. There's a difference."

"What's the difference?" I kept my eyes on the path, unable to meet Pierre's gaze.

"One means 'I love you'. The other means 'I think you're adorable.'"

"Doesn't it also mean something like 'I love you'?"

"Not really. It's what a man says when he's not serious about a woman."

My blood froze. *Je t'adore* sounded so serious. So adoring. How could it mean something less than the way it sounded?

"It is? But what about the way he was looking at her? He was practically beaming."

"A man doesn't smile like a hyena when he's telling a woman he loves her. It's a serious statement. You don't smile when you are trying to show someone you are serious, responsible, do you?"

I remembered Arnaud saying *je t'adore* to me. Had he smiled? Yes. Not unlike the way the man at the table next to us had smiled at his girlfriend.

"But the way he was smiling at her looked like he was crazy about her," I protested.

"Exactly. *Je t'adore* means he's crazy about her. Don't misunderstand. It means he likes her a lot. It just doesn't mean he loves her. In fact, he definitely doesn't, because he wouldn't say *je t'adore* if he really meant *je t'aime*."

"Well thanks for clearing that up." Something pinged inside my chest. Another balloon popping.

"You're welcome. I'm happy to explain to you the difference. It's an important one for a woman to know."

So he did care about romance, and about a woman not getting her heart broken. Did he have any idea what state my own heart was in at that moment?

"So, just to clarify, do you think a *je t'adore* sort of relationship ever turns into a *je t'aime* kind of one?" I hoped I didn't sound too interested to hear his response. It's just that I needed to know. Immediately.

He shook his head. "Not likely."

"Why not?"

"Because a man who says *je t'adore* to a woman without ever saying *je t'aime* is letting her know the relationship isn't on the serious track."

"Huh." There was so much to absorb, I couldn't do more than walk in silence for the next few minutes. "So then, how does the woman let the man know she is on the serious track? I mean if he's already said *je t'adore* to her. Like a number of times, say."

"Then she should dump him, I think you Americans say."

"Just like that?"

"After he's said it to her a few times, she needs to either confront him or just drop him."

"Oh." I had a lot to think about.

"Why do you ask?" he probed. Pierre Castel appeared to know something about romance after all. Talking to him was as easy as having a gab-fest with my singer/actress girlfriend, Jessica, back in New York.

"Oh well – I just know someone who –"

"Who said *je t'adore* to you?"

"No! I mean I know a girl – I have a girlfriend, I mean – who told me her boyfriend always says *je t'adore* to her whenever they say goodbye."

"So, she knows where she stands."

"Uh, I'm not so sure about that."

"I'm sure she does. If she didn't, she wouldn't keep seeing him."

"Well maybe she's still seeing him because there's no *je t'aime* kind of guy in her life at the moment."

"When he comes along, she'll dump the first one."

"I like your certainty."

"I like your smart questions."

"I like your answers."

"I like your songs."

"I like you," What had I said? " – in your jacket," I quickly added. Pierre wore an officer's jacket, dark blue with red trim. He looked dashing, as well as geeky and earnest. It was an adorable combination, except now I was suspicious of using the term 'adorable' in French in any context. I would ban it from my vocabulary until I figured out what it really meant.

"I like you," he responded, no qualifiers attached.

I was glad.

"But you don't adore me, right?" It felt good to get such a point straight from the start. Although this wasn't a start really, it was just the start of a friendship. Or something. Whatever it was, it felt genuine.

"Right." He smiled.

We continued on our walk – I, more grown up than I had been minutes earlier, and he, lost in whatever private thoughts he was having. Perhaps about mathematics. Probably about me.

CHAPTER FIFTEEN

La Décision

For the next two weeks, I performed at Teddy's on Wednesday, Thursday and Friday nights and for all six of those nights Pierre Castel showed up for part of the evening to listen, converse with me during my breaks and then leave. His elusiveness drove me crazy. The fact that I was Arnaud's girlfriend and I was supposed to be desperately longing for his return, but somehow wasn't, was also driving me crazy. Who was I? A lightweight? A will o' the wisp musician drifting along in the willow world of nightclub entertainment and nightclub mores?

On afternoons after my last English student left and evenings I wasn't working, Pierre squired me around town. His enthusiasm for everything we visited matched my own, probably because he wasn't a Parisian. We were both free to marvel at the wondrous beauty Paris offered, untrammeled by the mandatory blasé attitude of a native Parisian. *"Je m'en fou.* I could care less," the expression I'd heard used so frequently there, never once crossed either of our lips. We were like two outer borough New Yorkers romping around the island of Manhattan.

One mild early-December afternoon we decided to explore Montmartre, the hilly neighborhood where nineteenth and twentieth century artists such as Toulouse Lautrec and Modigliani had painted. It was a well-known tourist destination, which neither Pierre nor I minded, counting ourselves among them. We climbed the five hundred or so stairs to Montmartre's most famous landmark, the Basilica of Sacré-Coeur. There, in the main square before the enormous white church, a street performance was in progress.

Four acrobats, two men and two women, flashed back and forth across the square in dizzying gymnastic sequences. They wore black and white harlequin leotards with yellow-gold trim. Lithe and graceful, the entertainers teased the crowd, provoking, then retreating from the audience in a series of flips, cartwheels, and shoulder stands. Suddenly, the more attractive of the two female performers landed directly in front of us, breathless and flushed. Her animated eyes raked over Pierre, ignoring me altogether.

Like a déjà vu, the castle courtyard in Sancerre flashed into my head, where I'd watched Arnaud exchange looks with the court lady with the green scarf. The scene still smarted, although I knew it had meant nothing.

I glanced at Pierre, steeling myself to be strong. He was a French man after all.

But he wasn't gazing at the young, female acrobat only inches away, her not-unpleasant sweaty scent filling our nostrils. Instead, he stared bashfully down at the cobblestoned square like any homespun, right-hearted American man would do in the company of a female he was with and an attractive female stranger in front of him.

"*Ça va?*" he asked, his eyes sweeping up to mine. No guilt or hint of wandering attention showed there.

My heart warmed.

"*C'est merveilleux, non?* It's marvelous, isn't it?" I asked, meaning how he hadn't allowed his attention to be diverted to the lightly clad woman in front of us.

He nodded, breaking into a smile. The performer gave Pierre a disdainful look, then she cart-wheeled back to the center of the square.

The rest of that afternoon, I had plenty to think about. One month earlier, I'd been madly in love with Arnaud. But the logistics of loving someone who wasn't there and not in regular touch were having a not-so-surprising effect. In the absence of any sort of commitment between us, and buffeted by Pierre's discourse on the *je t'adore, je t'aime* distinction, my heart was no longer certain of Arnaud or of my feelings for him.

"So Pierre, what kind of woman do you date?" I asked, rather audaciously, a few days later, as we strolled out of Père Lachaise cemetery. We were planning to continue on to a nearby park that we hadn't visited before, the Parc des Buttes-Chaumont. Pierre had told me it featured Paris's highest elevation point, with a waterfall cascading from a man-made cliff that offered spectacular views of the city.

His smile was rueful, a tiny bit sad.

"Why should I tell you?"

"Because I want to know, that's all," I reasoned playfully, like an eight-year old having a talk with her big brother. It was delightful to spend time with him. We had no agenda. He was just visiting, and I was just waiting for Arnaud to return, so I could either have it out with him about the *je t'adore* track or suggest he take the fast track out of my life. It felt good to be beyond reach of Pierre – safe, protected and unafraid to say anything that might come into my head.

"*Bah*, what is it you want to know exactly?" His eyes twinkled as he looked at me. They were a prosaic shade of medium brown, unspectacular but warm.

"Well, have you been married?" With Pierre I was my curious, inquisitive, nosy New York self. I had nothing to lose, unlike with Arnaud, to whom I constantly tried to think of clever things to say in order to keep up with him.

Pierre shook his head.

"No. Never."

"Well, why not?" I prodded mischievously.

"Sorry, Ava. If I'd known you were going to ask, I could have gotten married just so I'd have a story to tell you."

"That's okay. Tell me your non-marriage story." As we exited the gates of the cemetery, it struck me that walking there with Pierre made me feel completely different from being there with Arnaud. I wasn't terrified of losing Pierre. I felt comfortable in his presence without the constant excitement coupled with anxiety I felt when I was with Arnaud. Spending time with Pierre was exciting too, but in a less flashy sort of way. Sort of like being in a Vermeer painting as opposed to a Toulouse-Lautrec one.

"Umm, well I've had a few girlfriends here and there," he replied hesitantly.

"And who was the most important one?"

How long would it take him to answer? If it was fast, he'd indeed had a serious relationship. If he took time to think about it, maybe not.

"*Ehh – crétin – comment vas-tu?* Hey – stupid – how are you?" a voice sang out. We looked around to see a figure waving assuredly at us from across the street. Arnaud.

In the strangest sort of way, I felt as if I'd been caught in the act. But what act? Arnaud had sent Pierre my way in his absence. Pierre had been a perfect gentleman, whose company I'd enjoyed. My heart sank at the thought our time together was about to end.

Arnaud crossed the boulevard, his cocky, confident stride announcing to all he was in full command. The show he put on was for everyone – not just me. I was a show person, too, a performer, but inside, I'd become more interested in developing the private, songwriting side of myself.

"*Eh, salut, fils de pute.* Hello, you son of a whore," Arnaud greeted Pierre, wrestling him into a giant bear hug. His casual, comfortable tone confirmed they were old friends.

Then he turned to me. Against his deep, golden tan, the blue-green of his eyes was even more vivid than usual. I thought of ice as I looked into them. He propelled me into his arms and against his chest. Petulantly, my muscles clenched, resistant to his embrace. He'd shown up at just the wrong moment – just when Pierre had been about to tell me something significant about himself.

Releasing his grip, Arnaud kissed me four times, twice on each cheek, but not on the mouth.

Strangely, I was pleased. I didn't want my mouth touched by another man in Pierre's presence. I stepped back, collecting myself. It wouldn't do to show my hand at this particular moment. Especially, since I didn't know what was in it myself.

"*Comment vas-tu, morceau de merde?* How are you, you piece of shit?" Arnaud roared, smacking Pierre on the shoulder. Pierre looked pleased, but he wasn't smacking Arnaud back. He said something jovial to Arnaud then looked at me. Suddenly, Pierre's expression changed, becoming more guarded.

My heart contracted. *Don't look at me that way, look at me the way you did five minutes ago, the way we look at each other every day when we're making silly conversation or taking a walk.*

"Let's go get something to drink. Come on, I need to find out what filth you've been up to while I was away," Arnaud said, draping one arm over Pierre's shoulder and the other around my waist.

Usually, I was starstruck in Arnaud's presence, mesmerized by his charisma, his conversation, anticipating with bated breath the audacity of what he might do or say next. But this time, his outrageous, larger-than-life patter wasn't working its magic on me.

He and Pierre babbled on in French while I evaluated the shift in my feelings. As we stood at the crosswalk waiting for the light to change, I felt Arnaud's left hand slip down my backside.

I moved it back up to my waist. It didn't seem to belong there anymore either. As the light changed, I realized so had I.

We took a table on the terrace of the café at the corner of Rue des Alouettes and Rue Fessart, around the block from Teddy's.

"So how was it out there? Where were you – Vietnam?" Pierre asked.

"Vietnam, Cambodia. Laos. Up in the Golden Triangle," Arnaud listed, looking around for the waiter.

He hadn't said a thing about travelling to countries other than Vietnam. It occurred to me I knew next to nothing about what he did on assignments – where he went or with whom. Just as he had no idea who came in to Teddy's on nights I performed, and what transpired between my audience and myself. How many admirers I had, which were there for my music, which were there waiting to find out what their chances were with the glittering girl from New York, bathed in spotlight at the piano. Our professional lives were mysteries to each other. As long as they didn't bleed into our personal ones, who cared?

But deep in my heart, I knew my performing career did bleed into my personal life. How could it not? It was the crucible on which my identity was now being forged. The larger-than-life artist's identity I wasn't feeling one hundred per cent comfortable in. I wasn't *bien dans ma peau* when I was on-stage. And that was precisely what Paris had taught me. What it was and how to achieve it. So, where was I now?

I looked over at Arnaud, his eyes flashing, hands gesticulating as he gave the waiter his order. Whatever he did was all show, but it wasn't inauthentic. It was one hundred per cent Arnaud being himself – his way of being, his way of expressing himself.

Next, I looked at Pierre. Without drawing attention, he gave his order to the waiter. No fuss, a minimum of hand gestures, just a purposeful declaration of what he wanted. Pierre being Pierre, *bien dans sa peau.*

An epiphany stole over me without warning. The only person at the table who wasn't authentically being who she really was, was me.

I gulped. Then I ordered a hot chocolate.

The men continued to chatter, catching up since the last time they'd crossed paths, a few years earlier. I wanted to figure out who I was, then be it. That was what coming to Paris had been all about. Paris had taught me what really mattered was to figure out how to be myself, and not someone else – or some aspect of myself I was trying on for size at a given moment. I wanted to be me in a place where I belonged.

Pierre caught my eye as Arnaud made a dramatic point, describing his time in Thailand's Golden Triangle, where the borders of Burma, Laos, and Thailand meet. I'd heard it was popular with tourists on recreational drug jaunts. Had he told me he was going there on this particular assignment? *Non.* Did I care? Quite honestly, *non.* I just cared that he hadn't thought to let me know. What else hadn't he let me know?

I returned Pierre's look. I wanted him to know I belonged to myself alone – not to anyone else sitting at the table. Would he get the message?

"Ava and I were on our way to Buttes-Chaumont," Pierre said at the next pause in Arnaud's soliloquy about his trip. "Do you want to join us?"

It was a challenge – *un défi.* Pierre hadn't allowed his friend's presence to change our plans. Feeling like the heroine of a Jane Austen novel, I feigned disinterest, as Arnaud paused before answering.

"*Bahh, Ava, que'est-ce que tu desires?* What do you want?" Arnaud responded, his eyes flicking across mine, cool, detached. Uncertain, perhaps?

The way the phrase came out in French suggested more than its intent. "What do you desire?" seemed a portentous question. Carefully, I answered.

"*Comme tu veux, Arnaud. Viens avec nous, si tu veux.* As you wish, Arnaud. Come with us, if you want." I made sure Pierre heard the us in my response.

"*Bon. D'accord,*" Arnaud agreed. His eyes glinted as he swung around and gave me a first full gaze since his return.

I returned it levelly, a cool, self-possessed American girl who knew her way around Paris as well as a man like Arnaud de Saint Cyr.

He seemed alerted for the first time to the *us* in our conversation. I watched as his psychic antennae waved in the air around him. I should have been overjoyed at our reunion, rushing to reunite with him privately, dumping Pierre curbside along the way, but instead I wanted to extend my time with slow, unexciting Pierre, who made me feel comfortable, safe. I was in no rush to be back in Arnaud's arms where, after initial elation again I'd feel insecure, anxious to always appear clever, scintillating, and attractive at every moment. How were those feelings consistent in any way with feeling *bien dans ma peau?* Comfortable in my own skin? It was time to make it happen.

We set off toward Parc des Buttes Chaumont, two blocks north of the café. As we walked, visions of *Pauline at the Beach* danced through my head. I'd seen the 1983 Eric Rohmer film in New York a few years back and had been awestruck by the way the beautiful, young blonde heroine had played with the affections of her two male admirers at the beach in the south of France. Adrienne Dombasle in the 1983 film had been gorgeous – blonde, lithe, and utterly sure of herself.

Sandwiched between two attractive men, part of me wanted to emulate Pauline and hone the skills my time in Paris had taught me. But the other part wanted to break away and run to the nearest metro stop. Who was I kidding? I was no Pauline. On the other hand, I hadn't felt like a Yalie the summer before freshman year, one decade earlier. But by the time I graduated, I did. "Fake it till you make it," I reminded myself. Or "fake it till you're not faking it anymore." I could do this. *Pauline at the Beach* move over. *Ava on Her Way to the Park* is here.

The conversation continued in French, peppered with regional words and phrases I couldn't understand. It was all I could do to process the knowledge that I was the object of interest for both men present. Two caveats kept me above water, just barely treading – the first was to hold onto my *sangfroid*, the second to remain fully present in the moment and not worry about anything else. I was young, relatively good-looking, and sought after by two single, attractive Frenchmen. Why was I uncomfortable?

Despite my resolve, thoughts, plans, and speculations escaped in all directions, like steam pouring out the sides of a lid on a pot of boiling water. If I left Arnaud for Pierre, Pierre would forever remember we'd begun our relationship when I was with another man. Not a good start. But didn't people do that all the time, especially in France?

If I stayed with Arnaud, I wouldn't be able to stop thinking about Pierre and what it might be like to be in a conventional, committed relationship – one that didn't involve months-long business trips away and the constant stopping and starting a long-distance relationship entailed.

I came up lightly behind the men, catching the tail-end of their conversation. They were talking about someone they both knew. Their hushed tones told me it was a woman.

"You saw her recently?" Arnaud asked, his voice for once not booming out, dominating the conversation.

"She passed through Chavignol about a month ago," Pierre said.

"Did she ask about me?" Arnaud's tone was serious, almost reverential. Quiet as a mouse, I tiptoed behind the men.

"I can't remember," Pierre replied.

"You can't remember what Mélanie said to you? I don't believe it," Arnaud said.

"We were at the *boulangerie*. It was crowded – we spoke in passing." Pierre looked around, spotting me then clearing his throat.

I walked quickly ahead, pretending not to have heard anything. My blood boiled to think of how vulnerable Arnaud's voice had sounded when he'd asked if whoever Mélanie was had asked about him. I'd never heard Arnaud utter a single word to me in a similar tone, not even when he'd said *je t'adore*.

Suddenly, I didn't adore him back at all. My feelings for him crumbled, as the scales fell from my eyes. He was carrying a torch for someone named Mélanie. And whoever she was, she wasn't me.

"*Always maintain straight posture at critical moments*," my grandmother's voice rang out inside. I straightened up, flicking my ponytail back to ward off the gnat of insecurity now buzzing behind me. Then it hit me – Mélanie was the name of the woman in the photo at Arnaud's country house.

Something tugged at my hair. I ignored it. Again, I tried to catch their conversation.

Arnaud had realized I was within earshot. Changing course, he began to describe a herd of elephants he'd seen in Cambodia.

I felt another tug. This time, I turned my face to the left, where Pierre's eyes caught mine. I lowered my own quickly, my pulse racing. He had been the one pulling my ponytail. Meanwhile, Arnaud droned on about yet another fascinating, obscure thing that had happened to him in the jungles of Southeast Asia.

Pierre lowered his eyes back at me and made an inaudible 'shhh' with his mouth.

My smile was discreet, unnoticed by Arnaud, who was now waxing rhapsodic about how baby elephants call for their mothers. Whatever.

It occurred to me things that happen to us don't really matter as much when they are not shared. If Arnaud had been watching baby elephants bawl for their mothers with me, for example, we would have shared the memory of such a charming scene forever, woven into the fabric of our relationship, however long it lasted.

Instead, it would be Arnaud telling his baby elephant story to others throughout the years, regaling strangers in bars with tales of wondrous exploits he underwent alone. So what? It all seemed like a big nothing to me.

"And then the female elephants all form a circle around the babies and bellow at the male elephants who try to charge the watering hole before the babies have had their drink. Yak, yak, yak, blah blah ..." Arnaud was now completely caught up in his anecdote, oblivious to Pierre's eyes flickering over mine, engaged, attentive, and fully present in the moment. "Be here now" was what Arnaud had preached to me.

But Pierre practiced it.

My mind wandered back to George Berkeley, the eighteenth-century empiricist who'd said "to be is to be perceived." He was one of my favorite philosophers. In my college philosophy classes, he'd been one of the few I'd fully wrapped my brain around, along with Hegel and his three-part dialectic. As a songwriter I could really get behind the concept of three – verse, chorus, bridge were the three components of just about every pop song ever created. It was inarguably a pleasing number, both to the mind and to the senses. No wonder God had chosen it to represent Himself.

But back to Berkeley's way of thinking – let's just say that Arnaud hadn't really seen those baby elephants, or heard them crying for their mothers, or seen the ladies get huffy with the males who tried to drink before the babies had their fill. Who would ever know? Since Arnaud witnessed this whole scene by himself, then who was to say it actually happened?

That's what Berkeley would ask and that was what I was asking now. If Arnaud chose to live his life in a way largely unshared by anyone who remained constant in it, then was there meaning in what he experienced? Frankly – who cared?

My body twitched, my conscience lashing out for the meanness of my thoughts. Still, they kept coming, like a refreshing shower washing away Arnaud's American girlfriend in Paris and leaving a new, stand-alone, self-possessed woman. I was beginning to see his reality was not available to be shared by me or by anyone else, for that matter. Despite being annoyed to hear him ask Pierre about Mélanie, I couldn't feel jealous. Méelanie probably hadn't asked about Arnaud, because she'd left him behind in the dust a long time ago when she'd realized how completely wrapped up in himself he was.

Pierre lightly brushed my left shoulder. Airily, I returned the touch. It was just the tiniest wisp of an interaction. Unlike watching big, dramatic elephants crossing our paths, we'd shared a small, simple interaction, no doubt to be remembered sweetly by us both. That's what I wanted for my future. I didn't want to view elephants in jungles all by myself. I wanted to take walks in homey, familiar places with someone I loved, who loved me back. That was all.

The park looked wilder than other Parisian parks I'd visited. Tall, bushy trees created a dense forest, above which a rocky cliff loomed, perhaps a hundred feet in the air. At the top stood a Grecian-style temple: cute, incongruous and not very French-looking. The setting reminded me of Belvedere Castle in Central Park, back in New York. An unexpected pang of homesickness twinged in my stomach.

Whatever Pauline might have done in a situation like this, I needed to do what was right for myself. Pauline enjoyed playing with the feelings of two men – both present, both interested in her. I didn't.

I turned and fled.

Running through the park, I quickly found my way to the gateway on Avenue Jacques de Linières. Behind me Arnaud's voice rang out, calling my name. The sound of it was sad, as if he already knew he'd lost something.

Once on the avenue, I turned down Rue Fessart, passing the café where we'd sat earlier. Not daring to stop or look behind, I ran all the way back to my apartment above Teddy's, dashing up the stairs then slamming the door, and bolting it shut the second I got inside.

To calm down, I took a shower, then tried to focus on my performance that night. Impossible. My mind awhirl, my thoughts confused, all I could think of was one thing. I wanted to go back to New York.

At Teddy's that night, I cringed every time a new customer came in. Inevitably, Arnaud or Pierre or both would show up. Then I would have to choose. As much as my feelings had changed for Arnaud, I didn't yet know what I felt for Pierre. And there was no way I was going to take up with a new man the moment I broke it off with another.

What would my grandmother have done?

To channel her, I played *Fascination,* the tune made famous by Hoagy Carmichael. It had been one of her favorites, along with *Liebestraum.* The classical piece wouldn't be suitable for a nightclub setting. And besides – if I played *Liebestraum,* I'd choke up at the thought of her sitting quietly in the living room armchair next to the piano at which my eleven-year-old self tried as hard as I could to ease her unhappiness. She'd smoke one of perhaps five Kent cigarettes she enjoyed per year and hum along while I played Franz Liszt's ode to love's dream. Inside, my heart would swell with joy. For a few brief moments, my grandmother would be at peace. And I was the one responsible.

As I finished up *Fascination* I felt her presence in the air. *"Do what your heart tells you, Ava. Don't make my mistakes. Go where you want to be and the right man will follow. Don't follow a man, follow your dream. And for God's sake, get a real job."*

This time, I listened. All the other zillion trillion times she'd advised me to get a real job, I'd covered my ears and immediately begun planning trips to Japan to teach English, or treks through India, seeing how many countries I could visit and for how long, armed with a Eurail Youthpass and a hundred dollars.

I'd smashed into oblivion my grandmother's dreams for me by becoming a singer/pianist/songwriter. But now, there was no more need to do that. My grandmother was no longer around, nagging, hounding, dictating what I should do with my life.

For the first time, I realized I might be ready to listen to some of the advice she'd given me. Because she'd known what would make me happy. Not a dramatic, over-the-top lifestyle like being a performer. And not at the side of a dramatic, over-the-top man such as Arnaud.

The burgundy velvet curtain rustled, announcing a new customer. My stomach lurched as I looked up. D-Day had arrived.

CHAPTER SIXTEEN

Being Where I Belong

"Ava, why did you run off like that? Was it something I did?"

"I wanted to be by myself. I'm sorry, Arnaud." We stood around the corner from Teddy's, outside the entrance to my apartment building. He'd waited out the duration of my performance at the bar at Teddy's then followed me outside. It was time to have it out.

"What do you mean, you're sorry?" His eyes searched mine. For once, I had his full attention.

"I mean — we aren't right for each other."

I'd said it. Thank God, I'd gotten what I needed to tell him out on the table before our conversation moved any further along.

"You mean you *are* seeing Pierre? That *con* bastard. I can't believe you'd fall for someone like him." Arnaud seethed, his face a mask of disgust. "He's dull, Ava. Conventional. Boring. Not like you at all."

"No. I'm *not* seeing Pierre. I just don't see myself with you anymore. It has nothing to do with Pierre." Okay, I lied a teeny bit. Realizing Arnaud wasn't right for me had a little something to do with Pierre entering the picture. But I wasn't about to jump into his friend's arms. Neither was I about to reconnect with Arnaud. I needed to reconnect with myself. But that was harder to explain.

"Of course it has everything to do with Pierre. We were fine before he showed up."

"No, we weren't fine. You were in Vietnam, or Thailand, or wherever, and I was here. You have no idea if I was fine or not while you were gone. That's the point."

"That's not the point. You know what my job is. I've gone on trips before and you were always okay with it. What's changed this time?"

"*I've* changed." I wasn't going to compete with anyone for Arnaud's affections - neither some woman from his past named Mélanie nor some turbo-charged version of myself I no longer wished to be.

"Well — what — how — what do you mean, you've changed?" he sputtered. I'd never seen him at a loss for words before.

"It doesn't matter. It just matters that I'm no longer someone who's meant to be with you." Actually, I couldn't think of anyone who might be meant to be with Arnaud. There was no other woman I could imagine being jealous of as Arnaud's girlfriend, now I knew what being with him was really like. If I continued seeing him, there'd be more loneliness. More long periods of separation. More *je t'adore* declarations diluted by *see you when I get back* ones. My heart shriveled at the thought. Whoever Mélanie was, the fact that she hadn't asked about Arnaud when she'd bumped into Pierre told me she wasn't in the market to be his girlfriend. Maybe she already knew it was an impossible job.

"Of course, you're meant to be with me, Ava. You and I are alike." He paused, apparently trying to think of some ways in which we were.

"Are we?" I didn't think so anymore. It had taken Pierre coming along to make me realize I didn't want to have to work so hard at being someone I wasn't. I just wanted to be appreciated for being not-so-clever, not-so flashy me.

"You're a performer, a star. I'm a peacock. See what I mean?"

He undoubtedly got the second half of that statement right.

"You *are* a peacock, but I'm not a pea hen. I'm a performer now, but I'm not sure I want to keep on being one. I 'm not star material." There. I'd breathed life into the thought that had been nagging at me for so many months. I wasn't Madonna, and I was never going to be her or anyone like her. It just wasn't me.

"Of course you are. That's what drew me to you in the first place." His eyes lit up at the thought of whatever glittering image he had of me when we first met.

"That was then, and this is now." I took off my black and white turban and tossed it in the trash.

"But what do you mean? You're a performer. It's your destiny to be a star."

"While you were away, I realized I don't want to be a star. I want to be a songwriter."

"*Eh voilà.* I'm a journalist, and you're a songwriter. Two writers who don't compete with each other. *Parfait.*"

"Not *parfait*, Arnaud. I'm going back to New York."

"But – then what about Pierre?"

"I told you this has nothing to do with Pierre," I yelled. I needed to get back to where I belonged, that was all.

"What has nothing to do with me?" a voice chimed in.

Sacré bleu! I looked around to see Pierre standing under the streetlamp, his brown eyes trained on mine with remarkable focus.

"My decision," I said calmly, although I felt anything but calm inside.

"What decision?" Pierre asked.

I took a deep breath.

"Arnaud and I are no longer seeing each other," I said, not daring to look at my former love.

I'd made more life-changing statements in the past five minutes than I had in the past five months. I was scared, but it was a good kind of scared. I had stood up for myself, for what I wanted out of life.

Pierre's eyes swiveled to Arnaud. Mine too.

"Is that your wish, then?" Arnaud asked, looking directly at me.

I nodded. No sound came out. There was no point to say anything more.

"Bon. *C'est ça.* Then we're done." Without so much as a glance at Pierre, he turned and walked away, his back straight, his stride jaunty.

It didn't fool me. He'd probably walked out of the life of the woman called Mélanie like that once upon a time. Then, he'd carried a torch for her forever after. Now, he could carry another one for me.

Pierre looked steadily at me. "I came to ask you something."

"Why I ran away – " I began. "I needed to – "

"*Non.* Not that." He cut me off, searching my face.

"Then what?"

"You know what."

"Do you mean, what's – "

"I mean, what's between us."

I nodded. Of course that's what he meant.

"What *is* between us?" I asked, wanting to hear him put words to what we already felt.

His hand slipped into mine as naturally as our feelings for each other had slipped into each other's hearts – without fanfare.

"Something, *non?*" he said, his face serious.

We stood there looking at each other a long moment. It was true, there was something between us. But now, there was something I needed to do for myself. *Go where you want to be and the right man will follow. Don't follow a man, follow your dream.* If whatever was between us had any legs, it would take us somewhere, down the road. Not now.

"Come on." I smiled to let him know his answer had been well-received. "Let's go upstairs." Arnaud had never bothered to visit my place. We had always gone to his.

Inside my flat, I poured Pierre a drink.

When he put it down, I picked up his hand with both of mine and looked at it carefully. It was strongly-built with squared off fingers and hairy knuckles. Unlike Arnaud's artistic hands, it looked down-to-earth, no-nonsense. Not much like a mathematician's hands either. But definitely hands that might belong to a French military officer. Or someone's husband or father.

Our embrace was warm and sweet, free from past hurts, firm from the solid friendship we had built over the past few weeks. And then we kissed.

It was dazzling, but I'd been dazzled before. What I hadn't been before, was grown up. Now, I was. If Pierre wanted to pursue me, I'd be receptive. But he'd have to follow me, because I now knew where I was going. And I was going to need some time to get over Arnaud.

"So tell me about going back to New York," he said, when we stopped kissing. We sat side by side, his hand covering both of mine, clasped in my lap.

"I need to be where I belong," I told him.

"Are you sure you don't belong here?" he asked.

"Yes. I'm sure. Paris is beautiful, but it will never be my home."

He nodded in understanding.

"I know the feeling."

"You do?" I was surprised.

"Yes."

"But you're French. How could you understand how it feels to be a foreigner here? Always learning new things, but always at a disadvantage to whoever I'm learning from."

"I know the feeling well."

"How could you?"

"I'm not from Paris. I'm from the provinces."

"But so many French people come here to live from the provinces."

"They do, don't they?" His smile was rueful.

"Like Arnaud." And Jean-Michel before him.

"Yes. They make their peace with the city."

I thought of both Arnaud and Jean-Michel. They led isolated, single lives in tiny studio apartments. It was a big-city lifestyle, not dissimilar to the way thousands of people lived back in Manhattan. But I belonged in Manhattan. And there were plenty of people who met each other and made lives together there. Not as foreigners, but as New Yorkers. Paris was different. If you weren't Parisian to begin with, you never were.

"And wouldn't you make your peace with the city?" I asked.

"If that's what I wanted."

We kissed again, this time more passionately.

"So what do you want then?" I continued.

He shook his head. "I don't know yet. But it's not living in a certain place I most want. It's being with the right person."

"The right woman?" It was a bold question, but the friendship we had built gave me the confidence to ask it.

"Exactly."

"And you?" What is it you most want?" He tucked me into his side, then stroked my chin, affectionately, like a father.

"I want to be *bien dans ma peau*. In a place where I belong. Where I won't be a foreigner forever."

"You're smart, Ava."

"And?" Sam had told me the same thing. Maybe it was time to believe them both.

"And I like smart women."

"I think you already told me that," I said, remembering our feather-light conversation on the grounds of the officers' club a few weeks earlier.

"*Non.* I told you I liked your smart questions."

"Oh."

"And that I like you."

"Oh."

"So go back to New York, smart girl. Take what you learned here and make it work for you where you belong."

"Pierre, you're a mind reader. That's exactly what I plan to do."

"Then may I help you with your plans?"

I looked at him surprised. Suddenly, we were having a very grown up sort of conversation.

"But how would you do that?"

"I'd come visit you in New York, for a start."

"You would?"

"Yes. I would. And then we would see what the next plan is."

The smile on my face sprang directly from my heart.

"I would love that," I said without thinking, meaning it as naturally as the words tumbled out of my mouth. It was easy to talk with Pierre about anything, everything – even the future.

"I would, too," Pierre said. "And now, I'm going to leave so you can get some sleep and be fresh to make more plans tomorrow."

"Where are you staying?" It didn't seem likely he'd remain at Arnaud's.

"I got a room at the officers' club this afternoon."

"And when are you leaving Paris?"

"Hopefully around the same time you leave for New York."

"Let's make that happen," I said, laughingly. I didn't need to know where he was going back to. It was enough to know I would see him again soon – in New York.

The next day, I went to Rue Scribe near Place de l'Opera, where the principal airline offices were located, and booked my return flight to New York.

John, the Englishman whose apartment I'd been staying in, was returning shortly after Christmas, to resume both his gig at Teddy's and teaching English to the aeronautical school students. I tidied up his small place, and by late afternoon, met Pierre again.

"So when are you leaving?" he asked, kissing me four times on the cheek and then once on the mouth.

"This Friday." It was still early enough in December for me to have caught a seat before the Christmas travel season began. "How about you?"

"This Friday, too. Right after I say goodbye to you at the airport."

The man knew how to make a plan.

We spent the next two days taking long walks, deep in conversation and not noticing the gray chill of a Paris December in the least. Then it was time to go.

On Friday morning, Pierre picked me up by cab at my flat, and we nestled next to each other on the long ride out to Charles De Gaulle airport. I wasn't sad. Looking into his steady brown eyes, I knew we would see each other again soon. Meanwhile, I had plans to plant myself again in New York, this time in a non-performing capacity. I'd heard from a regular at Teddy's that the United Nations hired scores of administrative workers for each of its annual General Assemblies. I would go there the following Monday to fill out a job application. If Albert Einstein had been able to come up with his theory of relativity while working in a sleepy Swiss patent office, then I could pursue a career as a songwriter while holding down a job as an international civil servant. An administrative position at the U.N. would be predictable and unexciting. I could hardly wait.

At the airport, I quietly leaned into Pierre's chest as we stood in front of the international departures gate.

"Remember, Ava. Take what you learned here and make it work for you where you belong."

"I will." It was nice to feel understood. I looked forward to getting to know this man who liked my songs and liked me. But in my own time, on my own turf. I kissed him hard, then walked through the gate without looking back.

Twelve hours later, I was out on the sidewalk, blinking in the crystal blue brilliance of a cloudless December day in New York. I had said *adieu* to Paris but the lessons I'd learned there would stay with me forever.

I stepped off the curb and raised my hand to hail a cab.

Glossary of French Terms

arrondissement - an-administrative district in Paris or neighborhood as in "a good one" or "a not so good one." Parisians know instantly where to place each other on the socio-economic ladder by which of Paris's twenty arrondissements they live in, a fact which can be instantly determined by an address's postal code. 75005 means the fifth arrondissement, a good neighborhood. 75020 means the twentieth arrondissement – not so good.

au pair - baby sitter, usually in her late teens to early twenties, who lives with a family in a foreign country, does some babysitting and light housekeeping and spends as much time as possible soaking up experiences, preferably with the opposite sex.

bien dans sa peau - comfortable in one's skin. An expression used widely in France and not used widely enough in the United States.

bien élevé - well raised, brought up properly, conversant in the art of social graces.

de bonne famille - well born, from a family of high social standing.

bordel de merde - dammit, literally "shitty screw-up."

boulevardier (also see *draguer, flâneur*) - a man who strolls along the street or sits at outdoor cafés attempting to pick up women through the use of idiotic, time-tested phrases that occasionally work (see *au pair*). Endemic not only to French culture, this type of male can be found in most Latin countries.

c'est pas normal - actually "ce n'est pas normal," an overused expression in France, meaning "it's not the way things are done."

à chacun son goût - to each his own, to each his own taste.

con - idiot, jerk (noun), stupid (adj.)

crétin - idiot, from French dialectic for deformed and mentally retarded person found in certain Alpine valleys.

doucement - gently or "easy does it."

draguer - a man who tries to pick up women on the street. Literally he tries to drag her home with him or at least somewhere dark. Sometimes works (see *au pair*).

fils de pute - son of a whore.

flâneur - a man who strolls the streets aimlessly, making comments to women and trying to pick them up. From *flâner* - to stroll.

fromage maigre - a creamy, white cheese with zero percent fat used by Frenchwomen to lose weight. Surprisingly tasty, especially when it comes in flavors such as strawberry.

gagner la vie - to make a living, literally "to win the life."

je m'en fous - I could care less, a frequently used expression, as well as mentality, based on the Frenchman's sense of entitlement supported by generous government social services.

jolie laide - literally a pretty-ugly woman, meaning an attractive woman who is not beautiful in a conventional sense, but who is perceived as beautiful because of the confident way she carries herself.

lardon - cubed or diced bacon or pork fat used by the French in salads (*lardon frisée*) as well as many traditional dishes such as spaghetti carbonara, *quiche Lorraine*, and *coq au vin* (chicken in wine sauce). Similar to pancetta.

lardon frisée - a classic French bistro salad served with French chicory (*frisée*) and warm *lardons* (French cubed bacon or pork fat bits).

louche - sleazy, dubious, of questionable taste, perhaps indecent. Almost always it connotes something exciting or forbidden.

minou or minouche - literally means "to caress" but used as a term of endearment meaning something like little cat or little darling.

morceau de merde - piece of shit.

moue - A pouting expression used to convey disdain or distaste.

porte-documents - (literally a "carry-documents") the French version of a briefcase, preferably sleek, supple and leather without handles and always carried under the arm.

sacré bleu - an ancient French oath that is actually never used by real French people. Refers to the color (literally "sacred blue") associated with the Virgin Mary. Frequently found in nineteenth century writer Victor Hugo's novels.

salope de putain - bitch of a slut.

sangfroid - literally "cold blood" (*sang* - blood, *froid* - cold), meaning coolness, composure, especially in trying circumstances.

savoire-faire - know-how, or knowing the correct way to do things, as in how to arrange a cheese plate, how to tie a scarf, how to open a champagne bottle, or how to make an entrance.

sturm und drang (German) - literally "storm and stress," meaning something that's a big deal.

Paris Adieu

Book Club Discussion Questions

1. Is Ava's character believable? Can you relate to her? In what ways does she remind you of yourself or someone you know?

2. Ava's first French boyfriend Jean-Michel advises her to be comfortable in her skin - *bien dans sa peau*. What does this mean? How does it differ from self-love?

3. How does Ava's character evolve from beginning to end of the story? Which events were turning points for her?

4. What does Ava's motto "fake it till you make it" mean for you? How is this consistent with her quest for authenticity, and if so, how?

5. What is your take on the French concept of *jolie laide*, i.e., a woman who is not a beauty by conventional standards but comes across as one (Chapter Three)? Do you buy it? Was there ever anyone in your life who struck you as a *jolie laide*? What celebrity or historical figure most represents a *jolie laide?*

6. How does the French ideal of female beauty differ from the American one?

7. In Chapter Three, Ava's French boyfriend Jean-Michel says "Men don't fall in love with a woman who is perfect. They fall in love with a woman who is specific. A woman who is comfortable with herself can be herself specifically. She is free to explore who she is, because she is not comparing herself to other women all the time, trying to be someone she's not." True or not? Discuss.

8. Ava arrives in Paris addicted to junk food. Her appetite is regulated not by how full her stomach is but how raging her desire for sweets is. By the end of three extended stays in Paris, she is no longer a slave to sugar and fat. What changed? How did Ava make food choices at the end of the story that differed from the way she made them at the start?

9. In Chapter Seven, Pascal hands Ava a hard-boiled egg to eat for breakfast at the counter of a workman's cafe. It's a watershed moment for Ava. Why?

10. "The whole point of having sex appeal wasn't really about making men happy. It was about making myself happy. Who knew?" (Chapter Eight). Do you agree? Which popular culture icons do you think have true sex appeal? Which historical figures do you think had true sex appeal? Why?

11. "Being here now never seemed quite enough in New York. In Paris, it did."(Chapter Ten). Do you agree? How does Ava's time in Paris help her learn how to live in the present moment?

12. "Have you ever been in love with someone who didn't love you back?" Sam asks Ava. (Chapter Thirteen). Have you? If so, what did you do about it?

13. Sam describes Paris as the Queen of Diamonds (Chapter Thirteen). What does he mean? Do you agree?

14. " 'Be here now' was what Arnaud preached to Ava. But Pierre practiced it" (Chapter Fifteen). What's the difference between the two men? Which one, if either, is right for Ava? Which one, if either, would be right for you?

15. Which actress do you see playing the role of Ava?

Rozsa Gaston is an author who writes serious books on playful matters. She studied European intellectual history at Yale, and then received her master's degree in international affairs from Columbia. In between Rozsa worked as a singer/pianist all over the world. She currently lives in Connecticut with her family.

Please visit www.parisadieu.com to learn more.